JACK PROBYN

Over The Line

Vinci Books

vinci-books.com

Published by Vinci Books Ltd in 2025

1

By Jack Probyn

DC Jake Tanner Crime Thrillers

Part 1: 1st Jan

Chapter One

DELIVERY

Perks of the job, he told himself. Or was it part and parcel?

Idioms had never been his strongest suit. Give him a piece of intricately written code and he could understand it faster than switching on a light bulb. But understanding the English language? That was a challenge in itself. And it didn't help that it wasn't his *first* language either. Born to a Polish father and an English mother, Roland Lewandowski had always found it difficult to fit in. At school, at university and in the wider world of work. Not that he liked to talk about it, but he felt himself in a perpetual state of judgement. That everything he said or did was criticised and ridiculed. Even though, deep down, he knew that probably wasn't the case.

Probably or possibly. Which one was it again?

The only place he felt comfortable, aside from his home and at his parents', was his desk at Bow Green. The people were friendly, the laughter heart-warming and the conversations enjoyable. It was just a shame that he hadn't developed those relationships outside the workplace, outside the confines of the brick cage they were all kept in for twenty-four hours a day at times. If he had, then perhaps he'd be welcoming in the new year a little differently: with laughter, celebration, alcohol, food and the warm embrace of social comfort.

Who was he kidding? In social situations, he was about as awkward as a nun in a brothel. Didn't know what to do or where to put his hands.

Give him a dozen computers and he would have a dozen new friends within a minute. And hundreds of places he could put his hands.

Instead of widening his social circle into double figures, Roland was set for a brief night in front of the box, a good meal and maybe even some time with his right hand for company. Maybe even throw in a beer or two as well. Not necessarily in that order.

Perks of the job, he blamed it on.

'Sorry, I can't come tonight. I've just got to finish this thing. Won't be done until late.'

'Sorry, I've got other plans.'

'Sorry, I promised my parents I'd see them.'

The excuse book was thick tonight.

But there was an element of truth to them. He *did* have things he needed to finish at the station. And, as was becoming increasingly frequent, he did have to bring it home with him.

Perks of the job.

Carrying his rucksack in his hand, Roland fumbled for his keys and entered his small maisonette. It wasn't much to look at, nor had he expended much effort in making it look more presentable; what was the point in prettying the house if there was no one to show it off to? But the rent was cheap. Surprisingly. And he was fortunate enough to have a landlord who not only didn't insist on hiking the prices every year but also included bills as part of the package. The man was fair, unlike some of the other con artists he'd had the displeasure of renting from, and Roland appreciated that. He paid on time every month, so there was no reason to cause concern.

He dropped his keys into a small pot on the kitchen counter and headed straight for the fridge. Empty. Except for the ten gallons of Coca-Cola and share bags of M&Ms – which, if he was being honest, were never big enough to share with anyone else anyway.

He reached in and pulled out a bag and, as he moved about the kitchen, started lobbing sweets into his mouth. There was washing-up that needed doing, surfaces that needed cleaning, old takeaway boxes of Chinese that needed binning.

But all of that could wait. He allowed himself a night off from the mundanity of chores. It was New Year's Eve.

Roland stopped by the oven and glanced at the time. Eleven. It had been a late one, later than he'd realised. With any luck, the mad rush of pizza deliveries would have finished and the heroes, as he liked to call them, would be winding things down, deliberating what to do with the leftover dough balls and unused ingredients. He grabbed his landline and dialled the number for Domino's. Speed dial. Number four.

'Hi, this is Domino's. Can I take your order?'

'Large Pepperoni Passion with stuffed crust, extra cheese and extra pepperoni, with a side order of cookies and a bottle of Coke please.'

His favourite.

Twelve slices of heaven.

And the Coke was free if you got it in a bundle.

'Delivery or collection?'

Roland considered. One of life's most difficult choices: succumb to laziness and endure a long wait, or get your arse out of the sofa and enjoy the delectable feast sooner than anticipated.

Perks of the job.

'Delivery.'

'That'll be ready for you in forty-five minutes.'

'Hero.'

Roland rang off and searched the fridge again. Hoping a different snack or beer or two had manifested since the last time he checked.

Nothing.

Sighing as he realised the irony of it all, he grabbed his car keys and headed to the off-licence round the corner, where he purchased a crate of Stella and a packet of Doritos. He was back within ten minutes, with another thirty-five to spare until the food arrived. Plenty of time to get showered and into something more comfortable. At this rate, he'd have twelve different kinds of friends to enjoy his midnight with. Each with different tastes and flavourings. Sometimes he liked to imagine they were his girlfriends. Some he'd get to spend the night with, others on a rare occasion he'd get to enjoy the following morning for breakfast.

It was just after half past eleven when he finally sat on the sofa, switched on the TV and opened a cold tin of Stella. Beside him was the laptop he'd brought home from the office. He kept it with him everywhere he went; in recent months it had demanded his entire attention. Both in and outside work.

A few months ago, his colleague DC Jake Tanner had approached him with a suspicious email. There was nothing in the email except for the header which read WE THANK YOU FOR YOUR SILENCE. At first, Jake had claimed it was the result of a phishing email, but Roland had been around computers and hackers long enough to know that wasn't the case – the degree in computer science also helped. Something else was happening. The problem was the sender's IP address and details were masked beyond comprehension. The emails could have been sent from space, for all Roland knew, but seeing it as a personal challenge, as well as a favour to Jake, Roland had embarked on a voyage of discovery.

And the information he possessed, the information he'd discovered, had the potential to rock the boat.

Rock the fucking *Titanic* more like, he thought as he opened the laptop, which was resting on his lap. An image of a tropical bird appeared, resplendent in its vibrant beauty and colours. In the background, the TV played, but it wasn't loud enough to drown out the cheers and music and jubilation coming from his neighbour. The heavy, repetitive vibrations thumped through the walls and were slowly beginning to infuriate him. It wouldn't be too long until the music was replaced with the loud snap and crack of festive fireworks.

Roland ignored the sounds and focused his attention on the computer. Beer in hand, he opened the email sitting at the top of his Drafts folder. The culmination of eight months' intense work. For the past few days, he'd been contemplating his wording; how it should be addressed, who specifically it should be addressed to and who it should be sent to.

A minefield of options and potential pitfalls.

Roland had heard of The Cabal before, thanks to Jake. His colleague had shared the horror stories of corruption, of The Crimsons, of how it was difficult to place his trust in people. But he'd never really believed in it.

Until now.

With the name of The Cabal staring him in the face.

Roland nestled the beer between a set of cushions and readied his fingers. At the top of the screen, in the Recipient section, he typed JAKE. The system auto-filled Jake's work email address, and Roland prodded Enter with an oversized thumb.

Then the doorbell rang.

He glanced down at the clock on the screen: 23:34. Ten minutes early.

They were called heroes for a reason.

Dragging himself out of the sofa, Roland caught the beer before it spilt on the cushions, then shuffled towards the front door. Behind the window panels was the faint dark blue shadow of the Domino's delivery driver's uniform.

Roland opened it. 'Hiya, mate. Wasn't expecting you so—'

The first thing he noticed was the colour of the man's eyes. Jet black, dark, empty, but also containing shadows of guilt and regret. Splinters of fear etched their way across his face.

The second thing Roland noticed, before the smell of the dough and grease and cheese and pepperoni hit his nostrils, was the reflection of the hallway light catching on the Glock in the man's hand.

'In,' the man said coldly.

Roland didn't need telling twice. He shuffled back into the house, instantly throwing his hands in the air in surrender.

Following him in, the man flicked the gun in the direction of the living room. 'There. Now.'

Roland listened to the man's voice. Recognised the hint of an accent. Faint, discreet, like the voice of a man who'd either spent many years in the UK, possibly from a very young age or was good at masking his identity.

Roland trotted into the living room and stood on the other side of the coffee table. Lying between them was the laptop and beer, a stream of suds descending the side of the bottle.

'Are you going to kill me?'

The only thing he could think to ask.

The man said nothing, just gestured to the sofa, and Roland sat, sinking into the cushions. There he was immediately compromised. Impeded by his weight and size, it would take a monumental effort to get him out of there to spring a surprise attack.

'What do you want?' he asked. 'I don't have any money.'

Except for the fifty grand sitting in his account for a rainy day. But the man wasn't getting his hands on *that*.

The man said nothing, checked his watch. Roland did the same, glancing at the time on the computer. Somehow, five minutes had passed, and it was now 23:39. Just over twenty minutes to go until the country welcomed in the new year.

If he made it that far.

And then it dawned on him why the man was checking the time.

'You can take what you want,' he began. 'I don't have much but... whatever you want, it's yours.'

'Shut up.'

Five minutes passed, and in that time, Roland thought of nothing. The computer in his mind had switched off and left him with nothing other than a black screen. During that time, however, his killer had been busy in comparison; he'd set the pizza box down on the coffee table, paced from side to side, and checked his watch several times a minute.

'No matter how many times you check it, it's not going to make time go any faster,' Roland said.

He was treated to a blank, cold stare in response.

The pacing from one end of the coffee table to the other concerned Roland. Either the man was nervous – holding a man at gunpoint for the first time – or he was afraid of being interrupted. Perhaps the real pizza delivery guys were on their way. The heroes coming to rescue him.

'Are we waiting for someone?'

This time, he was met with an answer: 'No. Waiting for *something*.'

'Will it be quick?'

Back to the stonewalling. Back to the pacing. Back to the gun glistening beneath the new energy-saving lights he'd recently fitted.

Back to the waiting for death.

And it was a long wait. A minute turned into two. Two into three. And before long, sat there, squashed between his cushions, he began to reflect.

He'd never been afraid of death – that was quickly eradicated after he'd first laid eyes on a set of crime scene photos. In fact, he welcomed it. Just another friend to add to the Filofax.

Instead, he was afraid of life.

Of how little he'd experienced. Of how much he'd wasted, thrown down the drain. Of how he'd failed to build long-lasting relationships with friends and colleagues and neighbours. Of how he'd failed to make an impact on other people's lives. Who in the world was going to know he was dead? He was a nobody, a piece of Sellotape on the wall –

invisible, yet right there, right in front of you. What did he have to show for his time on the planet?

Nothing. An unfulfilled life.

Then he asked himself: if he was spared tonight, if he was allowed to live and enjoy his dinner, what would change? Would he go round the neighbours and connect with strangers? Would he go to the pub after work with his colleagues? Or would he continue to waste away in front of the TV, with his appalling diet and lifestyle choices?

Sadly, he knew the answer: nothing would change.

Roland stretched his leg and in doing so nudged the laptop. The screen illuminated on the lock screen and displayed the time: 23:59.

One minute until his death.

Sixty seconds.

People usually ask: What would you do if you had a day left to live, an hour? But nobody asked what they'd do in a minute. Possibly (or was that probably?) because they'd spend the time trying to think of an answer, by which point they'd be dead.

But not Roland; he knew exactly what he would do: sit back, take a drink of his beer and close his eyes. Death was coming, death was knocking on the door. But if he couldn't hear or see it, he didn't have to answer it.

The sound of the laptop lid closing stirred him. The man was in the middle of placing the laptop in the pizza box. Outside, the fireworks began, large flashes of colour illuminating the window above the TV screen.

Here we go.

The man rounded the coffee table and looked at him, his expression cool, emotionless. He held the gun to Roland's temple, the cold from the nozzle searing his flesh.

'Sorry,' the man said.

So was Roland: sorry for neglecting the things that mattered in life.

'Just a perk of the job,' he said before the world went black, the sound of the bullet drowned out by the explosions outside.

Chapter Two

TWENTY-NINE

He liked the sound of silence. Welcomed it. A silence so profound, so deep it allowed him to drift through the clouds in his mind and focus on what was really important. But it was becoming increasingly difficult thanks to the fireworks detonating overhead.

He was inside his Mercedes C-Class. Not too conspicuous to raise suspicions as to how he managed to afford it, but not too drab or depressing either. He needed to keep it within his salary range, lest anyone begin to dive a little deeper into his income and expenditure. In front of him, illuminating the darkened high street, was a nail salon, its neon OPEN sign on the window beckoning half of London through its doors.

Unacceptable.

He had an audience waiting for him. And he didn't want that interrupted by some drunk bitch who thought she could get her acrylics done at the stroke of midnight.

New year, new me.

New you, dead you.

Deeply unimpressed, he climbed out of the car, brushed himself down and wandered across the street to the salon, failing to look either side of him as he passed. He approached the door. Knocked.

Within a few seconds, a figure appeared at the other end of the shop. His body was domineering, tall, broad, yet his movements were light, elegant, graceful, as though he'd been a ballet dancer in a former life.

'Dimitri.'

'Evening,' Dimitri replied, stepping aside and closing the door after him. 'Any trouble getting here?'

'None.'

He sauntered his way into the middle of the salon through the central walkway. Either side of him, running along the length of the wall, were the desks where the workers conducted their daily activities – filing, painting, trimming, glueing, all the while remaining perfectly silent and ignorant to the conversations around them. At the end of the walkway was Dimitri's seating area: a tall chair and wooden stand, the top of a computer screen just visible over the back of the stand. To its right were three leather chairs, with a sign above in incandescent lettering: PERFECT FOR PEDICURES. The smell of chemicals and other beauty products stung his nostrils.

He stopped and turned to face Dimitri. 'Downstairs?'

'Yes,' replied Dimitri.

'So why have we got the lights on?'

'It's midnight, nobody's—'

The look he shot towards Dimitri instantly silenced him. *You know better than to talk to me like that.*

Strike one.

Three and you're out.

At once Dimitri cowered, lowered his gaze to the floor

and hurried across to the front of the building. He opened an electric box, switched off the lights and lowered the shutters. Within seconds they were plunged into darkness, save for the ambient light from outside warming the desks and chairs slightly. He waited until his eyes adjusted to the low light before stepping aside.

'After you,' he said to Dimitri.

Dimitri, hands grappling for purchase on something, led him through a heavy fire door at the back of the room, into a hallway, through another door and down a flight of stairs – and down a few degrees centigrade.

They stopped at another door. A thin sliver of light chased the floor along the bottom, gently filling the stairwell with some form of illumination.

'Anything I need to know?' he asked.

'No change since this morning.'

'Number?'

'Twenty-nine.'

The age I wish I was. He nodded, gesturing for Dimitri to open the door. As Dimitri did, a torrent of light flooded into the stairwell, momentarily blinding him.

He blinked his surroundings back into existence, staving off the wall of dark pink and blue in his retinas. Then he crossed the threshold into the underground room. The mass of bodies – exactly thirty-one of them – all sat on the floor in the foetal position, with their backs against the wall, legs scrunched against their chest. Beneath them was a sea of mattresses, elevating them slightly from the cold hard concrete. To his right was a pile of discarded and loose backpacks and coats.

'Is that all of it?' he asked Dimitri, pointing at the pile of luggage.

'Everything.'

'Has it been checked?'

'It's on my to-do list.'

'Prioritise it.'

Dimitri said nothing, moved beside him, then reached down to the floor and picked up a black sack. He fanned it open until it billowed and filled with air.

'Up!' he screamed. 'Up. All of you. Empty your pockets. Essentials only. Personal items you want to keep. That sort of thing.'

For a while, nothing happened. Then Dimitri clapped his hands and, at once, the figures rose to their feet and shuffled towards him. Their arms were either pressed against their chest, hidden behind their back, or dangling by their sides. He made a quick count. Twenty-nine females. Two males. A good balance. But not the best.

He whistled. 'Get in a line. If no one wants to be first, I'll choose someone.'

As he took a step forward, everyone froze.

'I know you're afraid,' he began. 'You're in a new country. You don't know where you are. But that's what we're here for. We'll look after you.'

He continued down the room, ushering them into a single file queue.

'I'm going to look after you,' he continued. 'You can call me D – and that over there is Dimitri. You need anything, you go to him. If you think it's important, you go to him, and if he thinks it's important, then he'll come to me. I hope you all had a pleasant journey over here, and that it wasn't too cold for you.'

Now all of the recruits were lined up, he idled up and down the row, inspecting, observing, looking at their arms and hands – searching for Twenty-Nine.

'Please raise your hand if you can speak English.'

D stopped. Out of the thirty-one that were lined up, only fifteen raised their hands. Less than half. Below average. But he didn't discriminate. If they were willing to pay him money to get here, then he would have to work with what he had.

D made another quick check – still no sign of Twenty-Nine.

'You can lower your hands now,' he said as he continued back down the queue. 'For the next few weeks, this will be your new home. You will have access to washing facilities and toilet facilities, as well as basic food rations, over there.' He pointed to a hole in the floor in the corner of the room, protected by a thin sheet of plastic hanging from a fixture in the wall. Beside it was a bench containing basic rations. Their bathroom and kitchen in one.

'If you want water, there are perfectly good taps in the sinks. You are not, under any circumstances, permitted to leave the premises. If you try, you will be caught and an example will be made of you to the rest of your colleagues. These people around you are not your friends; nor are they your family – they are your colleagues. You do not know them. Forget that you've ever met any of them.'

He slowly made his way back to Dimitri, who continued to hold the black sack in his hands. A woman, whose arms were as thin as a snooker cue, clung to the necklace around her neck. Dimitri reached for it and yanked it. A nice little token of her appreciation for all the effort he'd gone to in getting her here. The woman let out a cry but her moans were stifled after she realised her battle was already lost.

'You will work when you are told, and you will do as you are told. You must wake up at six every morning. The salon will open at seven, and you'd better all be ready. With all that said, please raise your hands if you know how to paint nails in any capacity?'

Twenty out of thirty-one. Nineteen girls, one boy. The numbers were improving.

And then he saw her.

Twenty-Nine.

The problem.

Staring directly into the back of the head in front of her, giving him no attention at all. Hands by her side, chest gently rising and falling with every steady breath.

He surveyed her up and down. Small, petite. Her hair was tied in a ponytail, her make-up-less face was covered in scratches, yet there was something beneath the curtain of her eyes that attracted him. An incipient fire waiting to burst on stage and tear everything down. He loved that about women, the dominant ones. That he could take the power from them and use it against them.

Tonight, she was dressed in a baggy light purple hoodie and jeans ripped at the knee. She wore a small bracelet on her left wrist, and on her right, on the back, was The Company's symbol. Everyone who set foot through those doors was given one:

D approached her and leant into her ear.

He whispered, 'So, you can't speak English, nor can you paint nails. You're not much good to me, are you? I bet you're angry. The money you paid to get here – or the money your parents paid to get you here – all gone to nothing. This wasn't the life you were expecting when you got into the back of that container, was it? This wasn't what you wanted out of your new life in London, was it? But look at all of these other people. They paid the same money as you. They have to go through the same things as you. And none of them are complaining, are they?'

He grabbed her wrist and squeezed her skin. Twenty-Nine grimaced as his hand rubbed and twisted the abrasions from her freshly embedded tattoo.

'This is your first warning,' he said, giving it an even harder squeeze. 'You don't get any more after that. Why don't you want to follow instructions? You will get out of here, once you've paid off your debts. All of your belongings are mine, and every item that I sell of yours goes towards paying off your debt. But the more you antagonise me, and disobey me... the more your debt goes up. You don't want to work in the nail salon? Fine. We have plenty of other things we could have you do instead.'

His other hand moved towards her backside and squeezed. Her flesh felt soft under his grip.

As soon as he did it, Twenty-Nine twisted and raised her hand to defend herself. But she was too slow; he caught her hand and held it there. A collective gasp came from those around them. Her eyes widened with immediate fear.

'Tut, tut, tut,' he said, shaking his head. 'I'm the one who does the touching here. Nobody else.'

He turned his head to look up and down the queue. 'Do

you all remember what I said? If you disobey me, an example will be made of you. And her actions here have just added to all of your debts. How many of you want that?'

Nobody out of those that claimed they could speak English raised their hand.

'What if I told you that I could make it all go onto her debt so that none of you are affected?'

This time, there were more hands. Four. Then six. Until eventually everyone felt brave enough and all thirty turned against her.

He faced Twenty-Nine. 'Seems your colleagues have spoken.'

Twenty-Nine glared at him, her gaze unrelenting. He leant in again, this time pressing his cheek up against hers. Her skin was smooth, soft, despite the scratch marks. Which meant she took care of herself. Which meant she took care of every part of her body. D lowered his hand to her crotch and buried it between her thighs.

'You ever experienced a touch like that?'

She was shaking now, shuddering uncontrollably. Her breathing was rapid, bouncing in and out in short breaths, pain and discomfort etched over her face.

Using her power and defiance against her.

'Like I said, if you don't want to work in a salon, there are other things you could do.'

'No…' she whispered. Faint, almost inaudible.

Until she cracked…

Bingo.

'So you do talk? You do understand English?'

No response.

He wrapped his arm around her and escorted her out

of the room. 'Come on,' he said. 'There's a lot of stuff we can get up to. And a lot of it you can put towards paying off your debt.'

Part 2: 3rd Jan

Chapter Three

THE ONE YOU WANT

'You're bullshitting me, I know it!'

Jake Tanner offered the young boy a dismissive, disappointed look.

'Did you talk to your dad like that?' he asked, then immediately wished he hadn't.

Lewis Coyne's reaction wasn't what he'd expected. Despite his father dying a few months ago, and the fact he was still living with the raw emotions of it, he took it quite well. Jake knew, from the unending pain of experience, that nobody really overcame a bereavement. It was never that simple. Switch off and forget. There were always constant reminders living and breathing everywhere you looked.

'I think you already know the answer,' Lewis replied. His voice seemed deeper than usual. Perhaps it was because the question had caused a lump to form. Or perhaps it was because he was entering a new stage in his development into a young man.

'Well, I'm not your dad,' Jake replied, 'so you can't get away with using that language around me.'

Lewis grinned, baring his teeth. 'Yes, boss. Sorry, boss. Won't happen again, boss.'

Jake leant forward and grabbed the plastic cup on the table. He sipped, swallowed the cold water down his gullet and, as he placed the cup on the table, scanned his surroundings. The room they were sitting in was grand. Jake was on one sofa, Lewis on another. There was an empty fireplace in front of him, a metal gate stained black and white from years' worth of usage, debris and children's curious fingers. The wallpaper was a dark shade of pink and beginning to peel away by the ceiling, and the carpet was an equally garish colour of sunset orange. It looked like something out of a mad house at a theme park. Worse, a hallucination. And to exacerbate the horror of the room was the smell. It reminded Jake of his great nan's house: the perpetual state of *old*, of having been lived and breathed and sweated in for an eternity, of decay painted onto the walls. Of impending death.

'Seems nice here,' Jake said, breaking the uncomfortable silence that had formed.

Lewis rolled his eyes. 'Yeah, right.'

'I know it might not seem like much, but at least it's a roof. There are others in your situation that aren't so lucky. You have a lot to be grateful for.'

'If you say so.'

'What about the people? Are they nice?'

Lewis shrugged, defiant, like the teenager he was gradually learning to become. 'Miss Thomas is all right. She's been helping me with school and stuff.'

'That's nice of her.'

'She's tryna teach me how to play the guitar. She used to be in a band back in the seventies, but it's been a long time since she last played.'

'There are some things you never forget,' Jake said with a smile. He'd been looking forward to this meeting for a long time, and now he was finally here, he didn't want it to end. The event had been on his calendar for months, and for the past few hours, he'd been devoting his undivided attention to Lewis Coyne. His son that never was.

'What about the other kids?' Jake asked. 'You made any friends?'

Lewis dipped his head, stared into his lap and played with his hands, rolling his fingers over one another. It was amazing to think that, only a few months ago, Lewis had been witness to three horrific deaths – including his own dad's – and had been full of resentment and anger, not only at Jake as a police officer but also at the world. Lewis had seemed like a man then. Filled with bravado, a tough exterior. Having experienced and witnessed things no teenager should. But now, here he was, looking his age – and acting like it. The exterior – his resilient shell – was more than just an act; it was a defence mechanism, a layer of protection for the fragility that lay beneath. After all, he was just a child, and there was no amount of life experience or suffering that was going to change that. He needed help, just as much as all the other kids in his situation did.

'What's wrong?' Jake pressed.

'They're *different* here.' Lewis raised his head. 'All of them. They talk different. They talk about different things. It's like they're in their own little worlds.'

'You feel excluded?'

Lewis nodded softly.

'Have you tried to make an effort?'

'Well… I…'

'Maybe they're thinking the same as you, mate. Maybe they're waiting for you to make the first move. Speak with them, get to know them. I'm sure that after a while you'll find that you can get along. You shouldn't judge other people before you get to know them. But you also shouldn't change who you are just so that you can fit in, you understand? That's just as important to remember. If not more.'

Jake paused a beat to gauge Lewis's reaction – his attention waned as the lecture continued. Jake moved the topic of conversation along. 'And school? You got many friends there?'

'A few.'

'There you go. A few's all you need.' Jake tilted forward, lowered his voice. 'And, between me and you, nobody really likes the cool kids anyway.'

'You're only saying that because you were never one of the cool kids.'

'And it still pains me every day. Everyone just thinks they're dickheads.'

He winked at Lewis, eliciting a chuckle.

'Now who's swearing?'

Jake tapped the side of his nose. 'Do as I say, not as I do.'

Lewis chuckled for a little while longer, and then, like a switch had gone off in his head, he stopped suddenly. His demeanour dropped and he stared directly ahead, distant, his eyes burning a hole in the carpet. Twice that had happened, and Jake knew exactly what the young boy was thinking; he'd been thinking the same thing himself for seventeen years. Flashes of his dad in his vision, a random memory, a splinter of hope that he would manifest and appear through the door at any moment.

Jake shuffled across the sofa, moving closer to the young boy.

'It gets easier, kid. Trust me. It might not seem like it

right now, but you have to persevere. The feeling of hurt will never go away, but it will only last as long as you let it. All the pain and suffering we ever feel in our lives is controlled by us. If we let something disturb us for a long time, then it will. I'm not asking you to forget about him – you can't, and you'll never be able to. But take it from someone with experience that there will be tough times, but there will also be good times too. Every time I see Chelsea Football Club, I think of my dad. In fact, any time I watch or see anything to do with football, I think of him. But it doesn't make me sad; it makes me proud. You just have to find a way to turn your negative feelings into a positive.'

Jake paused to catch his breath. 'Listen. I know you've probably heard it a lot – I'm sure your therapist or social services are drumming it into you left, right and centre – but if you need to talk to anyone, know that there are lots of people out there that can help. You're not alone in this; none of us are. And you have my number as well, so you can call me if you need to chat. Sometimes I might not answer – too busy catching the bad guys – but I'll try to whenever I can. You understand?'

Lewis raised his head. Thin red snakes swarmed his irises and a thin line of liquid glistened at the bottom of his eyes.

'I'm fourteen. Not four.'

'And sometimes you act twenty-four. Which people neglect to acknowledge. You're a kid, Lewis. It's OK to act like one. No one's going to judge you for that. We were all kids at one point in our lives.'

'How are yours?' Lewis asked, his eyebrows rising, revealing more of the whites of his eyes.

Before he could respond, Jake's mobile vibrated. He removed it from his pocket and checked – a message, unknown number. Jake unlocked the device and opened the chat at the top of the screen.

The one you want is D

Jake hesitated for a moment, caught in a snapshot of confusion. The message appeared as though it was incomplete, that the sender had accidentally pressed Send by mistake. But when another one didn't appear ten, twenty, thirty seconds later, he began to suspect there was no mistake at all.

'Jake?' Lewis said, but he barely heard him.

The one you want is D…

D.

D.

The pool of people Jake knew that began with a D was limited to three.

Danny Cipriano.

Drew Richmond.

Darryl Hughes.

Two of whom were dead. One of whom was very much alive.

'Jake!' Lewis waved his hand frantically in Jake's face, eventually bringing him round.

Jake shook himself back to reality, replied quickly to the message, asking 'Who is this?', then focused his attention back to where it was needed. The young boy had been through so much neglect in recent months, jumping from foster home to foster home, Jake didn't want to add to that.

'Sorry, Lew, what were you saying?

'Your kids. How are Ellie and Maisie?'

An image of his daughters appeared in his mind and

brought a warm smile to his face. 'They're fine. Everyone's healthy.'

At that moment, the door opened and an elderly blonde woman wearing a bright red jumper entered. Her skin was red – the blood vessels beneath her skin exploding – and her nose looked like a pizza slice. It was the same woman who'd greeted him at the entrance to the foster home and shown him through to the living room.

'Sorry to interrupt,' she said. Her voice was hoarse and deep, a symptom from, Jake presumed, years of shouting and dealing with disobedient foster kids. 'But, Lewis, Miss Thomas has had to bring your guitar lesson forward. She's upstairs waiting for you.' She adjusted her head to face Jake. 'I hope you don't mind.'

Not that he had any say in the matter.

'But I...' Lewis began.

'It's all right,' Jake said, lifting himself out of his seat. 'Go to your lesson. I was just about to leave. Gotta get home. Think Elizabeth's making a pasta bake.'

'But...' Lewis pleaded, the whites of his eyes reflecting the artificial lighting overhead.

'Go on. Out you get. I'll be back to see you soon though.'

'Promise?'

'Promise.'

Lewis extended his pinky finger and Jake wrapped it in his. The woman ushered Lewis out of the room and he obliged, sulking away, with his head down and his shoulders hunched.

Jake fought the lump in his throat back to where it had come from. Seeing Lewis again caused many memories of his own to resurface. Most ferociously, the death of his father. It was a memory he'd repressed, and one that only ever haunted him in the darkest of times. He seldom let anyone into his mind or let them know what he was feeling. Not because he didn't want to concern them or burden them with his stresses, but because he could handle it on his own. He had a degree in psychology – he knew the ins and outs of his brain, his behaviour and his thoughts, so why the hell did he need to share them with someone else? Some said it was unhealthy, letting his demons nibble away at him on a daily basis, but he was on top of it. Making full use of his antidote: consuming himself with work to help drown out some of the noise.

The one you want is D…

'Is everything OK, sir?' the woman in the doorway asked.

Jake hadn't realised it, but he'd drifted into a reverie and was staring at the woman directly ahead, his shoulders slumped.

'Yes,' he replied. 'Everything's fine. I can show myself out.'

The woman exited the room, and the sound of the door closing sprang Jake into action. He reached into his blazer pocket and removed his phone. It was then that he noticed the deluge of notifications. Seventeen missed calls. Thirteen voicemails. All of which he'd missed because he'd been driving over here, his phone on silent and his blazer slung over the passenger seat.

'Shit,' Jake said through gritted teeth.

They were all from Elizabeth. The last time he'd received that many calls from her was the first time they'd celebrated the miracle of birth. Except, on that day, neither of them had been in the mood to enjoy it: Elizabeth, because she was pushing a baby out of her body and experiencing unnaturally high levels of pain, and Jake because he'd crashed his car on the way to the hospital.

He unlocked his phone and scrolled straight to voicemail.

Jake! When you finally get this, can you call me please? I'm on my way to the hospital. My dad's been rushed to A&E. I've got the girls with me – they're both fine. I'll call you when I get there. Please hurry.

Shit. As he lowered the phone from his ear, he checked the timestamp on the call. *Double shit.* It was from over an hour ago. Knock knock, a bollocking was coming when he arrived at the hospital.

Trying not to think about it, he pocketed the phone, rushed out of the foster home and raced towards his car.

He broke the speed limit every step of the way.

Chapter Four

INTO THE RING

'Alan Clarke,' Jake said to the member of staff behind the desk. 'My father-in-law. He came in here about two hours ago. Alan Clarke. Can you help me find him?'

Jake hoped his voice projected the urgency of the situation effectively, but the woman wasn't forthcoming with a response that easily.

'Are you a family member or a friend?'

'Family member. He's my father-in-law. I just told—'

'One moment, please. I believe he was… Yes, he should be in the east wing, Room 312.'

Jake thanked her profusely before shooting off towards the room. He traversed myriad corridors, several flights of stairs and passed through numerous sets of double doors, until eventually he found what he was looking for and burst into the room, disturbing the still and solemn air. A trio of bodies surrounded a hospital bed. Elizabeth. Her mum, Martha. And her sister, Tegan.

As soon as he entered, all their heads turned towards

him. Without saying anything, Elizabeth left her father's side and rushed over.

'Where have you been?' she asked, trying unsuccessfully to keep her voice to a whisper, and trying even harder not to swear.

'Working,' Jake responded. It wasn't a complete lie, even if the visit was purely personal. There was still a connection between Lewis and Henry Matheson's investigation; Jake just wanted to keep the visit a secret. After hearing what the boy had done and what he was capable of, Elizabeth didn't want Jake anywhere near him. Said that he needed professionals in his life, and Jake wasn't one of them.

Jake disagreed. What Lewis needed was a father figure, and Jake certainly *was* one of those.

'Did you not get my calls?'

'My phone was on silent. It was on my desk. I didn't hear it.'

Not all of that was a lie either.

Jake took Elizabeth's hand and peered over her shoulder. As he held her hand in his, he couldn't help but notice the lack of commitment and strength in her grip. It was almost as if she didn't care that he was there after all. Something to be called upon and pushed away just as easily.

'Is everything all right?' Jake asked, ignoring the destructive voices in his head. 'Is he going to be OK?'

'It's his kidneys. He needs a transplant.'

Jake turned his attention away from her father and focused on her. There was an ethereal hurt and suffering there that he hadn't seen before.

'What happens next?' It was the only thing he could think to ask.

'He'll go on a waiting list, and be on dialysis until he gets one.'

'How long can that take?'

'Weeks. Months. Years. Some people die without ever getting one.'

'Liz…' Jake said, stroking her arm and squeezing her hand again; this time she reciprocated. 'Are none of you a match?'

Elizabeth shook her head, closing her eyes.

'What about your mum? Your sister?'

'None of us. We've all got different blood types. There's a greater risk his body would reject the kidney.'

Jake hesitated a while, his mind blank. He looked over at Alan lying there on the bed, hooked up to the machines like he was in the Matrix. The man who'd walked his wife down the aisle only a few years ago, dressed tall and proud in his suit, reduced to a mess on the bed.

'What about me?' Jake asked. 'What about my kidney?'

'No,' she said. 'No way. I'm not having anything happen to *you*. I don't want to lose the two men in my life. What if something goes wrong?'

'That risk applies to everyone. It's not mutually exclusive to just me.'

'I don't like it.'

Jake ignored her and wandered over to Alan. It wasn't a case of what she did or didn't like – he wanted to do everything he could to help. At the bedside, he said hello to Martha and Tegan, kissed them on their cheeks and hugged them before returning to the other side of the bed.

'Liz said that none of you are a match for a donor. What about me? I might be able to give one of mine. It's not like I'm using it for anything!'

The dubious attempt at humour was met with unimpressed scowls. *Read the room, Jake. Read the room.* But before either woman was able to answer, the doors opened and a nurse entered, dressed in scrubs, and hurried across the room.

'Do you mind giving us a couple of minutes of privacy?' the nurse asked, skipping the niceties. 'I'm going to have to ask you to leave.'

'Yes, of course,' Elizabeth and Tegan said in unison. Only a few years separated them – Elizabeth being the elder – but they were alike in more ways than Jake could comprehend.

Slowly, Elizabeth, Martha and Tegan left Alan's side. Jake waited until they were out of the way before capitalising on his opportunity.

He spun on the spot, touched the nurse's arm and said, 'Hey, is it possible to... to test me for a transfer? See if I'm a match? Everything seems to be in good working order. I'd like to be able to help.'

'Jake...'

The weak, coarse, drugged-up voice came from Alan beside him. The early stages of stubble around his chin made it look as though he'd been in the hospital ward for days.

'You don't have to do that.'

'Yes,' the nurse interrupted. 'We can run some tests on you. There are no guarantees. And, right now, Mr Clarke, I think you should consider all possible options.'

The nurse turned back to Jake. 'If you wait outside I'll discuss the next steps with you once I've finished here. I've got a lot to get through and more patients to see.'

Jake said nothing further and acknowledged the passive-aggressive remark. An emergency worker himself, he didn't envy the role nurses and doctors played every day. Their job was more physically and mentally demanding than his or anyone else's in the services, so he forgave a little passive-aggression. He placed his hand on Alan's and stroked, feeling his finger run up and down over the prominent river of veins, then he departed.

As he closed the door behind him, Elizabeth stepped right into his face, and he caught a whiff of her Yves Saint Laurent Black Opium perfume. Every morning she sprayed a faint mist against her neck and chest, which was usually sufficient to last all day but was now as weak as Alan's grip.

'What did he say?'

'He's coming out in a second to discuss the options once he's done with your dad. Where'd your mum and sister go? And where are the girls?'

'They've gone to get a coffee. We're going to be here all night.'

'And *our* girls?'

'They're with your mum.'

'My mum's here?' Jake asked in disbelief. His voice carried up and down the corridor. 'Why?'

'I asked her to come. When you weren't answering your poxy phone, I needed someone to look after the kids. I'm sure she'll be the one to tell you that it's a ridiculous idea to give my dad one of your kidneys. You'll listen to her over me like you always do.'

Jake ignored the comment. Permitted it even. Her emotions were heightened. She was stressed, carrying her entire world's problems on her shoulders – he knew that. They'd been married long enough for him to know her words were spoken out of anger and frustration, rather than with any malice or intent. But that didn't make it hurt any less.

Elizabeth perched herself on a small bench and placed

her bag by her feet. Jake joined her and wrapped his arm around her small body. As he stroked her back, his fingers running over the bobbles in her top, she reached inside her bag to retrieve a piece of paper.

'This came today,' she said. Tears were forming in her eyes, and she blinked them into submission.

Jake took the letter and read. It was from their gas supplier, British Gas. Addressed to him. Mr Jake Tanner. In the top-left corner of the document were his address and his account number just below it.

At the top of the body of the letter, written in a bright, bold, unavoidable red font, were the words: NOTICE: ACCOUNT IN ARREARS.

Please, Jake thought. *Not now. Not again.* Just when, after months of trying, their finances were finally beginning to get healthy again. They couldn't afford to have another problem on their hands. His credit score was already as low as the numbers in his bank; a default account would only worsen it tenfold.

Money issues had been no stranger to them. They had four mouths to feed, a mortgage to pay, bills, other living expenses. And it was exacerbated by the fact Elizabeth had been out of work for the past few months. After failing to get her photography career off the ground, she had started working for a modelling agency. During one of the shoots, she'd been required to model bikinis for a company's summer collection. During the shoot, however, one of the photographers had liked what he'd seen too much and groped Elizabeth's breasts, violating her privacy and trust in the profession. But when she'd complained to the managers, they'd turned their backs on her and sacked her instead. Since then she'd struggled to find a job, so what little Jake earned was now being spent on covering the costs of everything – and put towards the possible costs of legal action.

'Why did you open this?' Jake snapped.

'What?'

'Why did you open this? It's addressed to me. I don't open your post.'

'You're turning this back on me? I thought everything was settled. I thought we'd cleared all the debt. I thought we were making payments – I thought *you* were making the payments.'

'I am! I have been!'

'Well, you're clearly not.'

'And what about your share of the bills? The water? The internet? Are *you* paying *those*?'

Elizabeth's face turned white with anger. 'Do you see any red paper statements? Or are they all in your name?'

That shut him up.

'The money is still in the joint account. Look—' He reached for his phone to show her the online bank accounts, but she beat him to it.

'No,' she said calmly, which was even more disconcerting. 'I want you to be honest with me. Honest. One hundred per cent.' She paused. Deep down he knew the question that was about to roll off her lips. 'Have you been using our money to gamble again?'

Jake tutted and shook his head. 'You're unbelievable,' he said. 'You seriously think I'm that stupid to throw away what little money we have on something idiotic like that? I never followed through with it last time, and I've not touched that account ever since.'

'Then how do you explain this?' She jabbed at the arrears letter repeatedly.

'How am I supposed to know? You've only just fucking given it to me!'

A welcome silence was a brief interlude in their conversation.

'Call them.' She said it with such finality that Jake knew it signified the end of the conversation.

Nothing more needed to be said.

Jake found a small quiet space in the corner of an empty room. The chairs were uncomfortable, and he could feel the metal digging into his back. A welcome distraction. Something to calm the frustration surging through his body. He wasn't angry at Elizabeth; how could he be? It wasn't her fault her dad was seriously ill. It wasn't her fault that their accounts were all in a state. Only he was to blame for that one.

But...

Have you been using our money to gamble again?

The accusation. The insinuation that he would jeopardise their situation so drastically. That stung deeper than any needle or incision.

He held the document in his hands, the giant red, scary letters shouting back at him.

Failure, failure, failure, they were saying.

And then, to exacerbate the thoughts in his head, Maisie and Ellie appeared, clinging to his mum's hands. Constant reminders of what was at stake if everything all went wrong.

'Daddy!' Maisie screamed and sprinted towards him. She leapt into his arms, knocking the bill onto the floor.

Jake embraced her and inhaled deeply. Her hair smelt of strawberries, and her clothes were freshly cleaned. She was wearing the new denim coat she'd begged for. Emblazoned on the back was an embroidery of the cast of Disney's *Tangled*.

A few steps behind her came Ellie, their youngest.

'How are my girls doing?' Jake positioned Maisie on one leg and Ellie on the other.

'We're OK, Daddy,' Maisie said. 'Hospitals are boring.'

Jake chuckled. 'They're not supposed to be fun, Maisie.'

'Why not?'

'Because sometimes people get poorly and they come here to get better.'

'Like Grandad?'

'Yes, like Grandad.'

'But getting better should be fun.' She cast her childish eyes about the waiting area. Jake could only imagine what she saw in the most intrinsically boring things: a chair morphing into a castle; vines crawling down the walls. A universe of wonderment and joy. All things corroded by the complexities and realities of modern life.

'Hello, Jake,' his mum said as she sat next to him.

Jake gave her a kiss.

'How's Alan?'

Before responding, Jake shifted the kids off his legs and told them to play on the chairs. Then he turned his attention to his mum.

'He needs a new kidney. I've thrown my hat into the ring.'

'How selfless of you. Have you thought it through?'

'Do I need to?'

'So long as you're aware of the risks. They can be dangerous.'

'So can brushing your teeth, driving your car, walking upstairs – but we do those things every day.'

She looked at him derisively, the way a mother does. 'Some things are more dangerous than others.'

'I'll bear that in mind.'

Denise placed a hand on his forearm. 'Everything all right at work?'

'Busy. As per.'

'Elizabeth said she'd tried calling you a dozen times.'

Try two dozen.

'I was at work.'

'Is that what you told her?'

'It was.'

'And where were you really?'

Jake glanced over to her, and she returned the gesture. There was an expression on her face that told him, somehow, that she already knew he was lying. A mother's instinct. A sixth sense they possessed for sussing out bullshit right from birth.

'I was visiting an old friend,' he said, then realised he'd made it sound like he was having an affair.

'Oh, Jake.'

'Not like *that*. The boy that got stabbed and was hospitalised, the one whose dad died in front of him. *That* one. I was visiting him, to make sure he's settled in his new foster home properly.'

'You were being his dad.'

'And?'

Jake didn't appreciate the accusation, but he could hardly deny its validity.

'Just don't forget you have a real family at home, Jake. Waiting for you.'

Inhale. In. Hold it. Out.

'Would you like some advice?'

When did anyone, ever, in the history of humankind, ever respond to that question with an affirmative?

Denise continued. 'You're just as stubborn as your dad. He was always like that, thinking he knew best. Wound me up at times. Sometimes, if you tell yourself the same lie over and over again, you start to believe it. That woman over there wants to help you. But if you keep doing what you're doing – being an *idiot* about everything – you're going to throw it all away.'

Chapter Five

ARREARS

The ringing tone sounded in his ear, deafening the thoughts of rage in his head. Another lecture was the last thing he needed. Too many times people thought it was OK to interfere in his marriage and his life, the reasons for which were unfathomable. They had no idea what was going on, just the same as he had no idea what was going on in anyone else's life. It wasn't his place; nor was it theirs.

So why did they think it was acceptable?

After his mum had finished berating him – something all the women in his life seemed to be doing this evening (except for Ellie; sweet, innocent Ellie) – she took the girls for another walk to keep them distracted, leaving him alone in the room.

The call connected.

'Good evening, this is British Gas. My name is James – how may I help you?' The man's voice was dry and dull and contained a thin hint of an accent.

'Hi,' Jake began. 'I have an account with you guys, and

I've just got a letter through the post. I was wondering if you could tell me what it's about?'

'Certainly, sir. What does it say?'

'It says my account is in arrears. I'm fairly sure I'm up to date with all the payments. I don't think there have been any issues.'

'I'll have to transfer you to our payments team. Would you mind if I put you on hold?'

'Not at all.'

A piece of upbeat music played in his ear, drowning out all thoughts of Elizabeth and his frustrations towards her. A few minutes later – after he heard the muzak loop through twice – another voice spoke to him. Another accent.

'Good evening, my name is Phillip from payments. How can I help?'

Jake explained the issue.

'Do you have the account number to hand? I just need to get logged into the account.'

Jake gave it to him, reading off the letter in front of him. In his ear, Phillip typed away on the keyboard.

'We're just going to have to go through some security questions if that's all right with yourself?'

'Yes, sure.'

'What's your memorable location?'

Jake searched his memory. 'Coffee.'

The name of the café where he and Elizabeth had met. Back when they were lost in blissful ignorance and didn't have any issues. Back when things were good.

'Thank you, that's great. And what's the name of your childhood friend?'

'Darren.'

'Lovely. And the name of your favourite sports team?'

'Chelsea.'

'Excellent. Last one. If I could just get you to confirm the last two digits of the sort code and account number that the payment comes out of, that would be perfect.'

Jake pulled his wallet out of his pocket, removed his debit card and called the numbers out.

'Marvellous. Thanks for that. All part of the security nowadays, unfortunately. The number of hoops you have to jump through,' Phillip explained.

Jake sensed he was trying to be nice and amicable, but he wasn't in the mood for it.

'I'm into the account now. Let's have a look... Right... Yes, I can see what's gone on now. It seems that, for some reason, you were sent the notice by mistake. There was an error with our system. It mistook an outstanding amount on your account for a defaulted payment.'

'Right...' Jake said, finding himself a seat on the nearest chair. 'So what does that mean? There's nothing wrong with the account? Nothing to pay?'

'Not quite, sir. There is an outstanding balance of two pounds thirty-eight left to pay for the month. Your latest meter reading showed that there was a slight miscalculation in your tariff.'

'All I need to do is pay that and then it's sorted?'

'Exactly. The direct debit will still be in place and the money will continue to come out at the same time every month. OK?'

Jake searched his brain for any reasons why that might be an issue. He found none.

'Do what you gotta do,' he said.

'Do you have your debit card to hand?'

Jake said that he did, then called out the sixteen-digit number on the front, the expiration date and the security code on the reverse. He paid the remaining two pounds thirty-eight and thanked Phillip for helping him.

'That should be everything sorted now,' Phillip said after the payment had finished processing. 'You shouldn't receive any more letters in the post. But if you do, please don't hesitate to contact us. Is there anything else I can help you with today?'

'No,' Jake said, shaking his head. 'You've been perfect. Thanks so much for your help.'

Phillip wished him a good evening and then hung up. A few seconds later, Jake received a text from British Gas, asking him to complete a customer satisfaction survey. He made a note to complete it later, pocketed the phone and headed back to look for Elizabeth. He found her bouncing Maisie up and down on her legs.

'And?' Elizabeth shot to her feet as soon as she saw him.

'Sorted. It was a mistake.'

'So we're not in arrears?'

'No. I just had to settle a small balance. But everything's fine.' Jake stopped beside her and looked at the doors leading to the ward. 'Where's your mum and sister?'

'They're in there with him. The nurse was looking for you.'

Maisie clambered down from Elizabeth's arm and reached up at him imploringly, begging to be carried. Smiling, Jake bent down and picked her up. He immediately felt the strain under his arms. Either he was getting weaker, or she was growing so fast that he hadn't realised it.

Juggling Maisie in his arms, he entered the hospital room. Just as he stepped in, he bumped into the nurse. The man's body was solid, taut. As though he had a real physical presence behind him that was betrayed by the fitting of his uniform.

'Just the person I needed,' the nurse said. 'You wanted some more information about the donation.' He handed Jake a handful of pamphlets. 'All the information you need is there. I would consider discussing it with everyone before deciding to go through with it. It's a big decision. Once you've made up your mind, we can get you booked in for a test to see whether your blood types are compatible.'

Jake gestured for Maisie to take the leaflets from the man. As she held them aloft, she asked, 'Daddy, are you sick?'

'No.' Jake chuckled. 'But I'm going to try and make Grandad better.'

'I want to make Grandad better too!'

'You are already,' Jake said. 'Just keep on giving him lots of cuddles.'

Jake lowered her to the ground and watched as she raced over to Alan, leap onto the seat beside it and climb onto the bed. Jake turned to the nurse. His decision was already made, and nothing was going to change his mind.

'Where do I need to go?'

Part 3: 4th Jan

Chapter Six

THE DREAM TEAM

The following morning, Jake was in the office early. Thanks to the aching sensation in his arm, he'd slept little. Typically squeamish at the sight of needles and injections, and the thought of something piercing his skin, Jake had needed calming down, and as a result, the nurse had found it difficult to control him – and to find a vein – so had prodded him extra harshly with the needle. At least, he considered, he'd saved himself the embarrassment of passing out. Just about.

Jake had just settled into his desk chair when the doors to the office opened. The building's facilities manager, the woman who was an ornate piece in the tapestry of the building, Lindsay Gray, entered, holding her laptop bag by her side. She wore her thick leopard-print glasses, black trousers and a black blazer. The same as almost every other day. But this time there was one subtle difference.

'New necklace?' Jake called over as she set her bag down in her office.

A thick black line circled her neck. She stopped and

held it, running it through her fingers, as though doing so conjured memories of a lost lover, a first date, a first kiss. A small heart was connected to the bottom of the necklace, holding three black stones inside. It was a disgusting piece of jewellery, but Jake didn't have the heart to tell her that.

'My husband bought it for me last night. It was our anniversary. Thirty years.'

'With one person? How do you do it?' Jake asked.

Lindsay smirked, removed her coat and placed it on the back of her chair.

'Trouble in paradise?' she asked.

At first, Jake was reticent to answer truthfully. He usually disapproved of converging his personal life with his professional – except for extenuating circumstances – but there was something different about Lindsay. She was the eldest in the office, and in a way, she reminded him of his mother. She was considerate, caring, attentive. She knew things. She had life experiences. She had the answers to questions he didn't even know needed answering yet. And there was the added bonus that she could tell him things and he couldn't get angry at her, which meant that he'd listen and pay attention.

Theoretically.

You're just as stubborn as your dad.

'It's nothing…'

Sometimes, if you tell yourself the same lie over and over again, you start to believe it.

'You sure? Doesn't sound like nothing. I can tell you've had a late night as well,' she said, slowly wandering over to him. She came to a stop on the other side of his desk.

'How so?'

'It's my job to know everything that goes on round here.'

Jake chuckled. 'There's nothing to tell. Coffee?'

'Is that even a question?'

With cowardice seeping through his mind, Jake lifted himself out of his chair and made his way to the kitchen. By the time he returned with the cups in his hands, Lindsay was already at her seat with her headphones over her ears, leaning forward so she was only inches from the screen.

'You seen your emails?' Lindsay asked as Jake started back to his desk.

'Not in the last five minutes, no.'

Lindsay pressed the button on her mouse.

'Darryl's just sent one. Looks like the two of us are going to be spending some time together.'

'Excuse me?'

She tilted closer, her nose now almost touching the screen. '"Morning all, please be aware that, in light of recent events, members from all teams within the building will be spending the day together in team bonding exercises. There will be four members in each team. Your teams will be attending an escape room, where you'll have an hour to escape. Now, as police officers, this should be something of a walk in the park for you – others, not so much. We've booked slots for you to attend in the attached document. Please familiarise yourselves with your teams and the time you need to be there."'

Lindsay finished and pulled her glasses off her nose.

'In light of recent events,' Jake repeated derisively.

'I think it's a good idea.'

Jake didn't. 'It won't bring him back.'

'But it might help the healing process.'

'So it's not a team-building exercise then. It's a grieving exercise. If a spade's in your hand, call it a spade.'

Lindsay looked up at him, head to the side, confused. 'I don't think that's the right—'

Jake held his hand in the air. 'You know what I mean.' Then he stormed back to his desk.

Ever since he'd heard the news about Roland Lewandowski's death, which had flooded through the building like the common cold, Jake had felt nothing but anger. Raw, unadulterated anger. That one of the nicest people he'd met in the force could be taken away from him, was unimaginable. That he'd died on New Year's Eve, the night of celebration and new beginnings, was even more profound. He and Roland had worked on several cases in the past, most notably when Roland had helped Jake catch the Stratford Ripper, a bloodthirsty and deranged serial killer who hunted and stalked women with the name Jessica via an online platform on the Dark Web. Roland had been instrumental in the case, and, more recently, Jake had entrusted him with finding the identity of The Cabal via a handful of emails.

What annoyed him more than anything was that the details about his death had been thin. In fact, they were almost non-existent. He was dead: that was all they knew.

The where and when were obvious; DS Brendan Lafferty had found Roland's body the following morning and was now on leave following the discovery.

The how was unexplained. The why was unaccounted for. The who was left to the imagination.

All the answers that Jake's insatiable mind required, missing, lost in the ether.

'I hope you're excited,' Lindsay called from her office.

'Why?'

'Because I'm in your group,' she replied a few seconds later. 'Along with Stephanie and Mason.'

'Mason? Hasn't he been signed off sick for the past three months?'

'Unfortunately, yes.'

'Looks like it'll be just the three of us then. The dream team.'

Those words were a struggle.

'Is that what we're calling ourselves?'

Jake shrugged. He didn't want to expend too much energy and thought on it. Aside from everything else going on in his mind, there was one thing that was a priority. Henry Matheson's trial. The former gangland crime lord was facing life imprisonment for a list of charges as long as Jake's arm. But the process had been delayed time and again while Henry attempted to obtain a suitable lawyer. Apparently, Rupert Haversham, the usual bicycle in the store of criminal masterminds, no longer wanted anything to do with him.

One day you're cock of the walk...

'What time's our slot?' Jake asked, gradually turning his attention back to his work. He had a lot to get through.

'Midday. Got a few hours to kill.'

'Only a few?' Jake replied sarcastically.

Chapter Seven

NAPALM

Henry Matheson was getting used to life on remand. He had a bed – albeit an uncomfortable one. Warmth. Access to TV, the latest sports programmes and even films. A room-mate who kept himself to himself, and was either oblivious to what was going on or simply didn't care. A pool table, table tennis. Sofas. Even the food wasn't that bad.

Most importantly, he had protection. Running the drugs and contraband through the prison, with a little help from some friends on the outside, had turned out to be easier than supplying to half of East London. The demand was higher, the supply constant. Both of which resulted in one thing: an accumulation of debtors that could repay in either cash or carrying out favours.

Favours, in the insidious world of incarceration, were the new currency. Favours were king. Favours exonerated you from getting into trouble. And there were no lengths people wouldn't go to in order to get their drugs. Combine highly volatile and destructive individuals with copious amounts of stimulants and chemicals, and you've got yourself a boiling pot of droogs ready to commit some ultra-violence.

Henry was lying on his bed, reading his book. *A Clockwork Orange*. The first book he'd held for a long time. The library contained an entire selection of books to indulge himself in, but this was a Penguin special edition – gold lettering, a textured case, aged and worn pages – and not least because of the packets of spice that were hiding in some of the pages. One of the many methods he had at his disposal.

This particular edition had been smuggled in by one of the latest additions to his team. Long gone were the days of calling himself the leader of the E11, his cadre. Here, he was king, but there was no need for a gang name; everyone knew who he was, everyone recognised the face, everyone understood what it meant when he spoke to them. He could protect them, offer them safety in return for favours. And if they didn't play ball, then their original problems would quickly escalate and change hands. *He* would become their problem, and he would make sure they learnt their lesson.

A knock came on the door. It was Jason, a former junkie whose love and adoration for drugs had been renewed since sparking a friendship with Henry. They'd become acquaintances when Henry had shared a room with him, and then their relationship had blossomed into friendship. Jason was jittery, unable to stand still, and his right hand was permanently crooked from where he'd apparently beaten someone to death. That was his crime. Death by fist.

But, as the saying goes in prison, he was innocent. Just like everyone else.

'All right, Hen,' he said, sniffing repeatedly. He scratched the back of his head with coarse fingernails. 'You got any gear yet?'

Not only was Jason Henry's number two, but he was also one of his biggest customers. The biggest coke-head Henry had ever come across; he spent nearly ninety per cent of the wages Henry paid him on the drugs that he was supposed to be shipping. Whenever a shipment arrived, Jason took most of it for himself and paid for his share. Somehow, unbeknownst to Henry, he always managed to come up with the cash. And if he couldn't, then the new currency would kick in. The only thing that could be said about their relationship was that Henry was grateful he'd never had him as a business partner on the outside. God only knew they would have been locked up within five minutes of working together.

'I've not got anything at the moment, mate,' Henry replied. 'Skinner's meant to be bringing some in Friday's lunch. Apparently, the shipment was delayed.'

'Ah, man. You not got no more lying around? I could *really* do with some. I know you keep your emergency stash somewhere.'

That was true. He did keep an emergency stash. But that was for emergencies.

'This isn't an emergency,' Henry replied. He dangled his legs off the top bunk and placed his book beside him. 'What's happening on the ones? The screws playing ball? Anything I need to be aware of?'

'Just some little fucker keeps asking about you.'

'What you mean?'

'Some bloke called Carlson. Won't give a first name. Only got here yesterday. Spent the night on the ones. Keeps asking me 'bout you. Wantsa know if he can chat you 'bout something.'

Henry hesitated a moment. It wasn't uncommon for inmates to want to speak with him and get a piece of the drug-filled pie. But when they were fresh meat, coming to him after only their first night... that was when the alarm bells started ringing.

'If he's got the balls to come up to me alone, I'll listen.' Henry wiped his nose with the back of his hand and cleaned it on his trousers. 'Anything else?'

Jason shook his head violently and scratched the back of his neck. 'Nothing, Hen.'

He scratched his neck harder. So hard, in fact, that Henry was able to hear it from his bed.

'What did I say about that? You'll make yourself bleed again. You'll infect everyone with your AIDS.'

'I ain't got AIDS.'

'You keep fucking all the new recruits in the showers then you will.'

'It ain't none of that *Shawshank Redemption* shit, Hen. We ain't do that sort of stuff.'

'Then what do you do? Sit around reading bedtime stories while you wank each other off?'

Jason lowered his hand from his neck and shrugged sheepishly. 'Sometimes we get the horn.'

'Jesus Christ.' Henry hoisted himself off his bed and arranged himself in his jogging bottoms.

Another thing he'd grown accustomed to in prison life was the attire. The ensemble of grey tracksuit bottoms and jumper wasn't his usual choice, but he'd found it surprisingly comfortable – especially when he was paying for the extra soft laundry conditioner in the washing room. Everything, and everyone, no matter who or what it was, had a price. And more often than not, he could afford it.

He moved closer to Jason, keeping just enough distance between them that he couldn't smell the other man's rancid breath.

'Come on, Hen. Tell me where it is. Where's your stash?'

'I told you, you ain't find it. And if I catch you looking for it, I swear to God, I will fuck you up like Mark got done. Think Biggie's knuckles are still sore.'

'Nah, nah, nah. I don't want none of that beef. *Come on.*'

'Where's yours gone anyway? Last shipment only came in a couple of days ago. I gave you enough to last you until the end of the week. You used it all up already?'

Jason stopped shaking and looked at the ground, like a child preparing himself for punishment.

'Jase? Jase, answer me. Have you used it all up?'

'Nah… Well… See… Kinda…'

'Where's it gone?'

'Dom took it from me yesterday.'

'That right?'

'He and his boys jumped me in the playroom when it was empty.'

'Is *that* why you were clutching your stomach? You said you had the shits.'

Already, a dozen ways to get payback were running through his mind. Recently, Dominic Radler, murderer and gang member from Liverpool, a truly nasty fucker, had been throwing his weight around. Nibbling away at Henry's business, crumb by crumb. First, it had been a shipment gone missing, then it had been a fight on the twos, something which was later reported as a bit of banter and sparring between two inmates. And now there was this. A line had been crossed, and it was time to do something about it. For good.

'What happened to your shiv? You lost it again?'

Jason lifted his head briefly then looked back down at

the floor again. 'I... I sorta lost it down the toilet the other day, Hen. Was tryna cut my nails with it.'

'While you were high?'

Jason nodded, a blatant look of shame and embarrassment on his face. He'd been entirely responsible for his own downfall.

Usually, Henry wouldn't feel sorry for someone so careless and stupid. But there was something different about Jason. He was like a small child who needed protecting. Like his sister. Sweet Danielle. Gone but never forgotten.

If there was one thing he'd learnt from being a gangland drug lord, it was that his enemies would always go after the things – or people – he cared about the most. That was why he'd made a concerted effort to distance himself from almost every aspect of his personal life. It was too dangerous for everyone involved, and the loss too severe. First, it had been Danielle, next would be Jason.

Saying nothing, Henry moved to the right-hand side of the room to the small kitchen area he'd manufactured himself. There he had a mug, a bowl, a kettle and a box of tea. Beside it sat two bags of sugar.

Henry filled the kettle to the brim with water from his toilet sink, placed it back on the stand then grabbed the bags of sugar, tore them open and emptied their contents into the bowl.

'Henry...' came Jason's tentative voice beside him. 'What're you doing?'

'Prepare the boys. Then find Dominic and report back to me. I'm going to need an extra set of hands,' Henry explained.

Jason nodded and backed out of the room slowly, keeping his gaze fixed on the bowl of sugar.

'Oh,' Henry called him back after he'd just left the

room, 'and I want you to find another shiv. I don't care who from, or what you have to do to get it – just find one. Then maybe I'll let you have some of my secret stash.'

At the mention of the secret stash, Jason's eyes widened and he bolted. Henry gave one last look at the twos – the name given to the floor that he was on – and the wire nets outside his room that were used to prevent suicides, then turned his attention back to the kettle. It had finished its boil, and a thin jet of steam whistled from the nozzle. He pulled it off the stand and poured the boiling water into the bowl with the sugar, mixing it with a spoon.

A few seconds later, while he was still stirring, a group of figures appeared in the doorway, Jason leading the pack.

Henry recognised them all immediately. They were his runners, the ones he employed to shot the food to the other prisoners on the ones and twos. Over Jason's left shoulder was Biggie, a six-four brute of a man whose only weakness in a fight was his abnormally long hair. Over Jason's right shoulder was Vinnie. He was the strongest of the three of them, and the most noticeable. He was the widest bloke in the entire prison and modelled his facial hair on Charles Bronson – which was apt because he was just as volatile.

Both of them were in there for armed robbery, although not together, and had been career criminals for a long time before eventually being arrested and imprisoned. Henry had employed them for their quick thinking and ability to worm their way out of sticky situations. Their size was also a contributing factor.

'All right, Hen?' Vinnie began, folding his arms so that his frame sealed the cell from external view. 'What we got?'

'A little task.'

'Who's the mark?'

'Dominic.'

Vinnie chuckled excitedly. 'About time. I've been waiting to get my hands on that cunt long enough.'

'No,' Henry said sternly. 'This one's Jason's. I only want you two to step in if he and I have any issues.'

'You're coming as well?' Jason asked.

There was an excitement in his voice Henry found endearing.

Just as he had on the outside, Henry typically distanced himself from any savage beatings and assaults. That way his hands stayed clean and the rest of the prison could continue to receive their deliveries. He was the one in possession of contacts, the snake's head, and if the head was chopped off, the rest of the body would slowly follow suit.

But this time was different.

'I've always wanted to see what sort of damage this can do...' He turned his attention back to the bowl of water. The steam rising in the air warmed the side of his face and hands.

'Are we gonna drown him?' Biggie asked.

'What?' Henry snapped.

'The water. Are we gonna drown him?'

Henry looked at him in disbelief. 'You ain't serious, are you? How long you both been locked up? This is napalm – water and sugar added together. Throw it over someone's face or their body, and it sticks to their skin. Throw something else – like a pillowcase or a shirt – and that shit ain't coming off. This'll make Dominic think twice about bending me and any of my boys over.'

Both Vinnie and Biggie smiled, baring their black-and-yellow-stained teeth. Vinnie clapped his hands and rubbed his palms together.

'Did you find him?' Henry asked.

'In his cell,' Jason replied.

'Have we got some of the boys keeping tabs on him?'

As soon as he finished speaking, another figure appeared in the doorway – Corben, one of the newest recruits. Henry had him doing the small-time stuff – proving himself, making sure he kept his loyalties in the right place – before he was able to work towards a promotion.

'Hen! Hen!' Corben said, panting. 'We need to hurry up. Minty said some of his boys are going into his room now.'

'Then we better get ourselves a mug each. But Dominic is still Jase's.' Henry turned to Jason. 'You find a shiv like I asked you to?'

Jason nodded, scratching the back of his neck again. As he pulled his hand away, Henry spotted flecks of blood on his fingers and fingernails.

Henry sighed. 'Come on, mate. Look a little bit livelier.'

He reached for a mug on the kitchen's surface, dipped it into the bowl of water and passed it to Jason. Then he filled the rest of the mugs on his table and passed them each to Vinnie and Biggie.

'What about you, Hen? Thought you were coming with us?'

Henry smirked, picked up the bowl in his hands, and said, 'Don't worry, I'll be right behind you.'

The four of them raced across the twos, heading towards Dominic's room on the threes, keeping their heads down. There wasn't a single screw in sight. Perfect. Someone on his books must have removed them from the equation.

Favours were the new currency.

Jason, Vinnie and Biggie kept their mugs by their hips, out of sight and away from any unwanted attention.

Meanwhile, Henry struggled behind, trying to keep up with the pace of the others in front, while trying to conceal the napalm in his hands. The last thing he wanted was for it to spill over the lip and onto his skin. Before leaving, he'd grabbed a tea towel and placed it over the top of the bowl, but it was proving ineffective; water continued to splash onto the cloth and seep through the rest of the material, rapidly soddening the towel. And his fingers.

As they traversed the strip, they forced other inmates out of the way with their presence, leaving behind them gossip, conversation and confusion. Before long, those that they'd passed on the way had formed a queue and were now following them, caught in the excitement of it all – even though they all knew better. Violence bred excitement. Excitement bred confusion. Confusion led to curiosity.

And too much of that could prove costly.

Vinnie was at the front, pulling ahead with his great strides. They came to a flight of stairs and climbed them. Henry's heart raced. For a split second, images of Frank Graham's burning body appeared in his mind. Followed by the smell, the sight, the taste, the sound of Frank's screams. He was transported back to that night on the Dunsfield Estate, getting revenge on the man who'd killed his sister. The excitement of it all, the heightened senses, the fervent feeling of immortality.

He revelled in it.

Adrenaline pumping, they breached onto the threes. Vinnie made a left turn and headed straight for Dominic's cell, directly ahead. No more than twenty feet away. Sounds of laughter and chatter and tinny bass music emanated from the small hole in the wall. Henry peered over Jason's shoulder. Osman, Dominic's second in command, was standing with his hands in his trouser pockets, laughing, leaning against the door.

As they neared the cell, Osman caught sight of them. But it was too late for him to react.

Vinnie was first into the room; he barged into Osman at speed and sent him flying into the opposite wall. Without wasting any time, he threw the cup of napalm onto Osman's face and started beating him. At once, the man screamed and threw his hands to his face. Heedless, Vinnie grabbed a pillow from Dominic's bed and wrapped it round the man's head, suffocating him, then kicked and punched his body into oblivion.

Meanwhile, Biggie tore in and saw to the other crony in Dominic's small army. The man was topless – showing off a tattoo of a wolf he'd recently had done – and Biggie threw the water against the man's chest. The napalm bounced off the flat surface and splashed into the air. Droplets landed on Biggie's arms and face, but he carried on regardless. He grabbed the man, kneed him in the stomach and thrust him down onto the bed, punching the back of his head repeatedly and pinning him into the mattress, using his monumental weight as ballast. The man's arms and legs thrashed and flailed, but it was futile.

Next, it was Dominic's turn to suffer. He was sitting on the right-hand side of the bed in the corner of the room with his back pressed against the wall, eyes fixed on the TV, then on the horror unfolding in his cell. His legs were scrunched up and pressed against his chest. He was cornered, and there was nowhere for him to go.

Jason was first to reach him; he poured his cup of water over Dominic's bald head, and, seemingly blinded by a rage within him, smashed the mug over Dominic's temple, immediately lacerating and breaking the skin. Dominic screamed in wild agony as the napalm seeped into the open wound, his hands flying to his face to protect his eyes and other exposed features. But it was no use. Jason had seen red, possessed by something deep inside him – the first time Henry had ever witnessed it. Jason looked ready to kill the man with his fists alone.

But as the saying goes…

Jason reached into his back pocket and produced his shiv. The metal razor blade had been attached between the bristles to the top of the toothbrush with tape, and Jason used it to slash at the man's skin. He struck and maimed repeatedly, narrowly avoiding Dominic's carotid artery before he moved down the body and started stabbing the man in the stomach, ribs, chest and the tops of his thighs, puncturing holes in his body like he was a microwaveable ready meal.

Meanwhile, Henry stood there patiently, holding the tub of water.

'Put him on the ground!' he screamed at Jason.

Jason didn't respond, he was too caught up in the moment of the attack.

'Jason!' Henry screamed again, his voice barely audible over the shouts and cries for help. Out the corner of his eye, Henry noticed the crowd outside the door, held back by some of his own men.

Then Jason stopped and spun on the spot. Small, pinpoint flecks of blood freckled his cheeks and nose and chin, and beads of sweat trickled down the sides of his face and the top of his forehead.

'Put him on the ground,' Henry ordered, nodding to the free space at his feet.

Jason did as he was told. He grabbed Dominic by his shirt, thrust him onto the solid floor and kicked him in the ribs. The man's white prison shirt was stained with flower blooms of blood.

'Lift his shirt up,' Henry ordered. All rationality had gone. He was consumed by the adrenaline of what was happening – and, more importantly, what he was about to do.

Frank Graham's burning body…

The smell, the sight, the taste, the sound of Frank's screams…

The excitement of it all, the heightened senses, the fervent feeling of immortality…

As soon as Jason pulled Dominic's shirt off, Henry balanced the bowl against his stomach, removed the towel and tipped the bowl's contents over Dominic's body, face and crotch. The liquid rapidly spread across his chest, and the smell of seared and burning flesh quickly filled the room. Dominic screamed, but his cries were stifled by a kick to the head from Jason.

Once all the liquid had decanted, Henry chucked the bowl to the side, grabbed the towel and wrapped it over Dominic's face. The fabric, combining with the napalm, clung to his skin and hair.

'Listen to me!' Henry screamed into Dominic's ear. 'Listen to me!'

He removed his foot and bent down by Dominic's side. A pool of blood was forming on the floor by his head and neck. He whispered, loudly enough for Dominic to hear above the noise of the room. 'You don't run this fucking joint. I do. So you're going to start treating me with the respect I deserve. And if you jump my friend again, I will make sure you never breathe another breath ever again.'

Chapter Eight

THE ROOM OF DOOM

Stephanie had opted to drive – it was her turn in the rotating cycle of carpooling responsibilities – and Jake and Lindsay were more than happy to let her. A few weeks ago, she'd ditched the Fiat 500 and opted for the new KIA Ceed, the only reason being she'd seen it on *Top Gear* as the reasonably priced car.

'It's not too bad a drive, to be honest,' she said as they pulled up to a set of traffic lights. 'Plus I got a good deal on the finance.'

'So it was more of a want than a need,' Jake said. He was finding the company a welcome distraction to his home life. 'I've still got my little Mini. My pride and joy that. Over forty years old and still running perfectly.'

'Sounds a little bit like you,' Lindsay said in the back seat. Jake had offered her shotgun, but she'd declined, saying she suffered horrendously from travel sickness whenever she was in the front.

'Watch it, you. I'm still a few years off forty,' he replied, twisting round in his seat. He thought about reciprocating the insult – adding a few more years to her age – but then realised he was better than offending an older woman. 'The doctor said I'm running perfectly fine, thank you very much.'

'Doctor?'

Ah, shit. Keeping last night's events a secret was going well.

'I went to the hospital,' he started. He trusted the two of them – in fact, they were about the only people he did trust – so what was the harm? 'Elizabeth's dad isn't well. His kidneys are on the brink and he needs a transplant. I offered one of mine.'

'Oh my God, Jake. That's big. Are you sure about that? Have you thought it through?' Stephanie asked as she slipped the car into first and pulled away from the lights.

'No, but it feels like the right thing to do. Besides, there's no guarantee it'll work. Our blood types might not match up and—'

'And what does Elizabeth say about all of this?' Stephanie asked, sounding like a concerned mother. Or nosy friend. The two weren't that dissimilar. 'I can imagine she wasn't too thrilled.'

'We had our fair share of arguments last night.'

'Trouble in paradise,' Lindsay said, although from her intonation it sounded as though she'd meant it as an internal thought, harking back to their earlier conversation.

Stephanie paused a moment and then continued. 'About this?'

Jake shook his head. 'Money issues.'

'Are you offering your kidney to make up for the argument?'

'No.'

But she didn't hear him and said, 'The things we do for love, eh?'

'I think it's a lovely thing,' Lindsay added, placing a delicate hand on his shoulder. 'Completely selfless and very brave.'

'Thanks,' Jake replied.

He wanted to move the conversation along, but Lindsay beat him to it. 'What's the latest? What juicy details have you got for me?'

'Excuse me?' Stephanie replied, glancing at the rearview mirror.

'About Matheson. I miss you guys sharing things with me now that Darryl's got you locked away.'

Jake hesitated, looked at Stephanie and caught her eye. The two of them had been working exclusively on the post-charge evidence against Henry Matheson, compiling all the evidence on the various MG forms that needed to be submitted to the Crown Prosecution Service. All their time had been consumed by one man and his empire of drug dealers and organised crime associates. Stephanie was the officer in charge of managing the investigation, with Darryl overseeing it all, while Jake was left to compile all the reports, which required him to pay close attention to detail on what he was doing. Something that, while the identity of The Cabal still remained a mystery, he found a struggle. The information contained in the investigation was registered confidential, and so they were sworn to secrecy.

But that didn't stop everyone else in the office trying to find out what they could. Lindsay was just another name on an already long list.

Jake reeled off his usual spiel. 'There's still a lot of

evidence we don't have against him for a lot of crimes we still don't know anything about. His criminal organisations stretch way, way back. There's still a lot of work to be done.

'Enough to sentence him for a long time though, right?' Lindsay asked.

'We'll have to see. Hopefully, we've done our jobs properly.'

'We'd better hope we had,' Stephanie responded, throwing in a little dig to remind him of the consequences if they didn't.

They entered Shoreditch, a few minutes away from Aldgate, where they were headed. They were ten minutes ahead of schedule, which gave him some time to mentally prepare himself for the next hour of his life.

'When's the court date?' Lindsay asked.

'Eighteenth,' Stephanie replied. 'A week on Monday.'

'Bet you'll be glad once it's all over.'

It'll never be over. Not until The Cabal's found.

A brief silence fell on the car, save for the ambient sounds of the car tyres rolling over the tarmac and the engine purring along as they navigated the stop-start traffic.

Jake was content to just sit there, without the need to make small talk and simple conversation. But he sensed there were things Stephanie and Lindsay wanted to discuss. It was only a matter of time, he realised, until they brought up the second topic of conversation.

The reason they were there in the first place.

'I'm still in shock,' Stephanie explained.

'It's horrendous,' Lindsay added. 'To think it happened when it did. We were all in the office with him hours before. It's crazy.'

The theory was that by talking through things with

others, it helped ease the pain, but Jake was struggling to find that the case. Roland's death was still raw in his mind, and the anger he felt was so strong he thought he might start arguing with them over something they said, no matter how minor. Instead, he decided to sit there, say nothing and agree politely whenever he was involved with the conversation. It was the bloke's way of dealing with it. Let it fester, and let it fall down, down, down until it was deep in the abyss somewhere.

That was the best way.

'If I could change one thing, I would've spent more time with him. I'd have liked to get to know him better,' Stephanie began.

Bit fucking late for that, Jake thought cynically but kept his thoughts to himself. In his experience, he'd discovered that death made people realise how much of a shitty human being they were, of how they'd become so self-involved that they'd forgotten about everyone else. Case in point: Stephanie and her posthumous desire to be friendly, to be kind to someone to whom she'd previously neglected to give any attention.

It was the hypocritical way of saying she was a good person.

'My dad always told me to be kind,' she finished. 'Sometimes it's easier said than done.'

Jake turned to face her. 'I think that's the first time I've ever heard you mention your dad.'

'Probably because if I told you where he was, you'd judge and have a lot of questions – and that's not something I'm prepared for. Maybe another time.'

The conversation ended there as Stephanie pulled into a lay-by on the side of the road. They checked the permitted hours, and Stephanie paid at the roadside machine. Jake offered her his share, but it was negligible. She suggested he buy her a coffee instead.

'You've got yourself a deal,' he replied as he stepped out of the car and closed the door behind him.

As they started walking towards the escape room, Jake's phone vibrated. He removed it from his pocket and checked the message.

Some people want to watch the world burn

Jake read it through a second time, a third. It was from the same mobile number as the night before.

The person you want is D...

But before he was able to dwell on it for too long, a hand appeared in his face. He hadn't realised it, but he'd stopped still, and both women were waving at him to hurry up. He apologised with a considerate smile then followed after them.

Shortly after, they arrived at a small building on the corner of the street. Its windows were blacked out with black sheets of A3 paper that had been Sellotaped together and stuck to the window. It was a shoddy job, which Jake assumed meant the interior was going to be just as amateur. At the top of the fascia was the company's name: Escape the Crazy Maze. Jake rolled his eyes and sighed. It was all a bit too much like Halloween for his liking. Good for one month and then outdated for the other eleven.

He hopped up the kerb and wandered to the building's front door. There was a button on the side of it. Stephanie pressed it, sounding a doorbell.

Within a few seconds, the door opened. They were greeted by a young girl with blood-red hair. Her frame was wiry and she had a mole on her forehead, just above her eyebrow.

'Hello,' she said. 'Grayson party?'

'That's us,' Stephanie replied.

The girl smiled, stepped aside.

'Welcome to the Room of Doom.'

Chapter Nine

SMASHING RECORDS

When they returned, just under an hour later, they were hailed as heroes. Everyone in the office had been surprised to see them back so soon, but Darryl most of all. The three of them had completed the escape room within a half-hour, something never before seen in the Room of Doom. With wit, intelligence and a keen eye for hidden details, they'd manoeuvred their way around the several challenges and escaped victorious, with the identity of The Butcher Killer – the psychopath they were hunting down – firmly in their grasp.

What they'd neglected to share, however, was the fact that Stephanie had already completed an escape room similar to the Room of Doom. They could have completed it within fifteen minutes, but they'd decided it would out them as frauds and cheats. So instead they'd set themselves a goal of meandering about, wandering vacantly at times, just so they could beat the world record by a modest few minutes.

'We'll have to see if Ashley, Oliver, Harriet and Azmi

can beat that,' Darryl said as he readied the next group to leave.

The office was looking sparse. Jake had worked busier Christmas Eve shifts than this. The idea of sending half the office out so they could connect with one another to mourn the loss of a friend still didn't make sense to him. They were all detectives. They were all numb to death and the pain it caused. But more importantly, they all had one thing in common: the understanding that the real sense of closure came from finding the killer responsible, from convicting someone for what they'd done. And Roland's death was no different.

The details were as scant as the bodies in the office, but that didn't mean that nobody was to blame. There were only a handful of people who knew what was going on – one was off work with stress, the other shipping people out on activities.

The one you want is D…

Speak of the devil and he shall appear.

Just as Jake, Stephanie and Lindsay were about to return to their desks, Darryl flagged them down and funnelled them into a separate room. Already sitting there, with a laptop open and a series of forms and letters resting neatly on the table, was Assistant Commissioner Richard Candy. Today, his hair was greasier than usual, his stomach bulging over the lip of his belt, and his hairy arms looked slightly more matted than normal. He wasn't an attractive man, but someone, somewhere down the line had found him some-what remotely good looking, as he continued to wear the ring his divorced wife had given him on their wedding day. Jake joked it was to fend off advances in the unlikely event of interest from the opposite sex.

'So very good to see you all,' Candy said, stepping out

of his chair and reaching for each of their hands. Jake was first, then Stephanie and finally Lindsay. 'How did you all get on at the escape room?'

Jake allowed Stephanie to bring him up to speed. She was the better storyteller.

'That's brilliant news. Knew I could rely on my best and brightest to bring the trophy home.' Candy offered Jake a quick nod. 'Especially with one of our officers of the year in the team.'

Jake flashed a coy smile as Darryl stepped around the side of the table and joined Candy, hands folded against his lap.

'Sorry for all the cloak and dagger, guys,' he began, 'but we wanted to do it this way to minimise the impact of what we're about to say.'

'It's about your colleague, Roland,' Candy muttered.

Darryl cleared his throat. 'As I said in my email, the escape room was to help you process and deal with the news. I thought that if you worked through it together, you might heal together. But after listening to some early feedback I've had on my emails, we've decided to go a little more in-depth which is why we're scheduling one-to-one meetings with myself and the assistant commissioner so you can discuss and share any thoughts and feelings and demons you may be battling.'

Jake didn't know what reaction Darryl was expecting, but judging by the shock on his face, it wasn't complete silence. He looked to Candy and they shared a message between them.

Darryl continued. 'We're putting together the rota for the meetings now, and we'll let you know once they're all confirmed. This has come as a shock to us all, and we'll all grieve and mourn in our own time.'

The biggest shock was the fact they were doing nothing concrete about it.

'Do you have any more information on what happened to him?' Jake asked.

Darryl hesitated at first, as though caught in a conflict of emotions, then nodded and reached across the desk for a piece of paper. 'Was going to wait until you were all back to share the news, but while you were gone, Poojah sent through the pathology report.'

'And...?'

Darryl dropped his head. 'There's no easy way to say this—'

'Just say it.'

'Between the hours of eleven pm and one am, we estimate, Roland committed suicide. A large quantity of paracetamol and ibuprofen was found in his system. And, to make matters worse, he pulled the trigger on himself.'

A knot formed in Jake's body. First his throat, then his chest, then his stomach. Each piece of rope tightening at different strengths, constricting his airways, bending him double.

It was unfathomable. Roland. Suicide. The two didn't – and should never – go together in the same sentence. In the time Jake had known him, he'd never expressed any concerns or feelings of depression or anxiety. Never had he had a bad day, appeared down or withdrawn. There was nothing to suggest he was suicidal. And given his understanding of psychology, Jake was fairly confident in his abilities to notice and acknowledge those types of things.

'Fucking hell,' Lindsay said, which was the first time Jake had heard her swear. 'Suicide? Really?'

Darryl pursed his lips and nodded considerately. 'That's

what it seems. You can never know what's going on inside someone's head. There's a lesson in there somewhere.'

Jake thought there was also. But not the same one Darryl was thinking about.

The one you want is D…

'What happens now then?'

'Now that the body's been released,' Candy responded, 'I've started work, with the help of HR, on the arrangements for the funeral. A death in the policing family is never an easy thing to comprehend or manage, but we're trying our best. So far it looks like we've got a venue sorted for this Thursday.'

Jake counted the dates in his head. Today. Wednesday. Thursday.

Two days.

'As far as we've been able to make out, Roland didn't have any living relatives whom we could ask to assist with the service. Poor bloke.'

The conversation came to a natural close as everyone absorbed and digested the information. Short and to the point.

One of their own.

Shot in the head.

Overdosed on painkillers and medication.

The assistant commissioner had been right when he'd said they were never easy to comprehend, but not for the same reason. Usually, a death in the force occurred in a freak accident with an armed robber or a murderer. Someone else was at fault, someone else to blame, and catching them would lead to the closure they all craved.

But a suicide… they were all culpable. If Roland really did have no one, no family, then his friends in the force were the only ones keeping him alive. And if they hadn't done that job properly…

'Jake,' a voice said, bringing him from his reverie. The owner of the voice fumbled with a piece of paper and placed it in front of him. 'We've got you down as our first meeting, if that's OK?'

Before he responded, he realised he didn't have much say in the matter. As Stephanie and Lindsay exited the room, they each placed a consolatory hand on his shoulders and offered him a warm, considerate smile.

Sadly there was nothing consolatory about the way he was feeling. Nothing to diminish the anger and betrayal and hurt and guilt.

And to make matters worse, he now had to spend the next twenty minutes telling other people what was going on inside his head.

Chapter Ten

ONE BIG FAMILY

'Please take a seat.'

The offer was non-negotiable. Darryl and Richard Candy were already in position, sitting opposite him, waiting until he sat. The atmosphere in the room had immediately switched from solemn and macabre to professional and procedural. And as he pulled the chair out from the table, Jake was beginning to feel like he was in the middle of a job interview. He had half a mind to ask for a bottle of water before they began.

'Before we begin,' Candy started, and Jake sensed it would be all one way from here – Candy at the forefront, in the headlights, Darryl in the background, thumbing the notes through – 'I'd like to say that this is a safe place. Nothing leaves these four walls unless, of course, you declare you're happy for it to. The aim of this meeting is to gather a better understanding of your mental well-being following the news of DC Lewandowski's passing. I understand you two had worked together for some time.'

Jake nodded politely. 'We were friends.'

'And is there anyone you can talk to about what's happened?'

Probably. Not that he would.

'My wife.'

Not that he'd tell her.

'It's always good to address these things. They can help ease the burden we place on ourselves.'

Jake knew. Jake knew all about this: about the stages of grief, of depression, about the way people felt and dealt with things. Now certainly wasn't the time for a lecture.

'Of course,' he said, feigning indifference. It was easier to play along than cause any issues.

'You're one of our best and brightest detectives,' Candy continued. 'First, the work you did on the Stratford Ripper, then all that mess with Liam and Drew and Pete, and lastly the officer of the year commendation. You've had a very successful couple of years with us.'

Jake sniggered internally. Success was a difficult aspect to measure. Was he successful because he'd helped capture The Crimsons on that ferry in Southampton? Yes. Was he successful because he'd helped save the life of a prostitute in Stratford from the menacing evil of the Stratford Ripper? Yes. Was he successful because, with the help of Stephanie, he'd uncovered a group of corrupt officers within the team? Yes. Was he successful because he'd helped arrest one of the worst and most organised criminals the city had ever seen? Yes.

To some, his record of successes was to be marvelled at. But not for Jake. It wasn't a case of modesty or ignorance. The truth behind it was simple; despite all of those successes, one problem still remained.

The Cabal. And he was no closer to finding him.

The one you want is D…

Jake slowly rotated his head towards Darryl, who offered him a friendly smile. Jake reciprocated facetiously. And then realised he needed to respond.

'Trying my best, sir.'

'As expected. And how are things at home? I understand you have a small family…'

'Not judging by the amount of food they eat,' Jake said, to a brief bout of laughter.

'They consume all manner of things when they're young.'

'You have kids, Assistant Commissioner?'

Candy shook his head profusely. 'No, no. But my step-brother came into the family when I was about ten. Old enough to understand that every last drop of food went on him, while we had to starve till the following morning.'

A real rags-to-riches story, Jake thought. But before he could respond, his phone chimed loudly. Then again and again.

'Think someone needs to get hold of you.' Candy nodded at the screen – it was lit with dozens of notifications and messages and missed calls.

'That'll be the wife. She's going through some stuff at the moment,' Jake explained, without really realising what he was saying.

The assistant commissioner readied pen to paper. 'Is that so?'

'Yeah,' Jake said, fixing his attention on the messages from Elizabeth. 'Her dad needs a kidney replacement, and I offered him mine.'

Jake's eyes fell on another message; this time it was from the NHS. 'Oh, and it looks like I'm not gonna be able to – our blood types aren't a match.'

'I'm… I'm sorry to hear that,' Candy said. 'But – and I hope you don't mind my saying this – I have an old friend from university who's a surgeon. He deals with this sort of thing. If you let me know your father-in-law's details, I'll see if my friend can do anything to expedite the process.'

'I… No…' Jake said. 'That's too… I couldn't possibly ask you to…'

'I'll see what I can do. We look out for one another here. We're like one big family.'

That they were. A dysfunctional one where they lied and betrayed, corrupted and bribed, neglected and disregarded, and even pushed people to suicide. What a family it was.

Jake thanked the man and shifted himself into a more comfortable position. He sensed that the meeting was over, that everyone had said what they needed to – which, in the grand scheme of things, was nothing at all. Jake didn't feel lighter about having shared his emotions (as he knew he wouldn't), and neither Candy nor Darryl had shared any further details on Roland's death. So in many respects, the quid pro quo had worked superbly. Just not in the way either party was hoping.

'Is there anything else you'd like to discuss?' Jake asked.

'Actually, there is.' This time the words came from Darryl. The Thumber had taken control of the microphone and was now owning the entire room. 'If you'll let me.'

Jake tentatively sat upright to listen.

'How long have you been in the force now?' Darryl asked.

'Just over five years.'

'As Richard said, you've accomplished a lot in that time. Considerably more than some of the rest of the team, with the possible exception of Stephanie. Those sorts of things don't go unnoticed,' Darryl explained.

He'd had Jake fooled. He'd been beginning to think they did.

'You're switched on. You've got your head and your heart in the right place – even though sometimes it might be *too* much in the right place. But that's something you can work on.'

Jake said nothing and waited for Darryl to continue. Smoke was blowing right up his arse, but he wasn't about to let it get to his head just yet.

'Richard and I have been thinking, and we wondered if you'd thought about going for a promotion to sergeant? I'd be happy to put you up for it. You'd have one hell of a glowing review. Your portfolio is astonishing considering the length of time you've been with us, in comparison to some of the others. I mean, first The Crimsons, then Liam, Drew and the rest of them, and now Henry Matheson – one of the country's most prolific criminals. You should be rewarded for your hard work and dedication. There would be a significant pay rise, and I know money is quite tight for you guys at the moment, but perhaps most importantly, you'd have more power and authority to do things quicker. Which would save us all a lot of aggro down the line. What do you say?'

The one you want is D…

D trying to butter him up.

D trying to throw him off the scent.

D trying to win him over.

Well, as far as Jake was concerned, D could go fuck himself.

'Can I think about it and let you know?'

Chapter Eleven

ONLY ONE

The decision in his mind, following his meeting with Darryl and Richard Candy, was simple. Solid. The complete lack of information regarding Roland's death had done nothing to settle his suspicions.

Roland wasn't depressed. Roland wasn't suicidal.

Roland got too close to the truth and he was silenced.

And there were only two people, as far as Jake was aware, that knew the answer as to what had happened to him.

One of them was off work with stress and the other was the woman who'd just inspected his body and conducted the post-mortem.

Poojah Singh was a pathologist who'd worked with Jake and the team frequently in recent months. At first, Jake and Poojah had been good friends, spending time together at the pub on the odd social occasion, but ever since Jake had blown the whistle on Liam and Drew, their relationship had become fractious. Unable to forgive him for what he'd done, and the investigations into her life his whistle-blowing had caused, she'd given him the cold shoulder.

It was fair to say that Jake had had his suspicions about her – about whether she was working with The Cabal, falsifying post-mortems on the dead to confuse the living. But after Stephanie's investigations into her had proven inconclusive, he'd let her off the hook.

Except now. Something was wrong. And in his mind, she was being leant on by someone much more powerful than either of them.

He knocked on her office door, tapping his feet while he waited. She opened the door, and as soon as she laid her eyes on him, they widened.

'Jake… what're you doing here?'

'Are you busy?' He peered around her and looked inside the room. When he saw she wasn't, he inched closer to the door. 'There's something I need to discuss with you.'

'I…' She hesitated but could tell it was worthless arguing and stepped aside.

Her office was small, which, when he thought about it, made sense. Everything she needed to conduct her day-to-day work was downstairs, surrounded by an assortment of weapons, chemicals and white coats. In the middle of the room was a desk and a computer with a bin beside it, filled to the brim with tissues and leftover lunch. The back wall was carved out by a window that looked out onto a residential street, a place where kids and adults lived and played knowing that dead bodies were dissected only moments from their front doors. Adorning the wall was a selection of family photos: the first of her children against a professional light blue background; the second with the family at Disneyland Paris. It was the first time Jake had been in her office, and the first time he'd ever seen any mention of a husband and kids.

'This needs to be quick,' she said, hurrying around the table as if to lengthen the distance between them. She placed her hands on the back of her chair. 'I have things to do. A lot to catch up on.'

'This will only take as long as it takes for you to tell me what I want.'

'What's that?' Although the intonation in her voice suggested she already knew what he was here for. And the relief suggested she was grateful for it.

'Roland. I need to see his body.'

Poojah scoffed. 'And I want to sleep with Brad Pitt, but that's not going to happen.'

'Why not?'

'Because he's way out of my league.'

Knives flew from Jake's eyes and punctured Poojah's resistance. 'I meant why can't I see the body?'

'Because, like Brad Pitt, Roland isn't here.'

'Where is he?'

'On his way to find out what a thousand degrees feels like.'

'Already?'

'His body was released about twenty minutes ago.'

'Just like that?'

'Yep. Just like that.'

Jake scratched the side of his chin and surveyed Poojah. Her stance. Her countenance. The way she spoke. The way she dealt with things and used humour as a defence mechanism. His intuition was telling him it was a result of avoiding the truth rather than dealing with the loss of a colleague.

'If I can't see him then I guess that leaves you to bring me up to speed,' he said finally.

'With what?'

'How fast the bullet was travelling when it killed him.'

'Jake, please.' This time there was hurt in her voice, something inside her calling out. 'Everything I uncovered was in my report. I don't know what else you want me to say.'

Jake pulled a chair out from the table. 'The truth.'

You're just as stubborn as your dad. He was always like that, thinking he knew best.

'That *is* the truth.'

'I think you once called me a bloodhound because I had a good nose for sniffing out bullshit. Do you remember that?'

Poojah confirmed she didn't.

'I know something's wrong. I worked closely with Roland. There was nothing that suggested to me he was going through a struggle.'

'And you think you're so mighty that you know exactly what everyone's going through at every moment of the day? We've all got shit, Jake. We've *all* got shit.'

Jake lined himself up for a punt. 'Is that how they got to you? They found out what yours is and exploited it?'

Poojah babbled, the syllables falling over her teeth.

'I know what these people are like, Poojah. I know what they can do. I know how *powerful* they are.' For the first time since he'd discovered The Cabal's clandestine network of corrupt officers and organised criminals, Jake truly felt like that was true. 'But that power comes at a price. And it can easily be taken away from them.'

'I don't know what you're…' Poojah closed her eyes,

inhaled deeply, held it, then exhaled for as long. 'You don't know what you're talking about.'

Jake sighed, then decided that if he was to get through to her, he'd need to mix it up. He unlocked his phone, scrolled through his camera library and showed her a picture of Luke Cipriano, the youngest member of The Crimsons, taken moments after he'd been shot in the chest. Then he showed her a photo of Danika Oblak, one of Jake's closest friends in the force, a photo taken of her brains blown out the back of her head, the bullet wound in the bottom of her chin. Finally, he found another photo, this time of Drew Richmond, another of his former colleagues, taken when Jake had discovered him the morning after his brains had exploded all over the floor, his body slumped in the chair in his kitchen.

'All of these people had secrets,' he began. 'All of these people had their demons, and all of them had one thing in common: they worked for the same man. The same man who had power over them, who threatened them, who controlled their every move.'

He flicked between the photos of Danika and Drew. 'One of these shot themselves in the head with a gun, the other was shot in the head by someone else. I don't think it takes a genius to work out which was which.'

He lowered the phone, pocketed it and stared deeply into her eyes. 'And I'm guessing the crime scene you saw in one of those photos was the same one you saw the other night. Is that right, Poojah?'

Jake typically avoided scare tactics where possible, especially when it came to his colleagues, but it was difficult to ignore the results. Poojah shuffled from foot to foot, avoiding his gaze, her head slowly turning towards the photo of her children.

Then to the photo with her husband.

'They're my kids,' she began. 'Hassan came into the picture shortly after they were born. My first husband died from a heart attack. He ate and drank horrendously, so it wasn't much of a surprise. But I never forgave him for leaving me and the girls alone. But that changed when Hassan came into my life. He was great with me, great with the girls. Loving. Caring. Tender. Completely selfless. We got married shortly after.'

Poojah moved closer to the photos as she left the room and disappeared down memory lane. 'We moved in together, even considered having a child of our own. But when... when we couldn't get pregnant, things changed. He started... hurting me. Hurting the kids. Nothing physical, at least, not to the girls. Most of it emotional. Calling me a piece of shit, cursing the children, cursing me.' She sniffed and wiped her face, out of sight. 'I guess they must have found that out.'

This was a completely new side to Poojah he was experiencing. No more was the dominant and quite frankly intimidating pathologist standing in front of him. Instead, she'd been replaced with a broken and fragile woman who needed support and attention. So he treated her with such.

'Who did, Poojah?'

'I don't know their names. I don't know anyone's name.'

'Tell me what happened,' Jake said softly.

Poojah hesitated, considered, licked her lips.

'One day, I got an email from an unknown sender. It didn't say much. All it contained was an image of me and the girls in the car on the way to school.' Poojah choked as she coughed the guilt and fear out of her throat. 'That was all. But it was enough.'

Roland.

'So I asked Roland to have a look at it for me. I told him I was afraid, that I didn't know who'd sent it. He was lovely about it. He told me that he wouldn't share it with anyone. Not until I was ready.'

Jake wished he hadn't heard that. What if he'd been upfront with Roland from the start, told him that the suspicious emails he'd received from The Cabal were direct threats on him and his family? Would Roland still be alive today? Would he know The Cabal's identity?

Jake didn't know what he was sadder about, the fact Roland was gone or that the identity of The Cabal had gone with him.

But that didn't bear thinking about.

'I think he was getting close,' Poojah continued, 'because he kept messaging me to meet up outside of work. But every time I met up with him, he never turned up. I think he was either afraid or busy with something. And then... and then I received the package.'

'Package?'

'Money. Drugs. And it had a message on it.'

'We thank you for your silence,' Jake finished. 'Yes. I've received them too. Several of them.'

'*Received*. Past tense?'

Jake nodded. 'The person sending them made it very clear that they're coming after me in a different way. I've yet to see how.'

That seemed to relieve Poojah slightly. That both of them shared this experience of a monstrous evil threatening them at every turn. That she could trust him.

'The other night,' she began again, 'I received another package. This time it contained twenty thousand pounds, but the note came through as a text message.' She reached for her phone and showed him the message.

Soon something will be required of you. Soon you will be able to leave your husband for a new life with your children. Soon you will know exactly what you have to do.

Jake lowered the phone onto the desk. 'So you were forced to rule Roland's death a suicide?'

She nodded.

'And cover up his murder?'

She nodded again.

Jake exhaled deeply and settled into the chair. 'What else do I need to know? Is there anything in his house I can use as a clue?'

He knew the answer as soon as he'd said it. If The Cabal was behind the killing, then he would have made certain there was nothing left behind that could incriminate him or whoever he'd ordered to carry out the hit.

Poojah confirmed it for him. 'I tried looking for his laptop, thinking he'd brought it home with him, but that was gone as well.'

'And it's not on his desk, either...'

Which meant it could have been anywhere, well out of his reach.

'Anything else?' Jake asked.

Poojah readied herself. 'Brendan Lafferty... he saw the body first.'

Jake tilted forward. 'Is he OK?'

'I don't know. I hope so. But I do know that he's not off work with stress.'

'Where is he?'

'I don't know. But I'm worried whoever's behind it all may have done something to him as well.'

She paused, swallowed away the fear and spoke clearly. 'Please don't say anything to anyone, Jake. You're the only one I trust. And you're the only one who can do something about this. But there are some serious things going on in your team. You need to be careful.'

Chapter Twelve

BROKEN INTO AND ROBBED

That evening, when he arrived home, Jake felt tired, mentally drained. Either that or he was monumentally distracted. The day's events had sapped all his energy from him like a leech. First, the escape room where, in truth, he'd found some elements of it enjoyable. Then the discussion with Richard Candy and Darryl Hughes. And then the meeting with Poojah. A lot for him to process. He yawned deeply as he stepped through the front door, struggling to free the key from the lock.

When he eventually did, he kicked his shoes off and dropped his bag to the floor. Usually, on his return at a civil hour, he was greeted by a flurry of excited faces. But tonight there was nothing except his drawn face in the hallway mirror.

'I'm home!' he called to no response.

Drifting from behind the kitchen door at the end of the hallway were the sounds and smells of dinner cooking. The deep, husky aroma of a beef stock cube marinating a piece of mince, lightly scattered with some spice, sizzling away in a frying pan.

Jake trundled towards the kitchen. There, Elizabeth was rushing from side to side, trying to handle the dinner and simultaneously feed the girls. A tea towel was flung over one shoulder, and a thin sheen of sweat covered her forehead.

'Daddy!' Maisie bellowed, spewing pieces of food across her chair.

Coming home always filled Jake with warmth. Especially after a long day. Seeing the faces of his little humans eagerly awaiting his return – it was what he lived for. Bending down, he gave Maisie and Ellie a kiss on the forehead each, then shuffled over to Elizabeth. He wrapped his arm around her waist and kissed her neck.

'Hi,' she said, flustered.

'How was your day?'

'Fine.'

'The girls behaving themselves?'

'Yeah.'

Uh-oh. We've been here before, Jake thought.

One Word City. Something To Say Avenue.

'What's wrong?' he asked, taking a step back so as not to add any fuel to the fire.

She didn't answer.

'Liz, what's wrong. Is everything OK? Is it your dad?'

'My dad's fine,' she snapped. 'I'll tell you after dinner.'

Dinner was delicious, one of her best. Not that she cared to hear it; she'd been too busy feeding the children and filling her mouth with food to listen to anything he had to say.

'My day was eventful, thanks for asking,' he said as he loaded his plate into the dishwasher.

No response.

'Went to an escape room, turned down a promotion, found out Roland's death was a suicide, found out that it wasn't a suicide.'

'You went to an escape room?'

'Out of all those things, *that's* the one you pay attention to?'

'Who did you go there with?'

Jake rinsed his hands under the tap. 'Stephanie and—'

'Course. Figures.'

He rolled his eyes but kept his back to her. 'Which means what?'

'Nothing. Why'd you turn down a promotion? Don't you know we need the money?'

Jake placed his hands on the edge of the kitchen counter and gripped. 'I don't need reminding. But it's not all about the money.'

'Says the only one in this household making it.'

'Besides,' he retorted, 'after tax, we really wouldn't be that much better off.'

'Every little helps, Jake.'

Not when it comes to arguments in a relationship.

'I'm happy doing what I'm doing,' he said, feeling as though he needed to defend himself. Which, he realised, he did. 'As a DC I do a lot more of the fun stuff. Any higher and you lose out on the operational side of the job. The higher you go, the longer you stay behind a desk. I don't want that. I signed up for this job because I want to make lives better, and where I'm at now, I can do exactly that. It's less about politics and strategy at my level, more about helping others.'

'Everyone except your own family,' Elizabeth whispered.

If she'd had no intention of letting him hear it then

she'd messed up. But if she had, then he hoped he'd given her the reaction she was expecting.

'The fuck is that supposed to mean?' He turned to look at her, scowling. This time she didn't protest about his use of colourful language in front of the girls.

Elizabeth reached beneath the laptop on the table and pulled out a piece of paper. Jake sauntered round the central island and snatched it from her. It was the letter they'd received yesterday, notifying them that their British Gas account was in arrears.

'I dealt with this yesterday.'

'No, you didn't. This is another one. Came through the post today.'

Weird.

'Maybe they sent it by mistake.'

'Maybe. Or you didn't sort it like you told me you had. Wouldn't be the first time.'

Jake bit his lip. Her accusations were becoming increasingly horrid and frequent, each one cutting away at him with immense pain. That he was gambling. That he was lying. Next thing, he'd probably be accused of being the head of a clandestine network of organised criminals and police officers.

Jake snatched the letter from her, stormed out of the kitchen and sat on the bottom step of the stairs. He unlocked his phone, opened his address book and tapped on the first number that appeared in his recent calls.

The ringing tone sounded in his ear, and as he waited, he picked at a scab on his ankle. A violent injury he'd sustained from tripping over one of Maisie's My Little Pony figures and kicking the TV cabinet on the way down.

'Thanks for your call,' came the automated voice on the

other end of the line. 'Your call is important to us. Please wait while we transfer you to a member of our team.'

Letting out a deep groan, Jake stretched his back against the steps, piano muzak playing loudly in his ear.

Three minutes passed.

Then five.

Seven.

Nine.

Ten.

After eleven minutes, he lost hope and tried again, this time double-checking the number that was on the letter Elizabeth had just given to him.

And then he realised, it was a different number.

Confused, he tried the new number, but the same thing happened. Except this time with a different canned response.

In the background of his mind, he began to panic. What was going on? Why wasn't he getting through to British Gas? Surely they couldn't be *that* busy at nearly seven o'clock? And why had they given him two letters with two different numbers to call?

In the end, after several more minutes of persevering, he found the number online from their website. Completely different to the numbers he'd just tried moments ago. Sceptical, he dialled.

Within seconds, he was through to an automated response. He followed the steps and waited.

'Hello, British Gas. My name is Jonathan. How can I help?'

Jake explained the situation.

'I see. Let me get logged into your account. Could you confirm the first line of your address and postcode please?'

Jake did.

'And please tell me the answer to your security question – name of first pet.'

Jake did.

'Excellent. Thank you.' Jonathan hesitated on the other end of the line. 'Unfortunately, Mr Tanner,' he continued, 'I can't see anything wrong with your account. There's nothing on here saying that you had any money owed, nor that your account was in arrears. Your payments have been going through fine and on time via direct debit.'

Jake's body turned cold. A lump formed in his throat and a great pressure squeezed his head like a baler machine as a dozen thoughts and questions swarmed his mind, paralysing him. He wanted to say something but couldn't. The words wouldn't reach his mouth, and he was beginning to feel physically sick. It dawned on him what had happened.

'Excuse me? Sir? Are you still there?' Jonathan asked, his voice distant, far off, like an echo.

'Erm… yes. Yes, I am,' Jake said, coming back to reality. 'I think… I think someone's hacked into my account. I called you guys yesterday. You took a payment from me and said that the account was fine.'

'There never was an issue with your account, sir. It is fine.'

'No, it's not. How can it be, if someone's managed to hack into it and pretended to be you! How has this been allowed to happen? Have you had a security breach?'

'Not that I'm aware of, sir.'

Jonathan continued speaking, but Jake was no longer paying attention. Instead, he was replaying the conversation he'd had with the British Gas representative yesterday.

How the man had asked him for his favourite location.

How the man had asked him for the name of his childhood friend.

How the man had asked him for his favourite sports team.

How the man had asked him the exact same security questions that he had for his online banking.

If I could just get you to confirm the last two digits of the sort code and account number…

And if I could get the details of your debit card…

'Sir?' Jonathan asked in his ear again.

'Yes,' Jake replied, closing his eyes. 'I'm still here.'

He pressed the bridge of his nose, attempting to block out the noise, get rid of it so that he could be alone with his thoughts. To come up with a contingency plan. Next steps.

'What happens now on your end?' Jake asked.

'The best thing for you to do, sir, is to speak with your bank. Make sure the accounts are fine and that nothing there has been compromised. If it has then they will launch an investigation with us and the police.'

'So there's nothing you can do?'

'I'm sorry, sir, I—'

'Nothing at all?'

'I'm afraid—'

Jake lost his temper. 'Thanks for fuck all.'

He hung up the phone abruptly then squeezed the device in his hand, his skin pressing the button that illuminated the screen. He unlocked the device, found his online banking and logged in.

He waited impatiently as the server logged into his account. Eventually, after what felt like an eternity, the screen loaded, displaying his account with Barclays. He had two – one for his personal account, and the other for their joint account.

The balance beside his personal account read: £0.

The balance beside the joint account read: £0.

All they had to last them till the end of the month. He'd been hacked, broken into and robbed of all his money. He felt violated, more so than if someone had broken into his home and stolen everything inside. It was incomprehensible – that his idiocy had been responsible for bankrupting them. If anything, this was worse than if he'd lost the money with the gambling he'd been accused of. At least then he'd have had a legitimate excuse – a problem, an illness. But this… this was different. He – and other police officers like him – were trained to notice and detect signs of fraudulent activity, phishing, email scams, personal identity fraud. He was aware of the methods that criminals and fraudsters used nowadays, but he'd been distracted and had completely overlooked them.

The pressure in his head worsened. What was he going to tell Elizabeth? He couldn't begin to think how that conversation would play out. It would put their marriage under even more strain than it already was. She wouldn't blame him for this, would she?

Of course she would. Who was he kidding? He *was* the one responsible. It was all on him.

Failure, failure, failure…

As he continued to stare at his phone, he received a text message from his network provider, telling him that he'd just incurred a charge of £144 for calling both incorrect mobile numbers. The bastards had even used a premium number to add insult to injury. Accompanying the message at the bottom was a gentle reminder that the money would be taken from his account within a few days.

Fury flared through his veins but he could be angry with no one other than himself.

And the people responsible.

Part 4: 5th Jan

Chapter Thirteen

LITTLE SUSIE

The screeching sound of the buzzer ruptured her ears. Her gaze darted towards the small door in the far-left corner of the room where, moments from now, her father would walk through. Her heart raced and her palms sweated with excitement, and she shifted in her seat, extending her spine and pushing her chest out. Just like he'd taught her.

The way you sit is sometimes people's first impression of you. Don't let them think you're lazy. It reflects badly on me and your mother.

A few seconds later, he arrived. His sweatshirt and jumper looked dirty again, dark, stained black across the shoulders, neck and waist. His arms were behind his back – more out of choice than any form of corporal punishment. His skin sagged, and it had lost colour considerably since she'd last seen him. Thin white whiskers sprouted from his chin like hairs on a potato. And he looked aimlessly around the place.

The only man in her life. Broken.

Her father moved about the room, followed by a stream of prisoners, and pulled his chair out from beneath the table. He slid into the seat and struggled a smile.

'Hey, Daddy,' she said.

'Leah,' he murmured, giving her a cold nod.

'Leah's not here, Dad. I'm Stephanie.' She surveyed him again, focusing on the frailty of his fingers and the way the jumper hung loosely from his shoulders. 'You're not eating again, are you?' she asked, filling her voice with concern.

'The food here's terrible. How can I?'

'You'll starve if you don't. And you're not washing your clothes either, are you?'

'I get other people to do that.'

'But you're not. I can see it in the clothes you're wearing. They're dirty.'

Her father leant forward, keeping his hands in his lap. 'It's a shithole in here, Stephie. They're all fucking psychopaths. All of them. None of them are guilty of anything.'

'But you're not, Dad. We both know that.'

Well, so far as she could tell. At present only one of them did definitely.

'And what're you doing about it?' he snapped. 'Two months I've been in here and you've not done anything. And you call yourself my daughter.'

The better daughter. The one who loves you while the other one's in fucking Paris riding some bloke's dick and getting used to not having you in her life anymore.

'I'm working on that, remember? It's difficult.'

In fact, it was proving more difficult than she'd anticipated. A few months ago, during the summer, her sister had found a few pieces of child pornography on their father's laptop – some graphic and nasty stuff – and quickly considered reporting it. But Stephanie had been the one to stop her. There was a fairly reasonable explanation, she was sure. And there was: the videos had been sent to him by a friend from one of his gentlemen's clubs, as far as his version of events had gone.

But Leah was having none of it, and subsequently reported their dad to the police. Now Stephanie had the job of proving that it was a one-time thing and that the other evidence she'd discovered on another laptop was all meant as funny jokes from his friends.

'They're always sending me weird things like that,' he'd said, 'but I never look at them.' She hoped, for their family's sake, that was indeed the case.

'The other day,' he began, lowering his voice to a whisper, 'one of them got beaten up in here. In their cell. They beat him and his friends up. Then they burnt him with water.'

Around them, conversations bustled and the room was soon filled with raucous laughter as friends and family members shared stories of the outside world, of a life without the prisoner in it.

Stephanie reached forward, placing her hand in the centre of the table in the hope that he'd take it and kept her voice low. 'Who did, Dad?'

'One of the guys in here. I don't know his name,' he replied. 'What're you doing to get me out? How long's it going to take?'

'I don't know. Hopefully not too much longer.'

'It's been two months already.'

'I know, Dad. I know. I'm working on it, I really am. You just have to be patient.'

'I hope you're working hard at work, Stephanie. I didn't raise you to be some sort of sloppy pushover.'

'I'm not. I got promoted to detective inspector. And I'm working in the Major Investigation Team now. I'm in a small team and it's much better than working at the IPCC. Are you proud of me?'

Her father grunted. 'You haven't got a boyfriend, have you? What did I tell you about boyfriends? They're no good. They'll distract you.'

'I know, Dad. I won't forget that sage piece of advice.'

'Good. Your sister always had boyfriends. I didn't like any of them.'

'Neither did she,' Stephanie said as a guard sauntered past with his hands in his pockets and his keys jangling by his hip. Stephanie eyed them, and for a split second contemplated stealing them, grabbing her dad's hand and carrying him out of prison so they could run away together. Go back home. Travel up north to Manchester, or go to the Lake District or the Scottish Highlands where nobody would be able to find them.

What a stupid fucking idea.

She turned her attention back to her dad.

'Do you remember the first boyfriend she had?' she began. 'The rugby player. Six foot fifteen or something like that. Remember when she brought him over for the first time and we had dinner together, the five of us? I'll always remember the look on his face when you told him you were a—'

'It's a shithole in here, Stephie,' he interrupted. 'They're all fucking psychopaths. But none of them are guilty though.'

'I know, Dad,' she said bluntly. 'You said.'

She glanced down at her watch and noted the time. Five minutes left.

'I miss her,' he said.

'Who?'

'Little Susie.'

Stephanie searched her memory bank of names. And then she had it.

'Little Susie from when we lived in Romford?'

A glaze washed over her father's eyes, and in an instant, he was out of the room and lost in his own world. 'She was a lovely little girl. So kind, so sweet. I miss her, I really do.'

Stephanie wasn't sure that the feeling was mutual; at any length, Susie Chaplain wouldn't have a clue who he was.

'Always so friendly. And she had a lovely smile. Such beautiful teeth.'

'That's enough now, Dad.'

She looked at her watch again. The time had disappeared just as fast as his memory. She didn't want to think about how quickly he'd deteriorated since the last time she'd seen him. Closing her eyes, she swallowed and said, 'I'm sorry, Dad, but I've got to go.'

'What are you doing to get me out? How long's it going to take?' His hand reached out for hers just as she retracted it from the table. His eyes shimmered in the fluorescent light. They looked distraught, but more importantly, she noticed there was fear in them – the paralysing fear that he would be in there for the rest of his life.

She had the fear too. Insidious. Paralysing. All-consuming. The one that kept her awake at night. She feared that she wouldn't be able to get him out, that she wouldn't be able to right the wrong that had befallen him. That she wouldn't be able to provide for him as he'd done for her all her life.

'You're going to get me out of here, aren't you?'

She struggled to look at him as she fought the lump in her throat. Blinking away the tears, she replied, 'Of course I am, Dad. I'm going to do everything in my power. And then we can be together like we were when Mum was alive. And then I can look after you. And then everything will be all right again. I promise.'

Chapter Fourteen

COMMAS AND ALL

Jake was in the office by six the following morning. The evening had passed in a blur. They'd eaten what was left of their dinner, put the girls to bed and then spent the rest of what precious little time they had together sitting on separate settees, both pretending to watch the first episode of the new series of *Sherlock*, the images of his empty bank account ingrained in Jake's mind as he tried to construct a way out of the thousand-pound hole they were in. Neither of them had said goodnight to one another as they went to bed, and when Elizabeth didn't ask why he was going in so early, he was grateful he didn't have to lie. Even though he already had one lined up. He'd decided not to tell her the truth, as he didn't want her to worry. Worse, he didn't want to give her any ammunition she could use towards him.

This was his problem, his solution.

And he was going to do it alone.

Right now, however, he couldn't think about Elizabeth's reaction. He was on the phone to the bank as he entered the office. It was quiet, save for the cleaner finishing her shift for the night; she was in the middle of wrapping the cord around the back of the hoover, a small plastic holder filled with cleaning chemicals and stained dishcloths by her feet. Jake paid her little attention. If this was any other occasion, he would have acknowledged her like he always did.

'Thank you for calling Barclays' fraud team. This is Alana.'

'Someone's hacked into my account. They've stolen all my money. I've got nothing left. I have bills that I need to pay. Kids that I need to feed.'

Alana sounded very concerned and asked him to pass through security.

'I…' Jake was hesitant. She was asking the exact same questions that he'd been asked a few days ago. 'Is there any other way you can get into the account?'

'Sadly, no. If you don't wish to discuss this over the phone, you can always pop into a branch and they'll be happy to assist you.'

Jake sighed and closed his eyes. He found his seat and slumped into it then bit the bullet.

'I don't have the time to go into a branch. Ask me the questions again.'

So she did, and Jake responded, just as he had done previously. Once she got into the account, he relaxed.

'I'm going to need a few more details, if that's all right?' Alana continued.

'Yes, sure. Whatever you need to know.'

He spent the next five minutes going through the process of raising a case. He told her in explicit detail what had happened, this time remembering more and more details than he had before. Like the intonation in the man's voice. The words he'd used and the way he'd answered the call. The background noise simulating a real-life call centre.

Whether or not it was useful for her, he didn't know. But by the end of it all, Jake felt exhausted.

'What happens next?' he asked. 'How do I get my money back?'

'From what I can see, the payments from your personal and joint account were made to a company called Candiru Limited.'

'Right.'

He wasn't sure what that had to do with anything. All he wanted to know was when he'd get his money.

'And... according to the login details, the payments were made while logged in to the same IP address as previous logins. Was this done on your desktop or laptop by any chance, sir?'

'I didn't make the payment.'

But somebody else did... On the street, in the house next door, outside the front window... Using my login details and my fucking IP address...

'Does anyone else in your family have access to your computer or laptop at home, sir?'

'Yes, but—'

'And is it possible they made the payment, sir?'

'What? No, nobody—'

'From what I can see in front of me, it appears that this may have been a scam where you or someone else in your household has knowingly paid the money into this investment account.'

Jake took a step back from his computer and clenched his fist. 'You've got to be joking me. So are you now accusing me of claiming this for some sort of insurance purpose?'

'Not at all, sir. I'm just telling you what's in front of me on the screen.'

Well, fuck your screen. And fuck you and your happy customer service voice too.

'So what happens now then?' he asked.

'First I need to give you a case number. Please keep a note of this, as this is the confirmation your case has been raised. Our investigation team will then look into this for you and contact you within seven days to give you an update.'

'I don't believe this. I can't wait that long. I need money now. I have two kids to feed. Petrol. Expenses. I can't do it all without any money.'

Alana continued, heedless. 'If the team do require any further information, they'll send you what's called a disclosure form. You'll need to complete it and return it within ten days or your case will be closed.'

'So what do I do in the meantime?'

'We'll put some temporary money in your account, sir. But please be aware that this can take up to forty-eight hours to process.'

Forty-eight hours without money.

Forty-eight hours to keep this clusterfuck of a situation away from Elizabeth.

Shambles.

'OK. That's fine. Thank you.' He quickly realised that he was using Alana as an outlet for his aggression and anger. It wasn't her fault, but she was the only one that he could take it out on right now.

He'd beaten himself up about it enough the night before.

'I wish there was something else I could do,' Alana said.

Her attempt at trying to appease him was worthless but appreciated.

'You've done everything you can. So, can I—'

Without warning, the call disconnected, and he heard two beeps in his ear. Jake pulled the phone away from his head and stared at the screen. In the top-right corner of the phone, where the signal bars should have been, was nothing. He tried placing the phone in flight mode and switching it back on again. But nothing.

He returned to the home screen and noticed a notification in his messages. It had come in while he was on the phone with Alana. It was from his mobile network provider, Vodafone.

Thanks for your recent SIM Swap. Your new SIM card will activate within the next 24 hours. Your number will remain the same. If you did not request this, please contact customer services on 209.

No mobile phone signal.

No means of communication.

Someone, somewhere in the country had swapped his mobile number to a new SIM card. Now they would receive all his incoming messages and calls. His entire identity gone, just like that.

He was at the bottom of shit creek, submerged fifty feet deep, and nobody was on standby to give him a paddle.

Jake swore, his voice filling the empty room. As he reached the crescendo of his cry, the office doors opened, cutting him off. Lindsay entered, briefcase in hand, looking as though she was wearing the same outfit as the day before.

'Everything all right?' she asked, standing in the doorway.

Jake froze. 'I'm just... I'm just having a bad morning.'

'Another one? Same thing as yesterday?'

'An extension of it,' he said, adjusting his tie, brushing it into place.

'Must be bad then.' She moved across the room. When she stopped at her desk, she asked, 'Anything I can help with?'

Jake hung his head in shame. 'Know anything about mobile phone signals? SIM swaps?'

'Not much. Why?'

'What about fraud? Know anything about that?'

'No, but I had a friend that went through it. Nasty. Really horrible experience. Her trust in everything disappeared after that. She's paranoid about everything now. She always carries cash.'

Jake grunted. He had no response. He knew how profound and overwhelming the situation was.

'Has something happened to you?' she asked.

Jake nodded. 'Everything's been taken.'

'Jesus. Sorry to hear that. How?'

'Pretending to be British Gas. Sent through a letter saying that my account was in arrears, and when I passed security with them over the phone, they took a payment from me to settle the *debt*.' Jake made inverted commas with his fingers as he said the final word.

'And they completely rinsed your account?'

Jake nodded again.

'They're so sophisticated nowadays. You have to be so careful.'

Thanks for the advice. Hadn't thought of that.

'I'm trying to get it back but nobody seems too bothered to help,' he told her.

'Have you tried the fraud squad? I'd have thought that would be your first port of call.'

'Sorry,' Jake said, grabbing a pen from his desk and drawing on his notepad. He scribbled, weaving the pen in and out in a figure of eight until the ink became dense and thick. 'It's just been a manic couple of days. Lots going on.'

'Anything else you want to talk about?'

Yes. Everything. He wanted to blurt it all out. Scream. Sprint up and down the stairs. Punch holes in the wall until he spelt: FUCK YOU, WORLD. Commas and all.

Instead, he composed himself. Inhaled, held it. And decided to keep it all bottled up – like the coward he was.

'I'm fine thank you.' Saying nothing further, he grabbed his phone, wallet and identification, and started out of the door.

'Where are you going?'

'Fraud squad.'

'What about your phone signal?'

Jake froze mid-step and glanced down at his screen. 'Erm... I'll fix it on the way. I'll use my work phone or something like that.'

'I think you need to make an appointment with the fraud squad.'

'Sorry, Lindsay, but right now I don't care. I'm going to speak to someone, and they're going to speak to me.'

Chapter Fifteen

MARSHMALLOWS

Henry could scarcely remember the last time he'd finished a book. Ten, twenty years ago? He hadn't touched one since he was fifteen, that much he was sure of – and that was only to give it to someone else so they could use the book cover as a roach for a joint they were making. Academics had always been a struggle for him. Maths, English, science – the ones you were always taught you *needed* to succeed in life – were out of reach for him. Just like history and geography and religious studies. He was an indictment of the English education system and had he applied himself better, he often wondered what life he would have led, what corporate ladder he would currently be trying to climb. Prison did that to a man – gave him lots of time to think. Lots of it. And if your brain wasn't stimulated in the right way, it could descend down a very dark path.

Fortunately for Henry, he was clever enough to apply himself to things. He had his business, and he had his books. The two main staples of ensuring his sanity survived while in prison.

Anthony Burgess had just delivered a beautifully written piece of Nadsat as Alex and his droogs readied themselves for some more ultra-violence when his cellmate trundled through the door – weak and distracted, as usual, shuffling about the room, looking into space as he did most of the day.

'What you sayin', Brian?' Henry dog-marked the page and set it beside his leg on the bed.

'Eh?'

'What you sayin'?'

The man shrugged. 'Not much.'

No surprise there. Henry remembered the day Brian had first walked through the door. He was Calvin Kershaw's replacement. That little fucker had got himself hooked on Henry's secret stash of spice and, while on a bad trip, started slicing himself with a razor blade. Blood and mess all over the place. Henry'd had to shower and clean himself three times and beg for his blood to be tested for AIDS. (Eventually, the guards had conceded and his results came back negative.)

At first, Brian had seemed kind, friendly, sprinkled with the usual dash of apprehension. But when the time came to find out what he was doing time for, he'd struggled to give a definitive answer. Fraud, he'd said. Responsible for embezzling millions into offshore accounts for the wealthy. And Brian had that air about him, the white hair, the well-groomed face, the middle-aged upper-class appearance that reminded Henry of Rupert Haversham, his former lawyer. But Henry prided himself on being a good judge of character, and he didn't for a second believe him. Of course, there was a multitude of crimes someone Brian's age could have committed: DUI, manslaughter, burglary, affray. But there was only one that Henry's men had uncovered.

Worse was the fact that someone on the twos had recognised him as the copper who'd arrested him. So the man was a nonce and a copper; it was a miracle – and an indictment of the criminal justice system – that Brian had found himself in with the rest of the population and not some sort of special section for the vulnerable and least popular.

Henry felt a duty to protect the man then. Not because he liked him or agreed with what he'd done. The opposite, in fact. Because, in their cramped cell, Henry could make life a lot more difficult for Brian than any other inmate.

'Who came to visit you today, Bri?'

Brian was in the middle of boiling the kettle. He stood with his back to Henry and tapped his feet as he waited, staring at a crack in the wall.

'Bri?'

'What?'

'Who came to see you today?'

'My daughter.'

'That's nice.'

'Yeah. Bless her, she's got a good heart on her, but she's so easily led astray by all these men. She's trying to get me out of here, you know.'

That was the first Henry had heard of it, which made a nice change from hearing the same stories again and again.

'Is that right? How's she doing that?'

The kettle finished its boil. Brian turned his back on it, rested against the bunk bed. He kept his voice low, down to a whisper. 'She's a police officer. Really good one too. I'm so proud of her. But she better not let any boyfriends get in the way of her career. Otherwise, I'll be furious.'

Henry took a moment to absorb that. His daughter was a police officer, working to get him out of prison. Whether it was a pipe dream that Brian truly believed or whether it was the truth, Henry didn't care. It opened up a lot of possibilities for him. Brian's daughter would be someone else he could lean on.

He turned to Brian and placed a hand on his shoulder. 'Boy, they really fucked up when they put you in here with me, didn't they? What's your daughter's name?'

'Stephanie. But I call her Stephie. She used to love marshmallows as a kid, my Stephie did.'

'I'm sure.' Henry scratched the back of his thumb. 'And what did you say your surname was, Brian? I can't believe I've never asked.'

'Grayson.'

Henry paused a moment. 'Of course it is,' he said eventually.

The names Grayson and Tanner were synonymous with Henry's PTSD from his arrest and subsequent induction into the prison system. Both of those surnames were responsible for putting him in here, and now, with somebody to lean on, they would be the ones to help him get out.

'Hey, Brian,' Henry called, tapping the man on the shoulder. 'How would you like a job, something to keep you busy in here?'

'Er…'

'Great! I just need you to do a couple of things. Nice and simple. I need you to be my eyes and ears around this place. There are a lot of bad people who will try to make life miserable for me, so I need someone to be on lookout.'

'I don't know…'

'Life can be very hard for you in here, Bri. Trust me. I know who you are and what you've done, and I have ways that I can get to your family.'

'Stephie…'

'That's right. We wouldn't want anything to happen to

Stephie, would we? So whaddya say? We could even have a little safe word if you needed it. How about… marshmallows?'

'Marshmallows…'

'Every time I say that word, it means I need you to do something for me. Can you remember that?'

'Of course I can. There's nothing wrong with my memory.'

Henry didn't believe that, but he did believe he had Brian wrapped around his little finger. To seal the deal, and to set something in motion on the outside, he removed his phone from his pocket and typed a message.

New lean on Steph Grayson. Stratford CID. Dad's in prison wiv me.

He hit Send but didn't wait for a response. Instead, he turned his attention back to Alex and his droogs, while Brian busied himself with washing his hands. Henry looked over at the kettle and mug beside it.

'Brian, mate… couldn't make me a cuppa, could you?'

Chapter Sixteen

BIGGER CRIMINALS

Jake was standing in the reception to the City of London police station, surrounded by acres of clean marble floor, waiting for Lindsay's contact from the fraud squad to speak with him. After his little outburst, she'd somewhat reluctantly given him DCI Aaron Beckett's information. She was unsure whether he still worked there – it had been a long time since she'd last had contact with him – but Jake was feeling lucky.

Like he'd just won the lottery – which he'd never taken part in seriously before but could really do with right now.

He paced from side to side as he waited, checking his watch every few seconds, then stopped and observed his surroundings. To his left was a flyer board. Hanging from it were dozens of leaflets and pamphlets. One stood out to him.

The side profile of a female police officer with another behind her dominated the space. Her features were blurred out, and beneath were the words: SOMEONE BLURRED THE LINES BETWEEN RIGHT AND WRONG?

REPORT CORRUPTION NOW. FOR MORE INFOR-
MATION PLEASE CONTACT THE INDEPENDENT
POLICE COMPLAINTS COMMISSION.

Beneath the text was the logo of the IPCC and their contact information.

Evidence of his handiwork.

A smirk grew on Jake's face. Since blowing Liam's and Drew's corruption into the mainstream media, an internal review of procedures had been conducted. The copious amounts of literature and educational material displayed in police stations across the city now was evidence of that. What Jake had done, without realising, was create a safe place for officers in a similar position to come forward and roll over on their colleagues or seniors. Two more officers in the wider team of the Met had been arrested and convicted of corruption in connection with Liam and Drew as a result of his handiwork.

Another success to add to his CV.

A voice distracted him. 'DC Tanner?'

A man wearing a sophisticated three-piece suit was waiting for him. He had a round bald head, with a full beard that looked as though it had been growing wildly for a long while, yet simultaneously looked perfectly manicured. His ensemble reminded Jake of a model for an independent barber company he'd seen on TV once.

'DCI Beckett?' Jake asked, rising from his seat.

'The one and only.' Aaron smirked, flashing a set of veneers. Jake found it difficult to place the man's age. He would have estimated early forties, had it not been for the teeth. But now he wasn't so certain.

'Thanks for meeting me on such short notice.'

'We don't usually allow this sort of thing. But Lindsay and I go way back. I owe her a thing or two. Shall we?'

Aaron gestured for Jake to lead the way. Together they walked side by side in silence. They took the flight of escalators to the first floor, then climbed the rest of the way on foot.

When they reached the fraud squad's offices, Aaron scanned his key card and a few hesitant seconds later, they entered.

The buzz and hubbub of the office filled the room. Talking. Phones ringing. Keyboards typing. Mice clicking. Printers printing. In the background of it all was the sound of the air conditioning blasting tepid air into the room. There wasn't a single open window in the building, so Jake could only imagine what sort of winter germs were currently being incubated.

Aaron led him around the outskirts of the floor and into a room tucked down another corridor. Before they reached it, they passed a row of major incident and debriefing rooms.

'They're for large-scale enquiries,' Aaron said as Jake entered. 'The major incident rooms that is. Things like corporate fraud. Such as if your billionaires and banks were trying to swindle more money out of the system.'

'I thought that was all part of being a billionaire.'

Aaron chuckled, clearly not willing to offer an opinion on Jake's comment.

'So you even go after the banks?' Jake helped himself to a seat. It was cushioned and though the back was decorated in thick, coarse material, it was more comfortable than he was accustomed to at Bow Green.

'Nobody's above the law, Jake.'

Aaron closed the door and grabbed the seat from beneath his desk. Mountains of paperwork and forms lay atop an organiser. Overflowing. Spilling.

Aaron must have noticed Jake looking at it because he tapped the top layer and said, 'One of my few bad habits. But sometimes we have to let the chaos in our minds come out one way or another, eh?'

Jake didn't know what to say. He wondered what the manifestation of the chaos in his mind would look like… In the end, he shrugged and settled with saying, 'I guess so.'

Aaron ran his hand through his beard. 'When Lindsay spoke to me on the phone, she said it was urgent.'

'It is,' Jake replied.

'Well, the floor's all yours.'

Jake then proceeded to explain to Aaron what had happened. How it had happened. Where it had happened. And when.

'I'm very sorry to hear that,' Aaron replied after Jake had finished. 'And there was nothing the bank could do?'

Jake thought back to his call. How professional Alana had been but also how infuriated she'd made him feel at the same time.

'Not as much I expected of them,' Jake said, making no effort to hide the bitterness in his voice.

Aaron shook his head. 'I mean, I know I probably shouldn't say it, but after years of working here – and working with the banks – I've come to realise that sometimes they're bigger criminals than the ones you and I catch.'

'So what does all this mean for me, sir? Can you help?'

Aaron pursed his lips. 'I'll be honest with you, Jake.' He was doing a lot of that. 'Ever since that lot came into power, our resources have been stretched – I'm sure you know exactly what I'm talking about – which has meant we've got fewer and fewer staff doing almost double the work, with even less pay. As it stands, I can almost guarantee that it won't be looked at until next week.'

Are you fucking joking me?

Jake was going the extra mile – as he always did – to find out what had happened to one of their own, Roland. Was it too much to expect the same in return, the one time he needed help?

'I wish I had better news for you, but as I said, the amount of constraints that are being put on us is overwhelming. In the last few days, I've had several people call in sick. Not to mention the amount of overdue annual leave that everyone's taking. And we're not getting paid overtime or being given any days off in lieu.'

I don't want to hear your sob stories.

'I was under the impression you'd be able to help,' Jake retorted.

'Like I said, we *can* help. We *will* help. We just won't be able to do it in the short time you want us to. I simply don't have the resources. I'm sure you can appreciate that.'

'With all due respect, sir,' Jake started, 'I thought we looked after our own. If someone killed one of the officers in your team – or, God forbid, if someone killed you – my team would be on it regardless. And we wouldn't stop until we found the person or people responsible. Do you see where I'm coming from?'

Silence crawled through the cracks in the room, sucking the energy from the place. The slight smile on Aaron's cheeks dropped and fell to the ground. He eased himself into the back of his chair, staring at Jake, his eyes burning holes in Jake's head. Then Jake realised what he'd done – what he'd said. *Oh, my God.* He sounded like Drew Richmond.

Almost verbatim.

Jake retreated into his memory and recalled one of the last conversations that he and Drew had had. Drew had told him that loyalty was everything. That they looked after one another. That they always had each other's backs. But his words had been laced with an ulterior motive: his own self-ishness. And so had Jake's just now.

What did that make him? Was he just as bad as them? Was he as bad as the people he'd been successful in catching? Was he just as bad as a criminal?

No, of course not. *You're just being paranoid,* he thought. Yes. That was right. He wasn't turning into Drew at all. For starters, he'd done nothing wrong. It was just his overly sensitive conscience contaminating his thoughts.

Aaron cleared his throat, bringing him back to the present. 'I'm sorry, detective, but if there was something I could do to expedite it, I would. But, as such, my hands are tied. Rest assured though that when someone does finally get round to it, I'll have my best guys on it.'

Jake rose, shook Aaron's hand and left feeling aggrieved. If nobody else was going to get him out of the situation then he was going to have to do it on his own.

Whatever it took.

Chapter Seventeen

EXTENUATING CIRCUMSTANCES

At the back of the queue, Henry sensed the contemptuous looks directed at him. The discreet and whispered conversations about him. By now everyone in the prison knew about what had taken place the day before. In fact, they'd known within ten minutes. And everyone knew that he was responsible – the small burns on his legs and arms were a testament to that – but nobody had been brave enough to say anything. Not the inmates, not the guards. But, to Henry's surprise, Dominic – and his boys – had also remained tight-lipped. Partly because he was in a hospital bed somewhere, hooked up on morphine while the nurses dealt with his injuries. And partly because, credit where credit was due, Dominic was intelligent enough to know when to keep his mouth shut. What happened was a freak accident. A minor oversight. That was all. These things happen.

The other layer behind the decision was fear. Fear of reprisal and suffering a similar fate. Or worse. Along with favours, fear was the next biggest currency in prison. Once you had a man worried for his safety, he was willing to do anything for you to protect himself.

Gradually, the queue shortened, and as he neared the long conveyor belt of food, his stomach began to talk to him, telling him that he was hungry. Starving.

First up on the menu was fruit. The chef working behind the counter grabbed a banana and apple with his grimy fingers and flung them onto Henry's tray. Henry grunted and then moved down. Next: crisps. Ready salted, same as always. Then it was time for the sandwich, his preselected meal. On the menu today was a cheese and ham baguette, wrapped tightly in cellophane.

Henry stopped and glanced up at the chef. He gave the man a curt nod, maintaining eye contact, and watched him reach for the sandwich at the back of the pile, and as he placed the sandwich on Henry's plate, he tapped the top of the baguette five times.

Tap.

Tap.

Tap.

Tap.

Tap.

'Thanks, boss,' Henry said, lifting his tray from the conveyor belt and stepping away.

He moved about the lunchroom, weaving in and out of the tables, conversations freezing the instant he walked past, and found a seat on an empty table with his back to everyone. He picked up the sandwich and unwrapped the cellophane, slotting it in his pocket. Then he split the sandwich in half, peeled away the layer of cheese and found what he was looking for: an extenuating circumstance. Five grams of spice. Just for Jason. Just enough to placate his cravings until the larger shipment came in later that day. Not to mention, he wanted to give it to his friend as a little reward – a job well done for sticking up for himself and nearly beating a man to death.

Henry wiped the bag of spice clean and placed it inside his sock. He made no attempt to hide what he was doing; he simply didn't need to. Nobody was in a position to confront him about it – especially now they all knew what he was capable of.

Silence fell on the cafeteria, and in the back of his mind, he became aware of it. Something wasn't right.

And then a figure appeared in the corner of his eye. A small, well-built individual. Hairy, yet well-groomed. Fresh-faced. And it soon became apparent that this was the guy Jason had been talking about the day before. Carlson. The new man on the ones.

The one asking all the questions.

Henry straightened his back and tensed his muscles, a muscle memory he'd developed from years of working on the streets, dealing drugs in the early days of his empire. Carlson carried himself well and walked with a certain air of arrogance, as though he thought he was the cock of the walk, the bravest and boldest. Well, it was Henry's job to knock the bird down a peg or two.

'All right?' Carlson asked. He had a thick estuarial accent, with a minor speech impediment on the pronunciation of his Rs.

'Yeah?' Henry looked up at him, letting the man know he didn't like to be interrupted.

Carlson sat down. 'You're just the man I've been looking for.'

Strange choice of words.

'Must've got me mixed up with someone else,' Henry said, taking a bite of his sandwich. 'I ain't nobody in here.'

'Isn't what I hear.'

'You'll wanna stop listening to Mark. He's been in here so long he thinks the walls in your cell are talking to him. You ain't careful, you'll go the same way. Poor sod needs help.'

Carlson laid a hand flat on the table. Henry looked at it, surveying it for a moment. A lot could be learnt from the shape and cleanliness of a man's hand: the dirt beneath the fingernails, the length of the nails, the cuts, scars, bruises.

None of which Henry could see in front of him.

Instead, he was faced with a well-manicured hand. Small fine hairs sprouted out of the top of his fingers, and the creases in his skin were delicate. They looked as though they'd spent several years behind a desk. At a keyboard. Holding a paintbrush or wrapped around a steering wheel. There was no life experience behind them. Except for one thing: the ghostly band of a missing wedding ring on his left hand.

'What're you doing?' Henry asked, returning his attention and focus to the sandwich.

'Talking to—'

'I mean, time. How long?'

'Four years.'

'What for?'

'GBH.'

Henry closed his eyes. If Carlson was going to lie, why didn't he insist on lying well? It almost made him feel bad for the way he was about to treat him.

'All right. And what do you wanna do with me?'

'I hear you're the man who runs things around here.'

'Like I said, don't spend all your time listening to Mark. He's a bad influence.'

'I want to join your group. I want *in*.'

'And what exactly is it you want *in* on?'

The man looked around, sheepish, his gaze skitting left and right. 'You know, drugs. Dealing. I want in.'

Henry took another bite, savouring it, purposely delaying his response. 'What's your name, kid?'

'Carlson. Owen Carlson.'

'All right, Owen. I'll let you in. But first I need you to do a couple things for me.'

This didn't seem to faze him. And perhaps it shouldn't have, given the fact he was a criminal and wanted to become a part of Henry's ranks. But Henry wanted him to squirm, to hesitate. He wanted another reason to suspect the man.

'Anything, Henry. Whatever you need me to do, I'll do it.'

And there it was. The reason.

Clear as the bag of spice in his sock that he reached for and placed on the centre of the table.

'You want me to sell it? Like a test?'

'No. I want you to *use* it.'

'What?'

'Snort it up your nose. Smoke it. Rub it into your gums. Shove it up your arse if you prefer. Just make sure it gets in your system one way or another. That's your first test. Now take it and get out of my sight.'

'And then I'm in?'

Henry sighed. Why couldn't he just eat his sandwich in peace? He looked at Owen.

'I'll have another task for you later.'

The moment Owen was out of his sight, Henry spun round on his chair and went in search of Brian. Fortunately, he found the old man wandering gormlessly in the centre of the ones, muttering to himself. Henry observed him for a few moments and noticed that every time Brian walked past a guard, he'd acknowledge them and shake their hand.

You could take the man out of the police, but you couldn't take the police out of the man.

Henry chased after him and tapped him on the shoulder. 'You lost, Bri?'

'Don't think so. There aren't many places you can go round here.'

'There are lots of hiding places if you know where to look. I'll have to show them to you some time.' Henry placed a hand around Brian's shoulder and led him in the opposite direction. 'Remember this morning I said I was gonna need your help?'

Brian replied with a tentative yes.

'Well, I need it now. There's this new guy that wants to get cosy with me. All I need you to do is follow him and report back. Reckon you can handle it?'

'Like a stakeout?' Brian's demeanour changed. His face flushed with excitement, and he became almost childlike.

You can take the man out of the police...

'Exactly. Like a stakeout.'

They came to a stop and Henry placed both hands on Brian's shoulders.

'Now, I need you to go and find him and watch him. In his pockets, he's got a pouch of drugs on him. I want you to watch what he does with it. But you'll have to be quick.'

'How do I know what he looks like?'

Henry explained Owen's physical appearance to Brian, who nodded accordingly.

'Reckon you got this?'

A nod. 'I got this.'

Henry gave him a wink. 'Good man. Come and find me as soon as you can, all right?'

Then he waved the old man off and watched him shuffle to the other end of the ones, this time walking with a sense of purpose, his back straight and his head swinging left and right in search of his new target. Call him the Messiah, but Henry had just breathed a breath of fresh air into the old man.

But his optimism was quickly stunted. Behind him, he heard footsteps. Loud, military-style boots pounding on the concrete.

Henry turned. Saw one of the screws coming towards him.

Williamson. Henry's favourite. The man was dressed in black trousers and a white shirt, with epaulettes on the tops of his shoulders. His hair was thinning, and he had a bald patch at the back of his skull. Williamson was Henry's biggest supplier – the one that facilitated everyone's drug habit. He made it possible for the shipments to come in, and he also made sure that they didn't go back out again shortly afterwards. To keep him on side, Henry paid him a monthly retainer with the understanding that, if the shit hit the fan and the warden found out what was going on, then Williamson would leave him 'high and dry out in the cold with his balls wrapped around his neck', as Williamson himself had so eloquently put it.

'Matheson,' Williamson called, his voice commanding and authoritative. It was abrasive – the result of years spent screaming at other inmates. 'A word.'

Excellent.

They crossed the ones and came to a stop by a set of heavy, six-inch-thick metal doors. Williamson scanned his key card and they waited for the doors to open. As he entered, Henry gave a curt nod to the stationary officers standing either side of the door with their arms crossed behind their backs. They paid him no attention.

Williamson then led him down a long, never-ending corridor. Henry had only ever been there once, and that was when he'd first arrived. He'd hoped that the last time he'd see it was when he was being escorted out of the prison gates for good. But he'd also wished for his cellmate to be a Victoria's Secret model, and look how that had turned out...

Once they reached the end of the corridor, Williamson scanned his key card and ushered him into a small square space, with three other corridors sprouting out from it like a spider's web. They were surrounded by walls and doors. But in this particular space, there were no cameras.

Williamson stopped and turned in front of Henry, keeping him at bay with an outstretched arm. Henry didn't like being touched, but he made an exception – Williamson was one of the few he made it for. He owed the man a lot.

'What the fuck you playing at?' Williamson snapped, his voice echoing enormously around the enclosed space.

'What do you mean?' Henry asked, taking a step back for his own safety as well as Williamson's.

'Don't play dumb with me, fuckwit. Yesterday – Dominic Radler. I know you and Jason were the ones responsible.'

'You come to tell me off, is that what this is? Put me on your knee and slap me?'

'I'm not coming for you. But others will if they catch wind of it. It's a warning – think of it that way. You're lucky the governor isn't about this week, otherwise, he really would have had your bollocks wrapped round your neck.'

'What did you tell him?'

'He doesn't know. I plan to get it all sorted out by the time he comes back. And that means I'm going to need double money this month. As an apology for making my life that little bit fucking harder than it already is.'

'No,' Henry responded, putting his business cap on. 'Double's too much. I'll give you an extra K.'

Williamson stepped forward. Henry matched him for height, but there was something in the man's stance that made him appear six inches taller.

'You really think you're in a position to negotiate? All it takes is for me to give permission to Dominic, and he'll be able to explain the entire thing. In exquisite detail, no doubt.'

Henry folded his arms. Threats. Empty threats. That's all they were. He'd experienced many before. But there was one thing that he was certain of himself – whenever *he* made a threat, he always followed through with it.

'How is he?' Henry asked. Now wasn't the time to pick a battle with Williamson.

The man sighed before replying. 'Not good. None of them are. His burns are bad – like, really bad. But he's being treated by one of the best in the country – a little consolation for what you did to him.'

'Why? He doesn't deserve that.'

'He does if you want him to keep his mouth shut. Oh, and I agreed that you have to keep him on a monthly retainer. Silence costs, mate.'

Henry exhaled deeply and fought the urge to roll his eyes. Williamson was eating his profits with all these unnecessary expenses.

'We'll see,' Henry said.

'No, no.' Williamson wagged his finger in the air and chuckled sarcastically. 'Don't even think about it, mate. If you want him to be quiet – and *stay* quiet – you'll do exactly as I tell you.'

'Like I said, we'll see.'

'Jesus,' William hissed, looking away from Henry.

'How's that other thing coming along?' Henry asked. He hugged his arms tighter around his body.

At the mention of it, Williamson became friendlier, more docile.

'You got an update for me?'

'Not a positive one.'

'Let me hear it.'

Williamson swallowed and looked around him, as though he'd heard someone sneaking into the confined space escaping their notice.

'Haversham's left the country,' Williamson said.

'He's what?'

'Gone. And no one seems to know where. I'm getting some of my contacts at Border Force to look into it.'

'Has he gone alone?'

Williamson shook his head.

'So he'll be coming back at some point. The kids'll have school and his wife'll get bored – trust me, I've met her and she needs constant attention. Rupert wouldn't have been able to escape the country that quickly – not if he wanted to start a new life somewhere else.'

'I don't know what you want me to tell you, Henry. I'm doing everything I can to find him. You still haven't told me what you want me to do to him when I do…'

Henry hesitated for a moment. He'd thought about his revenge on Rupert Haversham for a long time – ever since his solicitor had refused to defend him in the police station – but the present circumstances had forced him to re-evaluate his decisions.

'You know what happened to Dominic?'

'Yeah…'

'The specifics?'

'Yeah…'

'*That.*'

A look of confusion struck Williamson. 'My contacts will do some messed-up stuff, but they won't go that far.'

'Find him and leave the rest up to my guys. They'll take care of it.'

A silence fell on them both. A thought popped into Henry's mind.

'And the *other* thing?'

'I'm making some home visits over the next couple of days.'

'Good boy.'

'Anything else, Your Highness?'

'Actually, there is.'

'Seriously?'

'Shouldn't have asked if you didn't wanna hear it.'

'What now?'

'Owen Carlson. Cell thirteen. I want everything you've got on him. I got a feeling that little reprobate's gonna be causing me a few problems sooner than Dominic will be.'

Chapter Eighteen

ONE CONDITION

The Major Incident Room was the pivot of any major investigation. The hub, the focal point. Where the officers working the case spent the majority of their time consulting and evaluating evidence and strategies. Or, as Jake liked to call it, the black hole. Where information came into the room but never went back out. It was there, in MIR4, he found Stephanie working, sticking things to the walls with pins and Blu Tack.

Jake thrust open the door, his hand slamming down on the handle. The noise surprised her, and she dropped a piece of A3 paper onto the floor.

'Jake, what're you doing here? I tried to get a hold of—'

'I need to speak to you,' he said, closing the door behind him gently.

Stephanie stopped what she was doing and placed the sheet of paper on the desk.

'Hi, Steph, how are you? Haven't seen you all morning. Missed out on an important meeting with Darryl, but it's

OK – I'm here now and I need you to drop everything you're doing so we can have a chat,' she said, mocking him.

The guilt in his stomach wrapped itself into a neat little bow, a well-deserved present for his selfish and ignorant behaviour.

'I'm sorry,' he began sincerely. He knew that she was a good enough judge of character to see right through it if he'd been facetious. 'I'm sorry I wasn't about this morning; I've been busy with stuff. Issues with my phone, but they're all sorted now. How are you?'

'All about you, isn't it?'

'Stressful morning?' Jake asked, looking around the room.

'Yeah, because I've had to do all of this on my fucking own. With no help from you especially.'

This referred to the copious number of MG23 forms they were required to submit to the Crown Prosecution Service. Operation Cardinal, the investigation into Henry Matheson and his gang, the E11, had been one of the largest of its kind – several thousand hours had been dedicated to it, both by the Stratford CID team and others from further afield who'd been seconded in to help. The final product of which was sitting in the middle of the table: four six-inch-thick ring binders, bulging at the seams.

'Is this everything we have?' he asked.

'You should fucking know. You're the one making sure it's all there.'

Jake flashed her a cheeky grin, one he'd relied upon frequently in the past to worm his way out of tricky situations. 'Oh, is *that* what I'm supposed to be doing?'

Her eyes and brow narrowed. 'Don't fuck with me on this one today, Jake.'

'Three F-bombs in one conversation. Things must be bad.'

The two of them had worked closely with one another, confined to the same four walls for months and as a result had grown to read each other pretty well. They'd laughed, they'd shared, they'd shouted and they'd made up again. In short, they'd experienced all the emotional struggles of being in a relationship with one another, without ever having any of the physical connection. So Jake knew when she was having a bad day. And today was one of the worst.

'I'm fine.'

Translation: she definitely *wasn't* fine.

'What's happened?' Jake asked, hoping his cheeky smile would work. It didn't.

'Nothing.'

'You want to talk about it?'

'Obviously not.'

'Well you know where I am.'

She snorted. 'Good one. Nobody knew where you were this morning. I tried calling you several times but all I got was voicemail.'

That reminded Jake: pay a visit to the phone shop, sooner rather than later.

'That's what I needed to talk to you about,' he replied, pulling a chair out and sitting opposite her.

'Why do I get the impression I'm not going to like this?'

Jake tried the smile again. Still not working. Two for two failed attempts.

'How confident are you with the work we've done here?'

Stephanie's eyebrows rose. 'Depends on what you mean by confident. Am I satisfied that the work we've done is up to the standard? Yes. Am I satisfied that—'

'Do you think we've done enough? Is all of this necessary? If you had to put a percentage on it?'

'I don't like where you're going with this.'

Neither do I, but I have to.

'I need us to do a little something on the side. Some legwork on a new thing that's come up.' Jake used Stephanie's reaction as an indicator; there was none, so he took that as a good sign. 'We need to look into a fraud investigation.'

'That's completely out of our—'

'Remit, I know,' he interrupted, 'but it's a part of *my* remit – as a father and a husband – to investigate it.'

And then she realised what he was talking about.

'We're investigating fraud against you?'

Jake nodded.

'When? How? Where? Why?'

He answered all those questions in the order that she'd asked.

'Jesus, Jake. I mean… I wouldn't even know where to begin with that sort of thing. Surely the fraud squad can help? The bank even?'

Jake shook his head. 'Nope. Not quickly enough.'

'I wish… I wish I knew what to suggest.'

Jake leant closer into the table. 'You have contacts, right? Some of your old friends in the IPCC? They must have experience with this. They'll be able to help.'

'It's not that easy…'

He was losing her, and if he didn't pull it out of the bag, he knew he would lose her for good. She was his one last hope at a quick fix. What sort of father would he be if he waited and let other people get him out of his predicament when he had the resources and the skills available to do it himself?

In a last-ditch attempt, he turned to something he'd hoped he'd never have to. Begging.

'Please, Steph. You know I wouldn't ask unless I was desperate. They've taken everything – out of my account and also our joint account. There's nothing left in either. I'm so afraid of what's going to happen that I haven't even told Elizabeth yet. I've been avoiding her calls, and I've found out I can't offer her dad my kidney. Even if it were possible for me to *buy* him one, I can't. There really is nothing I can do. But I want to catch the people responsible for this. I want to get to them before they get to someone else.

'Together we can do that, while still keeping on top of everything to do with the Matheson case. And that's a promise. We can't afford to let that slip – I'm aware of that. And we won't. I'll make sure of it. I'll carry on the work at home. I'll do overtime – unpaid. I'll do anything I can to make it work. But I need you, Stephanie. I need your help to make it happen. Like we did with Liam. So... what do you say?'

Stephanie hesitated before responding. She swayed from side to side, shifting her weight from one foot to the other. Her eyes rose and fell over him like a bouncer on a night-club door.

'Does Darryl know?'

'No. And I'd like to keep it that way.'

'Why?'

'I have my reasons.'

'I'm not helping you until you tell me.'

'I'm not telling you until you tell me what's wrong with you.'

Stephanie quickly fell silent. Touché. Game, set and match.

'I fucking hate you, Jake Tanner.'

'You in?'

'I'm in. But on one condition.'

'Anything. So long as I don't have to tell you my reasons for not wanting Darryl involved.'

For the first time, they were going to have to work in the dark with one another.

Chapter Nineteen

THE FARM

After years of exposure to the smell of nitrocellulose, micas and acetone, Dimitri had grown accustomed to working in a nail salon. In fact, he spent so much time around it, he'd grown oblivious to the effects it was having on his body: the dizziness, the headaches, the sickness. Not to mention the fact that he liked the smell. Found that it soothed and relaxed him whenever he needed it.

Today the nail salon was busy. Appointments had been flowing constantly throughout the morning, with minimal waiting times. And so far, nobody had made any mistakes.

Happy customers. Happy boss. Happy workers.

The circle of business.

It was Dimitri's job, among others, to enforce a clean working schedule. They were to come up from their basement, looking presentable and ready for the day, and work their twelve-hour shifts in silence, offering little conversation to their customers.

And if they disobeyed his rules then... Well, he'd already warned them of the consequences: they would be taken out to the back and beaten where the wounds weren't visible.

To police them, Dimitri was at the back end of the shop, keeping a watchful gaze over them all while they worked. There was a social phenomenon that existed called panopticism: in the centre of a circular jail is a single tower, boarded and closed, with three hundred and sixty-degree views of all the cells and their inmates. The guards could see the prisoners, but the prisoners couldn't see the guards. The theory was that, for the inmates, they would police themselves and monitor their own behaviour out of fear of being constantly watched and caught in the act, despite not knowing who, if anyone, was watching. The act of self-governance was enough to deter antisocial behaviour and crimes from being committed. The modern-day equivalent was CCTV. Plenty of it, but not all of it necessarily worked. Dimitri liked to think of himself as the tower, the panopticon. And he wanted to make sure that all the inmates in his prison knew that he was watching. Everything, at all times.

Twenty-Nine had just finished with a customer. She took the money, pocketed it and waved goodbye before wandering over to him, shoulders slumped forward, gaze fixed on the floor. Dimitri didn't know what had taken place between her and The Cabal the other night, but it had been affecting her appearance. Drastically.

Her expression was upside down, defeated; she shuffled her feet, miserable and stared off vacantly into space, lost. But despite all that, she was still gorgeous. And he often found himself lost in her beauty. She was so angelic it felt precious, delicate to him, like an artefact that had to be preserved and kept in pristine condition. The way her hair was pulled back from her face, yet small strands dangled against her skin. The way her lips parted seductively as she listened to you speak. The way her eyes narrowed intently, as though she was paying attention even if she may not have been. And it wasn't just her beauty, her elegance; Twenty-Nine was the only inmate who didn't fear him, who treated him with natural respect. Everything about her was different. And had it not been for the barcode on her wrist, they would have spent the evenings together in a different setting, just like he'd imagined.

Saying nothing, Dimitri gestured for her to enter the back of the salon. The air inside the hallway was cold, blowing in through the fire exit beside them. Twenty-Nine stopped in the middle of the space and kept her head down.

'Give it here,' he said, extending his hand.

Tentatively, Twenty-Nine lifted her arm and released the money into his palm. The soft paper felt warm in his hand, fresh from her touch. He briefly counted the notes and realised there was an anomaly.

'And the rest of it?'

At first, Twenty-Nine didn't respond; instead, she kept her head down and her hands in her pockets, bridling from side to side.

'Give it here,' he pressed, trying not to sound too forceful.

Eventually, she reached into her jumper sleeve and removed the final handful of notes and passed them to him. He added them to the bundle and counted them thoroughly. Every hour they were expected to hand across all the money they'd earned in that time. And, so far, she'd been the slowest. Not to mention the fact she'd tried to keep some for herself.

Dimitri recalled what The Cabal had said: *If you disobey me, an example will be made of you.*

He didn't want to let that happen again.

'You're lucky I'm not going to tell D,' he told her as he pocketed the money in the back of his jeans. 'The last time someone tried to keep money from us, they died. This money is to pay off your debt, so I don't see what good it's doing by keeping it for yourself. Understood?'

Before she was able to respond, his phone vibrated. He answered the call and held her at bay, hovering his finger in front of her face.

'Yes?' he said into the handset, his voice deadpan.

'We're outside. For Twenty-Nine.'

'Why?'

'Because we have to.'

'What for?'

'You ask silly questions.'

Dimitri locked eyes on Twenty-Nine. 'Fine. I'll have her ready. Meet me at the back in five.' He hung up the phone before the person on the other end could. 'Grab your things. Get your essentials. You don't have long,' he ordered her urgently.

Twenty-Nine did nothing.

'Did you hear me? Get your stuff. D needs you. He has something else in mind for you.'

'I... I don't have anything,' she replied. 'You... you took it from me.'

Dimitri sighed and rolled his eyes. He reached into his back pocket, pulled out the notes, counted out a few then handed them to her.

'For emergencies. I don't know how you're going to use it. Or when. Or why. But you have to keep it safe. If they find it on you, they'll kill you.'

Twenty-Nine shook her head profusely. Perhaps she thought it was a set-up – that he was trying to plant the money on her so she'd receive a harsher punishment and slip into deeper debt. Or perhaps because she was a kind and selfless person who didn't like to accept charity. A part of him knew that giving her money was a bad idea – everything about it screamed failure – but it *felt* like a good idea. She was so beautiful, so fragile, so vulnerable.

He wanted to help her. Needed to help her.

'You have to take it. But you can't tell them I gave it to you.' He paused. An idea sprang into his mind. 'In fact,' he continued, 'give it to *them*. Use it as bargaining power. Tell them you stole it from the others to help pay off more of your debt. They'll respect that and be more lenient on you.'

It had worked once before, so why wouldn't it work again?

Twenty-Nine shoved her hands in her pockets, avoiding the money. Dimitri grabbed her wrists and forced the notes into her palms. Just as he was about to say something, a knock came on the fire exit door to his right. He froze, and his head slowly turned towards the grey rectangle in the wall.

He lowered his voice to a whisper. 'Take the money. Look after yourself.'

'Why you help me?'

Dimitri gave her a long look. The truth was he didn't know. He'd been in the game too long to start getting soft. But recently things had started to get to him, like what they were doing wasn't quite right. Like they were ruining lives for... for nothing. Money. Power. Fast cars and fancy clothes. Superficial items that deteriorated and depreciated in value as quickly as the cheap nail polish they were using.

Dimitri pulled the door open slightly. On the other side was a slim man with a dark navy turtleneck. He stood side on, a cigarette dangling from his lips. Dimitri didn't recognise him and in the back of his mind contemplated taking the man on.

One on one. A fight to the death. Winner gets to claim the girl.

Then he dismissed the idea.

'You have the girl?'

'Yes,' Dimitri said, stepping backwards and widening the door. He reached for Twenty-Nine, buried his fingers in her armpit and dragged her towards him. 'Where are you taking her?' he asked as he handed the girl over.

'No more silly questions. Fucking gypsies. Never listen, no.'

Dimitri swallowed the statement, allowed it to bruise his ego. It wasn't worth getting in an argument over. Saying nothing more, he passed Twenty-Nine over to the man, who grabbed her forcefully and shoved her in the direction of the Mercedes that was parked up a few feet from the door.

Before he could do anything that he knew he would later regret – even more so than he already did giving her the money – he closed the door and returned to the nail salon. It was unlikely he was ever going to see her again. And the sad reality of it was that if he were to see her again, it would be when she was dead, when he would be responsible for disposing of the body. As he had several times before.

The small bell dangling above the salon's door rang. A new customer wandered up to him.

'Have you got any appointments?' the young girl asked. He vaguely recognised her features. She was a regular.

'Someone has just finished. Please find a seat and the next server will be over to you shortly.'

The young girl thanked him, and as she wandered away, Dimitri's phone buzzed in his pocket.

'Hello?'

'Has she been picked up?'

'Yes.'

'Any issues? Did she put up a fight?'

'No,' Dimitri replied. Through the salon's windows, he saw the Mercedes float past. 'She was fine.'

'Good,' The Cabal replied. 'She must have learnt her lesson from the other night.'

Dimitri grunted. He had nothing more to add to the conversation.

'There's something else,' The Cabal continued. 'Tanner. Have you got the money? Did everything transfer correctly?'

'Yes. Everything was fine.'

The car disappeared out of sight.

'We managed to get everything?'

'Yes. Everything. He has nothing left.'

'And you followed my instructions like I said?'

He had, up to a point. The instructions The Cabal had given him were long and convoluted, too technical for his brain to comprehend. So he'd resorted to following the same process they always did. Easier, smoother, quicker. And just as secure. But if The Cabal wanted the job done properly, he should have done it himself.

'Yes,' he lied.

'Perfect.' There was a slight pause. 'And what about phase two?'

'It's beginning today.'

'Excellent. I need you ready and responsive in the next couple of days.'

'Why?'

'We have another shipment coming in. Soon, I'll be sending more men in to free up some space in the rooms.

But at least, for now, you've got Twenty-Nine off your plate.'

Dimitri swallowed at the mention of her name. He had a question in his mind that he was too afraid to ask – too afraid to know the answer to. But he wanted to know nonetheless.

He inhaled sharply before asking, 'Where is she going?'

There was a long pause on the other end of the line. The sound of heavy breathing coming from The Cabal told him that the man was still there.

'She's going to The Farm.'

Chapter Twenty

NEGLECT

'Come on, Dad,' Elizabeth said. 'Last step. Nearly there.'

Her dad yanked his arm away from her and shoved her aside. 'I'm not an invalid, Liz. I can look after myself.'

Alan Clarke was a very proud man. An investment banker all his life, he'd worked his way from the ground up. Starting on the trading floor to owning his own private company, where the roster of clients that had been with him from the beginning followed. His relationships with them were built on trust. They trusted him to invest their millions, and he trusted them to pay his commission and keep up the mortgage payments. Now in his early fifties, and in a comfortable enough position, he'd sold the company and retired. Since then, his hours had been spent collecting and building model railway sets.

Business empire aside, Alan Clarke was proud of his daughters. They were his life, and he'd always tried to give them everything they asked for. But when it came to money, that was where Alan drew the line. If he showered them in money and spoilt them, then they'd have no life skills, no perception of the value of things.

It was one of the things Elizabeth respected most about him.

'Nobody's calling you an invalid, Dad,' Tegan, Elizabeth's sister, replied. She was standing on the other side of Alan, holding his arm.

Letting go of her father, she watched him enter the house and kick off his shoes.

'Where's your mother?' he asked.

'In the car. You just saw her. You're not going senile as well, are you?'

'Piss off,' Alan replied.

Tegan ushered her father down the corridor of their new stately home in the Surrey Hills, just a few miles south of Croydon, and into the kitchen at the end of the hallway. Meanwhile, Elizabeth stayed behind and picked up the pile of post that lay at the entrance of the house.

'Is that all of it?' her mum asked, directly behind.

'I think so.'

'The post office are forever getting ours mixed up with the neighbours. Useless, honestly. How difficult is it to match the numbers on the door with the front of the letter? They all need re-educating if you ask me.'

Elizabeth hadn't, so she ignored her mum and turned her attention to the letters, searching for her name. Like she'd used to after school. Back then it had felt exciting to see her name in the post – a birthday or Christmas card, or perhaps a letter from her penfriend in France. Back then she'd felt a certain prestige at having her name in the post. It had made her feel special. However, once she was an adult, jaded and burdened with the weight of reality, she'd quickly learnt there was no glamour in it at all. Bills, bills,

bills… and more bills. Something she was beginning to realise was having an adverse effect on her marriage.

When she'd said her vows all those years ago, she'd never foreseen that something as petty as a gas bill could divide them so much. She missed Jake, missed talking to him, hearing about his day. The silence in the house had been unbearable, but it had also given her time to reflect and realise that she'd been in the wrong to accuse him of gambling again. The accusation was unfounded and unjust, and therefore a betrayal of her belief in him.

Fuck's sake, Jake Tanner, why do you insist on causing me so much stress?

'Come on,' Martha said, nudging her in the back with a plastic shopping bag. 'I need to put this down somewhere.'

Elizabeth moved aside to allow her mother to set the bags on the floor. Once she'd finished, Martha closed the door behind her, brushed her hands together and grabbed for the envelopes in Elizabeth's hand.

'Oh, joy,' she said, skimming through the letters. 'More things to worry about.'

'I'm sure they're not that important,' Elizabeth replied. 'They can wait.'

'Did Jake ever fix that electricity problem you had?'

'Gas, Mum. It was gas. But yes, he did,' she replied confidently. 'Apparently, it was just a mistake.'

Elizabeth bent down to pick up the bags from the floor. As she gripped one of them in her hand, Martha said, 'Good for him,' in her usual sardonic tone.

'Mum, stop it,' Elizabeth snapped. She hated it when her mother said that.

Good for him he's coming home early and spending time with you and the girls like a father should.

Good for him he's taking the girls out to a park, like a normal dad.

Good for him he's helping out with the cleaning.

Good for him. Good for him. Good for him.

Those three words had the power to incense her.

Her husband's and mother's feud had started on the night they'd first met – dinner round Elizabeth's parents', tucking into a home-cooked roast; Martha probing into Jake's life, Jake doing his best to answer the questions. But then they'd moved on to the matter of politics, and both had stumbled across one another's brick-wall point of view. Jake didn't like politics, nor did he like politicians. Martha, who herself was a politician in the housing department had, naturally, struggled to accept that. Neither of them were in the wrong, but it was a night she would never forget.

'He's been busy,' she said, continuing to defend him. 'But he sorted it out quickly.'

'He should never have let it get to that stage in the first place. Once you've got a black mark against your name on these things, it's incredibly difficult to get it off.'

Like you've been trying to prove your whole life.

'You're never going to approve of him, are you?'

'It's not that, my darling. It's just that there are things he does that I don't agree with. In some ways, he reminds me of your father – especially when it comes to you and the girls. Whereas, others—'

'He's incredible with the girls,' Elizabeth interrupted. 'He always makes time for us. He always puts us first.'

Martha moved in closer and placed her hand on her shoulder. 'Come on, Liz,' she said, her voice soft. 'I think you've been telling yourself that lie for a long time now, haven't you? You say he always makes time for you, but when? When do you see him? He doesn't appreciate you as much as he should.'

'He has to work. You know how much his job demands of him.'

'Yes. And I'm proud of him for that, but it doesn't justify him spending as much time there as he does.'

'I'm happy,' she lied, further suppressing the feelings she'd been burying for a long time. 'He even offered Dad his kidney. He wouldn't do that if he didn't care.'

'Yes, but one selfless act doesn't make up for a long time of neglect.'

Elizabeth's mouth fell open in shock. 'Neglect? What are you talking about *neglect*?'

Martha opened her mouth to speak, but Elizabeth cut her off.

'I don't want to hear it.' She shoved the letters and bag into her mother's chest. 'Here: you can take your post and Dad's medicine—'

'Where are you going?'

Elizabeth stepped into her shoes, grabbed her bag from the floor and slung it over her shoulder. 'I'm going to pick up the kids. Maybe even spend some more time with Denise. She's got nicer things to say about her son.'

Chapter Twenty-One

VENDETTA

Jake bounced his leg up and down, creating a loud, persistent squeak.

'Can you stop that?' Stephanie asked, lowering the papers in her hand onto the table. 'I like you and I think you're great, but I'm not afraid to kill you.'

Jake stopped and apologised. She thanked him – sarcastically, he noted – and returned her attention to her laptop. Then she grabbed the photocopies of the British Gas bills, shuffled them and spread them evenly on either side of it.

'What are you doing now?' he asked, the impatience within him bubbling harder with each passing minute.

'Tracing the mobile number,' she replied. '*Trying* at least.'

'Why?'

'I have to get it approved. But, obviously, that's going to take slightly longer than originally planned.'

'Is there a quicker way of doing it?'

Stephanie turned away from her computer and shot a

look at him. 'Is there a quicker way of you shutting up and letting me do what you've asked me to do?'

Jake retreated lower into his seat, attempting to hide from her scathing looks but failing miserably. In this small office, there was nowhere to run.

'Is there nothing you could be doing to help?' she asked.

Of course – plenty. Finding Roland's killer. Mending his fractured relationship with Elizabeth. Working on the Matheson trial.

But finding his money, and finding the person responsible for taking it, was his priority.

He reached across the table and picked up the original copies of the letters. To all intents and purposes, the documents looked real. The logo. The font. The formatting. They even had the company registration number at the bottom. Which meant that whoever was behind it was talented.

An individual – or individuals – who knew what they were doing. Who had the resources to make it look professional. Who had a personal vendetta against *him*…

Jake rested his arms on the edge of the table and, slouching his back, conducted an online search. His eyes skimmed the first page of Google and went no further.

Inspired, he conducted another search. The results were the same. The online forums on various websites told him everything he needed to know: in the history of British Gas, nobody had been subject to a fraudulent attack from the company in the way he had.

Phishing emails, spam phone calls, sure. But no such thing as spam snail mail. Which meant one thing: he was the anomaly. That he was specifically targeted. That somebody was out to rinse him of everything he had.

One name popped into Jake's head: *The Cabal.*

The one you want is D...

D for Darryl.

The faceless, nameless figure who haunted him and had made his career, and now his life, hell.

And then an idea flashed across his mind.

There was only one man who had worked with The Cabal and would be willing to speak to him. And he was sat behind bars.

Jake erupted out of his chair and grabbed the letters from his desk. He folded them in half and slotted them in the inside of his blazer pocket.

'Oh, so you're finished then, are you?'

'No,' Jake replied, making no attempt to hide the disdain in his voice at her insinuation.

'Where are you going then?'

'I'm going to visit Liam.'

Chapter Twenty-Two

GOLDEN ARCHES

Henry's stomach grumbled deeply.

He'd been in prison for months now. And he'd grown accustomed to a lot of things, things he could tolerate. The drab, lifeless walls, the constant screaming and shouting outside his cell at night and at all times of the day, the rigid and uncomfortable bed, the paper-thin pillow that was beginning to cause him headaches. Even the shitter in the corner of the cell was a surprisingly convenient appliance – and he had no shame so it wasn't a problem dropping his guts in the company of another man.

But what he couldn't tolerate, more than anything, was the food.

It was as bland and lifeless as the walls, and a few months ago, he'd set about trying to bring in something decadent and debauched – McDonald's, Nando's, Burger King, KFC – something that would remind him of the outside world and what it was like to feel human again. But the logistics of smuggling food meant he would no longer be able to bring in the spice and other drugs and trade on his favourite currency – favours. So in the end it had been a toss-up between drugs and food. And if you took one, you didn't need the other, which made the decision all that much easier.

On the outside, living off the fruits of his empire, Henry had known what it felt like to experience luxury, to indulge himself in the finer things in life. The Michelin-star meals that he'd only dreamt of eating when he was a kid. The thousand-pound bottles of wine and champagne at some of the most exclusive clubs in the country. In recent years he'd tasted some of the finest foods from the finest chefs, where so long as you paid the bill, there was no judgement as to where the money came from. For the first time in his life, he'd known what it was like to be at the top of society, the Bruce Wayne of East London. Billionaire by day, vigilante by night.

But despite all this, despite all the wine, the steak, the caviar, the lobster tails, the Wagyu beef – what he was really craving now was a large feast from the Golden Arches. With a side of chips, chicken nuggets and an extra-large Coke.

Sometimes the best pleasures in life were the simplest ones.

His stomach growled at him again.

'You hungry there?' Brian called from the bunk below.

'I'm always hungry, Bri. It's the reason I'm here.'

'You surrendered to avarice?'

'Sure,' he said, even though he had no idea what the word meant.

'It's been the downfall of many a man before you, and it'll be the downfall of many after you.'

Henry rolled over and peered down the side of the bed. 'You been reading philosophy in your spare time?'

Brian looked up at him with his weak, vacant eyes. The

life in them had gone, as though it had been sucked from the fore by his deteriorating brain.

'Helps me remember things,' he said. 'Books are wonderful like that. They transport you to places you've never been, let you meet people you've never met.'

Henry nodded and took the mantra with a pinch of salt; since Brian had become his cellmate, Henry hadn't seen him with a book in his hand once.

A figure appeared in the door frame, swallowing the light. Owen Carlson was out of breath, leaning against the door for support. He'd undressed and was now wearing a T-shirt, with his jumper wrapped around his waist. A droplet of sweat dangled on his chin, threatening to pluck up the courage and jump.

'I'm back,' he said.

'You don't ever leave this place. Not until you've done your time, or until they put you in a body bag,' Henry replied. 'What do you want?'

'The second task.'

'You've done the first one already? So soon?'

Owen nodded fervently, his eyes beaming.

Henry admired the man's courage in lying to him, but he hoped Owen's bravery was resilient enough to survive a few more days.

Shortly after sending him off on his mission, Brian had reported back to Henry. Brian had watched Owen disappear to his room, pace about for a bit, then flush the drugs down the toilet. That had been over an hour ago, so by everyone's estimation, Owen should have been in the middle of his trip, enjoying himself and *not* thinking about the second task.

Bravery one, intelligence nil.

'How was it?'

'Fucking. Amazing.'

'Yeah?'

'Time of my life.'

Henry cringed. In the history of spice, nobody had ever referred to it as the time of their life. It was an escape from reality, a deferral of existence from one physical plain to the next. For a brief moment, everything in the world seemed calm, serene, at peace. The complete opposite of the time of their life.

'I'm glad to hear it.'

'What is it? What's my next task?'

Henry jumped down from his bed and grabbed *A Clockwork Orange*. He sauntered towards Owen, studying the man's reaction. His face was jittery and his body rippled with the effects of something, but it wasn't the spice he'd been given.

Using his fingers, Henry gestured Owen closer. When the man was within a breath's reach, Henry opened the back of the book. Sitting there, nestled in the spine, was his shiv.

'See this? This is your second task.'

Owen grunted at it, eyes transfixed. Henry would have paid a lot of money to know what was going through his mind right then – so much so, in fact, he would have given up the Golden Arches for the rest of his life.

'Tomorrow morning,' Henry continued, 'when everyone's going for a shower, I want you to use it on someone.'

Owen reached for the knife. Henry snapped the book shut and smashed it round Owen's jaw. Shockwaves rippled through the pages and up his arm as the man's mouth ricocheted from the impact. This hardback was even more unique than he thought, insofar as it hit differently.

'Don't you fucking touch my stuff ever again, all right?'

Henry snarled, grabbing the back of Owen's head. 'Now, I want you to make your own. And once you've done that, I want you to find your own target. I don't care who. Could be someone you got beef with, could be your cellmate. So long as you find someone to hurt, and you hurt 'em good, you passed your second task. You understand?'

Wiping the blood away from his mouth, Owen nodded, his eyes giving Henry the answer he wanted without realising it.

Chapter Twenty-Three

FOLLOW THE MONEY

The best place on earth.

Nana Tanner's, according to Maisie. Aside from their own home of course. On the way back from her parents', Elizabeth had picked her daughters up from nursery and driven them to the promised land.

Nana Tanner's was a place of sweets, treats and a place to share the deets. And for the past twenty minutes, Maisie had been doing exactly that. Telling them about her day. Of how Florence, one of Maisie's best friends, had raised her hand in response to a question, but the teacher, Miss Cain, had refused to acknowledge it. Of how Timothy had picked his nose and wiped it on the carpet. Of how Eddie had chased after her around the playground and tripped her up, badly grazing her knee.

The playbook of school gossip already, and she was only four.

'You'll have your hands full with that one when she grows up,' Denise said as she gently rolled a sleeping Ellie back and forth in her carrier.

'That's what I'm worried about,' Elizabeth replied, watching Maisie dance around in the middle of the living room. She didn't have a care in the world. 'She starts school in September. Seems like only yesterday she was crawling out of her cot. Now look at her.'

Maisie, noticing the adults' attention was on her, finished her dance with an elegant pirouette.

'Same thing happened to Jake. Only last week he was screaming and crying in the middle of the shopping aisle.'

'Don't be under any illusion, Denise. He still does that.'

The two women shared a brief chuckle. Denise's house was much smaller than her parents', much more modest, but it had a far superior homely feel to it. Elizabeth felt comfortable there, and Denise always made her feel wanted, at home away from home. She was great with the kids, and she was one of the kindest and most caring women Elizabeth had ever met.

'I've never said this, but Jake's very lucky to have you as his mum.'

'And he's very lucky to have you as his wife. Even if it feels like he doesn't realise it sometimes.'

Elizabeth dropped her gaze to the floor. 'It's been feeling like that a lot lately.'

'I know,' Denise replied.

How?

But then she remembered: Jake and Denise had spoken at the hospital the other night.

'I told him, as I'm sure you have, that he's one stubborn boy. Just like his father. In fact, dare I say it, he's far worse. But I think he has reason to be. When he was growing up, he had to change very quickly. Looking after his brother and sister required him to do things his way or no way. And a part of that's been fed to his siblings. They're all a little similar. But that doesn't mean there isn't love there. If anything, he's doing it *because* of love.'

A lump caught in Elizabeth's throat. She quickly swallowed it down with a swig of tea. 'He says he's been busy at work a lot recently. But I still feel like there's a divide between us. Something neither of us are willing to confront.'

Denise offered her a warm smile and placed a hand on Elizabeth's knee. 'Take it from me – he loves you. And he'll do anything for you. He's afraid to lose you and the girls, and in his own little way, he thinks that absorbing himself in his work is showing that to you. But sometimes it takes a strong woman to sit him down, put their cards on the table and *teach* him where he needs to change.'

Elizabeth avoided Denise's gaze. Here they were bashing Jake when *she* was also part of the problem. They'd learnt to live together a long time ago now, learnt how to juggle their relationship and Jake's work, so why was it only becoming an issue—

Her phone started ringing, vibrating against her leg.

Mum Mobile. She ignored it.

Putting the phone back in her bag, she turned her attention to Maisie, who was now lying on the carpet, legs flapping in the air, busying herself with a colouring-in book.

Her phone rang again. This time she let it ring through to voicemail.

She apologised to Denise.

And then it rang for a third time.

'Yes?' she screamed into the handset.

'I need you to come over quickly.'

'Why?'

'Please, Elizabeth.'

'Is everything OK?' Now she was getting worried. Her

mum only used her full name when something was wrong. 'Is it Dad? Is he OK?'

'Just… Please… come quickly. And bring Jake.'

The heavy clunk of metal sliding into place jerked Jake into action. He was inside a small interview room, surrounded by four walls with no windows and only a single light dangling from the ceiling. He was facing the door in front of him, and he craned his head to look up at it. A second later, the door opened and in stepped Liam Greene, Jake's former manager.

Liam shuffled in, his trainers scuffing along the floor. Behind him was a prison guard, his uniform complete with tie and epaulettes. Liam's face beamed as he approached Jake. He opened his arms wide, revealing a series of red marks and abrasions on his skin.

'When they said I had a special visitor, I wasn't expecting you,' Liam said sardonically. His voice sounded deeper than Jake recalled, gruffer.

'Were you hoping for Kim Kardashian?'

'Come on, Jake, you know I don't know who the fuck that is.'

'Neither do I, but Elizabeth's obsessed with her.'

Liam pulled the chair out from beneath the table and seated himself. 'Are the kids well?'

'As well as kids can be,' he replied.

'I'm glad to hear it. Now tell me, why are you here?'

Jake lost his train of thought as he stared into Liam's eyes. He thought of all the moments they'd shared – the hours spent at the pub after a long shift, the banter they'd had with the rest of the team while working a case. And then his mind wandered to everything else that had happened between them. With Drew Richmond. With Pete Garrison. Danny Cipriano. Michael Cipriano. The Farmer. The death, the lies, the betrayal. At the end of it all, he'd been the only one to survive – to come out unscathed.

'I need your help.'

Liam rolled his eyes. 'No change from last time then. There I was beginning to think you wanted to see how I'm doing.'

'And how are you doing?'

Liam shrugged. 'Fine.'

'Glad we got that out the way. Would have taken all day otherwise.'

'Cheeky shit.'

'The cancer?'

'Still gone. Still have to spend the rest of my life here instead of getting a seat upstairs sooner than expected.'

'What makes you think you deserve a seat up there? The only place for you is down. Way down.'

'Thanks for that. Now, what do you want from me?'

'I need your help – I told you.'

'I know that. I'm not fucking stupid. What *exactly* do you need my help with?'

Jake considered for a moment. Since the last time they'd met, only a few months ago, and under similar circumstances when Liam had helped Jake capture Henry Matheson, the seed of a question had started to germinate in his mind. He wanted to ask it before he moved on to the real reason he was there.

'Why?' he asked.

'Gonna need a little more than that, Jake. Why *what*?'

'Why did you protect me for so long when we were working together? As soon as you disappeared, the packages started. And before that, you had the perfect opportunity to get rid of me along with everyone else. It's the one thing I've never been able to understand.'

'You came all this way for some closure?' Liam replied, although he said it more as a statement than a question. 'I could have saved you the trip and told you over the phone.'

'Just answer the question,' Jake snapped. 'Why did you protect me from The Cabal?'

Another smirk grew on Liam's face. 'Ah, there it is – the Freudian slip. The real reason you came. You want to talk about The Cabal.'

Liam hesitated. Jake remained stern and gave away nothing in his facial expression.

'He's coming after you again, isn't he? But now Henry's out of the way, it can't be the packages… it can't be the drugs or money. So it's something else, isn't it? He's coming after you a different way, isn't he?'

'Answer my question and I'll answer yours,' Jake replied.

Liam hesitated again, sat upright in his chair and cleared his throat before beginning. 'Do you know how I ended up here?'

'Yeah? I—'

'Not your version. *Mine*. Do you know how I started out in all of this?'

Jake fell silent. When he didn't respond, Liam took that as his answer and continued.

'I told you about my wife, didn't I? Beautiful woman she was. Gorgeous. She gave me the world, and I tried to give her mine. She died when we were only young. Thirty-one. Cancer. The same thing I got rid of took her. Fucking ripped her straight from me.

'After she died, I had nothing left except for work, so I spent all my time working, trying to forget, trying to heal the pain. But I knew there was no fix, no quick and easy solution. And that's when the drinking and drugs started.

'It became my everything. I never signed up for the service with the intention of becoming a bent copper. It may come as a surprise to you, but when I joined I was full of spunk and desire to exceed the expectations that I'd placed on myself. I wanted to be the best officer I could. Shit, I even wanted to be the best officer in the force. But after Molly died... that fell out of the window, and I quickly realised that my pipe dream didn't exist. I had nothing else to live for. I needed the drugs to keep me happy, and I need the money to pay for the drugs. So that's when I became affiliated with The Crimsons. I helped them on their first heist in Newcastle, and I helped them for the rest. When it came to Guildford, I was the one who roped in Bridger. You know the rest.'

Liam's mouth seemed to have turned dry as he swallowed harshly, the bulge in his larynx bouncing up and down his throat like a yo-yo. For a while, Jake sat still and absorbed everything Liam had just told him, replaying it all in his head.

'That didn't answer my question. When we were working in the team, you had every opportunity to get rid of me,' Jake said.

'And you had ample opportunity to get rid of me sooner than you did. And do you know why you didn't? I think it was because you still had hope that there was some good left in me. The same way I saw there was good in you – an unprecedented amount. Every time someone tasked me with killing you or driving you out of the team, I couldn't do it. I saw too much of myself in you – that drive, that determination to succeed and be the best. Just like I had. But the only difference was... with you, you had everything else going for you. The family. The wife. The career. You actually had a chance of realising your potential.'

'So you decided to let me live?'

'I'm starting to wish I hadn't if you're going to be this ungrateful about it.'

It wasn't every day Jake was told that people wanted him dead – let alone being sat opposite one of those very people – but it was very humbling to hear.

'I guess… I don't really know what to say.'

'You can tell me what The Cabal wants with you now.'

Jake reached into his pocket and produced the British Gas letters. Upon his arrival, the prison officers had requested photocopies be made, lest Jake had surreptitiously laced them with drugs. Jake laid them out on the table, face up, and eased back into his chair.

'I got them the other day,' he started. 'I called the customer service number, paid a small fee, handed over my financial details. And now everything's gone. I thought you might know something about it.'

Liam pursed his lips as he read through the letters. 'I think we both know who this is.'

'Can you give me a name?'

Liam shook his head. 'The answer's still no, Jake. That's the last thing I'm going to do.'

'After that lecture you just gave me?'

'Correct.'

'Why? Why won't you help me?'

'You still don't get it. After all this time I'd have thought you'd pick some of this stuff up. How many times have you been warned? There are people like me who know too much information. Whenever those people open their mouths, look what happens to them – they die. I was the one tasked with making sure that was the case. You saw it first-hand. But now that I'm in here, I don't want you to think that means nobody's stepping into my shoes, because trust me you'd be wrong. There will always be someone to replace someone else in this business. I'm being watched constantly by everyone and everything in here – including the guards. They're all reporting back to The Cabal. All of them.'

'So what's incentivising you to keep quiet?'

'I've got it pretty good in here. I'm well looked after, considering I'm a former cop. The people in here have a certain predisposition to police officers, as I'm sure you can appreciate. But I get the respect I'm owed, and I will continue to do so, as long as I keep my mouth shut.'

'So you won't tell me anything?'

Liam shook his head and skimmed the piece of paper across the desk.

'The only thing I will tell you is if you want to catch him then follow the money. It's left a trail somewhere – all you have to do is find out where it went. And, I'll be honest, you won't like where it leads.'

Chapter Twenty-Four

FIRST DIBS

'I'll be there as soon as I can,' he'd told her.

That had been over two hours ago, and there was still no sign of him. Stratford to Reigate was an hour's journey. Max. So where the hell was he? Maybe something had happened to him. Maybe he'd been involved in a car crash. A high-speed pursuit. A stabbing. A fight. A kidnapping.

Or worse, maybe he's shagging a witness. Someone from the office. Or someone he'd met at the pub one evening after work.

The swimming tank in her mind was beginning to fill with paranoia. And lots of it.

'We'll have to wait for Jake,' Elizabeth had told her family.

She was back in the Surrey Hills, in the kitchen with her dad and mum; meanwhile, her sister was in the living room with the girls, climbing higher on the Best Daughter leader board.

'Where is he?' Martha asked.

'I don't know,' she replied, pouring herself a glass of

filtered water direct from the tap. She necked the drink and licked her lips clean. The chilled liquid soothed her throat as it descended.

As she set the glass down on the draining board, the doorbell sounded.

'Daddy!' came the cries from the girls in the other room.

Elizabeth spun on the spot and raced towards the front door, adamant she was going to be the one to open it. Trailing behind, erupting from the living room, was Maisie.

Elizabeth threw the door open.

'Daddy!'

Jake's face beamed and he crouched down to give Maisie a kiss.

'Hey,' he said with that smile. That fucking smile. The one where nothing was wrong and everything between them had been kissed and made up. 'Sorry I took so long. Work.'

He leant in and kissed Elizabeth on the lips.

'Right,' she replied, unsure whether she believed him or not.

'What's happened? Is it your dad?'

She said nothing, turned her back on him and started towards the kitchen. Jake followed her, Maisie by his side.

The atmosphere inside the kitchen was stale. Everyone was in there now, Tegan included. The Clarke family on the right-hand side, the Tanner family on the left.

Jake greeted everyone with a wave. Usually, he would have hugged them or shaken their hands, but this situation felt different, and the tension in the air was palpable.

'What…' he began. 'What's going on?'

Elizabeth took control of the situation. She placed her hand on the island in the centre of the kitchen and looked at him.

'Mum and Dad had a little visitor today,' she began.

'Right…'

'The postman,' she replied and reached for the envelopes lying on the surface. 'They found this…'

She handed him a letter, and from his immediate reaction, it was clear he knew exactly what it meant.

'You didn't call the number, did you?' Jake asked, lowering the sheet of paper to his side.

Out the corner of Elizabeth's eye, on the other side of the room, her mother nodded.

'No,' Jake cried. 'No, no, no. Please tell me you didn't.'

He slammed the sheet on the surface and massaged behind his ear.

'What's the issue?' Martha asked, beating Elizabeth to it.

'Did you pay anything? Did they ask you to make a payment?'

'Yeah. The girl on the phone said it was a small fee that was outstanding on the account.'

'Ah, Christ.' Jake lowered his hand from his head and used it to massage his chin. 'And you gave them your financial details? Everything?'

'Everything.'

Elizabeth stepped forward. 'What's going on, Jake?'

For a long while, he said nothing. He placed his palms on the edge of the island, stepped back a few paces and dropped his head to the floor. As he sighed heavily, she thought he looked as though he was about to start a hundred-metre sprint. To get away from the family and the situation.

'Jake? What aren't you telling us?'

He kept his head down.

Coward.

'We've been hacked,' he replied.

'What do you mean *hacked*?'

'Rinsed. Robbed. Ransacked. What other word do you need to describe it? Whoever I spoke to on that call the other day took down our details and stole everything from us.'

'*What*?'

'They asked me to make the payment over the phone, so I did. I answered the security questions. I gave them everything they needed to be able to log in to my online banking and take everything. From the joint account and my personal account. All of *our* money... gone.'

'Have... have you gone to the police?'

'I *am* the police, Liz.'

She'd realised it was a stupid question immediately after she'd said it, but she didn't need Jake reinforcing it and reminding her. Especially when it made her feel small and insignificant in front of her family.

'You've lost all of our money,' she retorted, her aggression taking over.

'Come on,' Jake replied. 'That's not fair. I was targeted. I did a quick search online and nobody else has had this happen to them.' He turned to face her parents. 'But now they're coming after you as well.'

'Why? What reason would they have for coming after *you* in the first place?'

Jake looked pensive, as though he was thinking of all the lies he could spew to avoid the question. 'I've upset a lot of resourceful and powerful people in my career, not least Henry Matheson. It's possible that he wanted to get back at me.'

'What are you going to do about it?' Martha asked, stepping forward, hands on hips.

183

'I've been to the fraud squad. I've been to the bank. Both were less than useful.'

'Are they going to give you your money back?'

Elizabeth sensed the worry in her mother's voice; it was the same as when she'd called Elizabeth the other night telling her about her father's situation.

'They're investigating.'

'What does *that* mean?' Elizabeth interrupted.

'It means the exact same thing it does when we say it: we're looking into it, amongst the other mountain of things we're looking into.'

'Seriously. Is that it? Can *I* not do something? I can raise a claim, make a job of getting them to do something about it.'

'Just… trust me… please.'

She wasn't sure how much more of that she had to spare.

Jake continued, 'I can handle this. I can make sure we get our money back.'

'But what about *us*?' Martha asked, pointing at her chest and then over at Alan, who was propped against the kitchen counter. 'We've got far more at stake than you two have. All of Alan's business money is tied up there…'

'Call them. Tell them you think there's been suspicious activity on your account. They'll be able to block your cards almost instantly.'

'And if they can't?'

'Move the money out of that account. Put it in any other accounts you might have.'

Martha shook her head and glanced back at Alan. 'Why would they want to come after us as well, Jake? Why are they taking all of our money too? Have you pissed them off again?'

'*Them?*' Jake asked, beating Elizabeth to it.

'Yes. You know. Them.' She hesitated. 'Anyone that you've managed to piss off in the past.'

'That's a long list,' Jake replied. 'And it keeps growing.'

This isn't a time to satisfy your ego, Elizabeth thought. There were bigger things to worry about.

'What effect is this going to have on us, Jake? The kids? We've not got any money for food, drink, petrol. And our credit cards. The mortgage. We can hardly afford anything as it is. How are we going to manage until the end of the month?'

Jake approached her and placed his hands on her shoulders. He gently squeezed them and said, 'It's fine. Honestly. I'm sorting it. I'm finding out who's responsible. Stephanie and I are working on it.'

Of course you and her are.

Bet you were fucking her just now, weren't you? That's why you were so late.

She was always conscious and wary of Stephanie's relationship with Jake. He didn't necessarily talk about her frequently, but she was always jealous when he did. They spent a lot of time together – which was due to work, she knew – but she'd seen the way Stephanie acted around her husband, and she didn't like it. She didn't trust her… and now they were spending a lot more time together, she wasn't sure whether she could trust her husband either.

Time to put your cards on the table, Elizabeth.

But before she could, Jake's mobile rang, breaking the silence in the room and snapping Elizabeth out of her thoughts.

'Hello?' he answered immediately. 'Oh, hello, sir. How are you doing? Is everything OK?'

Jake moved about the kitchen and rested against the

dishwasher. 'Yeah, sorry about that. I've had a few technical difficulties with my number. But I managed to sort it,' Jake continued, bringing her attention back to the present.

'Oh… Oh, really, guv? I… I mean, that's fantastic! I don't know what to say! Well… yes, obviously. I'll let them know now. Brilliant. Perfect. Thanks once again, sir. And when did you say it would happen? Cheers, guv. Honestly, thank you so much. I'm with them now. They'll be so thrilled.'

Jake rang off and dropped his phone onto the kitchen surface.

'Well…?' Elizabeth asked, filled with hope.

'Fantastic news. Your dad.' Jake turned to Alan. 'I spoke with the assistant commissioner. Told him about what was going on. He—'

'Why would you do that?' Elizabeth snapped.

Jake darted his head at her, scowled and then returned his gaze to Alan.

'I told him about what was going on. Turns out he's very pally with one of the best surgeons in the country who deals exclusively with kidney and diabetes patients. And he's just managed to get you higher up on the waiting list.'

'How long did he say it would take?' Martha asked. She inched gently towards him and eventually touched his arm.

'They've got to find a donor first, but you've got first dibs when one becomes available. So keep an eye on your phone. You don't want to miss out on your new kidney.'

Chapter Twenty-Five

ERRANDS

In the time that Henry had been a resident at Wandsworth prison, confined to the same four walls, with nothing but the soft glow of the light pollution to illuminate his cell, his ability to see in the dark had vastly improved. Plain grey walls took on new colours. Obstacles adopted new positions and appeared clearer in his vision. Almost like a living superhero.

At the end of the long corridor was a thin strip of light. In front of him, keys jangling, boots echoing, was Williamson. The man had dragged him out of his cell and led him to their usual meeting spot.

They came to the end of the corridor. Williamson opened the door and ushered Henry through.

'You're not gonna like this, Hen,' Williamson said as he shut the door behind him.

'I don't need to like it. I just need to know what you know.'

Williamson inhaled deeply. 'I did some talking earlier.

My contacts spoke with their contacts, and their contacts spoke with—'

'I know how communication works, dickhead. Just tell me.'

'He's working for The Cabal.'

Short and sweet. Rip off that plaster, Williamson.

'How do you know?'

Williamson surveyed the hallway. 'Because my sources tell me they've seen him working with the Flying Squad. One of them even said he recognised the face.'

'From where?'

'An OCG. Mr Carlson was working undercover with my contact, trying to get in a drugs gang.'

'So he's an undercover officer…' Henry said, before drifting off into his thoughts.

And not a fucking good one.

'Plus, and this is the funniest bit, on his emergency contact numbers, the fuckwit was stupid enough to put The Cabal's number down. I checked it against the number you gave me, and it was the same one.'

Henry took a moment to digest the information.

The cheeky fucker. Sending in an undercover officer and thinking he wouldn't notice.

Now there was no doubt in Henry's mind that Owen was there for one thing and one thing only. His instincts had proven right, and he was glad he'd trusted them.

'In the morning I'll arrange for him to be removed from here and transferred somewhere else,' Williamson whispered.

'No. That won't be necessary. Let me take care of our new friend.'

A noise sounded behind Henry, distant, as though it had travelled through six sets of steel doors to reach them.

'You'd better go. Are we done?'

'Yeah, we done.'

'Good. Because I've still got some of your fucking errands to run.'

Chapter Twenty-Six

PERFECT LITTLE LIFE

Little Susie.

Little Susie from down the road at number nineteen. Little Susie with the dog and the swing in the back garden.

Sweet, innocent, lovely Little Susie.

Stephanie remembered her fondly. Even more so since her and her father's conversation earlier that morning. She'd replayed it in her head several times over, each time picking apart the meaning of his words, the smile on his face as he'd spoken them. She'd tried to imagine the images and scenarios that were playing back in his head, but then she realised that was a potentially dark and terrifying place she didn't want to visit.

The allegations against her father – the child pornography, the indecent content – was already too much for her fragile mind to comprehend. That the man who'd been her guiding light throughout her life, her inspiration for getting into the police force, was a sex offender and paedophile frightened her more than any disease, illness, plague or form of torture ever could. The man she'd placed on the highest possible pedestal collapsed to the ground.

The thought of it made her feel sick, and as she sat there, staring up at the house with its lights on, the crippling acid in her throat burnt, the sensation almost unbearable, her palms and the back of her neck laden with sweat.

It hadn't taken long for her to decide on a plan of action. And in between helping Jake with his finances and compiling the evidence against Henry Matheson, she'd dedicated some time to finding Little Susie.

After calling in a couple of favours, and creating new ones for some old friends, the evidence of her investigation was right in front of her.

By now Little Susie wasn't so little. Instead, she was twenty-five, living with her husband in a two-bedroom semi-detached property and with a mortgage to her name. A quick search of her online social media profiles had confirmed that she was a successful communications grad-uate working at managerial level for a Fortune 500 company. She had the world at her feet and everything going for her.

It was times like this when it was virtually impossible for Stephanie not to evaluate her own life in comparison.

There she was, sitting in her reasonably priced car, living in a one-bedroom flat above an off-licence, single, with only a stray cat for company, and working as a detec-tive inspector for the Met. Her social life was non-existent, and her sex life even more so.

Stephanie was in a different part of the rat race entirely, and at the moment there were no signs of her ever catching up.

Feeling slightly depressed at the thought, and with a

mild dose of jealousy bubbling inside her, she clambered out of the car and shuffled towards Little Susie's house.

Little Susie's perfect little life.

The sky overhead was pitch-black, and the bitter, wintry chill chewed at her fingers and nose, gradually numbing her to the pain of her own life.

Eventually, she came to a stop outside the front door. Waited, waited. Hoping the courage to knock would be summoned from somewhere inside her.

And then she found it.

The knock seemed to echo up and down the street and split the still air in two. On the other side of the door, through a thin sliver of glass was darkness. A second later, a light flashed on, and a shadow emerged from behind it.

Then the door opened.

Little Susie was much prettier than her social media photos suggested, even with all of her make-up removed as it was now. Her hair was tied in a bun and she was dressed in jogging bottoms and casual wear, yet she managed to pull it off seductively – something Stephanie herself had never managed. In the bright light, her eyes were the colour of a tropical forest – deep, dark and with an uncertain complexity to them.

Just from looking at her, she wasn't surprised that Little Susie was successful and in the position that she was.

Stephanie cleared her throat.

'Hi,' she began and then choked on her words. 'You might not remember me, but my name's Stephanie Grayson. We lived on the same road together about fifteen, twenty years ago. Me, my sister and my parents.'

Susie hesitated, nodded. 'I remember,' she said, her voice soft, delicate.

That was what she'd been dreading.

Stephanie said, 'I was wondering if I could come in? There's something I need to speak with you about.'

Chapter Twenty-Seven

DOWN PAYMENT

Williamson was seldom allowed time away from the prison. Budget cuts and the responsibilities of the job meant he spent most of his waking moments there. But whenever he did get time off, he always tried to make the most of it with his family. He hardly saw his three children at the best of times, and his biggest regret was missing their formative years. Their first words, their first steps, their first laughs, their first forward rolls. Sometimes he felt like a stranger in his own house.

On the other hand, he was making an extra hundred grand off this little job – with the potential to earn considerably more – so he was willing to make another sacrifice. After all, what was a couple of days in the grand scheme of things? With that new money, he could take the boys on holiday, buy them those toys they wanted, that new Xbox, a TV. Maybe even give up the job for good and find a more convenient career. Then he'd be the best dad in the world. And then he could turn his attention to spoiling his wife.

It didn't matter that their love was bought with dirty and

corrupt drug money. What mattered was that, in years to come, his family appreciated his hard work and realised it was to provide for them and give them the best life possible. Because that's what he was doing. Slaving away with some of the country's most violent and dangerous criminals in return for a shitty salary but a wonderful investment: his pension. He didn't want to spend the next twenty years counting down the days until he got to cash in on it.

A hundred thousand, he told himself. *A hundred grand*.

In this particular instance, the reward certainly outweighed the risk of what he was doing.

The house was in a cul-de-sac. The road stretched far back, and the end was shaped in a circle, like the head of a pin. The house he was looking for was on the right and surrounded by expensive cars. It looked as though it was an advert for European engineering. Maseratis. Mercedes. Ferraris, the only exception being a Range Rover Sport sitting on someone else's drive. And as he approached the front door, he couldn't help wondering whether the money he had in his pocket would make any difference to the family on the other side. Perhaps it would better serve an impoverished family down the road. Still, now wasn't the time for ethics; nor was it the time to be charitable.

He had a job to do.

Williamson pressed the doorbell.

'Hello?' A tentative and apprehensive voice emanated from an intercom system at the bottom of the doorbell. He hadn't noticed it at first, and it made him wonder what other technological set-ups they had. 'Who is this?'

'My name's Simon. I'm with the Home Office. I'm here to speak with Amelia regarding her upcoming jury duty.'

'One moment please,' came the voice, and within a few seconds, the door opened.

Standing on the other side was a small woman. She looked no older than sixteen, and at first, he thought that he was speaking with Amelia's daughter.

'Hi,' he began. 'Is Amelia in? Can I speak with her?'

'I'm Amelia.'

Williamson took a step back and eyed her up and down. She was five foot five and looked as though she weighed next to nothing. Her skin was pimply, and her hair – a thick, vibrant, oak-brown colour – flopped to one side of her face. It was safe to say that she wasn't what he'd been expecting. He'd been in the prison service for fifteen years, and in that time he'd only ever heard of someone under the age of twenty sitting on the jury once or twice.

'You're scheduled for jury duty on the eighteenth of January?'

'I am.'

'Do you mind if I come in? There have been some developments with the case that are too sensitive to inform you of by email or post.'

'Why?'

'Someone in a higher position than me has decided they're scared it might be intercepted. I'm just the messenger.'

'And I'm not supposed to shoot you, right?'

'Exactly,' Williamson replied with a disarming smile.

Before she allowed him to enter, Amelia asked for some identification. Williamson produced the forged Home Office ID that one of Henry's contacts had produced for him, and after a few seconds of surveying the card, Amelia stepped aside to let him in.

As Williamson crossed the threshold and entered the foyer, his feet echoed on the laminate flooring. To his left was a staircase that looked as though it had been sculpted from marble, and at the top of the steps, the landing stretched across the width of the house. His eyes followed the length of the landing and back down the building to Amelia.

'Nice place you got,' he said.

'Thanks. It's my parents'. I just live here.'

'Rent free, I hope.'

He couldn't think of a teenager in the world who could afford a place like this without the bank of mum and dad. When she only offered him a weak grin in response, he reached into his coat pocket and produced a thick Jiffy bag.

'This is the message,' he said, handing it to her.

Amelia eyed the package suspiciously, took it from him and pulled out the first half of the thick wad of cash inside.

'What am I doing with this?' she asked, as if she wasn't fazed by the amount of money she held in her hands. This was going to be tougher than he thought.

'It's a down payment,' he replied.

'For…?'

'Not convicting the accused, if you're selected.'

'I don't…' She hesitated and pulled more of the money out. 'Are you paying me to stop a guilty man from going to prison?'

'You don't know he's guilty—'

'Come on, you wouldn't be here if he was innocent.'

'Either way,' Williamson continued, ignoring her, 'you're going to vote not guilty. Understand?'

Amelia shook her head. 'I don't want it.'

'You don't have much of a choice. Like I said, I'm just the messenger. And I have another message for you. Would you like to hear it?'

Eventually, after some time, she dipped her head.

'The people who gave me that,' he said, pointing at the

money, 'also told me that if you vote guilty instead of not guilty then I'll be back. But this time it won't be with money. It'll be with some other friends. Some who aren't as kind as me. Some who like to break the bones of anyone they're told to, including little children. Some who like to rip off fingernails and toenails without so much as an afterthought. They're dogs, and they don't mind staying that way in order to get what they want.'

Williamson hesitated and licked his lips. 'You're an impressionable young girl. I'm sure you can understand what the correct decision is. Maybe you could take the money and go on a holiday with your friends. Treat yourself to a new car. Maybe use it for a deposit on a house so that you can move out and stop living off Mummy and Daddy. The choice is yours. But remember what I said – make the wrong one and I'll be back.'

Chapter Twenty-Eight

MR FORGETFUL

The empty multi-storey car park groaned and whistled as gusts of wind battered and blustered through the open spaces. A ghostly chill crept along the floor towards her, freezing her breath as it left her mouth. Outside light filtered in and illuminated the markings on the wall, and in the distance was the sound of cars rolling on tarmac as delivery drivers and taxis went about their jobs, mingling with the sounds of partygoers and drunkards on the street. The scum of society. With her arms folded against her chest, hugging her puffer jacket against her body to insulate her, she fought off the chills climbing her body.

She checked her watch – 00:02.

He was late.

Martha Clarke hated when people were late. It was inconsiderate, bad-mannered and made you look like an arsehole. She had no time for people who couldn't keep to a schedule, regardless of who they were. If the Queen were late to a meeting, Martha would have believed it well within her rights to stand up, walk out and ask to reschedule.

After ten minutes of hating on the world, the sound of car tyres screeching reached her on the top floor. Martha trained her eyes on the gap in the concrete where, soon, the car would appear.

A few seconds later, it arrived, swung round the corner and parked in the opposite bay. The car door opened, and a giant figure appeared.

'You're late,' she said.

'You're still married.'

Assistant Commissioner Richard Candy stopped by her side, placed one arm on her shoulder and kissed her left cheek and then her right. Martha remained stern, solid, still.

'Does your husband know you've come all this way to meet me?'

'He doesn't need to. He trusts me.'

'I'm sure he wouldn't if he knew the truth.'

Candy took another step back and placed his hands in his blazer pocket, leaving his thumbs to hang over the side.

'What's going on, Dick?' Martha asked.

'You know, you're the only person who calls me that.'

'Like I care.'

Candy licked his lips. 'I love this. Just like old times. The animosity, the hostility. I've missed it. And I bet you have—'

'Shut up,' she said, raising a hand in the air. 'Just answer my question. Why are you getting involved with my family?'

'What do you mean?'

'You know exactly what I'm talking about. Don't play Mr Forgetful. Not again.'

'I have no idea what you're talking about, Martha,' Candy replied, raising his hands in surrender.

The movement transported her back to the playground, to their first argument in secondary school. She'd just caught him flirting with another girl during lunch and launched a verbal assault on him. He'd been an arsehole then, and he was still being an arsehole forty years later.

'Why *now*? After all this time. Why are you trying to help my husband of all people?' Martha realised that her intonation and pitch were increasing with every syllable; she made a conscious effort to lower her voice. 'You've had years to make up for everything.'

Candy chuckled and took a step closer to her. 'You know,' he began, 'that was one of the things I loved most about you, Martha. You were very proud – you liked to do things on your own, by yourself without any help from anyone else. But, sometimes, you need to wake up and smell the shit. There are people out there who want to help. It's time to learn to accept it when it happens.'

'You still haven't answered the question. Why now? Why are you helping us?'

Candy took a while to respond, and in that time, she got lost in his eyes. The irises were pitch-black, contrasting with the brightness of the whites surrounding them. But there was more to them; she'd known him for so long and had maintained infrequent contact – behind Alan's back – and she knew of the hurt behind them. The relationships he'd had in the past, his stepbrother, his father. The passing of his mother when he was young but old enough to process the pain and suffering and hurt of loss.

'We're both old now, aren't we?' he started.

'Speak for yourself.'

'It's not worth keeping the petty bullshit in the back of your mind. You grow up, and you grow out of it. Your son-in-law is one of the best officers we have in the field and I make it my mission to look after all of our employees. I was in a position to help him, so I did. I had the contacts, so I used them. I don't see what the issue is.'

A silence fell on them both as Martha contemplated what to say.

In the end, Candy finished with, 'We can't afford to lose Jake, Martha.'

And there it is. The real reason he'd employed the doctor to help them. The real reason he'd returned to her life.

'I think that's the first time you've ever given me an honest answer. You're looking out for yourself and whatever's good for the police. I wonder if you've got a promotion coming up any time soon?' Martha folded her arms and raised her left eyebrow.

'What importance does that have on anything?'

'You love your ulterior motives. This has something to do with it.'

Candy removed his right hand from his blazer pocket and pointed it at Martha's face. 'And what are you going to do? You're not in a position to refuse the surgery. That's your husband's choice. And how suspicious will it look if you speak with him in the morning and tell him to decline the operation? He's going to die if you don't do anything about his kidneys. And that will be on your head. Imagine what impact that will have on your relationship if you tell him the truth about where this help is coming from. And what if I speak to him, spill the beans on all the times we've seen each other, all the times you've found yourself in places you don't want to be? The truth won't set you free, Martha. Instead, I think the truth will kill you inside... and it will definitely kill him.'

Part 5: 6th Jan

Chapter Twenty-Nine

DOGHOUSE

The monumental weight of the money he'd lost descended heavily on Jake's mind when he awoke the following morning. He yawned and stretched his body, elongating his spine and legs. Not so long ago, he'd thought about taking up yoga so that he could alleviate the desk-induced pain in his back but if he couldn't find enough time to spend with the girls, he didn't know how he'd manage to spend hours stretching and putting his body into strange and uncomfortable positions.

Jake rolled over to the other side of the bed. Empty. He held his breath and listened. Sounds, distant, emanated from the kitchen downstairs. Coffee mugs crashing on the surface. Plates and drinking glasses clanging against one another. The sounds of someone unloading the dishwasher. Forcefully.

Sighing, he rolled himself out of bed, wandered into the shower and then readied himself for the day ahead. Today was Roland's funeral, and he dressed in his smartest black suit and the shoes he'd worn on his wedding day. Due to the unprecedented stress of the past couple of days, with no money and no one willing to help him, except Stephanie, Jake had almost forgotten. It wasn't until she'd sent him a message late the night before that he'd remembered. Sometimes he wondered what he would do without her.

It was 6:36 a.m. by the time he was downstairs. Four minutes ahead of schedule.

'What're you doing awake?' he asked Elizabeth, shutting the kitchen door behind him.

Elizabeth, busying herself with putting the dishes away, turned to him and dropped a coffee mug antagonistically.

'Careful! You'll wake the kids!'

'I'm glad you managed to sleep all right,' she replied.

'What's that supposed to mean?'

'While you've been snoring all night, I've been worrying about everything. You don't seem to be that fazed by it, Jake. We have no money left – except for the little that *I* have. And you and we both know it won't last us very long. And now my mum and dad might not have anything left either.'

Eat. Sleep. Argue. Repeat.

'I told you I'm working on it. I've got Stephanie involved. She's got contacts who can make things happen faster.'

'I'm sure that's not all she can help with.'

Elizabeth threw a tea towel on the kitchen surface and stormed to the other side of the room where she pulled out a chair from beneath the table and sat.

'Not this again,' Jake said, rolling his head back and staring up at the ceiling.

'I don't want you to rely on her – or someone else – to resolve *our* issues. Not to mention the fact that I don't want anyone else knowing about our financial problems. You talk with people at work, which you're entitled to, but whenever I want to talk to you about things, you're never here. I'm stuck inside all day, every day.'

'What about the girls?' Jake asked as he tentatively moved closer towards her.

'They're all busy. Tash, Hannah, Emma – they've all got their own lives. None of them can spare any time for me. So who do I have to talk to about things? Ellie? Maisie? Be serious. And the last person I want to talk about this sort of stuff to is my mum. So I've got no one. And I feel like I'm slowly going insane here.'

Jake sensed that she was, for the first time in a long time, putting all her cards on the table and addressing the mighty African mammal in the room.

He hesitated before responding. 'What about... what about your photography? I know you're still coming to terms with what happened, but... you need to get yourself out there, build up the portfolio. Find some extra clients. Even if you sell some images of the plants outside. Make some money that way.'

Elizabeth's face turned pale. She sat up straight, her eyes wide.

'You didn't just...? Pah! You're unbelievable. It's that simple, is it? Take a few photos of some blades of grass, upload it to a stock image website and then sit back and wait for the money to roll in. You're even more stupid than I thought if you think that.'

Now it was getting bitchy. He'd tried reasoning, offering some advice and help, and this is how she wanted to react?

Two could play that game.

'Well, I'm sorry,' Jake said sarcastically. 'I can't help the fact that I need to be at work as much as I am. I can't help that it takes up so much of my day. That I feel physically exhausted as well as mentally drained by the time I come home. I can't help that I've never taken that much of an interest in your photography. I…'

That woman over there wants to help you. But if you keep doing what you're doing – being an idiot *about everything – you're going to throw it all away.*

Jake caught himself before he said anything more he would regret. He'd just overstepped the mark, and he was fully aware of it.

He swallowed hard and felt a warm wave of guilt consume his body. He wanted it to swallow him up and take him back in time to a few minutes ago. Shit. If there was a graduate degree for Fucking Things Up, he'd get a first-class honours and a graduate job directly in The Doghouse.

'Liz…' he began, dipping his head in shame.

'Get out. I don't want to see you right now. Go to work. Spend some time with your other family. I hope you have more of an interest in what they're doing than you do me. I might not be here when you get home,' she replied, her voice deadpan, devoid of any and all emotion.

'Where will you be?' Jake asked. His voice was weak with sorrow.

'Away from here. Away from you. Just let me know when we get all of our money back.'

Jake walked to his car slowly, burdened by the weight of his missing money and the even bigger fracture in his relationship. It was now the size of a glacier's crevasse, and it was growing wider and deeper every day. He fought the urge to glance back at the house, to see if Elizabeth was peering through the curtains, resplendent, both of them immediately regretting their argument, falling madly in love with one another again and going back to the way things were.

But he wasn't naïve enough to think it would be so easy.

He likened their argument to a criminal investigation: first you had the argument itself, which was typically the victim. Then you had to build the case, which required speaking with witnesses, investigating leads, interviewing suspects. Which, in Jake's analogy, was just another way of saying sitting down and talking with one another, discussing the issue with friends and looking within themselves to find the root cause. The outcome of the case, whether they were able to arrest their own demons, depended on how well they could come together to get the desired result as a team.

As he climbed into the car, he should have thought about some of his own witnesses and suspects. Of how Elizabeth was the love of his life and he'd been out of order. Of how he'd dug himself an even deeper hole than he knew possible. But first, in his mind, were the other things he needed to worry about.

He removed his phone from his pocket and placed it on the dashboard. As he set the iPhone in position, the screen illuminated, revealing several messages and one missed call from Stephanie.

Starting the engine, he called her back.

By the time she answered, he was already at the end of his street, pulling the car onto Norton Road.

'Jake?' she answered, the voice echoing around the vehicle via the loudspeaker.

'Hey, what's going on?'

'There's been a change of plan.'

'Oh?'

'You're coming to mine, and then I'll drive you to the funeral. You can pick up your car on the way back.'

An inconvenience but far less serious than returning home to the silence and space between him and Elizabeth. To the place he wasn't wanted.

'I'll be there as soon as I can.'

'OK. Hurry. I've got an update for you. It's important.'

Chapter Thirty

BRICK WALL

He's working for The Cabal.

Henry had spent the past few hours repeating those words in his mind, staring at the blank ceiling above his bed. While Brian had been snoring loudly, possibly dreaming of little children or fond memories with fellow police officers, Henry had been formulating a plan.

The task was simple: silence Owen Carlson before he had a chance to silence Henry.

Fortunately, he'd already laid the foundations, thanks to his intuition, which had not only suspected Owen of being dodgy in the first place but he had also instructed Jason, Vinnie and Biggie to enter the showers at the same time as Owen. More of a scouting mission than anything else originally. But now that needed to be escalated, and the boys needed to be brought up to speed. The only problem that remained was finding a way to do it. The rooms were locked, and the rest of the inmates were sleeping.

As soon as everyone was awake, he would hurry out of the room and brief them.

In the meantime, with the wintry darkness slowly beginning to recede, he continued with his book. As he read, he ran his fingers over the shiv taped to the back cover, reminding himself that it was still there – and of the pain it could inflict.

He always enjoyed the moments before the screws came and opened the cell doors – they were always the quietest, the time he could reflect. Everyone had either exhausted themselves to sleep or they were so excited about being let out for the day that they didn't want anything to jeopardise that moment (some screws would punish you if you caused too much disturbance in the morning).

When the cell door did finally open, Henry jumped out of the bed, placed his book on the mattress and hurried out of there, leaving Brian to get up in his own time. Keeping his head down, he paced towards Jason's room. The man was in there alone, lying on his bed with one arm behind his head, the other scratching himself.

'All right, Hen? Weren't expecting you here this early. We still on for—?'

Henry held a finger in the air, silencing Jason. 'I need you to go in with some metal, all right?'

'You what, Hen?'

'You need to be carrying. That fucker's in here to kill me, all right? I want you and the boys to finish him.'

'What about you though?'

'I'm gonna be in my room. Reading my book. Away from it all. Tell the boys. Make sure they're prepared.'

Before leaving, Henry gave his partner a nod. Jason was fully aware of the task, and now it was up to him to spread the word.

By the time Henry returned to his cell, Brian was out of bed and staring out of the window.

'Look sharp, Granddad,' Henry called, clapping his hands together. 'Brand new day ahead. Eighty down, another five hundred to go.'

Brian mumbled, shuffled his feet and turned to face Henry. Confusion was painfully drawn in his expression, and at that moment he didn't look as though he knew what year it was.

Henry let him be and turned his attention to his book. He was making good progress and was intrigued to find out what sort of life Alex would live after serving his prison sentence and finishing his treatment. Grabbing the book, he hopped onto the bed and opened it to his previous page.

He made it as far as the second paragraph before a knock came at the door.

Henry sighed, lowered the book, froze.

Standing in the door frame was Owen, eyes bright with excitement.

'What're you doing here?' Henry asked, rolling his legs off the bed.

Owen's gaze bounced between Brian and Henry. Henry sensed he wanted Brian to leave, which left him feeling torn. Firstly, because what was about to happen was no sight for a man in Brian's position. On the other hand, Brian was a witness, and if anything were to happen to Henry, Brian was backup. A weak and feeble form of backup, but backup nonetheless.

In the end, he said, 'Brian, mate, can you give us a minute? See if they've got any marshmallows for breakfast for us, could ya?'

At first, Brian didn't react. But then as the words slowly digested in his brain, he shuffled out of the room, muttering to himself. Whether or not he'd understood the meaning of their code word, Henry didn't know. But it was a bad morning to rely on someone in his condition.

'Marshmallows?' Owen asked.

'His head's going a bit. Spent all night talking about them. They were his daughter's favourite.'

Owen stepped into the room, shoulders puffed out, muscles tensed. 'I wanted to show you something.'

Tentatively, Henry nodded, secretly trying to slip his finger through the back page of his book.

Owen pulled out a shiv from his sleeve. It was almost identical to the one Henry had. Same coloured toothbrush, same wear on the string used to bind it.

And then Henry realised. It *was* his shiv. The same one he'd had less than five minutes ago.

'Looking for this?' Owen asked.

Before Henry could react, Owen lunged at him, swinging the blade across his vision. Henry reacted on instinct and raised a hand to block the attack, but he underestimated the man's strength and stumbled backwards into the wall. Pinned, with his arms up by his chest, Henry pushed, all those years of bench pressing finally paying off. Their hands were locked in a battle for the trophy: ownership of the shiv. Achieve that and the game was over.

Then he felt the explosion in his stomach, engulfing his organs.

Owen brought his knee down and readied himself for another attack: a headbutt. But in his time, Henry had suffered, and inflicted, a few of those, so he knew the warning signs. The readying of the neck, the eyes widening for that extra bit of power, and then the final assault.

Still reeling from the blow to his stomach, Henry was bent double and able to counteract it; he ducked and dodged his head to the side, narrowly avoiding the man's chin. Instead, Owen's head clattered into the wall. In the misguided attack, he dropped the weapon and staggered back, throwing his hand to his forehead.

Brick wall, meet skull.

Skull, meet pounding headache and disorientation.

Henry capitalised. He rugby-tackled Owen, picked his legs up and dropped him onto the concrete floor, a move worthy of entering the WWE Hall of Fame. Owen's head ricocheted like a rag doll's. Now he had double the headache. Front and back. Stars would be swimming in his vision, and if he wasn't careful, he'd pass out.

But that wasn't enough for Henry. The bastard had tried killing him, stabbing him with his own weapon. And in doing so Owen had just signed his own death warrant.

Henry grabbed him by the scruff of his jumper, dragged him out of his cell and down to his cell.

Thirteen.

Empty, but the door had been left wide open.

Henry threw Owen's dazed and almost lifeless body into the cell, shut the door and paused. He sensed he had a few seconds to gather himself, to scout his surroundings, to find what he was looking for – anything that could be used as a weapon given that he'd had to leave the shiv behind in his haste.

The cell was a mess. A small table in the corner was littered with paper and pens and leftover food. A row of shelves was filled with books and dust. But there was nothing he could use.

Except...

Except...

Resting on Owen's bed was a large plastic bag. New inmates brought them into their cells on their first night. It usually contained a spare change of clothes and some other essential items, and everyone in the prison typically destroyed it before the end of their first week out of boredom. But not Owen. His was in almost perfect condition.

No holes. No tears.

A solid, sturdy plastic bag.

Henry stomped on Owen's stomach and lunged for the bag. Grabbing it with both hands, he jumped onto the floor, wrapped his legs around Owen's chest, pinned his arms in place and ballooned the bag over Owen's head.

Consciousness slowly returned to Owen, and he clawed weakly at the bag. To combat the attack, Henry tightened his legs and arched himself backwards, making it harder for Owen to reach back. The added pressure on the man's neck drastically shut off the oxygen supply in the bag.

Through the plastic, Henry could hear the muffled and disjointed breathing, the gasps, the murmurs for mercy, the regret and retribution.

Too late, motherfucker.

The man was suffocating faster and faster. Faster and faster.

After a thirty second struggle, Owen's body started turning limp. But he wasn't out yet. He just needed a helping hand: a punch in the face or two. Something to disorientate and asphyxiate the brain quicker.

Then, after another thirty seconds, Owen's body lay completely still, the fight in him gone. Nothing but a mass of skin and bones and muscle on the floor.

Slowly, preparing himself for a sudden rebirth and reanimation, Henry released his grip on the bag and gasped, panting for breath. He stared up at the ceiling. In all his years, out of all the people he'd killed, that had been the most intimate. The one where he'd come within inches of death himself. The one that would live with him for the rest of his life.

Breathing heavily, Henry unravelled his legs, removed the plastic bag from Owen's head and climbed to his feet. Before leaving, he lifted Owen's body into his bed and placed a pillow over his face. It wasn't the perfect cover-up, but everyone in the joint knew that Mark, his cellmate, was deranged and wild enough to do such a thing.

Double-checking everything was as it had been when he'd arrived, Henry slipped out of the cell and hurried back to his own. There, he found a lighter beneath Brian's pillow – a few inches from where all the other drugs were stashed – and set fire to the bag. Toxic smoke quickly spread through the room, filling his lungs and making him nauseous, but it was a necessary consequence. His fingerprints and DNA were all over the bag, and it was the only thing connecting him to the crime. And if anyone asked, he'd accidentally set fire to a plastic bottle of soap.

Once the bag was nothing more than disintegrated embers, he flushed it down the toilet and hopped into bed to spend some time with Alex and his droogs before Owen's body was found and it all kicked off.

Soon, as time went by, and as Henry's adrenaline levels dissipated, he felt confident enough to send a text message. He reached inside the hollow metal of the bed frame and pulled out the device, found The Cabal's number and sent a message. Short and sweet, enough to convey his feelings.

Ur mans dead. Fuck u

Chapter Thirty-One

NIGHTMARE

'What was so important you couldn't tell me over the phone?' Jake asked as Stephanie nursed her reasonably priced car into the left lane of traffic.

Roland's funeral was being held a few miles away from Bow Green at Forest Park Cemetery in Chigwell. A bulletin had been placed on the police internal news board, and it was expected that dozens of other members of the force would venture out to pay their respects.

One big family.

'Where do you want me to begin?'

Stephanie was dressed in a slim black dress, with a blazer draped over her shoulders. Her make-up was minimalist and understated, and her hair was tied in a simple bun. She looked elegant and pretty, although the make-up had done very little to hide the bags under her eyes.

'From the beginning,' Jake replied. 'I want to hear it all.'

'I'm not sure if you've heard, but there have been a few developments with Matheson on the inside...'

He hadn't. 'What's happened?'

'Napalm – you ever heard of it?'

Jake shook his head.

'Sugar in boiling water. Nasty substance – burns the skin horrifically. The other day, some inmates were attacked with it. Naturally, we suspect Matheson was behind it all. But CCTV footage of the attack has magically disappeared, and the guy who got hit isn't saying a word.'

'A turf war in prison? That's just asking for danger. What's this got to do with the case?'

'Nothing. At least not directly. Darryl wanted to warn us, to make us aware of the lengths that he can go to – and *will* go to – in order to protect himself. He says we and our families should stay vigilant and safe.'

'I'm well aware of what Matheson's capable of.'

And I don't need parenting lessons from Darryl, thank you very much.

'But it got me thinking,' Stephanie continued. 'If Matheson's been able to eradicate the CCTV footage, then it's clear to me that he's got someone on the payroll. Matheson's a man of resource, and if he can pay someone on the inside, then he's going to have absolutely no issue paying someone on the outside.'

'What are you saying?'

He was beginning to feel like there was a lot more she wasn't telling him and getting the information out of her would take up all his time and energy.

'It's come to our attention that Henry Matheson is in the middle of paying off the jurors.'

'Whose?'

'Excuse me?'

'Whose attention? How do *you* know?'

Stephanie stuttered. 'Darryl. He's got…'

But Jake blocked her out, his mind beginning to list all the reasons why Darryl would want to share that information with Stephanie. He remembered what Liam had told him about Henry and The Cabal's relationship: it was fractious, a clash of egos. Now with Henry in prison, their partnership was finished, and so was their respect for one another. By arming Jake and Stephanie with this information, they could then flag it and make sure that his jury was clean and unbiased. With the evidence they had, it almost guaranteed a guilty verdict.

The Cabal pulling his strings to get Henry Matheson out of the picture – for good.

'So what do we need to do?'

Stephanie rubbed her eye delicately, mindful of her make-up. 'I've requested the list of jurors already. Once I've got that, I'll be calling round to find out what they know. As for the rest of them, we're working out who's responsible for dishing out the bribes. If we can find them, we can put a stop to it.'

'So what do you need *me* to do?'

'Nothing. Yet. But we need to work faster and harder. There's talk of bringing Matheson's hearing forward. The quicker we can get the jury pool put together, the less time Matheson has to convince them he's innocent.'

'Jesus,' Jake whispered under his breath. Another thing to add to his stress and the pressure of everything else he had going on. Another thing he had to worry about. 'So when's the new date?'

'Monday. As in, this Monday.'

Jake double-checked the date on his watch. Alan's operation on the Friday. Henry's trial on the Monday.

'What a fucking nightmare,' he said.

'They don't last forever.'

'Mine is,' Jake scoffed. 'And I'm beginning to feel like I might never wake up.'

Chapter Thirty-Two

ATOMIC NAILS

The cold, wind and rain had done nothing to deter the turnout at the funeral. Dozens of police officers, most dressed in suits, with the exception of a handful of uniformed officers wearing their full gear, had attended the burial, with even more arriving throughout the procession.

One big family.

Jake could hardly fault them for turning up late, given that it had only been arranged the other day.

As he stood there, hands crossed in front, staring into the crater in the earth, he reflected. About how he didn't think the hole in the ground would be big enough. About how Roland had always worn a smile on his face, how he never appeared to be down or depressed, how he was always approachable and amicable, regardless of who he was speaking with. How he treated people with kindness and adoration. How he was a fantastically intelligent and bright individual. How, despite all that, someone had ripped him from them unexpectedly and way too soon.

Jake was sick of burying people. Especially those he

knew fondly. In the past few years alone he'd already buried two: Danika Oblak and Drew Richmond. Both of whom had been corrupt. Yet they were also vulnerable individuals, people who'd been preyed upon and exploited by The Cabal. But Roland... Roland was different. The third police funeral in as many years. Third time lucky, whereby the only morsel of luck that could be gleaned from the situation was that Roland was close to uncovering The Cabal's identity.

The first and last person to do so.

An excellent officer, an excellent friend and an even more excellent human being. Gone. But not forgotten.

With a wave of his hand and a slight bow, the vicar signalled the end of the procession and gestured for the visitors to return to the church. Because Roland had no loving relatives or next of kin – they had all either died or were unreachable – there was to be no wake, no time to share stories of him and continue his memory.

So long and farewell. The quickest goodbye known to man.

Stephanie by his side, Jake shuffled back to the church, under the safety of an umbrella, walking arm in arm with her. She was a blubbering mess, gently dabbing under her eyes with a sodden tissue. Her grip around him was strong, as though she never wanted to let go. Jake didn't know the extent of her and Roland's relationship, but it didn't matter. What mattered was that she'd come and that all the other officers had as well.

Stephanie opened her mouth to talk but quickly stopped. After several more attempts of trying, while fighting off the sniffles, she said, 'If he saw how many people were here today, I don't think he would have done what he did.'

It took a while for the comment to register in Jake's mind. And when it finally did, he slowed and leant closer to her ear. 'I don't think he…'

But then he lost track of his thoughts.

Surrounding him at various angles were small knots of people, walking in twos or threes, heads dropped low, hands in pockets, meandering back to the church, each carrying the solemnity of the morning on their shoulders.

Except for one.

A figure, standing on the other side of the graveyard, hiding behind a parked car, getting assaulted by the cold, wind and rain. His features were distorted by the elements and Jake's weakening vision. But he was fairly confident he recognised who it was.

What are you *doing here?*

Before he could think to ask in person, the figure turned his back on Jake and slipped into the car. A pair of eyes illuminated at the front of the vehicle, bathing a gravestone in light, then the car pulled away slowly.

Jake intently watched it disappear then felt a tap on his shoulder.

'Jake, what are you doing? Are you all right?'

'Yeah.'

'You sure?'

'Yeah.'

'What were you going to say?'

'I'll tell you on the drive back to the office.'

They were in the car within fifteen minutes of the funeral ending. So long, farewell, but now back to work. The criminal world wasn't going to stop for anyone.

'What were you going to say?' Stephanie asked as she twisted the temperature knob up to max.

Jake steadied the ship amongst the tide of thoughts in his mind. 'I can trust you, can't I?'

'What?'

'Trust. I can trust you?'

'Of course you can. What sort of question is that?'

An important one.

'Roland's death wasn't a suicide,' he said.

Stephanie opened her mouth to talk again, but this time was impeded by shock rather than grief. 'How can you... How do you know?'

'Because I spoke with Poojah. She falsified the pathology report to make it look like a suicide.'

'That b—'

'You can't say anything to anyone.'

'Try and stop me.'

Jake placed a hand on the steering wheel. 'I said no. She's being leant on by The Cabal. He's got something over her. The Cabal made her do it.'

More shock, more silence.

'The Cabal... Killing Roland... Why?'

Jake removed his hand. Stephanie slotted the car into gear and pulled out of the church behind Darryl and Ashley, who were carpooling together.

D for Darryl.

'Because he got too close to the truth, Stephanie. Roland was trying to find out the name behind it all, and I think he did, and that's what got him killed.'

'And it's what'll get you killed if you aren't careful.'

Jake's selective hearing came to the fore. 'It's all connected somehow.'

'What is?'

'Roland's death and me losing everything I have.'

Stephanie fell silent again. But this time it wasn't due to shock or grief; it was because she was summoning the courage to say something. Jake could see the struggle in her face.

'That reminds me...' she said.

I've got an update for you. It's important.

She cleared her throat, signalled and overtook a bus. 'One of my contacts came back to me,' she started. 'They did as you said and followed the money. It took them a while, but they got there in the end. Apparently, it went to an unregistered offshore account then bounced back to the UK.'

'Where?'

Stephanie didn't immediately respond.

'Where, Stephanie?'

The answer to that question told him where he needed to go next. The answer to that question told him where his money was and what it was being used for.

'It was transferred to a company bank account registered in the UK. A little nail salon in West Ham.'

'What's it called?'

'Atomic Nails.'

Chapter Thirty-Three

SECTION 13

The nail salon was situated in the middle of the high street, sandwiched between an off-licence and a small, independently run café, where the metal chairs outside were in desperate need of a clean. Immediately outside the front of the salon was a bin, overflowing with uncollected garbage, and a disused phone box that had its windows smashed in and a white tape flapping lazily around it in the wind. The salon's location didn't exactly scream high-end luxury, but judging by the number of patrons coming in and out – ten in the last hour – it turned over a good bit of business.

Jake was seated in his car, parked a little farther down the road, just out of the vicinity of anyone exiting the property. Trained on the entrance was his smartphone camera. It was all he had with him that would take decent enough photographs. And the last thing Jake wanted to do was return home to borrow Elizabeth's professional camera. For a multitude of reasons.

He inhaled deeply. Exhaled. Prepared himself to disembark the car and come face to face with the owner of the salon. With the person who'd stolen all his money.

Jake pocketed his phone, switched off the engine, and exited the car. He brushed his suit down, making sure his tie was within the lapels of his jacket and started towards the salon.

Looking both ways as he crossed the street, his heart started to pound in his chest, and his mind raced with potential situations.

Walking through the door and being gunned down instantly.

Walking through the door and embarking on a high-speed foot chase through the back-end streets of West Ham.

Walking through and being jumped, abducted and taken to a random location where he'd find himself abused and tortured.

Or there was the much more favourable scenario: coming head-to-head with The Cabal and arresting them once and for all.

The one you want is D.

Finding the identity of the individual who'd caused so much harm and devastation would be the pinnacle of his career, and he'd be happy if nothing topped it. Three years in the making, dozens of lives lost, a handful of arrests, all for one person.

Jake entered the salon. The first thing he noticed was the smell. The dizzying, putrid smell of nail varnish, remover and a whole concoction of other nauseating chemicals. Jake inhaled then wished he hadn't. The toxic fumes immediately knocked his senses into disarray, as though he'd just been punched by a heavyweight. Same sensation, except without the blinding pain.

Jake came to a stop in the foyer and absorbed his

surroundings. To his right, by the door, was a row of coat pegs. Several coats dangled next to an oversized philodendron that ate into the walkway. Its browning leaves suggested a good watering was overdue. Orange and pink stars and paper snowflakes dangled from the ceiling on pieces of string, leftover from Christmas, and the walls were decorated in a dark maroon colour. In the main section of the building, skirted along the walls in the shape of a horseshoe, was a conveyor belt of workers, meticulously painting customers' nails. Each of them wore face masks to protect their lungs from inhaling too many chemicals. None of them said anything. Jake had only been to a few nail salons in the past, and in his experience, they always bustled with energy and life; conversations conducted between employee and customer, with the odd shout or command bellowed across the room from employee to employee. But this place was the complete opposite. The ambience was non-existent.

Thanks to one man at the head of the room. Sitting behind a desk. Keeping everyone in check. Laptop and a large notebook in front of him.

Jake glanced up at the man. As soon as he did, a figure walked in front of him, disrupting his view. The figure of a man, whose hair was greasy and slicked back, his beard unkempt and his skin yellow, as if he had liver disease. The figure of a man who had no right being there.

'Excuse me,' Jake asked, waving at him to flag him down. 'Can I—'

The man spun on the spot and froze. His eyes the size of the moon with shock, he looked as though he'd been deaf his entire life and this was his first time hearing someone. The man pulled his face mask over his nose, and as he lifted it, Jake caught a glimpse of the man's wrist. The number fourteen was tattooed on the underside of his wrist in indelible ink; the skin surrounding the tattoo was still red, and there were signs of an infection, from where he'd lost against the struggle to refrain from scratching it.

'Where's your manager?' Jake asked, trying to make his voice as soothing and calm as possible.

The man said nothing, rotated his body slightly and pointed in the general direction of the man behind the plinth.

'Him,' he said. His voice was hoarse and weak, barely audible even over the silence of the nail salon.

Jake peered around the man's shoulder and locked eyes again with the man behind the altar. Then he thanked the worker and headed down the length of the salon.

The manager was balding with a thick head and an even thicker neck. His skin was tan, and a fuzzy black beard hugged his chin tightly. Through the hair, his expression looked as though he was discontent and pissed off with everything in the world. A thick vein bulged and throbbed at the top of his forehead.

'Can I help you, sir?'

He had a thick Eastern European accent, foreign to Jake's ear, so he was unable to place it.

As Jake approached the reception desk, he seized up and froze. The man was taller than himself, and not only that, he was wider than Jake by a few inches. But it wasn't fat behind him; from the contours and rolling hills on his sculpted body, it was muscle. Thick, dense, grisly muscle. Staring up at him, Jake suddenly came to the realisation that he wouldn't be able to take him on. The man outweighed and outmuscled him two to one.

'Excuse me? Sir?'

'Yes. Hi. I was wondering if I could speak with the owner?' Jake asked.

This was it. He was in uncharted territory now. He had no Plan A. No Plan B. Not even a Plan C. He was potentially staring at the man who'd stolen all of his money, and Jake didn't know how to react. He wanted to beat the man, smash his face in until it was nothing but a bloody mess. The other part of him wanted to arrest him there and then, on the spot. Make sure there was nowhere else for him to go. But what if this was an innocent man? What if Stephanie – or her contact – had made a mistake and sent him to this nail salon due to misinformation.

'Is there an issue?' the man asked.

Jake listened intently to the sound of his voice, to see if he recognised it.

'I would like to speak with the manager,' Jake insisted.

'Are you a customer of this salon? I have not seen you before.'

'So *you're* the manager.'

'How may I help you?'

And then Jake had it. Something in the back of his brain told him that the person he was speaking with right now was the same one that he'd spoken to over the phone.

My name is James – how may I help you?

Jake said nothing and reached into his back pocket. He paused. Locked eyes with the owner. Gripped his warrant card in his fingers. Remained still.

He was torn. If he arrested the man now or asked him to come down to the station for a voluntary interview, which he was absolutely certain the man wouldn't do, then it would be an unlawful arrest. If he left now, keeping his identity hidden, then there was the risk that the man would be gone by the time he returned, armed with more evidence and more support.

But then Jake remembered something. Section 13 of

PACE granted him the right to arrest an individual if he had reasonable grounds to believe they'd committed a crime or were in the process of committing a crime.

Yes. That was it. That was his answer. His justification. He just hoped it would stand up against the custody officer.

'Sir,' the man said, breaking Jake from his reverie. 'If you are not a paying customer or you do not have a complaint you would like to raise then I must ask you to leave. Your behaviour is concerning me, and my staff and clients are feeling unsafe.'

So cool, so collected. As though he'd practised it a thousand times before.

The man held out a hand, gesturing towards the door. His hand was so big and his arm so long it nearly hit Jake in the face.

Then Jake reached for his other pocket and produced a set of handcuffs that were concealed beneath his blazer. He unlocked them and slapped them against the man's wrist.

'And I'm going to have to ask you to come with me.'

Chapter Thirty-Four

MAN ONE AND MAN TWO

As soon as her eyes opened and she regained consciousness, she thrashed her muscles. But something tight was gnawing away at her skin, holding her back. Blinking away nausea, she realised she was pinned to a bed, her arms spread either side of her as if she was on a crucifix, and her legs spread open. She was naked too, which was even more concerning, save for a thin cloth that hovered gently over her groin, while her breasts listed to the side slightly.

She was surrounded by darkness, save for the weak, dim glow of a light bulb dangling over, blinking randomly, as if speaking to her in Morse code. A slight draught wafted in from somewhere, gently kissing the tops of her shoulders and arms. She craned her neck to glimpse where it was coming from.

Groaning as she bent her neck into a position it had never been in before, she caught sight of a door over her left shoulder. Her escape. Her chance at salvation. But first, she needed to break free from the ropes. Whoever had placed them around her wrist had not been kind, for they were tight and digging into her skin.

She twisted her head to the side, surveying the knot in the low light. It was a constrictor knot. One of the hardest to master – and even harder to escape from. In a past life, she'd been an engineer, working on the ships in Constanta, her home city. As one of two women in her team, she'd made it her life's mission to succeed at everything in front of her, to be one step ahead of the men in the same role. Yet, after achieving near-perfect scores on her exams, and achieving one of the highest degrees her university had to offer, the one thing she'd neglected to study perfectly was rope knots.

She thought back to Hamsik, her favourite colleague and best friend at work. He was the master of knots, and so, whenever she was faced with a knot obstacle she didn't know how to hurdle, she'd always left it up to him. Occasionally he'd try to teach her with several demonstrations, but she'd never listened, her mind distracted by his thick hands and arms, his thick shoulders and chest, his bulging thighs…

Hamsik, her Achilles heel.

Voices emanated from the other side of the door, carried by the draught. As she lay there, she tried to recall what had happened to her before she fell unconscious. She closed her eyes and thought hard.

She remembered being in the salon. In the corridor with Dimitri. He'd offered her the money. Yes, that was right. But then somebody had come to pick her up and take her away. They'd walked her to the car… And then another image appeared in her mind; when she was being escorted to the back of the Mercedes – they didn't have many in her country as flash as the one she was thrown into – she'd punched her captor and tried to make a dash for it, an escape. But it had quickly been thwarted and she fell and collapsed to the ground, grazing her hand.

She clenched her fist, and as the skin creased, a stinging sensation tingled the palm of her hand. And then the crease in her elbow burnt. Her eyes moved up the length of her arm until they reached the crease. A large red lump had formed, surrounded by a patchwork of blue-and-purple bruising.

Then she remembered. Moments before the world had turned black, her captor had grabbed her by the hair, reached into the boot and jabbed her with a needle. Knocked her straight out.

And now here she was. With no idea where 'here' was. With no idea how long she'd been here. With no idea what was going to happen to her next.

The money that she'd been given had been taken away from her. Now she had nothing to use as leverage for her escape.

Before she was able to dwell on it even further, the voices coming from outside grew louder. Laughing, cajoling. Footsteps. Laughter. Footsteps. Laughter.

Nearing.

Nearing.

Nearing.

Her heart pounded, and a faint sheen of sweat formed on her thin, supple body.

The door opened, flooding the room with light. It blinded her, burning a distorted rectangle in her retinas.

'Looks like the subject's finally awake,' a voice said. Unknown. Unfamiliar.

She opened her eyes and watched two figures, nothing more than silhouettes, enter the room.

One of them moved to the other side of the room and twisted the dimmer switch on the wall, and she groaned as the light above her face intensified, blinding her even more. She winced and turned her head but there was no escape. The light was all-consuming so she was forced to close her eyes again.

The other voice spoke this time. Also male. Deeper than the first. 'Aww, would you look at her – she's starting to sweat.' A finger touched her skin, picking up the beads of liquid across her stomach and running them down to her pelvis. 'Being scared only makes it worse.'

With her eyes still closed, she felt the presence of the other man join her opposite side. She blinked away the harsh light, but it was no use; her vision was still distorted and densely populated with swimming stars.

She mumbled, groaned, gasped.

A hand was placed over her mouth gently, stifling her discomfort.

'Shh… Shh… It's OK, my little butterfly,' man one said.

'Butterfly?' man two, with the deeper voice, added. 'Really?'

Man one moved his hand up her face and stroked her hair. 'It's what I call all my patients. Especially the younger ones.'

'Kids, you mean?'

'Sometimes. Sometimes the adults like being called a butterfly too. I tell them they're elegant and graceful. That as soon as they wake up from a long sleep, they're no longer the ugly caterpillar they once were – they become so much more, so much prettier, so much *better*.' His hand moved to her ear, stroking back several strands of hair behind it. He addressed her directly. 'Do you like butterflies?'

She decided not to answer.

'I think they're elegant creatures. The way they blossom and bloom in magnificent colours. Don't you agree?'

She said nothing.

'One of these days you'll learn to appreciate what I'm telling you. And one of these days you'll learn to appreciate what I'm going to do to you.'

She inhaled sharply and closed her eyes. Her body tensed, and her muscles turned taut, rigid. Preparing herself for what was about to come. To suffer in silence. Alone.

Suicide would solve it all. She could kill herself now and save the days, weeks, months – potentially years – of abuse that she was going to suffer while in this situation. She could stop it now. End it all.

But then they'd win. They would have defeated her.

I didn't come this far…

'What… what you do to me?' she whispered.

Man one gasped and flicked his gaze to man two.

'She *does* speak. For a second there I thought we were going to have to look at her voice box.'

He let go of her ear and moved to a corner of the room, out of sight, then returned a few seconds later with a scalpel in hand. 'There are a lot of sick people out there. Unhealthy. Dying. Some of it's genetic, some of it's the result of their own sin – greed, gluttony, that sort of thing. But there are also healthy people who can help cure the sick.'

'That's where we come in,' Man Two finished. 'And that's where *you* come in.'

She could feel the vein in her neck throbbing out of its skin, bursting in an attempt to escape, her body releasing oodles of sweat everywhere, her stomach bouncing up and down like a trampoline. Her heart working on overload.

And a part of her hoped she would slip into a powerful cardiac arrest. Sudden. Fatal.

But then she remembered her promise to herself. She would not be beaten. She would not let them win.

She was going to survive. And she was going to make them suffer for what they'd done to her.

'How...' she said, struggling to say the words; a ball of phlegm and saliva had formed in her throat, and she swallowed it down. 'What are you...?'

Neither of the men said anything. Man two on her right crouched beneath the bed and reached for something. As he extended his legs, she caught sight of what was in his hands.

A tank, with a tube connected to a mouthpiece.

'Twenty-Nine,' the man on the left began. 'Have you ever gone under the knife before?'

Man two placed the mouthpiece over her face. She panicked, started thrashing, her breathing turning rapid. She tried to fight and shake off the mouthpiece, but her efforts were pointless. Within seconds, the world turned black again and she was wrapped in the envelope of unconsciousness.

Chapter Thirty-Five

STRIKE TWO

Dimitri Romanoff. That was the name of the big bald man opposite him. A quick check of his possessions and his driving licence had confirmed his identity.

Beside Dimitri was a familiar face – Veronica Bateman. The same solicitor who would be defending Henry Matheson in court. The backup option to Rupert Haversham. Already, alarm bells were ringing in Jake's mind; whenever Rupert was concerned, or whenever somebody wanted the defence solicitor to represent them, there was always a wider-scale operation going on, an indisputable and tangible link to The Cabal.

And now it was time to find out exactly what that link was.

He pressed the record button on the digital recorder.

'Welcome,' Jake began. 'I trust you have everything you need? Water? Coffee?' There was no response. 'I'd just like to remind you, Dimitri, that you are under arrest under section two of the Fraud Act 2006. You do not have to say anything. But it may harm your defence if you do not mention when questioned something which you later rely on in court. Anything you do say may be given in evidence. Everyone on the same page?'

Dimitri's face remained placid.

'Halfway through the book,' Veronica replied.

'Then I think it's about time we began.' Jake pulled out his notebook containing the files that he'd rushed together after signing Dimitri in at the custody suite. 'I have here a copy of a letter that I received in the post a few days ago. It was notifying me that my gas account was in arrears. Do you recognise this document?'

Jake slid the piece of paper across the table towards Dimitri. The man ignored it and continued to stare into Jake's soul.

'I proceeded to call the number suggested on this document, which took me through to a member of customer support. There, I was informed that all I had to do was settle a small balance of two pounds fifty-eight. Like any good customer, I paid. Unbeknownst to me, after I'd given my card details across, along with the answers to my security questions, my bank accounts were hacked and my money disappeared.'

'This isn't an episode of *The One Show*, officer,' Veronica interrupted. 'We don't need to hear your life story. Please could you get to the point?'

Veronica was just as much of a bitch as he remembered. Rude, arrogant and only slightly better than the dirty protest one of the prisoners had smeared on the walls the other week.

Jake cleared his throat. Breathed. Calmed himself. 'I'd like to point your attention to the evidence that has already been presented to you. Article Tango-Echo-Four-Charlie. A copy of the bank account where the money was taken from. On it are the details for the account that the money was paid to. Do you recognise these details, Dimitri?'

Nothing.

'Because we were able to trace the money to an offshore account called Candiru Limited which has links to several businesses in the UK – one of them being your nail salon, which, according to Companies House, you are the director of. Do you know how that money got paid to you?'

Nothing.

'Do you know where that money came from, Dimitri?'

Still nothing. Jake shuffled the papers on the desk and turned to Veronica.

'I might remind you and your client that a failure to mention anything may be used against him in court.'

Veronica's face remained placid. She turned to Dimitri then back to Jake.

'I have a question for you, Detective Tanner,' she began.

Great. Here we go.

She continued without giving him a chance to respond.

'When you arrested my client, and when you brought him into the custody suite, did you or any of your other colleagues give him the opportunity to have a translator present? Did you take into consideration his needs?'

Jake hesitated. He searched his mind. Had he offered a translator's services? Had he neglected one of the rights available to a suspect?

Had he just made the arrest unlawful?

He spoke perfectly good English when he spoke to me in the salon.

'That's exactly what I thought, Detective Constable Tanner.' Veronica pursed her lips and wiped her hands on her knee.

Smug bitch.

'That will make things interesting if you decide to take this further.'

Jake shook his head. *No, no, no.* She wasn't about to let him get out of this. His own mistake!

'If you knew he needed a translator then why didn't you say anything?'

'I'm not here to tell you how to do your job. And don't even *think* about trying to tell me how to do mine.'

Jake sighed, scratched the side of his chin. Screams and shouts erupted in his head as he chided himself for his mistake. A rookie mistake, one born out of ego, impatience and complacency.

'For now,' he started, 'we will be releasing you on bail, pending further investigations, the particulars of which will be laid out by the custody officer. Interview terminated at three thirty-three p.m.'

Veronica climbed out of her chair, grabbed Dimitri under the arm and hoisted him to his feet.

'I'd like my client to be left alone while I get him out of here.' She walked past Jake and stopped by his shoulder. 'Oh, and if you continue the way you are, I won't be afraid to file for a harassment case against you, Jake. We both know how obsessive you can become.'

Veronica shut the custody cell door behind her, locking them inside the small cell. Dimitri stood in front of her, hands in pockets, looking like a rebellious teenager.

'We done?' he asked.

'Not nearly as quickly as you'd like us to be.'

'I have to go back to the salon.'

'Right now, no. Soon, yes. There are a few things I have

to take care of first – like getting you out of here. I need you to stay put.'

Dimitri grunted by way of response.

'The alternative is that you stay here and I let them sentence you to fifteen to twenty years in prison? No skin off my nose what happens. I get paid the same rate either way.'

'Even if you do shit job?'

She nodded. 'Even if I do a shit job, yes.'

Dimitri shrugged and rolled his neck from side to side, the joints clicking with every roll. 'The Cabal can fix it. He can get me out.'

'Not when there's nobody left, he can't. All his contacts are gone. He's doing all of this on his own. And do you know who's responsible for it?'

Dimitri's expression remained impassive. She was sure he didn't care about the answer, but she was going to give it to him anyway.

'The officer that you tried to steal from. He's the one crushing your operation into the ground. And if it weren't for his mistake then you'd be a part of it too. Whatever you and The Cabal are working on now, he would have put a stop to it.'

Dimitri peered over his shoulder at the bed that stretched from one side of the room to the other and sat on it. 'What are you waiting for then? Get me out of here.'

Veronica scowled at him. She hated being told what to do. Even more so when it was from a second-rate criminal like him. Henry Matheson? Sure. But him, the balding Romanian? No.

'One last thing,' she said, taking her mind off what she really wanted to say. 'Under no circumstances are you to make contact with The Cabal. At any point. Not until he makes contact with you. I will tell him everything in the meantime. The police will track your activity as soon as you leave here, which means where you go, who you see, what you do and what you say to people. If you notice anyone loitering around or tracking your movements, then let me know. It's called police harassment. Tanner's the most susceptible to it. But don't give him a reason to suspect you even further. Understood?'

Dimitri looked at her blankly. It was some time before he responded.

'I'm not an idiot,' he replied.

Sighing, she rolled her eyes and thought, *Why do I even bother?*

'I need a fucking holiday,' she whispered under her breath as she turned and started towards the door.

She knocked and waited for one of the uniformed officers in the custody suite to let her out. A few seconds later, a bolt turned and she crossed the threshold, ignoring the officer, then exited the station and headed towards her car.

Dialling The Cabal's number, she slid inside. He answered as soon as she shut the door.

'It's never good when you call.'

'I imagine one of these days I'll have good news for you.'

'What is it now?'

'Dimitri. He's been arrested.'

'I see,' came the response.

The Cabal sighed heavily through the phone, and she knew him well enough to know how he was reacting – he would be closing his eyes and rubbing his left eye. It was a small tell he'd developed, and one that she'd picked up on shortly after getting to know him. 'Let me guess. Someone without a penny to their name found out?'

'You know better than anyone that you shouldn't have

hit him like this. How many times have you been warned against the softly-softly approach?'

'Not enough times evidently.'

'Evidently.'

Two officers emerged from the station, descended the steps and hopped into a police vehicle.

'You seem rather optimistic about all of this,' she continued.

'Tell me what happened in detail, and then we'll see how I feel.'

Veronica then proceeded to inform The Cabal of everything that had taken place – for the parts of the story that she didn't know, she simply relayed the information Dimitri had given her. If it was in any way wrong, that was on him.

'How long till you can get him out?'

'Couple of hours. probably.'

'Do everything you can.'

'What do you think you're paying me for?'

He welcomed the silence following the call. Processed the information he'd just been given. Placed it in the Filofax of his mind and slotted it into the folder reserved for Jake Tanner, the biggest one in there.

Somehow, Jake had managed to put the pieces together, and they'd led him right to them. The only possible explanation was if Dimitri had been lazy. And *that*, in every possible way imaginable, was unacceptable.

Strike two.

Three strikes and you're out.

But there was a bigger problem to worry about than Dimitri.

Jake Tanner. The problem that was becoming like the

eczema on his hand, unending, enduring and a bitch to get rid of. And no matter how hard he tried, it always found a way to crawl back.

This time it was spreading.

Jake was a good detective, granted, but he wasn't omniscient. He didn't have eyes and ears everywhere. Instead, he had a helping hand.

Someone, somewhere in the team, was helping him get closer and closer.

Closer and closer…

A second problem.

And he knew exactly who it was.

Which meant it was time to get the cream out and eradicate both problems for good.

Chapter Thirty-Six

THE CYCLE OF LIFE

Jake made no effort to hurry back to his desk. The opportunity to catch and arrest the person responsible for stealing his entire life's worth had slipped past him. And he was the one responsible for it. Nobody else except for him.

You're shit, Jake. You're a massive shit.

Cock-up from start to finish.

The one you want is D…

D for Dimitri.

D for Darryl.

D for Danika.

D for Danny Cipriano.

D for Denise, his mum.

D for the next person who tried to speak to him.

How could he know who to trust anymore, if he didn't even trust himself to do the basics? The parasite of paranoia and doubt was festering in his mind, burrowing deeper and deeper. What was Elizabeth going to say? Fuck that – what was Stephanie going to say? She'd been the one involved in helping him root out Dimitri. She'd been the one to invest her time and risk her career for him. If anything, he'd let her down the most.

Jake scanned his key card and shuffled into the office. As he stalked along the corridor, he allowed himself a moment to relax, and he eased the tension in his shoulders and focused his attention on the door to MIR4.

'Tanner!' a voice called, bringing him to an abrupt and shuddering halt.

Straight away he knew who the owner of the voice was.

'Everything all right, guv?' Jake asked, hesitating before he summoned the courage to spin round and face his boss.

'I think you and I need to have a little chat.'

The one you want is D…

D for Darryl.

Darryl's office door closed with such finality that it scared him. Jake had been in this situation before, where he was about to be reprimanded for his actions, but he'd never been as frightened as this. He'd made a genuine mistake rather than telling the white lie he was best known for.

'I've been hearing a few things around the station, Jake. And I want to understand what's going on,' Darryl said as he walked past Jake's left-hand side.

'What do you mean, sir?' he asked, hoping that by playing dumb he could diffuse some of the malice in Darryl's voice.

'I think you know what I mean. Acting the fool isn't going to fly with me, not when we've got the assistant commissioner so close to us. I've got him breathing down my neck almost every hour of the day, reminding me of the importance of Matheson's hearing.'

So we've forgotten about Roland already then, have we? That didn't last long.

'One of my jobs as a manager is to take all the flak from up above and make sure very little of it filters down to you guys.'

Jake raised his eyebrow. 'I thought that was the whole point of being a manager? You get to unleash the torrent of shit on us. Tenfold.'

'And make you hate your job so much that you either quit or take it out on everyone else? You're my responsibility, so it's only fair that I have to deal with your slack. You don't perform, I don't perform. And then when you continue to fuck up, you get put on a performance review and then we say bye-bye. I replace you and then the process recycles. It's as simple as that.'

The cycle of life.

Come to work, lose your job, repeat.

Until you eventually kick the bucket.

Darryl continued, 'The moral of the story is to do your job properly. And thoroughly. Which, from what I hear, you've not been doing either.'

Darryl took a step closer to his desk, releasing the tension between the two of them. 'What were you thinking, arresting that guy? You're not supposed to be getting involved with other departments, nor are you supposed to be getting involved with your own investigation. There's a clear conflict of interest. Not to mention it's taking time away from the Matheson trial. You left Steph all on her own.'

Jake recalled something Darryl had said to him a few months back, while he and Ashley were in the middle of an unauthorised surveillance operation outside the Cosgrove Estate, Henry Matheson's home.

The office has ears, Tanner…

Stephanie had been the ears then, but… Surely she couldn't be now, could she? Jake dismissed the thought. Stephanie was helping him of her own accord. She may have protested and appeared aggrieved by the work he was making her do, but she wanted to help him.

She wouldn't do something like that.

No. Darryl had his own ears all over the place.

The one you want is D…

'This is affecting my family, guv,' Jake said as calmly and politely as possible. He didn't want to let on that he knew Darryl's secret. 'I have to get involved. Surely you can understand.'

'You're not Batman, Jake. You're not some sort of vigilante who seeks his own justice. It's not part of your remit. Convicting Henry Matheson is. Once that's all over, you'll be able to focus your undivided attention on getting the people who took your money from you. But, until then, I want you to prioritise the Matheson case. It's as simple as that.'

Jake nodded slowly, pretending he was listening. Even though both men in the room knew he wasn't.

'What if my investigation into Dimitri Romanoff uncovers something else – something larger, something I hadn't accounted for?' Jake said, images of the numbers and barcodes he'd noticed on the salon employees' wrists flashing across his mind.

Darryl folded his arms. An eyebrow rose. 'What have you found?'

'Nothing,' he lied. 'I was just saying.'

'Well until you can give me something concrete, I won't allow it.'

Concrete, like Danny Cipriano's tomb.

Jake smirked. 'Cool. We done? I've got Matheson's investigation to get back to.'

Darryl hesitated a moment. His face flushed red, and his lips narrowed slightly. 'Thin ice, Jake. Thin fucking ice if you step out of line and talk to me like that again. Watch your place please, son. Now get out and get back to work.'

And Jake did, but not the work Darryl wanted him to do.

Chapter Thirty-Seven

EMAIL

When Jake entered the Major Incident Room, he found two new additions to the team. The help. DC Ashley Rivers, whose first day had coincided with the beginning of the Matheson investigation, and another young detective constable named Nancy. She was slight, of similar build to Ashley, and seemed nervous to be in his company.

But there was no Stephanie.

'You come to help?' Ashley called from across the room.

'And ruin all the hard work you guys have been doing? That wouldn't be fair on you.'

'Maybe you should invest some of your manpower and give us a hand,' Ashley snapped.

Ouch.

It was the first time he'd had any sort of confrontation with her, and he didn't know how to respond to it. Had it been Stephanie or Darryl, he'd have felt comfortable enough around them to argue back. But because Ashley was still so new to the team, he wasn't so sure he could.

'Where's Steph?' he asked instead.

Ashley thumbed towards the room next door. Jake thanked her and skipped into Major Investigation Room 4.

There, he found her in the centre of the room, sitting behind her laptop, headphones plugged into her phone that lay on the table surface. Either side of her was a pile of laptops and a mountain of lever arch files. The manual age versus the digital age. And she was the master of both.

'Can I have a word with you?' he asked.

She snapped her head away from the screen and scowled at him. 'You're back. Darryl called round earlier. Asked me where you were…'

'Yeah, he found me.'

'And what did he say?'

'This and that. Something about a conflict of interest.' Jake shrugged like a teenager.

'When's that ever stopped you before?' Stephanie asked, paused, then scratched a mole on the side of her cheek. 'I've known you for some time, Jake. And I've never seen you act like this. Ever. You're an arsehole, granted. But I've never seen you work this hard at something, especially if it breaks the rules on *so* many levels.'

'Right…' Jake said, unsure where the conversation was going.

Just before she was about to continue, her laptop chimed. The notification caught her attention. She clicked on something and then stared at the screen, her eyes transfixed on the pixels. She continued to stare at it for an abnormally long time as if hypnotised.

'Steph?'

Nothing.

'Steph!'

The loud sound brought her out of her stupor. She shook herself back to the present and apologised.

'Important?' Jake asked.

'Just… just another… email.'

'Right. Well, you were saying?'

'Saying what?'

'You called me an arsehole…'

Her face lit up as she remembered. 'I can cover for you without you here, but I'm not a magician. You'll still have to show your face now and then.'

He was an arsehole. But a lucky arsehole.

Maybe that was the only way to get things in life.

'So you're giving me free rein to do what I want?'

'That selective hearing of yours coming through again, is it? You completely missed the bit about you showing your face around here. Don't make me take back what I just said.'

'Sorry…' Jake held his hands up in surrender. 'What do the others think? Ashley snapped at me just now.'

'She'll get over it. I think she's just sick of everything to do with Matheson.'

'Aren't we all.' Jake smirked at her and received one in response. 'Is there anything else I need to know? Any update on the jurors?'

Stephanie shook her head. 'We're looking into that today. It's taking a while to get the list from the Ministry of Justice. As soon as we get that, we'll have something to dig our teeth into.'

Jake thanked her and told her he needed to get out of there.

'I'll try and cover for you as much as possible, Jake. But don't take the piss. Once you betray my trust, that's it. Gone.'

Jake stopped on the half-turn and faced her. 'Noted. With thanks.'

Her body was cold. Colder than cold, in fact. Frozen, below zero.

The email had sent her into a frenzied state of shock, delirium, paranoia.

She hadn't known how to react, and so she hadn't reacted at all. Simply stared at it.

And now what was Jake thinking? That she was weird? That she was somehow working against him?

But that was the least of her worries.

Fuck Henry Matheson.

Fuck Jake.

Fuck Darryl.

Fuck the team.

Her main priority was the email.

Sitting at the top of her inbox, opened, flagged as important. No email header, no sender's address. It was a ghost in the system. But unlike a ghost, the message inside it was visible.

Etched into her brain.

Hands shaking, she reached for the mouse and moved the pointer across the screen. Inhaling deeply, holding it in her lungs until she was ready to burst, she clicked on the email again.

Several images appeared.

Several images, heavily pixelated and blurry, of her father. Sitting in his prison cell. Dressed in his prison uniform. Wandering aimlessly around the place, looking as though he wanted to get involved with a game of pool.

The final image showed the outcome of that request – her father pinned against the wall, pool cue pressed against his chest.

Tears swelled in her eyes. How could they be so monstrous?

At the bottom of the email were the words:

WANT HIM TO BE COMFORTABLE? MORE INSTRUCTIONS TO FOLLOW.

Almost as if someone was behind her, watching her every move, her mobile bleeped. It vibrated on the surface, the screen illuminating.

Tentatively, afraid it was going to detonate if she touched it too violently, she lifted it and opened the message.

Another unknown number.

The Cosgrove Estate underpass. E11 4QZ. Midnight.

Chapter Thirty-Eight

NAOMI

It took Jake thirteen minutes to make it back to the nail salon. As he arrived, he slowed the car to a steady halt and left the engine sitting there, idle. Just as with earlier, there was no game plan, no Plan A, B, C, or any of the other twenty-three letters in the alphabet.

All he knew was that the salon was where his money was kept. That it was a stronghold of The Cabal's. That there was a mountain of evidence and information there, waiting to be plucked like cotton in a field.

And without Dimitri there to reign over it, it was fair game.

A sound distracted him. The noise of glass smashing and a table collapsing.

Jake slipped the car into first and nudged further forward. Amidst the foliage of the plants and trees of the entrance, Jake saw a figure throwing the contents of the salon to the floor.

Creating chaos. Overturning the place. Destroying evidence.

Seeing it, Jake killed the engine, jumped out of the car, sprinted the short distance to the front door and... hesitated.

Something overcame him. A wall of white. A flashback to when he was cocooned under a sheet of snow in an avalanche in the Alps. A squeezing sensation surrounded his body as if he was being hugged to death. A tightness in his chest. A strong grip around his throat.

Closing his eyes, he inhaled sharply, fighting against the sensation. He inhaled further until his lungs were at full capacity. Held. Exhaled. Long, smooth, slow.

Just like that, the panic attack had disappeared almost as quickly as it had begun. Jake placed his hand on the door and shoved it open so hard that it bounced against the adjacent wall and collided with his shoulder. Paying it little heed, he crossed the threshold into the building and stopped in the middle of the walkway.

The salon had been turned upside down. Tables overturned, dozens of nail polish bottles strewn across the floor. Chairs. Acrylic nails. Desk lights. Everything. And in the centre of it all was a man wearing a balaclava and brandishing a baseball bat. In the background, by the other door at the end marked with a fire exit sign above it, was another man wearing a balaclava; this one held one of the employees from the nail salon in his arms. Jake recognised him immediately. It was the man he'd bumped into as he'd entered the salon the last time. The one who'd looked petrified as soon as he'd laid eyes on Jake. The one with the number fourteen and a barcode on his wrist that made him look like an item in a grocery store.

For a long time, Jake just stood there, staring at the man with the bat. Staring into his pitch-black eyes while his mind worked overtime, absorbing all the entry points into the building, as well as the possible exit routes. There were two in total. Front and back.

His peripheral vision scanned the large pieces of debris, the trip hazards, searching for anything that he may fall over in hot pursuit. And, similarly, he looked for anything that he could potentially use as a weapon, a means to defend himself. Currently, it was a baseball bat versus bare hands, and he didn't like those odds.

Slowly, Jake reached into his back pocket. He'd never been in a situation like this, and he needed to stall for as much time as possible. His hand fumbled inside his pocket for his warrant card. He found it and pulled it out.

'My name is Detective Jake—'

Baseball Bat attacked, affording Jake no time to prepare. He charged towards him, covering the short distance in a matter of steps. Jake moved his right foot backwards, readying his stance and tensing his muscles.

The man raised his arm and swung the bat down at Jake.

Jake ducked, narrowly avoiding the blow to the head, though he heard the whooshing sound it made as it buffeted past his ears.

Poised on his front left foot, Jake pivoted his body like a boxer, bouncing beneath the blow, and swung his right foot in a sweeping motion at the man's legs. Their ankles collided, knocking the man off balance slightly. Then Jake placed his hand on the man's shoulder and pushed; Baseball Bat collapsed to the floor in slow motion. The bat clattered to the ground.

As Jake hovered over the assailant's body, bending down to handle him and arrest him, Baseball Bat kicked Jake in the chest with both feet. The impact was too strong, and the force of the blow sent him stumbling backwards. His feet caught on an overturned plant pot, and he crashed through the glass shop window, his arms flailing as he staggered back and rolled onto his shoulder. The window splintered into thousands of shards that rained down on him.

'Bollocks,' he growled as he staggered to his feet, using his forearm to protect himself from the glass.

By the time he was in the salon again, Baseball Bat was already on his feet, sprinting towards the other end of the shop.

Skipping and hopping over the debris strewn across the floor, Jake chased after the attacker. His legs and arms pumped, and within a few seconds, he tore through the fire exit and arrived into a small square space. To his left was an open door that looked as though it led down to a basement. To his right was a flight of steps leading upstairs. Directly ahead was a door that led outside.

Jake jumped into a small private car park at the rear of the shop. There were two vehicles twenty or so yards away from him. A Transit van and a Mercedes. As he breached into the open, the Transit pulled away, the screech of tyres piercing the air.

The man with the baseball bat was running towards the Mercedes. He raced to the driver's side and hopped in. Jake sped after him, but just as he reached the car's door handle, the vehicle darted off.

Within seconds, the Mercedes was at the end of the small parking lot behind the row of shops. Before it disappeared out of sight, Jake squinted and made a note of the number plate – CM08 BY2.

Gotcha.

He spun on the spot and stared back at the deserted nail salon then pulled his phone out of his pocket and dialled 999.

'This is Officer Alpha-Charlie-Three-Four requesting emergency backup. Atomic Nails, Bremington Street, Stratford. SOCO assistance required also.'

Jake made sure they received the message clearly then pocketed his phone and started back towards the salon. Alone. With no idea what was waiting for him on the other side.

Chapter Thirty-Nine

BELLY OF THE BEAST

Jake made a point of always keeping a pair of rubber gloves in his Mini in case of emergencies such as this. They were the only thing separating him from the evidence used in criminal court cases. Too many times he'd heard of investigations going wrong due to the mismanagement and mishandling of evidence by those who were either new to the job or just downright stupid; pieces of evidence that intrinsically linked the suspect with the crime. There were procedures in place for a reason, and it was only right to follow them.

Kettle, pot called: you're black.

As he stepped into the salon, he noticed that a crowd was beginning to form on the outskirts of the property.

'This is official police business. Could you please step back?' Jake called to the ten or so people that had started to hang around the salon's entrance.

Without needing a second warning, the onlookers retreated to a respectful distance.

Jake turned his back on them and deleted them from his

mind. If he spent too long dwelling on them, he wouldn't have enough mental capacity to focus on the job at hand. And he needed to focus as there was still a lot of work that needed to be done. But first, he had to make sure there was no further threat to life. That nobody was lying in wait in the property.

Shards of glass crunched underfoot as he walked gently, delicately through the building, as if too much sound would disturb the internal foundations and send them plummeting beneath him. He came to a stop beside the baseball bat and inspected it then retrieved his pocketbook from his blazer, tore off a page, folded it in half and placed it on the floor beside the bat. It would come in handy later for when the scenes of crime officers arrived.

Jake extended his legs. The muscles in his thighs screamed in agony, and the joints in his knees creaked. He was getting old for twenty-six.

Brushing down his trousers, he moved towards the back of the premises, body tense, mind on high alert. His senses became tuned to his surroundings. A painting of a picturesque landscape somewhere in the world swung from side to side on the wall. Behind him came the chatter from the onlookers outside. In the distance, he heard the sound of several police cars converging on his position.

Jake stepped through the building tentatively. His eyes scanned the floor like a metal detector, sweeping from side to side, searching for anything that may indicate who was behind the attack and why.

There was nothing. At least to the naked eye.

Then he came to the end of the salon. He stepped into the small space and looked to his left. The door leading down to the underground basement was ajar. Jake shuffled towards it, pushed the door open and descended the steps.

The stairwell was poorly lit, and the smell of damp and sweat immediately hit him in the face. The stench was sitting at the bottom of the stairwell, where it had been left to fester. Jake had witnessed dead bodies at various stages of decomposition, and this smell reminded him of the latter stages.

There was a door that opened at the bottom of the steps. From his position, Jake was unable to recce the inside of the room. He didn't know whether anyone was in there or whether it was completely deserted. And he wouldn't know either until he was inside.

The belly of the beast.

Using his left hand, lest anything jump out at him and he needed to defend himself with his right, Jake pushed the door. It swung open slowly, hinges creaking.

He waited, listening for any sound or sign of life.

Nothing.

Holding his breath, he entered the space.

The room was large. Thirty feet by sixty. Jake presumed it stretched beneath the shop next door. The air inside was cold, the walls were bare – painted a plain, uncreative white – and a single light dangled from the ceiling, the room's only source of illumination. To his right was a toilet and a showerhead, open plan. Not even a curtain to pull across. And a hole in the floor where the water should have descended. But there was an issue. A dark brown puddle soiled the plug and surrounding area.

To the side of the shower, running along the wall, was a small table. Plastic cups of varying colour and degrees of cleanliness rested atop it overturned, their contents spilt onto the wood. Then Jake's eyes fell on the back of the room. Occupying the entirety of the floor was a series of mattresses that had been heaped together to create one giant bed. Clothes, pillows, pants, socks, shirts all lay in a pile at the foot of the bed.

Jake stopped and counted the number of pillows.

Thirty-one.

One for every person who works here, he thought.

And then he realised what sort of place he was dealing with. What sort of place he was inside.

People were living there. Sleeping there. Eating there. Showering there. Defecating there. Working there.

And Dimitri was the man in charge of it all.

Now Jake knew what his money had been stolen for. It had been used to fund a human trafficking slavery ring. Shipping them and ferrying them from one country to the next. Selling their bodies into a life of misery and torment.

And these were only the ones Jake knew about. It didn't bear thinking how many others had been held captive there – or for how long.

Chapter Forty

TWO FOR TWO

Amelia Wilmot. Eighteen-year-old university student, studying Business Hospitality at the University of Greenwich. Lives with her parents in what could only be described as a mini-mansion.

Stephanie was in awe of the cars on the street and the style of houses towering over them. In this part of the city, where crime was rife and burglaries were the most popular pastime, she thought it stupid to flaunt your money and privilege in such obnoxious ways. But then again, she'd never had money, so how could she know what it was like? Her father had always taught her to live within her means, and if that's what these residents were doing, with their hundred-thousand-pound cars, who was she to judge?

Although, if she found out that the Ferrari belonged to Amelia, an eighteen-year-old who'd only recently learnt to drive, then there was no other option for Stephanie but to judge. What eighteen-year-old deserved a car like that? Now that *was* ignorance.

Darryl had received an anonymous tip-off that Henry

Matheson was paying off his potential jury members with large sums of money. He didn't say how he'd found the names of those in the pool, but all she knew was that she'd been instructed to investigate anyway. After a long day of requesting the files, and with the right sign-off from Darryl and the higher echelons of the Met, the names of the jury pool for Matheson's trial had been given to her. And at the top of the list was Amelia.

Stephanie, perhaps rather naïvely, hadn't been banking on Henry's bribers to work through the list any other way than alphabetically, so she'd made the executive decision to visit Amelia Wilmot's house first, in the hope that she was only one night behind them. Darryl had given her strict instructions not to call ahead, and not to let on what was happening, lest she called at the wrong time and one of Henry's workers was there.

The identity of the individual carrying out Henry's dirty work was still unknown. Although Stephanie had a suspicion it was Reece Enfield, the teenage drug dealer who'd fled Stratford after being accused of several counts of murder. He was still at large, and his face was known to every police officer in the city, and further afield. Yet, somehow, in the months since Henry's arrest, he'd still managed to avoid capture, and his current whereabouts were unknown.

So it wasn't completely unfeasible to suggest that he was working for Henry again.

For the second time in two days, Stephanie lumbered out of her reasonably priced car feeling inadequate and with a sense of self-loathing, and shuffled towards Amelia's house.

As she approached the front door, she heard sounds of excitement and conversation, of the TV playing loudly in one room, music blasting through a set of high-quality speakers in the other.

It was a miracle anyone heard the doorbell.

Standing in front of her a few moments later was Amelia Wilmot, who looked even prettier than the photos on her social media page.

Why was that the case so frequently? Amelia had made it two for two. First Little Susie, now this. Nobody looked like they did in real life based on their social media profiles, but those two girls did. And then some. It disheartened her, but not nearly as much as the comments that some of her past dates had made about her appearance. 'You don't look anything like your profile picture,' one unlucky conquest had told her. 'Oh, I thought you… You look different, that's all. Different nice obviously. Just…' had said another.

Just not what I was expecting, she'd finished off for him.

'Can I help you?' Amelia answered. Her voice was deeper than Stephanie had been anticipating. Much deeper, in fact. Almost boyish. At least that was some consolation, she supposed.

Stephanie pulled out her warrant card and showed it to the young woman. 'Am I right in thinking you have jury duty soon?'

Amelia eyed the document suspiciously and nodded.

'May I come in?'

Amelia held out a hand, keeping her at bay. 'What's this about? Am I under arrest?'

'Nothing like that. I just need to ask you a few questions. It's come to our attention that the man being accused has found out some of your details, and we need to make sure you're safe.'

Amelia seemed to consider this a moment. She looked down at her half-eaten nails and picked at them. 'I didn't touch the money,' she said. 'I didn't want it. I haven't spent a single penny of it.'

Bingo. Honesty was always the best policy. Eat your heart out, Jake Tanner.

'There's nothing to worry about,' Stephanie said. 'Can I come in?'

Amelia led her into the living room, where MTV's latest instalment of *Teenage Mums* was playing loudly on a seventy-inch flat-screen TV. A set of patio doors opened onto a vast expanse of green, illuminated by a motion-sensitive light. Outside in the garden, a golden retriever sprinted from one side to the other, getting a much-needed runaround, giant plumes of cloud vapour expelling from its mouth. Indoors, the atmosphere was much warmer. Scented candles and diffusers from the White Company sat proudly on bookshelves on either side of the TV. Three white leather sofas worshipped the flat screen, and in the centre was a marble coffee table, another diffuser sitting atop it. Adjoining the living room was the kitchen, where Amelia was struggling to use a coffee machine.

Money could buy you a lot of things, common sense not being one of them.

'Need a hand?'

'Stupid thing doesn't work.'

'Water will be fine.'

'No, please. I insist. I'll make it from the kettle. Make yourself comfortable.'

Money may not have been able to buy common sense, but Amelia's politeness clearly came from somewhere.

'Where are your parents?' Stephanie asked as she seated herself on the leather sofa, looking straight at a teenager pushing a pram along a busy high street. She could get used to this.

'They're out somewhere. Working, probably. We don't see them much.'

'We?'

'My brother. He's the one playing that shit music upstairs. You can hear it coming down the street.'

Less than a minute later, Amelia set a steaming cup of coffee on the table, retrieved the dog from outside and sat on the sofa to her left, the dog draped over her legs, her fingers stroking its gorgeous fur. A queen and her loyal protector in command of the castle.

Stephanie tilted forward, removed her pocketbook and pressed pen to paper. 'Can you explain to me what happened when you received this money you spoke about at the door?'

Amelia nodded. 'It was last night. I was watching *The Only Way is Essex*. This knock came at the door and I answered it. Mum and Dad were out again so it was just me and Ryan. There was this big, tall bloke standing there. He claimed to be from the Home Office or something. We spoke for a bit and then he handed me a package.'

'Of what?'

'Money.'

'Do you still have it?'

Amelia shooed the dog from her lap, leapt off the sofa and hurried to the bookcase in the left corner of the room. At the bottom of the unit was a drawer. Amelia reached inside, removed a Jiffy bag and placed it on the table.

Stephanie tilted it to the side to inspect the contents. Money. Lots of it. She left it there.

'And nobody's touched it?'

'Nobody knows about it,' Amelia replied.

'Good. I'm going to need that. We'll have to test for forensics.'

With any luck, her already stupid criminal would have left incriminating fingerprints.

'What happened after he gave you the money?'

Amelia returned to the sofa, but the dog looked afraid to climb back up again, hurt after the last time it had been thrown off.

'He threatened me. Told me that if I told anyone, they'd come back and hurt my family.'

Stephanie paused a moment, a pain in her wrist flaring from the note-taking.

'Then… why are you telling *me* everything so freely?' she asked. In her experience, people who'd received those sorts of threats were cagey, timid, reserved and would do anything possible to escape from telling the truth.

'Because…' Amelia reached for the remote and turned the volume up. Then she climbed off the sofa and sat next to Stephanie. The girl's perfume was understated, yet smelt expensive. She had to talk loudly over the noise of the TV. 'I trust you.'

'Why?'

'Because you're a woman. This morning someone else came to the house, another police officer, asking the same questions as you. But I didn't tell him anything.'

Money may not have been able to buy common sense, but she was surprisingly street smart enough to know who to place her trust in.

'What did he want?'

'He just wanted to make sure someone had been, that I'd been given the money, that I understood what it was for. Then he told me, and I thought this was really strange, to ignore everything the man the night before had told me, and to vote guilty instead.'

'Did he say why?'

'Only that it was for the best and that the man on trial was very dangerous. Then the conversation moved on and he asked what I was planning on doing with the money. I don't know what it was, but something seemed off. He seemed... weird.'

'Weird how?'

Amelia shrugged. 'You know, like the kind you get in bars and clubs.' She searched for the word. 'The leering type.'

Stephanie knew all about them. Experienced her fair share too, as had Amelia no doubt.

'Can you remember what both these men looked like?'

Amelia nodded, held out a hand and led Stephanie to a small office along the hall. Inside, it looked like something out of a James Bond movie. A wall of computer screens flickered and displayed various angles of the house, both indoors and outdoors. In the top-left corner was Ryan, Amelia's brother, playing on his Xbox, controller in hand, headset around his ears, sitting on his bed.

Her eyes roamed over the images. Of the master bedroom, Amelia's room, their en suites, the guest room, the office, the landing, the games room, the kitchen and the living room, where the wisps of steam coming from her mug were as clear as if she were holding the thing in front of her.

'Dad's anal about security,' Amelia said as she sat at the desk and logged in to the computer. 'Says most people don't have it turned on, they just use it as a deterrent. "Little good that'll do them when everything's stolen," he says.' The young girl's impression of her father reminded Stephanie of her own; of how she'd mock him for giving her the life lessons she later came to appreciate.

'And you record everything?'

'Yep.'

'And you have footage of last night and this morning?'

'Yep.'

This morning, she thought, her mind whirring. Trying to think of who could have possibly come round to speak with her at a similar time to Roland's funeral.

And then she found out.

First, Amelia started with Henry Matheson's man from the previous night. Then she moved on to the second individual.

The second man she knew straight away, standing there in the camera lens buried into the front door. But the real surprise came when she realised she also recognised the first man.

Two for two.

She checked her watch – 5:05 p.m.

Seven hours to go until she was needed elsewhere. Plenty of time to process what she'd just seen.

Chapter Forty-One

ORDERS

'Sir, you're going to have to wait.'

Jake was becoming irritable. Irate. The SOCO had been examining his body, his clothes, his hairs, and his hands for forensic evidence for the past thirty minutes. He was a crime scene himself, and he needed to give everything on him up to the jobsworth who insisted on taking forever. She was probably doing it out of spite, sadism, getting a sense of satisfaction by antagonising and delaying him even further. But what she didn't realise, and what he didn't want to tell her, was that a group of trafficking victims were being transported somewhere. For all he knew they could have made it out of the country already.

'I'm afraid I'm going to need to take your clothes, sir,' the SOCO said. Her face was covered by her mask, and her hair was mostly hidden beneath the hood of her white over-suit, just a few small tufts of blonde protruding from beneath the white line.

'I don't have a spare change of clothes.'

'We've got some spare jogging bottoms and a jumper

you can wear,' the man beside her said. He was the one responsible for logging every piece of evidence that was submitted for investigation. He pulled down his face mask and said, 'The quicker you do it, the quicker you can get out of here.'

Jake sighed, rolled his eyes and removed his blazer.

'Will I ever get it back?' he asked as he passed it to them and started to undo his tie.

'You know how this works. I hope you've got spares.'

'And if I don't?' He placed his tie in a separate evidence bag.

'Expense it. Not your fault you're a crime scene. Line of duty 'n' all that.'

Jake said nothing more as he decanted the rest of his clothes into individual evidence bags. The female SOCO disappeared to fetch him replacement clothing, returning by the time he was down to his boxers.

'What about the shoes?' he asked.

'Afraid so,' the loggist replied.

Jake kicked them off and dressed in his new attire. The jumper was a snug fit, the trousers even tighter against his thighs, and his sleeves climbed back up his wrist as he extended his arm.

'They were the only size I had,' she said.

'It's fine. It'll do.'

'Sign here for me.' The loggist held a form in his face. 'For the evidence bags, and also the new kit we gave you.'

'You're not expecting it back, are you?'

'If you could be so kind. It's been in the family for years.'

'I'll give this back when I get my things returned to me.'

'We'd appreciate it if you could wash it beforehand.'

Jake grunted as he left them and raced back to the car.

There was nothing else left for him to do there. The basement was under forensic examination, and he was already painfully aware of what had been going on inside it. All he could do now was wait for the forensic report to come in, and he could take it from there. He was better served back in the office, where he could develop and continue the investigation.

By the time he eventually arrived, the dark orange hue from the oncoming street lights illuminated the dashboard, and the lights inside the city's skyscrapers looked like mini fireflies in the sky, twinkling and sparkling. Just as the lives and hopes and dreams of those trafficked into the country once had.

Jake pulled up to the station, hopped out of the car and stormed through reception. He ignored the reception staff as well as the custody officer and climbed the steps, deliberately avoiding the lift.

He scanned his identification card in the small slot on the wall, stepped into the office and headed straight for the kitchen. His mouth was parched and his throat sore.

Grabbing a glass from the kitchen cupboard, he put the tap on, running the cold water through.

'I was going to ask where you've been, but your change in outfit tells me it wasn't the shopping centre.'

Jake turned. Standing there in the doorway was Darryl.

'Either that or you've been arrested and managed to convince them to let you keep the shitty uniform,' Darryl said, rubbing his chin.

Funny, Jake thought, his sense of humour severely lacking. *Really funny.*

'I'm impressed,' Darryl continued. 'It only took you a couple of minutes to completely disobey my orders – again. I think that's beaten your record.'

Jake didn't appreciate his boss's passive-aggressive remark. To demonstrate his discontent, he remained silent and chewed the inside of his lip.

'Well?' Darryl said, stretching his arms sideways. 'Care to explain yourself?'

Jake sighed heavily through his nose before responding. He had to calm himself and swallow away all of the anger and frustration he was prepared to unleash on Darryl. It was neither the time nor the place.

'Guv, I think I deserve some extra credit, at least. Yes, I appreciate that I completely ignored everything you told me. But look what I found. A potential human trafficking ring in the Stratford area. And the man I arrested was using *my* money to fund it.'

'That's beside the point.'

'Please explain.'

Darryl counted on his fingers. 'First, you arrest him unlawfully, which I'm *astounded* by. And then, what's even better is you went into that nail salon without a warrant. Your being there wasn't exactly lawful.'

'But I had probable cause. I drove past and I saw people were smashing up the place. How is that not reason enough? Don't do that to me, Darryl.'

'I'm sorry, Jake. It's borderline harassment.'

That word pricked Jake's ears. Harassment.

If you continue the way you are, I won't be afraid to file for a harassment case against you, Jake.

The one you want is D…

D for Darryl.

Darryl helping Veronica push all the right buttons to exonerate Dimitri. Darryl evacuating the victims inside the nail salon before his arrival. Darryl The Cabal.

We both know how obsessed you can become.

'I want you to go home, Jake. I can't let you work on the Matheson case right now. It's suffered enough with you clusterfucking everything up. I've got the assistant commissioner coming down hard on me constantly. You're not helping things. Besides, look at you. You're not in any fit state to work in those clothes. You look like you haven't slept for days. I need you focused and at your best. You can't be doing that when you're dressed like this. And it pains me to say it, but I can't trust you to do a good job at the moment. You've ignored me countless times, and I don't know if you're going to do it again. I need you to go home. Maybe take a couple of days, if you need to. But this time it's an order.'

Chapter Forty-Two

COMFORTABLE

A wind, as cold as the way she felt towards her father, buffeted through the underpass, wrapping its claws around her bare ankles and climbing up her legs. She hugged her coat tighter against her body, fending off the chill, but it had little effect.

Ten minutes had gone by and there was still no contact from the mysterious sender.

Ten minutes of letting the cold nibble deeper and deeper into her bones.

She was in the middle of an alleyway, several hundred metres from the Cosgrove Estate – or The Pit as it was more affectionately known amongst the uniformed police officers charged with frequenting it. Graffiti covered the walls. Some of it was good and worthy of her admiration. Some of it profane and the work of an immature teenager who'd just discovered what a penis was.

But the mind of a thirteen-year-old boy was the least of her worries; being alone in such close proximity to The Pit was a danger in itself.

Let alone the fact she had the unfortunate circumstance of being a woman.

Not long after she'd arrived, anxious and caught in the anticipation of meeting the mysterious email sender, a group of boys dressed in hoods and tracksuit bottoms had idled down the alleyway, one of them on a bike, the others fighting to keep a mouthy pit bull on its lead. She'd kept her eyes down and avoided their gaze, but she'd felt them undressing her and imagining what disgusting things they'd do to her. It was a miracle that someone else, a complete stranger who looked as frightened as she did, had walked down at the same time, possibly saving her from a brutal rape or murder.

She hadn't seen him since.

And she was starting to wish he would show his face.

Funny, she thought, *the security we feel amongst strangers when we're desperate.*

Like clinging to the passenger next to you in a turbulent aeroplane. Like embracing a nurse in a hospital after a terrifying diagnosis. Sometimes the touch of someone could be all we need.

Except here, there was no one to touch. No one to cling to. No one to embrace.

As another gust of wind ripped through the alleyway, her mobile started to ring. A knot formed in her throat and she struggled to breathe as she looked at the screen.

UNKNOWN NUMBER.

'Hello?' she answered, unable to hide the fear in her voice.

'I bring good news. Would you care to hear it?'

As he spoke more, the image of the man she'd seen on Amelia's screen flashed in her mind. Now she had a face to the voice.

A face to The Cabal.

'Yes…'

'There's no need to sound afraid. My bark is much worse than my bite. Until I'm pissed off.'

Jake. Oh, Jake. What have you done?

Jake had tested The Cabal's patience, and now they were both witnessing how strong the man's bite was.

'I'm sorry about your father,' the voice continued. 'Must be horrible. I can't imagine what you're going through, let alone what he is.'

Stephanie blinked away a tear and sniffed. Swallowed.

'But with your help, I can make sure he's comfortable. Do you know who he's sharing a cell with? Henry Matheson. I know, I know. What a fuck-up, an indictment of our criminal justice system. And believe me, that's a lucky coincidence, depending on which side of the coin you're viewing. Now you and I both know what Henry Matheson's like. But so far, Henry seems to be warming to him. Though I can't promise it will stay that way forever. As your dad's mental health deteriorates, so will Matheson's patience. You *do* want your dad to be comfortable in there, don't you?'

Stephanie dropped to the ground, sliding her back against the wall. The bottom of her coat dragged and got caught in a puddle of rainwater – or worse, piss. But right now she couldn't care less what it was; all she could think about was her dad. Sharing a room with Henry Matheson. Living every day in fear of being around hardened criminals when he was anything but.

'He must be so scared in a place like that,' The Cabal continued. 'As a fellow colleague, I'd hate for something to happen to him. Your dad is a good man.'

The tears streamed down her face, ruining what little make-up she had left on her face.

'What do I need to do?' she asked, even though she was certain she already knew the answer.

Part 6: 7th Jan

Chapter Forty-Three

RULES

He drummed his finger on the steering wheel. Tapped his foot on the accelerator. Checked the time on his phone.

Finger. Foot. Phone.

Finger.

Foot.

Phone.

It went on like that for five minutes, until he got bored and decided to deviate from the norm by checking the dashboard: 2:07 a.m.

Two hours since he'd given the all-or-nothing ultimatum to Stephanie. Two hours since he'd crushed her world and everything in it.

Stupid bitch, putting her trust in the wrong people. Believing that Jake Tanner could somehow help her with her life's problems. 'The ones you love always find a way of hurting you in the end,' he'd told her before ringing off. To which she'd had no reply. As though it was something she already knew but had never wanted to believe or admit to herself. A truth so deeply ingrained in her it had disappeared.

If she ever wanted to see her dad comfortable in prison again, she'd do as he asked.

The irony of her putting her trust in him, the least trustworthy person, however, wasn't lost on him.

He looked upwards at the pitch-black sky, the clouds illuminated a soft grey from the pollution below. A few thousand feet beneath the clouds were the giant, booming floodlights of Tilbury Docks, its cranes and structures bathing the area in a milky white glow.

Situated less than a mile away, the ambient light reached him. A little over a hundred yards ahead was an overgrown field of marshes, separating him from the docks, and behind were a series of warehouses, towering in the darkness like monsters in the shadows of a child's bedroom.

He glanced at the dashboard again – 2:10 a.m.

Ten minutes late.

Unacceptable.

Second time in a row.

Three strikes and you're out.

Kenny, his contact, was letting him down more times than a blow-up doll. And he *hated* being made to look the fool.

Then, almost as if on cue, two white dots appeared in his rear-view mirror. *Finally*, he thought as he watched the lights cut across the tarmac and pull up behind him.

The Cabal hauled himself out of the car, slammed the door behind him and strode over to the vehicle. The window rolled down as he arrived.

'Who the fuck are you?'

'Nice to meet you too,' the woman in the driver's seat replied.

'Where's Kenny?'

'In bed. Sick as shit. Not in a good way. He told me to do the job instead.'

The Cabal didn't like that.

A thousand different names and faces appeared in his mind. Everyone he'd ever worked with. Everyone who'd ever worked at the Met. Everyone who'd ever potentially seen or recognised his face in his entire life. He'd forced himself to remember what they looked like. With the right training and the right amount of practice, it was a skill that could be learnt.

He searched his memory bank for her face.

Was she undercover? MI5? National Crime Agency?

In the end, he determined that she wasn't and that he'd never seen her before.

But that didn't make him feel good about using a stranger for the job. She already posed a massive security threat by just having seen his face.

There was a perfectly good handgun in the boot of his car, waiting to be used.

'Who are you?'

'Claire.' She opened the door and stepped out, holding her hand out for The Cabal. 'I already know who you are.'

The Cabal eyed her hand with grave concern. Her breath fogged in front of her mouth, and she was wearing a thin, brown overcoat that fell to the top of her shins. It was impossible to tell if she was wearing a wire.

'Take it off,' he ordered.

She opened her mouth to speak but he cut her off.

'Take it off,' he repeated. 'I don't want to see any wires.'

'Is this how you treat all of your contacts?' she asked as she started to undress.

First, she removed her coat and placed it over the frame of the car door.

'It pays to be paranoid in this business,' he replied.

Then she removed her top, a stretchy, black nylon jumper that reached up to her neck, and draped it over the coat. All that was left was her bra and a mole beside her belly button. But no wire.

'And your trousers,' he said, gesturing with his finger.

She shrugged, wrapped her fingers around the button, and said, 'You know, if you wanted to sleep with me, all you had to do was ask.'

'Very good. Now get on with it.'

Claire rolled her eyes, scoffed and then threw her trousers down. Her legs were thin, covered in bruises, and she wore a matching set of underwear. The Cabal gestured with his finger for her to spin around, which she did.

'Satisfied?'

'Very.'

Within seconds, she was dressed and ready to go.

'What's the plan?' she asked.

'Kenny didn't fill you in?'

'Well… up to a point.' She hesitated. 'My husband's good at many things. Communicating is *not* one of them. All he said was to come here, meet you, pick up the delivery and then drive it to where it needs to go.'

'And you have experience driving HGVs?'

'Got my licences. Done and done.'

'And you think you can handle this?'

'Don't sound like rocket science.'

'You know the drop-off location?'

Claire nodded.

'Good. Get in the car. I'll drive you.'

'What about mine?'

'That's your problem. Not mine.'

The Cabal moved to his car, started the engine and waited for Claire to join him. Once she was inside, he turned in the road and headed deeper into the industrial estate, where they were soon dwarfed by monsters lurking in the shadows.

They snaked in and out of the network of roads until they came to the skeleton of Handy Man Scrap Services, a large, disused warehouse. The gates were opened, blue and white POLICE tape spread across the perimeter of the building, blowing listlessly in the breeze.

'What is this place?' Claire asked. 'It's got police written all over it.'

'You ever heard of Henry Matheson?'

'Yeah, I seen his face a coupla times on the box.'

'Well, he owned this place. Stored millions of pounds' worth of drugs here. It's now under police occupation twenty-four hours a day, seven days a week. But sometimes they're partial to a small bribe to convince them to fuck off for a few hours and come back when everything's done.'

Which reminded him. They didn't have too long left.

The Cabal pulled into the warehouse car park, and the two of them alighted the vehicle. The Cabal led the way and showed her round to the side of the building. The shutters that stretched across the length of the warehouse were open, and inside was an 18-wheeler articulated lorry, a giant green container sitting on its back. Prepped and ready to go. Delivered only half an hour earlier by another contact working at the port.

He reached inside his pocket and dangled the keys in front of her face.

'Just like that?'

'Just like that.'

As he dropped the keys in her hand, a sound emanated from within the container. Like a dull thud.

'What was that?' Claire asked.

'Something might have fallen.'

'But it's stationary—'

'You know the rules, right? Your husband explained them to you?'

'Do the speed limit. I never saw you. Cover my face at toll booths. As few stops as possible.'

'Piss yourself if you have to. But you're forgetting the most important one.'

She hesitated for a moment and looked back at the green metal box in front of her. Pensive. Contemplative.

'You've lost me,' she said.

'Whatever you do, don't look inside the container.'

Chapter Forty-Four

CURIOSITY

Don't look inside the container. Pah! Yeah, like that was going to happen. The container was hers for the next couple of hours. She could do with it what she wanted and nobody would know. There could be all sorts in there. Drugs. Televisions. Mobile phones. Weapons. The lot. It was part of human nature to be a little curious, so what was the harm?

Nobody would know, she told herself.

And if they ever did find out, then she and Kenny could escape the country and jet off into the sun together using the money The Cabal had already paid her. Now *that* had been an oversight on his part. Perhaps he'd been distracted by the striptease, she thought as she pulled out of Tilbury Docks and started towards the A13. *Paranoid old fart.* Why on earth would she be carrying a wire on her? Why else would she be in the middle of nowhere in the dead of night? She was desperate for a shag but not that desperate.

Oh well. She had the container now. All she had to do was drop it off at the location, come back to the docks, pick up her car and drive home again. Plenty of time to think of all the things fifty grand could buy. Breast implants. Botox. Nose job. Lip fillers. Her whole body could be restructured and remoulded to what she wanted, to what *Kenny* wanted of her.

And then he might finally fuck her like he used to. Before the kids, before the weight.

Claire drove for the next hour, heading north counter-clockwise on the M25, around the top of London. She was sitting in the slow lane, idling along at the designated speed limit. Following her instructions. And then she started to think about what was in the back. What that noise had been. And why The Cabal was willing to make sure the package was picked up successfully in person whereas most of the other jobs that she'd done had been left completely down to her.

A sign appeared on the side of the road. South Mimms services. One mile away. Just on the outskirts of Potters Bar.

Claire switched on the indicator early, keeping her eyes peeled for the turning, paranoid she might miss it.

She didn't.

The service station was large. The car park was the size of a football pitch, and the petrol station inside was just as big. A large, incandescent sign protruded from the top of the building, signalling to patrons what was inside. M&S. WHSmith. KFC. Burger King. Everything a ravenous driver, and ravenous families, would need. On a usual shift, Claire would have stopped and treated herself to the unhealthiest option on the menu – it was her one cheat meal, her one chance to act and behave and eat like a slob without Kenny monitoring every calorie or gram of satu-rated fat that went in her mouth. Except now she wasn't feeling hungry at all.

She swung the lorry to the left, into the designated

HGV section, and slammed on the brakes. The momentum sent the small Homer Simpson bobblehead spinning.

Then she killed the engine and slid out of the cabin. Leaving the door open behind her – it would only be a sneak peek, after all – she stalked along the length of the container slowly, rubbing her hands up and down the grooves in the metal. She held her breath and listened beyond the sound of the motorway in the distance, tilting her head closer to the side of the container.

She heard nothing.

Claire reached the end of the container and fumbled for the keys. The Cabal had given them to her before she left so she could pass them on to the next driver, the next link in the chain.

Eventually, after thumbing through the keys in the dark, fighting off the cold in her fingers, she found the one she was looking for. As she readied herself to insert it into the lock, she dropped the set.

Dopey bitch.

Bending down to pick up the keys, she heard another dull *thud*. This one sounded as though it had come from the front of the lorry.

Her senses became acute. All she could hear was the sound of her breath amidst the rustling of the leaves nearby. To her right, in the distance, a car drove past, the headlights stretching shadows along the pavement. She ignored it and focused her attention on the keys.

Found the correct key again and slid it into the lock. It *clicked* with such finality it sent shivers up and down her spine. Something about this seemed like a bad idea. Like all her nightmares coming together at once. And she rapidly began to regret her decision. But it was too late now. She was too far gone to change her mind.

Curiosity was eating away at her like a disease, and she was struggling to fight it off.

She grabbed a metal lever and slid it across the face of the door until it stopped. Then she grabbed another lever, lowered it till it was perpendicular to her and slowly opened the door. The sound echoed around the container, signalling to her that whatever was in there didn't occupy all of the space – in fact, it sounded like it didn't occupy much space at all.

Grabbing the door, paying little attention to what was inside, she walked round to the side of the container and sealed it in place, lest a supernatural gust of wind sent it flying back at her, knocking her out. As she rounded the back of the lorry, she grabbed the other door, swung it open and locked it in place. Now she would have a full view of the container's contents.

Claire stepped into the middle of the open doors, keeping her head down. She wanted to look up at the last moment, starving herself of that curiosity for that little moment longer, making the pay-off even sweeter.

She lifted her head and looked inside the container. All the light from around her had filtered into the darkness. A torrent of cold air rushed out of the container and set the hairs on the back of her arms on end. What she saw inside made it worse.

Right in front of her was a sea of dead bodies, lying atop one another, dressed in thick jackets and jogging bottoms. A hand had fallen over the lip of the container and dangled there, still, lifeless. She had no idea how long they'd been there – all she knew was that they'd been there long enough to die. It was impossible to gauge how many lives had been lost inside. Perhaps twenty. Perhaps thirty.

Forty. Fifty. All together in the sub-zero temperatures, their skin pale, bordering on an ice blue.

Before she could do anything, a gust of wind attacked her. Followed by another. And another. Concerned for the door, she started towards it.

As she stepped to the side of the container, the lock fell open and the door smashed into her face, driven harder by the wind behind it. The metal collided with her head, breaking her nose and throwing her to the ground. The last thing she saw was a wall of white as pale as the bodies in the back of the container.

Chapter Forty-Five

MEET

The muscles in Jake's right wrist screamed in silent agony. For the past two hours, he'd lain awake in his bed, squeezing the grip strengthener Elizabeth had bought him as a joke on his birthday. He'd never found the occasion, nor the desire, to use it, and so it had since been sitting in a drawer collecting dust. That is until he needed something to soothe him, to take his mind away from the anger and fury bubbling away in the pit of his stomach.

When his alarm sounded at 5:30 a.m., earlier than usual – not that Elizabeth would notice; it had been another night of being ignored, another night of sitting in silence, another night of eating alone – Jake switched off the alarm, rolled out of bed and got himself dressed for the day ahead. Not that he had anything particular planned. After Darryl – that prick, talking to him like that, treating him like that – had sent him home, Jake had been forced to reassess the investigation and what he knew.

It was clear he was getting too close to the truth, too

close to the identity of The Cabal, and being sent home was a way to deter him.

D for Darryl.

Somebody had stolen his money and killed Roland. That same person was working for The Cabal. And that individual was operating a human trafficking network in East London.

D for Dimitri.

The only problem that remained was finding out where he was, where the operation was and who was at the top of it all.

Kill the head and the rest of the body follows.

It was six a.m. by the time Jake was dressed and ready, sitting there at the dining table, staring into the radiator on the wall. His mind blank, devoid of any and all thought.

Until his phone vibrated. For a moment, excitement surged through him. Perhaps it was Stephanie notifying him that they'd found The Cabal. That Darryl had been arrested and charged. That Henry Matheson was going to prison for the rest of his life.

Sadly, it was none of those.

Instead, it was a message from an unknown number.

Another one, another addition to the mess of cryptic clues and disjointed and fragmented thoughts.

Meet at the place nobody would think to look. The place nobody would know to look.

As usual, the complete message came through in a series of texts, each containing a few words to build the bigger picture. So far, in the past few days, he'd received several, each more confusing than the last.

The person you want is D.

Find the key.

Some people want to watch the world burn.

Never forget the code of ethics.

When one disappears, another appears.

But now he realised what they were: a series of clues. The person on the other end was trying to help him but was too afraid to share their identity.

And now there was this one: *Meet at the place nobody would think to look.*

The place...

The place where...

He trawled his memory, clawing for conversations, for locations in his mind.

And then he knew exactly where he needed to go.

Chapter Forty-Six

PRESS SEND

Farnham Golf Club, a place he'd visited only twice before, both of which had been under extremely different circumstances. The first was during a hostage negotiation, his first day on the team with Surrey Police. The notorious organised crime group, The Crimsons, the group that had started this entire odyssey into the unknown, had raided a jeweller's, taken a hostage, placed a spiked collar bomb on her neck and left clues around the county that detailed how to disarm it. The second clue had led him to the golf course. Eighteen holes of pristinely manicured lawns and trimmed-back trees.

The second time he'd visited was for a rendezvous with a former colleague, the one he was expecting to meet this morning.

Shortly after the first series of messages, another had come through telling him to arrive by nine, just before the premises opened for the day's round of golf. He was one minute early.

He climbed out of the car and meandered towards the

entrance, surveying the grounds and the car park around him. The usual suspects in their Audis and Mercedes and BMWs and Range Rovers were beginning to pull in – the morning's business on the stock exchange having finished already, it appeared.

The clubhouse was split into two parts: the shop, where you could buy the latest clubs and clothing, and the restaurant at the back. Jake headed towards the latter. On the way through, he passed James Atwood, the owner.

'Been a while,' James said, giving him a nod.

'Not long enough. He here?'

'On his way.'

Jake ordered a fresh orange juice at the bar then found himself a seat, looking out onto the green, watching the early risers slowly filtering onto the holes like flies swarming a dead body.

Then he sensed a presence.

Keeping the glass of juice in his hand, he slowly rotated his head towards the restaurant entrance.

At the sight of the man standing before him, he nearly dropped his glass. Since the last time Jake had seen him, he'd gone to serious lengths to obscure his identity, yet Jake was able to see right through it.

'You're not who I was expecting,' Jake said, finishing off the last of his juice, wishing it was something stronger.

The man just pointed to a bench on a patio outside the restaurant. 'Shall we?'

Jake felt as though he didn't have a choice.

'Are you the one I've been speaking to?' Jake asked as he seated himself on the bench.

Dimitri perched himself beside him, his body reeking of strong cologne. Perhaps to mask the body odour. Or, more pertinently, perhaps to mask his sins.

'No, but I've been monitoring your phone. And following you. You're an easy man to hack, Jake.'

It was almost laughable, but for some reason, he didn't feel any animosity towards Dimitri for what he'd done; instead, he felt an odd sense of calm – respectful. The real person Jake's anger lay with was the one orchestrating it all, not the pawn in The Cabal's manipulative and malicious game.

'Why are you here?' Jake asked.

'To give you a message.'

'From The Cabal?'

Dimitri turned to face him for the first time. 'Yes.'

A representative from one party meeting the other. Two rival superpowers coming together on neutral ground.

'And then what?'

'You go your way, I go mine.'

'And then what?'

'That is up to you.'

Jake nodded, absorbing what that meant. 'Go on then. Out with it.'

Dimitri reached into his coat pocket and removed an iPad, unlocked it and loaded up the home screen. While he watched, Jake's eyes scanned everything. There were the usual apps on there: Camera, Safari, Mail. But Jake looked for the anomalies, the rogue members.

Facebook, Instagram – even criminals needed social lives. Spotify, Amazon, Kindle. *Candy Crush, Kingdom of Empires* – they also needed entertainment, something to keep them entertained.

But there was nothing that caught his eye.

A second later, Dimitri loaded the photo library and tapped on the bottom image. Jake recognised it immediately from the thumbnail.

'The message is simple, Jake,' Dimitri began. 'And it's one I'm sure you've heard many times before. Stop what you are doing. Let us continue our work, and there will be no need to harm you or your family.'

'You already did that when you stole everything I own.'

Dimitri lifted the iPad in the air. 'Then perhaps a threat to your career will make you listen?'

Then he started to scroll through the images. And Jake was transported back to that night on the embankment of the River Thames, walking and talking with Henry Matheson, discussing what would happen if Jake didn't leave him alone, fearing that any moment might be his last.

And now here he was, history repeating itself.

'All I have to do is press send and these images go to your boss. You can talk yourself out of a lot of situations, but you can't talk yourself out of this one.'

'And then what?'

'We go our way. You go yours.'

'That can't happen.'

'Do I need to show you the photos again?'

Jake inhaled, steadied himself. 'I know what you're doing, Dimitri. The nail salon, the people you had living in there. I know about it all.'

'Congratulations. But only *you* know it. And if anyone else finds out then it'll become *your* problem.' He tapped the top of the iPad to highlight his point. Not that Jake needed reminding.

Before he was able to respond, cries sounded from behind him, seeping through the glass windows. He shuffled round in his seat and saw several people standing in the middle of the bar area, staring up at the TV screen. Then he squinted to see what the commotion was; something in his gut told him it was important.

And then he read it. Rolling along the bottom of the BBC News homepage.

FORTY CONFIRMED DEAD IN LORRY CONTAINER

Above it, several angles of a green-and-white articulated lorry surrounded by white tape and dozens of police officers flashed on the screen.

Jake turned back to Dimitri and pointed at the TV. 'Don't think it's your problem now?'

Chapter Forty-Seven

HEAVY CONSCIENCEVILLE

Stephanie's eyes were lost in the computer screen, the pixels and colours pulling her deeper through the looking glass. Minutes, hours, she didn't know how long, had drifted by without her doing anything. Not even a notion of rational thought crossed her mind in that time, as though it had been lost in an abyss of despair.

The bustling sound of movement and hard work distracted her. She landed back in the MIR, where DC Ashley Rivers and two other constables whose names continued to escape her were working on the Matheson case.

As a team, they were nearly there. Ninety per cent. Ninety-five. Ninety-eight.

They just needed that last push, and then they'd be over the finish line.

Somebody in the room whistled. A hand waved in front of her field of vision.

'Earth to Stephanie,' Ashley said. She perched herself on the edge of the desk, stretched her legs and placed her palms face down on the top. 'I bet you can't wait for this to be over.'

Stephanie blinked again, several times, until she became fully immersed in reality. She glanced up at Ashley's face and noticed a cold sore forming on her bottom lip.

'Make the most of it while you can,' Stephanie said. 'There'll be another case just like it soon, no doubt.'

'That's mighty insightful of you,' Ashley said, smiling. She placed a hand on Stephanie's shoulder and squeezed. Her touch was soft and strangely comforting. 'Are you all right though? You look like you haven't slept in days.'

'That's because I haven't.'

'I think we're mostly done here,' Ashley replied, easing the grip on her arm until eventually, she let go. 'You can take some time off if you want? Recharge a little. Not going to be much use to us if you're exhausted on the day of the trial.'

'I'll be fine.' Stephanie shuffled in her chair, stretched her back upright and straightened her arms, waking them up from their nap. 'Any news on Jake?'

Ashley pursed her lips and replied, 'Not that I know of. Think I heard someone say he hasn't bothered coming in this morning.'

Oh, Jake. Why are you doing this to yourself? When will you understand you can't always be the fucking hero?

'Did you see the news?' Ashley asked.

'Regarding the lorry situation?'

'Yeah.'

'I saw it. Has anything changed since it came out?'

Ashley shook her head. 'Not much more than we already know. Information's sort of got a lock on it at the moment.'

'Has anyone been down to Matheson's warehouse?'

'Should we have, ma'am?'

'It's our crime scene. It's part of an active investigation. If the container was picked up in that area, one of us should be making sure there isn't anything suspicious going on.'

'Would you like me to go, ma'am?'

'Please.'

At that, Stephanie leant forward, printed the document on her screen, launched herself away from the desk towards the printer in the corner and waited. For a short while, nothing happened.

'I'm sure these things are slow on purpose when you need them most,' she said.

Then the machine hummed and whirred into life, and shortly after, the document printed. All nine pages of it.

With the evidence in hand, she closed the lid of her laptop and grabbed her cold mug of coffee.

'Going somewhere important?' Ashley asked, still sitting on the side of her desk.

'Somewhere you'd rather not be, I can tell you that much.'

Stephanie turned on the spot and headed for the door. She held it just as it was about to shut and called back to Ashley. 'I might take you up on that offer of a break,' she said. She was going to need something stronger than coffee. 'Visit the warehouse in the docks. The rest of the team should be able to help, should you need it. If not, only call me in an emergency please.'

'Cross my heart.' Ashley flicked her hand across her chest as a way of saying goodbye.

Stephanie was outside Darryl's office less than a few seconds later. She hovered by the door, her right foot drumming on the floor, conjuring the strength and courage to knock. Eventually, she found it. The sound echoed through her mind. *Dumf. Dumf. Dumf.*

Guilt knocking on the door, ready to send her to Heavy Conscienceville.

'Everything OK, Stephanie? You know this is *my* office, right?'

'What?' she said, her mind slowly moving away from her body again.

'You look like you're searching for something else.'

A reason not to have to do this.

'I need to speak with you. It can't wait,' she said without giving him the opportunity to avoid what was about to come. He'd made excuses once before, and she wasn't willing to let him make them again.

'Yes. Certainly. Of course.' He opened the door for her and gestured her in. 'Is… is everything all right at home? Is it your dad? Is he OK?'

Stephanie grabbed a seat. 'It's about Jake.'

'Has anything happened to him?'

Stephanie glanced up at Darryl and then down at the table. 'Please… just sit down.'

Tentatively, Darryl moved across the room. He ran his index and middle fingers along the length of the table. Stephanie could feel his eyes staring into her, probing her for answers.

As soon as he was seated, she set the file on the table.

'Sir, I'd like to raise an investigation into the professional conduct of one of my colleagues.'

Chapter Forty-Eight

GREATEST NATION ON EARTH

His name was Huang Mei, meaning *phoenix* in Mandarin, and he had no recollection of how he'd got to wherever it was he was being kept. After he and the rest of the men and women had been trundled into the back of the vans, a drug had been administered into his bloodstream, and then soon after he'd been graced by the darkness and welcomed into the depths of hell.

Now, here he was. Alone. Clueless. Afraid.

There was no window in the room. No ambient light. No sense of time of day. No up, nor down. He was seated on the only item in the room: a sofa. It was a welcome luxury in comparison to the sea of inch-thick mattresses that he and the rest of the immigrants had been forced to eat, sleep and, in some instances, piss themselves on. It was a degrading and humiliating start to life in this beautiful country.

Still delirious, his vision slightly blurred from the effects of the drug, Huang Mei rubbed his forearm down to the back of his hand. He glanced down at the lines on his skin and felt a flash of pain swell on his wrist. The tattooist had been brash and hurried, stabbing and abrading his skin with the needle. The barcode and number was a constant reminder of the pain and suffering, and the endurance and mental resilience it had taken to travel halfway across the world.

Back home he'd been a farmer, like his father and his father before him, and had lived on the farm with his wife. But shortly after his wife's untimely death, he'd found himself managing her debts and the secrets she'd never told him, some of which he'd still been unravelling a few days before he flew to Europe. With the weight of fear and punishment and insurmountable debts looming over him, he'd sought a new start, a fresh life in the land of prosperity in the West. A place he could earn his money doing what he loved when he wasn't farming: painting. And so, with the savings that hadn't already been collected by the loan sharks, he purchased the VIP package from a contact in his village and embarked on the five-thousand-mile journey from his hometown in Dacheng to London, the greatest city on earth.

And now, as part of that package, he'd been stripped of his identity and reduced to a statistic, a single number that was easily replaced and disregarded. Like the names on a footballer's shirt.

He scratched the irritated skin. He was certain it was infected. But nobody was willing to help. Not the organisers who'd brought him into the country, nor even those he'd shared the experience with. Just like the numbers on their wrists, they were all different, all removed from one another by a single digit which meant, for some unknown reason, they couldn't help.

Perhaps it had been the fear of getting caught that prohibited them from easing his pain.

Or perhaps it was because, like him, he'd learnt the severity of their mistake. And that, from now on, it was survival of the fittest.

And he would survive, rising from the embers, reborn, like the phoenix he was.

A door opened in the room, flooding his vision with harsh light. A silhouette, tall and narrow, entered, his features indiscernible.

'Sit up,' the man said gruffly. His voice sounded as though he'd been shouting for a long time and was in desperate need of water.

Huang did as he was told.

The man stopped in front of him and held out his hand. He was holding a brown envelope with '39' written in large handwriting on the front.

'What this?' Huang asked, pointing at the envelope.

'It's your new life,' the man said, his face still covered by darkness.

As he said it, Huang recognised the voice as belonging to the man who'd abducted him from the salon and thrown him into the back of the van. He remembered those eyes, those piercing black eyes – lifeless, devoid of any emotion.

'Everything you need. Passport. National Insurance number. Driving licence – can you drive?'

Huang remained silent.

'Fine. You don't need that one then. The rest are in there though. Bank statements. Utility bills. Payslips for the past six years.'

Huang didn't know what to say. He was flattered. Flabbergasted, in fact. He was getting out of here! They were giving him a new life!

Rising from the embers…

'I… I…' he stuttered, overcome with emotion and trying hard to fight back the tears of excitement. 'I pay off… I pay off debt?'

Silence fell. And whatever hope and enthusiasm he had left rapidly dissipated the longer the silence remained. Huang's body turned cold and the muscles in his legs tensed. A stabbing pain swarmed his stomach and made its way up his body. The acid in his vomit burnt his throat as he swallowed it back down.

The man crouched, rested his elbows on his knees and slapped Huang's cheeks gently.

'Far from it, mate. You've got a very important job to do. There's a trial coming up at the Old Bailey shortly. One of the jury members has sadly dropped out because they didn't do what they were told, so you're going to fill in for them. And you're going to give the verdict not guilty. Everything you need to know, everything you need to say, is in this folder. Nice and easy. There's a good boy.'

The man gave him another slap on the cheek, this time harder. Then he rose, wandered towards the door and switched a light on.

'Oh,' he began as he hovered in the door frame, 'and you've got a new name as well. Something a little more English. Welcome to the United Kingdom, Jimmy Wu, the greatest nation on earth.'

Chapter Forty-Nine

OFF THE LEASH

'Are you sure you want to do this?'

For Darryl, the answer was a simple yes. For her, it was a no. Except it was more complicated than that. Far more complicated, and if the sensation in her stomach worsened, she was worried she would vomit the complications onto his desk.

'I am, guv. I've thought about it. A lot.'

We can make your dad really comfortable…

Darryl sniffed away the cold, wintry air that had crept into the office like a bad omen and dropped his gaze onto the letter in front of him.

'Is there anything else I need to be aware of?'

So comfortable he won't even know he's in prison…

A better life is what she hoped for. Both for herself and for her father, whether that was inside prison or on the outside. And if it came at the expense of a good friend and colleague, then so be it.

It was time she put her dad first. It was time she put

herself first. Rather than Jake Tanner and his fucking First World problems.

All you have to do is raise a case against Jake...

'Everything you need to know is in there.'

The evidence had been easy to come by. It was so profound the amount of unlawful behaviour he was responsible for, she could hardly fathom it. When she'd first met him, he'd been a respected member of the police service, someone who played by the rules and threw the rule book at people when they didn't oblige by it themselves. Now he'd gone one-eighty and joined what she liked to call the dark side.

She slid the face-down sheet of paper across the desk. Darryl took it and examined it.

For a while, she wondered what he was going to say, but then she drifted off. Thinking about her dad sharing a room with Henry Matheson. Afraid, scared, and in need of medical and professional help.

This was the right thing to do.

Yes. Of course it was. The right thing.

He deserves to rot in fucking hell... The words of her sister echoed in her mind, quickly drowned out by Darryl clearing his throat.

'Leave it with me. I'll see to it that the appropriate channels are notified and the relevant action taken.' He folded the note in half and placed it in the notebook on his desk, seemingly smiling at a thought that had just popped into his head. 'I know I'm supposed to remain impartial to these things, and that I shouldn't be discussing them with you, but I think what you're doing is probably for the best. Jake's been let off the leash for too long. It's about time we reined him back in.'

The news of the monumental clusterfuck had reached him almost immediately. His contact in Watford had called him in the small hours of the morning, just after he'd started to nod off, complaining that the shipment hadn't arrived.

There were two 'worst-case scenarios' for that, the first being that Claire had somehow been involved in a car crash, the odds of which seemed low, due to the time of night and lack of motorists on the motorway. The second was that she'd driven to a different location, in the hope that she could steal the contents of the container and sell the goods on for herself.

Both times that had happened in the past, he'd been notified first and had been able to deal with it. People he didn't know trying their luck, which made trust even harder to come by.

But what he hadn't been expecting to hear – from his contact, the police officers on his payroll and through the grapevine – was that Claire had opened the container door in the middle of a service station and passed out. The fact the entire shipment was full of dead people was another layer to the blow, like the addition of a knuckleduster to a fist fight.

Death came as part and parcel of trafficking. An occupational hazard. But now it had left him with one big meteoric mess to clean up.

He punched the wall of his office again, worsening the already broken blood vessels in his knuckles, then paced from side to side. In the background, hanging from the wall, was a flat-screen TV, playing the BBC News. The breaking news had just been announced to the world, and aerial images of the container appeared as a helicopter circled the crime scene.

Forty confirmed dead in lorry container.

Hyperbole dripped from the news reporters' mouths.

Worst crime scene the country's ever seen...

Tragedy strikes North London...

Sympathy pouring in from all over the world...

Largest murder investigation of its kind set to be launched...

But where was *his* sympathy? He'd just lost out on half a million pounds. More if you factored in the lifetime value of forty individuals working for him every day until they died.

And nobody would want to use his services to smuggle them into the country if they knew it resulted in death. The revenue lost from that was even more significant.

He pinched the bridge of his nose and thought for a moment. The lorry was sitting there, in the middle of the service station. Where it wouldn't be for too long. The police would have to move the lorry, with the bodies inside, to a secure location where they could begin the investigation and identification process. Each body would have to be removed and their belongings examined. At least a day's worth of collecting, collating and confirming. Maybe more.

Which meant he had a day or two to get himself out of the clusterfuck and over the other side. Sever all the ties connecting to him.

But where to begin?

The immediate problem was making sure Claire didn't speak. She'd seen his face. She'd heard his voice. She could identify him with ease if she ever saw him again. The only positive was that she didn't know his name – nobody did.

Claire. The only thing keeping him from being connected with the crime.

Then the solution presented itself to him: kill Claire, kill the connection.

But before he could think of anything else, the door to his office opened.

'Everything all right, guv?'

'Yes,' he lied. 'What's up?'

'Things are crazy down here. It's like seven-seven all over again. I've got someone on the phone for you.'

'Who?'

'They didn't say.'

He sighed and strolled to his desk, sat and hovered his hand over the phone. 'Put them through,' he ordered.

The girl disappeared and a few seconds later, the phone on his desk rang. He hesitated, summoning the courage to answer it.

'Hello?'

'I need to speak with you,' came the voice; he recognised it instantly. 'There have been some developments.'

Not good. Never good.

'OK. I'll be there shortly.'

Chapter Fifty

SELECTIVE HEARING

Mile after mile of waiting. Three lanes of traffic filtering into one on the M25 between London Colney and the motorway service station. A backlog of dozens of police vehicles and ambulances on the closed lanes. Of course, curiosity had got the better of the general public and everyone was eager to see what was going on, which meant the queues to get past were even longer than necessary. Faces of all descriptions, sizes and ages stared vacantly out of their windows, gossiping as they drove past, trying to aim their mobile cameras at the container in the car park.

Jake rolled the car along the hard shoulder until he eventually parked at the back of the queue. Half a mile away. The longest walk ever to a crime scene.

After hearing the news at the golf club, Dimitri had sprinted away and disappeared in his car. Jake had half a mind to follow him, but in his Austin Mini Cooper, the chances of catching up were nil. The other part of his mind told him that, sooner or later, their paths would cross again.

It was inevitable. And Jake was no longer worried about the threat of the images being leaked to Darryl, or worse, the press – Dimitri had a more immediate problem to worry about.

A hundred yards into the walk, the number of police cars in front seemingly never-ending, his phone vibrated. He checked the message.

Liar. Y was he there?

At first, Jake didn't know what the mysterious sender was referring to. But then he realised that his appointment had been interrupted by Dimitri. Jake replied, apologising.

not gd enuff, came the response.

Without realising it, Jake neared a group of four uniformed police constables, far away from the entrance, floating in the middle of the road like a lonely cloud. Perhaps they were there as muscle, Jake thought sardonically.

'What we got, gents?' Jake asked, flashing his warrant card before they asked him for it.

'Filthy one, mate,' the second man said. Jake assumed him to be the most senior – or cocky – of the four.

'Oh yeah?'

'Proper grim,' another said. 'Load of 'em in the back of a lorry. All Asian from what I'm hearing.' He scoffed. 'Fucking serves them right, don't it? Guess this is what they get for trying to come over here and live off the state.'

Them. The only word people seemed to think was an acceptable substitute for a racist term. As though the word itself hid and excused any notion of racism or xenophobia.

Jake despised and disagreed with everything the man said. He had little time for people like that. Even less so when they were part of the same family as him. It was ignorant, obnoxious and abhorrent.

The four men in front of him struck him as the type to enjoy game shows on daytime TV when they weren't working. They also looked like they'd tried applying for a few in their time as well. And Jake had the perfect game show for them: make them spend a month in the deceased person's shoes, to see how long they lasted living in whatever poverty and conditions they'd originally sought to escape.

I'm a racist, get me out of here.

Jake made a mental note of the officer's staff number and moved towards the third guy at the end of the row. He was holding a clipboard in his hand and held out a pen.

'Sign here for us, mate,' he said.

Jake took the pen and scribbled on the page. The man lifted the tape and Jake dipped beneath it.

The car park of the service station was filled with more emergency vehicles and clusters of uniformed constables and emergency response teams huddled together, discussing the situation. The sensitivity and enormity of the case demanded the utmost respect and consideration – something the first four cops had failed to do – and so the rest of the car park had been evacuated and the service station shut down, except for a back door that remained open.

Sitting in the middle of it all was the lorry. The vehicle of death. Surrounded by more than twenty men and women dressed in their white forensic suits.

Jake stopped at the top of the slip road, his eyes scanning for a person of authority. A uniformed officer wandered past him, the sound of her kit and keys jingling by her leg.

This one seemed more approachable and less reproachable than the first four.

'Excuse me,' he asked. 'Where's the SIO?'

The officer stopped, turned and pointed to a woman dressed in a suit. Her hair was in a bob, and she wore a police cap on her head.

'Superintendent Pemberton,' the officer responded. 'But if I were you, I'd only speak to her if you *really* need to. This isn't the type of case you can ask for autographs, if you know what I mean.'

Jake chuckled, thanked the officer and then started towards the SIO. At first, the name of the superintendent didn't register with him. It wasn't until he neared her, and her features came into view, that he slowly began to recognise her.

'Excuse me, ma'am,' Jake said politely after she'd just finished speaking with another uniformed officer.

Detective Superintendent Pemberton stopped what she was doing and turned to face Jake. Her eyes widened and the blood rushed to her cheeks.

'You!' she exclaimed. Immediately, her expression of abject horror turned to delight. 'Good to see you again.'

They embraced.

'Why is there always trouble when you're involved, Jake?' Nicki Pemberton asked as she pulled away. She nodded towards the lorry full of victims.

'It has a habit of following me.' *And sticking like shit to carpet.*

'How have you been?' he asked.

'Good. Brilliant actually. After what happened post-Candice Strachan – and everything else that followed *that* shitstorm – I decided I needed to start again. There was nothing keeping me in Guildford so I moved here.'

'And what about you and... your husband?'

'Divorced. Shortly after he found out about the affair. I've met somebody new now.'

'I'm happy for you.'

And he was. He and Pemberton had met on Jake's first day at Surrey Police in Guildford. She'd been a detective chief inspector then and had led the investigation and capture of The Crimsons, the organised crime group responsible for several armed robberies up and down the country. With Jake's help, they'd arrested two of the brothers responsible and in the process uncovered a spider's web of corruption. The events of that long, sweltering summer's day had been the starting point of the mission Jake was now looking to conclude.

'What about you?' she asked. 'I hear you're doing well. In fact, I *know* you're doing well. The news can't seem to get enough of you.'

Jake shrugged. 'Comes with the territory.'

'Modest as ever. Good to see that hasn't changed.'

'My tendency to follow the rules hasn't either.'

'I don't like the sound of that, Jake.'

He offered her a smirk filled with a dark premonition – and he could tell by the look on her face she sensed it as well.

He turned and pointed to the lorry. 'I think I'd prefer a bank robbery to this...'

'It's a cleaner mess to tidy up, I can tell you that much.'

'What's the latest?'

'Forty dead. No idea who they are or where they've come from – we're having trouble identifying them at the moment.'

'How did they...' Jake swallowed. 'How did they die?'

'Frozen to death. We estimate the container reached

321

temperatures of thirty below. They're usually used for meat and things, not humans.'

Livestock, Jake thought.

Horrible. Truly horrible. That they should be subjected to those conditions in the first place. He imagined the victims during transit, the temperature gradually dropping, their clothes becoming less and less effective, resorting to huddling together for warmth.

Until those around them started to turn cold also.

He spared a moment of silence for them then asked, 'Timeline?'

Pemberton wasted no time in telling him. 'Call came in just after four this morning. Reports suggest the container may have come in at Tilbury Docks around about midnight. And we've had a handful of people come forward saying they saw it outside a place called Handy Man Scrap Services.'

Jake couldn't believe it. A link, no matter how tenuous.

The Cabal was using Henry Matheson's warehouse facility for storage. Whether it had been ongoing or just a one-off, Jake didn't know. But it was evidence enough to suggest the two were connected.

'Who's come forward?'

'There was supposedly an officer keeping guard while it remained a crime scene. Said that he was approached by someone and paid to leave it for a couple of hours. He's being investigated in connection with it all now.'

A kaleidoscope of thoughts spun in his mind. Different colours and shapes morphed from one image to the next as he plotted out the night's events.

'I need to speak with him,' he said. 'And the driver.'

Pemberton folded her arms across her chest. 'Explains why you're here then. I thought you were just a hand.'

'You know that if it's connected to Matheson in any way then I need to be involved. Either myself or someone from my team. If we can find a link between Matheson and this, it'll be like giving a nuclear warhead to a toddler – shit is going to get fucked up.'

Pemberton sighed, and the muscles in her face contorted into a frown. She lowered her hands onto her hips – her trademark stance – and looked around her as if searching for an escape out of this predicament that Jake had placed her in.

'Jake, I have a serious investigation to deal with…'

'And so do I. We can work together. I just need to know what they know. Matheson is one of the country's—'

She held a hand in his face, stopping him abruptly. 'I'm sorry, Jake. I can't.'

Jake took a step closer. A fraction of an inch, just small enough to let her know he was more than serious.

'You owe me,' he told her.

How could she forget?

'I… You…' She inhaled deeply, composed herself.

He hadn't wanted to play that card so soon, but it was necessary.

'I returned that favour when I transferred you to Stratford.'

'That's not the same thing. And you know it.'

'Whatever. I can't.'

'Would you like me to tell people the truth? Maybe they'll frown upon your involvement with Mark.'

To a select few, Pemberton's affair with DI Mark Murphy had been a secret. And she'd wanted to keep it that way. *Begged* for it even. And Jake had kept his mouth shut and his lips sealed since. But sometimes lips had a way of coming loose.

When she didn't respond, he continued, 'It'll be brief. Ten minutes. Tops.'

Pemberton sighed and tapped her foot on the ground repeatedly.

'Five minutes,' she replied. 'And then I want you out of there.'

'Never to return again.'

'Cross your heart?'

Jake made a small cross on his chest where his heart was. 'Hope to die.'

Pemberton shook her head in dismay, reached inside her pocket and produced a pen and notepad. She wrote the police station address and name of the interviewing officer on a sheet and tore it off. Jake snatched it from her and read; at the bottom of the document was her signature.

'Just in case anyone argues with you.'

Jake smirked. 'I can't see that happening, to be honest.'

'You were never this cocky before,' Pemberton mused. 'Whatever happened to you?'

'People began to blow smoke up my arse… eventually, it starts to get quite light up here.' He pointed to his head.

'Oh,' he continued, 'and before I forget, the person who bribed the officer…'

'Don't even go there. We don't know anything about that yet. Nobody's giving that up.'

'They must be a loyal bunch of people. There's only one person I know who's got a following that loyal…'

Pemberton shook her head. 'I hate to break it to you, Jake, but The Cabal is just a myth. Is now and always has been. Nobody has that much power over that many people.'

Jake smirked. 'You didn't think I did a few minutes ago – now look where I've managed to end up.' He waved the piece of paper in the air. 'I'm getting close, Nicki. Trust me. I'll find him soon enough.'

Jake started walking away.

'But what'll it cost you?' she called back to him.

He chose not to hear her.

Chapter Fifty-One

GOOD SOLICITOR

Jake didn't think much of the bent police constable that he'd finished speaking with a few minutes ago. The man had confirmed everything Jake already knew or was already suspicious of – in recent months, an unknown source had started approaching him and blackmailing him, throwing in a lot of money as an extra incentive. All the constable had to do was turn a blind eye to the various shipments coming into the warehouse. He didn't know what was in them, where they'd come from, how they'd got there, why they were there – and he didn't *want* to know any of those things either. The less he knew, the better.

In front of him now, however, was someone completely different. Her name was Claire Fox, a thirty-three-year-old from Wolverhampton. She'd spent the majority of her life behind the wheel, in various types of vehicles, and her weight had suffered as a result. After being checked over for a concussion, she'd been cleared for interview.

The two of them were in the interview room alone, and

Jake had asked for six minutes, one more than Pemberton had originally allowed.

Up until this point, Claire had been hugging a box of tissues against her stomach and given the interviewing officers everything they needed. She hadn't asked for a solicitor and demanded that she didn't receive advice either.

An easy nut to crack then. The easiest he'd had in a long time.

'How are you feeling?' Jake asked, trying to make his tone as open and welcoming as possible. 'Are you being looked after?'

'As much as I can be,' Claire replied.

'Now, I'd like to remind you that you're still under caution, but over the next couple of minutes, I'm going to ask you specific questions regarding the individual you were with when you picked up the lorry. Do you understand?'

'What makes you different?'

Jake retreated in his seat and sat upright, subtly moving further away from her.

'You've lost me.'

'How come you and I are only talking for a few minutes? The others have kept me in here for much, much, *much* longer than that.'

'I get different privileges,' Jake replied.

'Are you the one they call Tea Boy?'

Jake shook his head. 'No,' he said, 'I get to do things like this.' He reached across the table and depressed the button to pause the recording. 'While this button's down, anything you say can't be used to incriminate you any further. No one's going to know what you're saying. Just you and me.' He hesitated and leant back in his chair as if to accentuate his authority. '*Those* sorts of privileges.'

'What do I get out of it?'

Shit. She'd asked the question he'd been hoping she wouldn't ask. The one that meant she would call his bluff further down the line. If he lied and promised her something he couldn't fulfil, it would backfire on him, and then he would have Darryl – and Pemberton, and Candy, and everyone else in the team – knocking on his door with a regulation notice and anything else they could try and throw at him. Technically speaking, what he was doing now was unlawful, against procedure but he was doing it for valid reasons.

Identify the name, identify the individual. Identify the individual, identify The Cabal.

Sever the head, and the rest of the body dies with it.

'I'm afraid I can't offer any legal advice,' Jake said finally.

'So the same rules don't apply to you then?'

'Which rules are those?'

'The ones that you've just made up. I'm allowed to say anything I want and not worry about no backlash, but you can't? Pah, you're a hypocrite just like the rest of them.'

'Not as much of a hypocrite as the person who dropped you in this situation.'

'How do you figure that one out, lad?' Claire asked. She stroked a piece of strawlike hair behind her ear and rubbed her nose with the back of her hand.

Jake folded his arms across his chest and crossed his legs over one another, making himself comfortable. 'You know he's a copper, don't you?'

'Oh, I do like a man in uniform.'

'What about a prison uniform?'

'I can imagine him in it now. The grey would really bring out his blue eyes,' Claire replied.

Bingo, Jake thought. Slowly, the mental image of The Cabal was becoming firmer in his mind.

'I imagine you feel betrayed. I would. He's not even trying to help you. And he's a copper, which means he's not going to. But if you give me his name, I can make sure you don't go down for this. After all, all they've got on you is the fact that you picked up a lorry. That's it. You didn't know what was in there. If anything, you were trying to save the lives of everyone inside. It's not your fault they were already dead by the time you opened that lorry. All I need is a name, Claire.'

'Willie Nelson,' Claire said. A small smirk grew on her lips. 'That's a name for you. One of my favourite singers as well.' Then, without warning, Claire broke out into a rendition of 'Always on My Mind'.

Jake sighed and sniffed. He placed his elbow on the arm of the chair and rested his head on his hand.

'Twenty years,' he said. 'That's what you could be looking at. Upwards of thirty, but, given the circumstances, I'd say you're looking at twenty. Have you got any kids, Claire? A family that depend on you?'

For the first time, Claire didn't respond to his question with a witty remark or a hint of sarcasm and he could tell he'd struck a nerve.

'You're going to be in your fifties by the time you get out, and that's if you appeal and get out on good behaviour.' Jake licked his lips. 'You'll miss your kids growing up. And your husband – do you think he's going to wait that long? I mean, how must he be feeling right now, knowing that you're here. He must be scared. I imagine the police are already speaking with him. And, if they haven't, then they're certainly going to. Things like this are never easy on a marriage. I've seen it before. They can tear it apart. My suggestion to you, in order to alleviate some of that damage, is to plead guilty, get yourself a more lenient sentence and just keep your head down while you're in there.'

When Jake finished speaking, the room filled with silence, save for the echoing sounds of movement and footsteps and conversation coming from outside the room. Jake waited and waited for Claire to respond; he wasn't going to be the first to break the deadlock. But her reply never came; instead, the HGV driver laughed. At first, it started as a small chuckle, the type you make when you're trying to stifle it in the back of the class, and then it grew into a deep howl that echoed around the room.

'Something funny?' Jake asked, his left eyebrow raised.

Then, just like that, she stopped, and the creases in her face disappeared. She leant forward and gestured with her finger for Jake to do the same.

'Has it ever occurred to you that I have no idea who you're referring to? That perhaps I was never given a name? That I showed up on the night, took the lorry and then drove off. Have you ever thought about that, Detective?'

Jake checked his watch. Thirty seconds remained. He placed his hands on his knees and bounced out of his chair, the joints in his knees creaking. He leant across the table and hovered his finger over the Record button.

'Find yourself a good solicitor, Claire. You're going to need it.'

Chapter Fifty-Two

GOING SOFT

'Please wait while we connect your call.'

Jake closed his car door as the automated system put him through. In less than thirty seconds, he started the engine, set the phone on speaker and was already on his way to Bow Green, snaking his way through the traffic outside the police station.

'People are gonna start talking, Jake, if they find out you're calling me this much,' came Liam's voice on the other end of the line. It was muffled and crackly, the connection between them weaker than an addict's willpower.

'Were you starting to miss me?' Jake asked.

'Don't flatter yourself,' Liam replied. 'If anyone hears this conversation, I swear to God I'm coming for you when I'm out of here. They'll beat me up.'

'Just don't drop the soap.'

'Someone's getting too big for their boots. Twice in two days? Must be important.'

'I need to pick your brains about something.'

Again.

'So long as that's the only thing you're picking.'

'How much do you know about human trafficking?'

As soon as he mentioned it, he heard a click, and for a moment Jake thought he'd lost the call. He glanced down at the handset resting on the dashboard and saw the duration of the call climb. They were still connected but there was no sound.

'Liam… you there?'

'Jesus fucking Christ's sake, Jake. You're aware these calls are monitored, right? You better not be incriminating me any more than you already have!'

Jake breathed a sigh of relief. 'That's the last thing I want. I mean, how much do you know about Matheson being involved with human trafficking? We've got forty dead bodies inside a container that was discovered northbound on the M25, and it smells like you-know-who is all over it.'

Liam lowered his voice to a whisper. 'What's that got to do with Matheson?'

'The vehicle and container were picked up at Matheson's old warehouse which, I might add, is currently under investigation pending our trial with him.' He slowed the car as he came up to a set of traffic lights by a roundabout off junction nineteen. The lights changed and he turned right, doing a one-eighty and heading east on the motorway.

'So someone must have paid him off…' Liam said, lost in his thoughts.

'Ten points if you can guess who. But you already know who, don't you?'

'Jake…'

'When you worked for him, did you know this was going on? Did you have any inclination that this is what he was capable of?'

As Jake heard himself say it, he realised how stupid he sounded. The Cabal was capable of hiring organised criminals to rob banks and jewellery stores, to sell drugs and destroy hundreds of lives, to hire hitmen to silence those who opposed him; trafficking humans into the country was just another feather in the cap.

There was a brief silence before Liam responded. The longer Jake waited, the more respect he lost for his former friend and colleague.

'The Cabal always maintained that there were three areas of the business.'

Another quick break in the conversation, and for a moment Jake thought he'd lost him again. But then he heard the sound of Liam talking with someone in the background.

'Listen,' he said, returning. His voice sounded as though the microphone was pressed right against his lips. 'I can't talk for much longer. But, as I was saying, The Cabal focused on three main areas of business. The first was where I came into it all. "Smuggling the valuables" he used to call it which is why I was looking after The Crimsons, making sure they didn't get arrested, making sure they stayed quiet. Then you had Matheson. He was responsible for smuggling in the drugs. His favourite phrase for it was "smuggling the delectables". And then, finally, you had the aspect of the business that he's taking care of now. He always referred to it as "smuggling the detestables" but I never knew what it meant. You've just answered that for me.'

A cry sounded in the distance.

'I've got to go,' Liam finished. 'You just need to carry on doing what you're doing, Jake. That son of a bitch has fucked up too many lives, yours included. If you catch him the same way that you did me and the rest of them, you won't have any problems. But be safe please.'

Jake felt the stress in his shoulders dissipate. Another clue. Another step in the right direction.

'Are you getting soft on me, DCI Greene?'

'Fuck off.'

'It's a shame you went down the path you did. I reckon we'd have made a good team.'

'Wanker.'

Chapter Fifty-Three

THE LONG LIST

Stephanie returned to her desk shortly after speaking with Darryl. If ever there was a time she'd thought that she was at her lowest – like the day her dad had received his sentence or when her mum had died from a brain aneurism – she'd been terribly mistaken. There were no words to describe the guilt and turmoil swirling around her every fibre. It was as if the entire playbook of terrible things that had happened to her in her life had culminated in one ball of shit and planted itself in the pit of her stomach.

She adored Jake; he was her closest friend, closest confidante, the person whom she could rely on the most. Someone she could trust unequivocally. But she'd discovered only recently that he was also someone who was capable of betraying her trust, abusing it. Just like her father, and just like all the other men that had come and gone in her life. There was no excusing it. Which was why it was necessary to do what she'd done. Not only was Jake becoming a liability to himself – there was no doubt in her mind that he was responsible for his own financial ruin – but he was also becoming a liability for the team.

The one condition she'd given him before agreeing to help him, the simple task of arranging the M11 forms in alphabetical order, had been neglected and as a result, picked up by someone else. Not only was he jeopardising his career, but hers too. The thin promise of promotion had been presented to her throughout several meetings with Darryl in the past few weeks – he wanted her to succeed, grow, develop – but the likelihood of her applying *and* succeeding hinged on the outcome of the Matheson investigation.

Hinged on Jake doing the fucking basics of his job.

Why then did she insist on helping him so much? That was a question she'd toyed with time and time again. And still, an answer eluded her.

Everyone needs help, even those who can't be saved. Even those who were poison to themselves and those around them.

Jake's been let off the leash for too long. It's about time we rein him in.

Stephanie eased herself into her seat in the Major Incident Room, acknowledging those still there. Fortunately, Ashley was no longer there to ask her why she hadn't taken that break. The honest answer was because she needed to keep her mind busy and stop thinking about Jake, about Darryl, about her father. And instead focus her attention on another man she couldn't trust: Henry Matheson.

She asked the team for a quick update, and they informed her that nothing had changed in the twenty minutes she'd been gone.

The twenty minutes that felt like twenty hours.

'Sorry,' she said, opening her laptop. 'Good work, guys. Keep it up.'

Stephanie opened her mail program and waited for the internet to connect. When it did, an email came through from DCS Dremel, her former senior from her time at the Independent Police Complaints Commission.

The subject read: ANOTHER DOSE OF EXCITEMENT.

At first, she'd thought he'd been subject to a phishing email, caught a virus and then sent it to the rest of the police force – all forty thousand of them. But then, as she opened the email, she realised she was wrong.

Hey, Steps,

Not sure if it's related to what you asked for the other day, but thought I'd flag anyway. Somebody else has just raised another case to investigate the banking history of Atomic Nails and Candiru Limited.

Yesterday, Atomic Nails received a large deposit – much larger than the original deposit you asked me to investigate – of £100,000.

The transaction was then forwarded to another bank account, the details of which I'll investigate if you want me to.

Hope you're keeping well. Perhaps we should meet up some time for a catch-up?

Thanks,

Leyton

Stephanie scanned the message again.

Meeting up for a drink with an old colleague was the last thing she wanted to do. Not least because he'd tried it on with her every other month they worked together. She supposed now they no longer saw each other every day, he thought he might stand a better chance.

Sadly, life didn't work that way.

What stood out to her most was the transaction that had been paid into Atomic Nails' bank account. A hundred thousand pounds. An enormous amount by anyone's estimations.

Which meant that the person it had been taken from was either someone who wouldn't notice it was missing or it was everything they had.

Stephanie supposed the latter; she remembered the other morning, on the way to the funeral, Jake had mentioned something about his in-laws being affected by the same British Gas scam.

Before she could do anything about it, the door opened and Jake entered, his hair dishevelled and windswept, his face flustered, as though he'd just sprinted a mile or so without stopping. His blazer was pressed against his body, and his tie was loose at the collar.

Where the fuck had he been all day?

Jake's been let off the leash for too long.

'Afternoon,' he said, waving as he approached her. 'How's everything going?'

She hesitated before responding. What was she going to say to him? If she didn't tell him what she'd done then surely she was just as bad as he was? What if she gave it away without realising?

'Earth to Stephanie,' he said, waving his hand in her face. 'Anybody home?'

'Yes…' It didn't feel like it. 'I… Sorry, uh…' She swallowed. Continued. 'Where have you been?'

Jake asked the two officers in the room if they could

have a moment. They obliged without question or interference, and Jake closed the door behind them.

Jake's been let off the leash for too long.

He pulled out a seat and shuffled under the table. 'You know that container that's been all over the news?'

'Yes…?'

'I paid it a little visit.'

It's about time we rein him in.

'For fuck's sake, Jake.'

'Hear me out, all right. Before you get all shouty at me. I get enough of that at home, I don't need it here too.'

Jake scratched at the scar on his chin, and she remembered the story he'd told her about how he'd got it – being pulled by his dog and falling onto a gravestone. How terrified he must have been.

His voice brought her back from the memory. 'It's all related. Roland, me losing the money, the nail salon, the people kept in the back of it, the container, Matheson's jury – it's the final strand of The Cabal's business.'

'How can you possibly know?'

'Because I wasn't born yesterday. I know more about this than anyone, and I know the signs. This morning I was due to meet someone, someone I believe to be helping me with all of this, just like you are. But when I got there, they didn't show. Instead, Dimitri arrived.'

She found herself leaning forward on her chair. 'The same Dimitri that…?'

'The very same. If not, he's got a fantastic doppelgänger. As you'd expect, he threatened me, said he'd ruin my career if I interfered.'

It seemed like the whole world was out to get him. Oddly, that made her feel less guilty about her actions. She was also amazed at the fact he was sharing these details with her; so far the communication channels had only been one way. Perhaps he was finally letting her in.

'When we both found out about the news, he panicked and fled. He's working with The Cabal on it, and something's gone wrong. That's no coincidence.' The excitement in his face reminded her of the same expression on her father's when he'd spoken about Little Susie.

Little Susie who wasn't so little anymore...

'I tried speaking with the driver, but she wouldn't give me a name. In fact, she didn't even know a name. And then after all that I called Liam.'

'Jake...' she said, trying not to sound like a concerned mother.

'He confirmed my suspicions. He was never fully involved, but he knew that something dodgy was taking place. Smuggling the detestables, he called it – The Cabal's words, not his.'

Smuggling the detestables. Smuggling the monsters. Smuggling the others. Those in search of a better life.

'We're getting close, Steph. I can feel it.'

Before she had a chance to respond, the door opened and a red-nosed officer stuck his head in. 'Sorry to interrupt, ma'am,' he said, his inexperience and youth coming through in his voice. 'ANPR has just pinged for the vehicle you asked me to track.'

'Which one?'

'The Mercedes.'

'The Mercedes?' Jake asked energetically.

'Is there more than one?' the officer asked, his eyes widening at the thought he'd made a mistake on his first week.

Stephanie raised a hand. 'No. You were right to follow the one you did.'

'You mean the plate wasn't fake?' Jake asked, his eyebrow raised.

'Evidently not,' Stephanie replied sarcastically, nodding at the young detective. 'Where was the last ping?'

'Birmingham.'

'And that's the only one?'

The officer nodded.

'When was the last ping?'

'A few hours ago.'

'Location?'

'Nearest we could get was a small section of the M42, but we followed it on CCTV to an industrial estate nearby. I'll send you the address now.'

Jake thanked the young detective and, as soon as the man was gone, leapt out of his chair. She found herself joining him, her muscles moving independently from her brain.

'I want you to come with me,' he said.

They stared at one another for a moment.

'What?'

'Birmingham. I want you to come with me.'

'Why? I don't…'

Jake's been let off the leash for too long.

Had he finally reined himself in? Had he finally come to his senses?

'As a thank you,' he told her. 'For all the support you've given me so far. You've been great, and I could really do with your help on this. Besides, last time they had baseball bats and threw me through a window… I could do with the muscle.' He gave her a wink, but she took it seriously. She *had* been working out recently, whenever she could find the time. Had he noticed?

She contemplated for a moment. Was this him being

nice? Was he leading her into some sort of trap? Or was she overthinking it all?

She recalled what Darryl had told her: to get close to Jake, to keep a keen and constant eye on him for as long as was possible. Was she going with him for Darryl or herself?

'I don't think I'd be able to sleep at night if I let you go alone and something terrible happened to you,' she said.

'Excellent,' Jake replied then fished in his pockets for his car keys. 'Do you mind driving? My car's got hardly any petrol left, and… well, y'know… Sorry, Steph. You know I would usually offer.'

'It's fine, Jake. Honestly.'

'Sure?'

'It's not a problem at all. I'll just add it to the long list of favours you owe me.'

Chapter Fifty-Four

DRINK

Jake's eyes felt heavy as he and Stephanie sped along the M3. More than eighteen hours awake, for several days in a row, with little breathing time in between was finally beginning to catch up with him. And deservedly so. Stephanie the Saint had afforded him a moment of respite from their unending conversation. He didn't think it possible for someone to talk so much for so long. It was exhausting. They'd gone back to basics, back to first-date territory even. Discussing school, college, university, to the embarrassing moments, to family trees and individual family members' life stories. Filling in the gaps they didn't already know about each other. Right up to the point he'd started falling asleep.

'Is it seven already?' Stephanie asked, pointing at the dashboard. 'Feels like we've only been driving for thirty minutes.'

Jake opened his eyes to find himself surrounded by darkness, save for the blinding glare emitted by the street lights and traffic lights racing past them. Clouds hung low over the road, as if slowly pouncing on their prey, and a light drizzle smattered the air.

'It was dry when I closed my eyes,' he said, rubbing them, blinking himself awake.

'You've only been out for half an hour. As soon as you closed your eyes, you were gone.'

Jake opened his mouth to speak but was interrupted by a yawn. He stretched his arms in the air and flexed his body, feeling his muscles awaken.

'Time really does fly, doesn't it?'

'Unless I bored you to sleep. Hmm?'

Jake turned to face her. 'Never.'

'Well, you'd better wake up and be ready for action – we're here.'

As soon as she finished speaking, they pulled off the motorway, rolled up at a junction, turned left and went back on themselves until they headed towards a small industrial estate. The estate, if it could be called that, consisted entirely of a timber yard, Dale's Yard – the reason they were there – and an old car sales forecourt in a cul-de-sac. Litter, broken pieces of metal and overgrown weeds hugged the concrete, burrowing deep into the cracks, and an eerie, supernatural chill crept along the road, rolling through with the clouds.

'Looks like a good place to live,' he said. 'Nice neighbourhood.'

To his left, a wire mesh fence ran along the length of the road until it disappeared behind Dale's Yard. Smashed cars with their roofs crumpled and tyres removed were stacked atop one another. In the centre of the estate was a large crane, its pincers dangling stoic, firm against the wind. In the background, Jake heard the sound of cars speeding past on the motorway. The light rain that had followed them from the motorway now worsened, freckling the windshield. Within a few seconds, it turned into a downpour, the sound of the water bouncing off the roof echoing around the vehicle.

'Hope you brought a coat,' Stephanie said.

Jake reached into the footwell and held her coat aloft.

'We can't both wear it,' she said.

Before Jake was able to answer, his phone vibrated. An image of Elizabeth's face with the girls on either side of her appeared on the screen. Jake held a finger in the air, placing their conversation on pause.

This'll be fun.

'Hey, babe,' he said, unsure why he'd said that. He'd never called Elizabeth 'babe' before.

'Where are you?'

'Birmingham...'

'Seriously?'

'What's the matter?'

And then it dawned on him.

'Liz... Oh my God, I'm so sorry,' he said, rubbing his left temple with his free hand. 'I completely forgot. What time's the operation?'

'Now.'

'It's been a mental day,' he began but was interrupted again.

'Who are you with?'

'Stephanie. But—'

'Save it, Jake, I don't wanna hear your bullshit excuses anymore.'

Jake opened the door and stepped out into the rain, leaving the coat inside. The rain lashed at his face and he quickly became sodden, thin lines of white slicing his view from every conceivable angle.

'Liz, what are you—'

'Don't come home tonight, Jake. Don't come to the hospital. You won't be welcome here. I don't want to even think about you right now.'

'I can explain—'

'You've already said enough. And this time you didn't even need to open your mouth.'

Elizabeth rang off. The disconnected call sound amplified in his ears. He stared off into the drain cover in front of him, gradually lowering his arm. Heavy drops of water clung to his eyelashes before falling to their deaths. Gusts of wind battered his soaked clothes from every angle, filling him with a bitter chill as his body turned numb – his hands, ears, neck, chin.

But it was nothing compared to the immense pain and hurt he felt from Elizabeth's words.

You won't be welcome here.

The rain continued to pelt him, the wind rapidly lowering his body temperature. Like he was stuck thirty-five below. In the back of a shipping container. Trapped beneath a mountain of snow, caught in an avalanche, surrounded by cold and wet and white.

And then it hit him.

Jake swayed from left to right, the world around him spinning in a carousel of grey and white. His breathing became infrequent. Rapid. Slow. Rapid. Slow. Pressure, the weight of the moon, grew in his head. The world was closing in on him, and there was nothing he could do to stop it.

'Jake?' Elizabeth called.

But then he realised it wasn't Elizabeth. It couldn't have been. She was over a hundred miles away, sitting in a hospital room, wishing he were dead.

'Jake? Are you OK?' the voice called again.

Jake found the energy within himself to turn and face the source of the voice. It was Stephanie, her eye make-up running down her cheeks.

He smiled at her. It was a weak smile, one that didn't reflect how he felt about her.

God, he fucking hated these panic attacks. Sometimes he wished they would just claim him for good and put an end to it all.

Someone, somewhere was listening to him…

Just as she rushed over to him, a wall of darkness descended over his eyes and sent him into the land of sleep.

Stephanie fucking Grayson.

Stephanie the Innocent. Stephanie the Righteous. Stephanie the Helpful. Stephanie the Saint. Stephanie the one she was constantly told not to worry about.

Now look where that had got her: sitting in a hospital room just as her dad was about to go under the knife, while Stephanie the Saint was with her husband in Birmingham.

Probably spending the night together. Probably getting drunk in the hotel bar. Probably touching each other, already undressing one another.

Holding Jake… Kissing him… Before sliding him into—

She closed her eyes and banished the images from her mind.

A doctor walked into the room, a nurse wading behind him.

'Everything's ready,' he told them, matter-of-factly, before turning his back on them and heading through another set of doors.

In and out. Just like that.

Just like Jake. In and out of Stephanie.

In and out of their marriage.

'How are you feeling?'

Elizabeth looked up to see the nurse had stayed behind. She stood with her arms folded across her front and the same warm smile she'd walked around with all day. The same one Elizabeth had been doing for so long. Putting on a brave face, smiling through the pain and torment to keep up appearances. To remind herself that everything was all right. In the vain hope that one day it might be. Or that she'd end up believing it forever.

'Fine,' Tegan said beside her.

'Nervous,' her mum said on the other side.

Nervous was an understatement. They were all petrified and had together spent the past several hours thinking of the worst-case scenario. At two to three hours long, a kidney transplant was every bit as complex as it was scary. The thought of her dad being in pain, of having a serious illness that could kill him... it was too much.

What she really needed right now was the man she loved, the man she'd married, the man she'd promised to spend the rest of her life with.

But he was with his new wives. The job. And Stephanie the Saint.

'I'll grab Alan,' the nurse said. 'You can wave him goodbye before he goes into the operating room.'

After she'd heard that, Elizabeth pulled herself together.

She didn't need a man to console her; she was capable of looking after herself. She'd been doing a good enough job of it without Jake at home recently.

No, she had her girls, her sister, her mum and her mother-in-law. All the women she needed.

Yet, as her dad rolled into the waiting room, covered in

a white sheet, hooked up to tubes and pieces of machinery, she was unable to shake the image of the one woman she didn't want in her life.

And what she was probably doing to her husband right now.

Jake's body weighed a ton. *What have you been eating?* she thought as she hooked her arm under his armpit, around the front of his chest and buried her hand in his other armpit, using her other hand to support herself and drag him backwards. The rear passenger door was only a few feet away, but it felt ten times that.

'Don't worry, Jake, you'll be all right. I'll get you somewhere safe,' she said as she climbed into the driver's seat.

She, along with a few others in the team, was aware of Jake's relationship with panic attacks, even though he never liked to mention them nor acknowledge that they existed. Indeed, she wasn't completely sure he'd told the necessary people that they existed. There had been a few occasions in the past where Jake had teetered on the edge of passing out but had staved it off. She'd implored him to report it, but both he and she knew that wasn't a good idea; it meant the possibility of more desk work. The bane of Jake's professional existence.

Stephanie pulled out of the industrial estate and headed towards the train station. There was bound to be a hotel there. Right now Jake needed warmth and someplace dry.

It was only when, five minutes later, she pulled into a Premier Inn car park that she realised what it must have looked like on the CCTV, dragging an unconscious man from the back of her car. As rain continued to pummel the exterior, she reached over to Jake's neck and checked his pulse, just in case he'd died in the back of her car.

The verdict: he was still breathing and his heart rate had returned to a regular pattern.

As soon as she pulled her fingers away from his neck, he stirred.

'Jake? Jake? It's me, Stephanie. Can you hear me?'

Gradually, his eyes opened and he blinked himself awake. Groaning, he rolled and turned to face her.

'You didn't drug me, did you?' he asked, a smile creeping over his face. His voice sounded weak. 'Where are we?'

'Premier Inn. You need a bed. You need to rest. I'm not having you go home like this.'

'I'm fine,' he said and he clambered to his elbow. As he reached an upright seated position, he swayed, held his head in his hand and collapsed back into the seat.

'You're definitely not. You need rest. So stay here while I find us a room each.'

'OK. But after that, we're getting a drink,' he said. 'Christ knows I need one.'

Chapter Fifty-Five

LOYALTY

In the world of drugs, criminal gangs and postcode wars, there were only a few aspects of an individual's personality that rang true. Sure, you could be tough, brave, unafraid to put your life on the line to defend the gang's reputation. But nine times out of ten that was a suicide mission, conducted by those at the lower levels, the ones on the frontline who didn't have anything else about them and were happy to put their lives at risk for the cause. But if you wanted to work yourself up to the higher echelons then you needed to demonstrate a different type of bravery.

Loyalty.

Not an easy trait to come by – even harder to know whether to trust it. Many in Henry's experience had proclaimed to be loyal, that they would defend him when necessary, but as soon as the pressure had been applied, whether from rival gangs or the police, their true colours had shown. They caved because a part of their brain switched. The amygdala, the part responsible for controlling fear. It tricked them into forgetting their loyalties and betraying Henry.

But there were some, those who needed more protection than he, that didn't possess that fear, those whose amygdala was damaged or broken. And they were the most dangerous. Loyalty meant everything to them; it surpassed every other basic need, and by the end of it all, they were bowing down at his feet, like he was some sort of deity.

On the outside, back at the Cosgrove Estate, hordes of men and teenagers had begged to worship him and do everything they could for him. But inside, in prison, those types of men were few and far between. Many of the other inmates had become hardened to the techniques and methods he used and so were harder to convince. He even felt dubious about trusting Jason, Vinnie and Biggie, for fear of them betraying him somehow. The life of an inmate was a boiling pot, and at any moment the heat could get too hot, and it would all boil over.

But not for the man pacing about his room now.

Brian Grayson, for the past twenty minutes, had been shuffling his feet on the concrete, pausing every time he reached one end of the room before turning back on himself. The noise of the gentle movements didn't disturb Henry – he was still reading his book – except now, however, it was feeling a little lighter. He'd thrown the shiv out of the window right after the incident with Owen. With his fingerprints all over it, it was too obvious a connection between Henry and Owen's murder.

Since then, Henry had stayed in his room, reading. Now nearing the final third, the part where the plot met its end, Henry had found himself hooked and unable to put the book down, something he'd never thought he'd say.

The only thing linking him to Owen's murder was his

DNA and fingerprints, but given that the cell doors were usually open for the majority of the day, it wasn't inconceivable to assume there were dozens of other prints in there and on Owen's body. The other possible thorn in his side was the few working CCTV cameras dotted around the prison. For a long while, Henry had pondered it, fearing that he'd been caught dragging Owen into his room moments before he'd died. But since a whole day had now passed, and there'd been no sign of retribution, he allowed himself to relax.

Everything was under control. Williamson had taken care of it. All that remained was making sure it stayed that way.

'You enjoying yourself over there?' he asked Brian, who was fiddling with a bag of sugar by the kettle. 'Thirsty?'

'No.'

'Would you mind making me one?'

A sound erupted outside on the twos, echoing all the way to their room. Henry ignored it.

'Milk, one sugar, right?' Brian asked.

'You remembered?'

Brian shrugged. 'Of course I did. It's only tea, isn't it?'

'Do you know what I miss, Bri? Hot chocolate with milk and marshmallows.'

'Marshmallows?'

'That's the one. Remember what we said about marshmallows?'

Brian paused a moment. Dropped the sugar. 'Yeah. I remember.'

'Good, good.'

Just checking.

The sounds outside drew nearer and nearer. Footsteps. Murmurs. Mutterings.

As Brian switched on the kettle, the sounds stopped right outside their cell.

Shit.

The door flew open. Standing in the doorway was Perry, one of the screws. Behind him were several others. Williamson was nowhere to be seen.

Double shit.

Had they found out he was responsible for Owen? Or had they found out about the jurors?

Neither. If either of those two were the case then they'd be dressed in full riot gear. But if they weren't in their gear, then what were they—

'Turnover,' Perry said.

'You what?' Henry asked, rolling his legs off the bed.

'Both of you. Out.'

'But we were talking about marshmallows.'

'I don't care. Out. This is a random search.'

'But you can't—' Henry began to protest.

'We can and we are. Now, both of you. Out. If I have to ask again, we won't be gentle.'

Grabbing his book, Henry jumped off the bed and started out of the door, but Perry stopped him halfway through and ordered him to leave the book on the shelf. Reluctantly, he stepped out of the room, where he was watched and guarded by one of the other screws in the team. Brian joined moments later.

And then the guards set to work. Dismantling everything, searching inside the kettle, emptying the bags of sugar and other condiments onto the floor, unscrewing the back of the TV, tearing through the pages of his books, shoving a hand down the U-bend of the toilet. Turning over every inch of the place.

They found nothing.

Until they turned their attention to the bed. The only logical place he could think to keep the spice and the mobile phone. The only place it would fit.

But despite his supposed ingenuity, the screws found the phone and drugs with ease; some of them were buried in a slit in Brian's mattress, while the rest were hidden in the hollow metal of the bed frame.

Perry charged towards them, brandishing a small packet of powder and the phone. 'Whose the fuck are these?'

Henry shrugged and stepped away. 'I ain't never seen that before in my life, sir.'

'Grayson?' Perry asked accusatorially.

'Sir?' The old man sounded infantile, confused.

'Are these yours, Grayson?'

'Brian, please,' Henry implored. 'Tell him the truth. They're not mine. So they must be…'

'Mine,' Brian said, dropping his head. 'They're mine.'

With that, Perry and the other officers wrapped their arms around Brian and led him up a flight of stairs.

'Hey, Bri!' Henry called before his cellmate disappeared out of sight. 'When you're back we can finish making those marshmallows.'

Nothing like the loyalty of an old man who didn't know what he was doing.

Chapter Fifty-Six

TEETERING ON THE PRECIPICE

For the second time that evening, her arm was wrapped around Jake, supporting him, feeling her fingers hugging the muscles in his body.

'Easy does it,' she said as they entered the bedroom. A bathroom was to their immediate right, a wardrobe and towel cabinet to their left, and beyond that, on the right was a double bed. At the back, a small sofa. The Premier Inn's iconic deep purple bathed the walls and furniture and reminded her of a scene from *Charlie and the Chocolate Factory*.

'You might have to help me with my clothes,' Jake slurred as she let go of him and bounced him onto the bed. There he lay flat and sprawled his arms wide across the duvet. 'You can start with the shoes and blazer. I'm sure I can do the rest.'

That was the drink talking, she was sure. After she'd paid for the rooms on her credit card, they'd found some seats at the bar. It was warm, comfortable and the drinks were surprisingly cheap. There they'd spent the past few hours talking, laughing and touching.

Stephanie stared at him for a little longer than was usual, comfortable. It wasn't that she didn't want to help him undress – she was more than happy to if it meant that he was warm and safe – but she didn't want things to become difficult between them.

She didn't want the dynamic to change.

She hoped…

Talking, laughing, touching.

Jake groaned and lifted himself to his elbows. 'I'll do it myself then,' he said.

Was that an attempt at goading her into helping him?

'It's fine. Let me…' she replied and bent down by his feet, undoing the laces and placing his shoes neatly on the floor beside the wardrobe.

As she spun on the spot to help him some more, his phone chimed.

'Elizabeth?' he asked animatedly to no one.

Stephanie rose to her feet. Watched. Held her breath.

Slowly, as if he were being hoisted by a rope pulley, Jake sat upright and perched himself on the end of the bed. Then his face dropped and his eyes turned dark.

'Everything all right?' Stephanie asked tentatively, her curiosity getting the better of her. 'Is she OK?'

She took a step closer.

For support. Moral and emotional.

'It wasn't Elizabeth,' Jake replied, his voice deadpan, almost emotionless. 'It was Darryl.'

Oh shit.

Jake's been off a leash for too long. It's about time we rein him back in.

Jake let out a big sigh, his entire body deflating.

'Just thought he'd let me know that someone's launched a complaint against me. My *unprofessional* conduct. There are several instances of it apparently,' he said sardonically. 'Fucking unbelievable. Jobsworths, the fucking lot of them.'

Another sigh, this time deeper. 'Don't suppose you know anything about this?'

His hurt puppy-dog eyes looked up at her, and for a moment she said nothing, as a storm of irrational thoughts clouded her mind. Did he know it was her? Had she given him any reason to suspect her?

'No!' she said as she placed a hand on his shoulder and sat beside him. An anthem of guilt played loudly in her head.

You did this. You're responsible. You destroyed this man's career, this man's life.

'This is the first I've heard of it.'

'Why is it so fucking difficult?' Jake asked, gesticulating wildly with his arms. 'Why does it feel like everyone's out to get me. Nobody wants me to succeed. I'm just trying to do my fucking job. Why is that so hard for people to believe?'

'I know,' Stephanie said, at a loss for words to console him. Had it been anyone else and any different situation, she would have known what to say, but because it was him and the situation was already complex enough, she had nothing.

'This is the last thing I need. With everything else going on. Fuck…'

Jake dropped the phone to the floor and ran his fingers through his thick black hair.

Stephanie gently moved her hand across his back and over to his other shoulder, her fingers moving over the grooves and rivulets of his muscles. Soft yet firm at the same time – reassuring, comforting.

She squeezed his shoulder.

'Everything's going to be OK,' she said, even though she knew it wasn't. A black mark would be an indelible stain against his name until the day he retired, or worse, was dismissed from the force.

'How can it be?' Jake asked. Something was caught in his throat and he swallowed to clear it, but it was still there when he continued. 'Work was the only thing going right for me at the moment. Elizabeth, the money, the operation, that was the part of my life I'd chosen to ignore. I didn't want to come to terms with what was happening. But now…'

For the first time since she'd known him, Jake Tanner cried. In fact, he bawled. His body jerked as he sobbed and hyperventilated, rubbing his eyes with his thumbs and forefingers.

She'd never seen him cry. She'd never seen him show a single splinter of emotion, whether it be for his family or his work. He'd never let her into any of his world with The Cabal, despite how much she believed him. But in the past few hours, while they'd been drinking at the bar, he'd opened up to her and introduced her to everything. His emotions. His heartache. His faults. His fallacies. His weaknesses.

He'd laid it all out on the table for her.

A cry for help.

And she'd stomped all over it when she'd agreed to destroy him like this. For who? Her father, the man she felt like she barely knew anymore?

One man was leaving her life, while another was entering it.

Stephanie wrapped her arm tighter around him. And tighter. And tighter.

'It's been a stressful day,' she whispered. 'Maybe you should get some sleep.'

At that, Jake's head tilted towards her, their faces separated by a few inches. For a long while, neither of them said anything.

Stephanie stared into his eyes. It was the first time she'd studied them, the first time she'd ever got close enough to be able to. They were like a treasure chest, brown on the outside, but inside were dazzling sparkles of white and gold, surrounded by rivers of red snakes coming to protect them. Her gaze fell down his face, over his bridged nose, down his nostrils and then settled on his lips. So delicate, so tender, so inviting. Pink, bordered by a thin red outline.

Jake sniffled heavily. The sound he produced should have grossed her out, but it didn't. All essence of time had flown out of the window. How long they'd been staring at one another like this, she didn't know. Didn't want to know.

She didn't want it to end.

Stephanie's eyes moved up to his, and then back to his mouth, the sexual tension between them undeniable, palpable. For so long she'd denied it, thought it a waste of time, believed nothing could happen between them. For so long so she'd put her job and her father first. But now, in this tender moment, losing herself in his powerful gaze, she realised he must have felt it too.

Now it was staring them in the face, there was no denying it.

It was real. Very real.

It was also wrong, very wrong.

But it felt so right.

Stephanie closed her eyes, leant forward slightly, and the next thing she knew, her lips touched his. She hovered there for a moment, teetering on the precipice of right and wrong, and then kissed him.

Yes, Jake had been let off the leash for too long. But only *she* was going to be the one to rein him in. And not in the way Darryl wanted.

Part 7: 8th Jan

Chapter Fifty-Seven

DALE'S YARD

The severity of the events of the previous night should have dawned on him sooner than it did. The night had passed in a mirage of beer, shots, more shots... and tequila? He remembered sitting in the bar, laughing with Stephanie, enjoying her company.

Now he was in the shower, trying to wash the hangover away. The beating in his head was incessant, like a bouncer knocking on the door, doing everything in its power to blast in. His muscles felt fatigued, and he struggled to squeeze the shampoo bottle the hotel provided without his entire arm shaking. And his teeth felt dirty and rough – the hotel didn't provide the appropriate amenities, so he had gone to bed without brushing his teeth, one of the things he hated most. He could only imagine how vile his breath smelt.

Jake switched the tap off, stepped out of the shower and reached amidst the clouds of steam for the towel dangling on the back of the door. Grabbing it, he wiped his face dry and placed his hand on the sink beside him. Blood rushed to his head and he felt dizzy, light, almost as if he wanted to pass out. Then he leant forward and retched. His body was usually good at reacting to hangovers. But that had been a long time ago; he wasn't nineteen anymore, and only now was he beginning to feel the full effect of his drinking.

He didn't like this. Not one bit. The nausea, the headache, the cramp in his stomach, the dryness in his throat, the sensation of feeling like the walking dead. This was something else. *What the fuck happened last night?*

And then, as he stared at the steamy mirror, his features nothing but a blotch of pink and black, Jake remembered. Stephanie. His bedroom. His bed. The kiss.

Wiping his mouth with the towel, Jake hurried out of the bathroom, threw his towel onto the bed and reached for his underwear resting atop the small desk. As he dressed and pulled what few layers he had away from the desk, he noticed something on the table. A small sheet of paper folded in two. Jake grabbed it and pulled out the seat beside him. He switched on the light. The words came alive on the page.

Jake

I'm sorry. That's all I know what to say. I know it isn't any consolation, but I'm sorry for what happened between us. It was a mistake, one that will live with me for the rest of my life. I don't think either of us meant for it to happen, but it did. I've convinced myself that it meant nothing – you have a family and a wife who adore you.

I won't say anything to anyone, not unless you want me to. By the time you read this, I won't be in the hotel anymore. I'm sorry to leave you in Birmingham alone, but there's money in the drawer for you to get back to London. It's not much, but it was all I had.

If you choose to stay and finish what we came here for, then please be safe. I hope you're not feeling too bad, and I'll see you soon.

Sorry.
S

Jake set the note down on the table and reached inside the top drawer. In there he found a pristine and untouched copy of the Bible. Jake removed it and opened the cover. Found a collection of tens and twenties sitting inside, their corners and edges crumpled from the haste with which they'd been placed in the book. He withdrew the money and dropped it onto the table.

Trying to buy him off like that, who did she think she was?

He'd cheated on his wife and family because of her. She'd destroyed his relationship with the only woman he'd ever loved, the only relationship that had ever mattered. How the fuck was he going to explain that?

Jake slammed his fist on the table. The plastic tray of glasses and mugs and sugar sachets shook violently. He reached for the handle and launched the tray off the edge of the table. The contents scattered across the floor, the mugs and glasses bouncing on the carpet, causing no real damage.

There's money in the drawer for you to get back to London.

Pity money. Guilt money. Sorry for ruining your marriage money.

He wasn't going to use it. He didn't need it. He was a grown man. He could make his way back without the help of anyone else, because if he could help raise his brother and sister without their dad, if he could overcome everything The Cabal had thrown at him, if he could help raise two wonderful children – then he could do *this*.

Trying to force the images of Stephanie – and that night, and the bar, and the touching, and the drinking, and the laughing – from his mind, Jake grabbed his meagre possessions and headed to reception to check out.

Outside, rain continued to fall, except now it had become a slight drizzle, causing infrequent ripples on the puddles in the car park.

Jake glanced up at the sky in search of an answer. He had no concept of time. His phone was dead and he had no way of communicating with the outside world. And he'd chosen a bad period in his life to stop wearing his watch. All he knew was that it was light, which meant that it was some time after eight a.m.

Huffing, he plunged his hands into his pockets and started walking. A few hundred yards away was Birmingham Central train station. He watched the trains slow down as they approached, their lights cutting through the mist. He probably had enough to purchase a ticket with Stephanie's money, but he was opposed to the idea.

No. He needed to do something else. Something that would clear his head. Something that would make him forget everything that had happened.

If you choose to stay and finish what we came here for, then please be safe.

Dale's Yard.

With the pounding in his head unrelenting, Jake started towards the repair shop, using his hazy sense of direction from the night before to guide him.

Chapter Fifty-Eight

MONEY

The smell of stale sweat seeped through the furniture in the room, as though it had been inhabited by a thousand individuals before her and would continue to inhabit a thousand after her.

That was assuming she was able to leave with her life.

Perhaps they bring people here to die. Perhaps they bring people here to recover. Perhaps they bring people here to *move them on.*

The only problem was she didn't know exactly where *here* was. All she knew was that she was somewhere high, surrounded by a lot of tall buildings. In anticipation of her journey to the United Kingdom, she'd undertaken hours of extensive research: places to stay, places to visit, places to settle down and find a job and a nice property to rent. And as a result, she'd seen the wonderful architecture that London had to offer. And in front of her right now were two prime examples: the towering Lego metropolis of Canary Wharf to her left, jutting out of the skyline, and the skeleton of The Shard.

Shortly after the procedure, she'd woken up and taken the men around her by surprise. Too woozy from the effects of the anaesthesia, she'd struggled to defend herself and try to escape. And the last thing she remembered before more of the drug was administered, was a man in a balaclava explaining that she going to a special place.

A place where people came and went. A place where things went on behind the walls. A place where money was exchanged.

The furniture in the room was consistent with that of a bedroom. It had a bed and bedside table. But beside it was a bucket filled with cold soapy water and a sponge.

She stood by the window, gazing down at the tiny ants moving fifty or sixty feet beneath. As she leant against the windowsill for a better look, the skin on the back of her hand creased and burnt. Before she could do anything about it, the door opened slowly, letting her know that someone was coming in.

Standing in the middle of the door frame was D, dressed in the same suit as last time she'd seen him. She noticed he looked a lot greyer, more stressed.

'I've missed you,' he said, crossing the threshold into the room. 'Amidst all the other fucking madness that's going on, you seem to be the only good thing.'

He sauntered up to her from behind and placed his hand on her right flank, where the searing pain was, and had been ever since. She flinched.

'Did the operation go well? I've heard you were brilliant throughout the whole thing.'

He placed his chin on her shoulder and moved his hand closer to her crotch. Her vagina throbbed and swelled, sending bullets of pain worse than her abdomen deep into her stomach. It had first started after the operation when she'd known something wasn't quite right and had been aching ever since.

'I'm proud of you for doing what you did,' D said. 'You helped save a dying man. He and his family are eternally grateful to you.' He kissed her neck. 'As am I.' He ran his free hand up her body, over her breasts, and wrapped it around her neck. She felt his prick bulge against her lower back. His breathing intensified in her ear, and he made low, soft groaning sounds.

And then, just like that, he released her.

'There's been a change of plan,' he said, easing his body away from hers. 'This isn't a place for you. It's not the right environment for you to thrive in. You're an A girl – this is where we keep the Fs and the Gs... And I don't just mean their bra sizes either.'

Her skin crawled. She understood every word but wished she didn't. Wished she wasn't here, listening to the men behind the walls groaning and moaning. Wished she didn't have to deal with the pain anymore.

That it would just end.

'Do you remember when I first met you?' he continued. 'I told you that if you paid your debt then you would be free to go. Well, there are several ways to do it. Working in the salon takes the longest and is the most boring. But what I've got planned for you now contributes more to your debt, so you'll pay it off quicker. And because you've been so well behaved, I'm letting you out.' He hesitated. 'But there are some conditions...'

She tensed her body in anticipation of what was to come. The last time he'd said that he'd violated her intimacy and destroyed her innocence.

'You're going to be meeting a lot of new people. Sometimes they'll come to you, but mostly you'll go to them.

You'll be taken to the locations by one of my men, and then you'll be left alone with the people you meet.' He placed his finger on the nape of her neck and ran it down her spine; she shivered.

'These people, the ones you're going to meet, have all been vetted. You cannot say anything to them, you cannot tell them anything, because they already know who you are, who I am, what you do and what I do. It is pointless to think otherwise. Your every movement will be watched, every word and syllable recorded. Your freedom comes at a cost and this is it.'

He moved his hand away from her back and slapped her backside. 'You'd better get yourself ready. You've got a client waiting for you now. Your driver will explain everything to you when you get there.'

He started from the room, paused, and then returned, this time holding money in front of her face. 'We found this down your knickers the other day. And I thought you might like it back, as a reward.' He groaned in her ear and sniffed the pieces of paper. 'Mmm... still smells like you.'

Chapter Fifty-Nine

DIAMOND GEEZERS

What felt like six hours had passed, and Dale's Yard was still closed. Jake was beginning to feel like a teenager again, loitering outside closed businesses in the middle of nowhere to meet up with his mates and drink alcohol in a secluded part of an industrial site. Granted, he'd only done that on two occasions, but the sense of juvenile delinquency and antisocial behaviour ignited a childish spark inside him. He was perched beneath a tree, sheltering from the rain. He'd managed to convince a taxi driver to give him the journey's fare for free after he'd shown his warrant card. Urgent business, Jake had said.

An unethical abuse of power? Yes.

Absolutely vital he get there in time? Also yes.

Yin and yang. Two opposites cancelling each other out.

Eventually, after what felt like another six hours of waiting, a white van arrived and turned into the garage's entrance. On the side of the vehicle was the company's logo and contact details. At the metal gates, a man dressed in an orange high-vis jacket hopped out of the cabin. Jake pounced on him as the man fumbled with a heavy keychain filled with more keys than a piano.

'Excuse me, mate,' Jake said.

The man, startled and perplexed, studied Jake as though he were a homeless man. 'All right?' he said with trepidation.

'You work here?'

'Five days a week.' The man lowered his arm holding the keys.

'Are you the manager?'

'His son. Carlton Junior. But you can call me CJ.'

Saying nothing, Jake reached into his pocket and flashed the warrant card in CJ's face. The man's eyes widened, and he stepped back.

'What's this about?'

'I need to have a look at a vehicle that came in here the other day. I need to know who brought it in and what's happened to it.'

'Erm… I'll have to speak with—'

'There's no time, mate. Sorry. I'll be in and out before you know.'

For a long while, CJ said nothing while he surveyed Jake up and down. Jake did the same. The man was no older than his mid-twenties, his body slight, and his hair scraggly, save for the meagre whiskers growing on his chin.

CJ opened his mouth and said, 'You're not… you ain't working undercover, are ya?'

'Yes,' Jake replied without hesitation. 'I can't say too much, but it's imperative I get in there and have a look right now.'

The man shuffled the keys through his fingers methodically until he found the correct one, shoved it in the lock and opened the gate. Jake didn't like to prey on people's innocence, but if it got the result in the end, then all that was holding him back was his morals. And the way he was feeling, he didn't have any left. The message last night had seen to that.

'Follow me,' CJ said, then led Jake through the forecourt, round the side of the main building, and to a mountain of scrap metal behind it. 'This is where we keep the cars that have been pressed.'

'Pressed?'

'When they come here, we press 'em down into little squares using the baling machine over there.'

Jake cast his eyes to the right. Adjacent to the mountain of metal was a large machine that looked as though it were a lorry container with an open roof. Attached to the top of the container were two metal plates that pivoted at an angle.

'I need to know everything you've got about a Mercedes C-Class.'

'Reg?'

'CM08 BY2.'

CJ told him to wait a moment then scurried away to the office. While he was gone, Jake used the opportunity to wander around, scanning the pyramid of crushed cars in front of him, each block of metal varying in colour placed atop one another. Debris scattered the ground. Dolls. Broken CDs. And then, as he approached a white box of metal, something caught his eye.

Just as he bent down to inspect it, CJ returned, clipboard in hand.

'Came in yesterday. Don't know who dropped it off. I weren't working. Was already pre-booked.'

'Name?'

'Danny Cipriano.'

Jake's face fell flat. It seemed Danny was still haunting him from beyond the grave.

'Everything all right, mate?' the guy asked, pronouncing thing as 'fing'.

Jake nodded. 'What else you got? Address? CCTV?'

'None of that. Dad don't trust it. Says it's unlikely anyone's gonna wanna come in here and nick something.'

'Is your dad working today?'

CJ turned over another page on his clipboard. 'Nah. He's on holiday in Spain at the moment. Jammy bastard.' Another turn, another page. 'Here we go. It was all paid for in cash.'

'How much?'

'Just a little over two bags of sand.'

Jake hoped the confusion on his face was obvious.

CJ chuckled, bubbles of phlegm spewing out the sides of his mouth. 'Cockney rhyming for grand.'

Two thousand pounds.

The same amount that had been stolen from Jake's debit accounts.

Perhaps his money hadn't been used to fund the nail bar. Perhaps it had been used to launder money instead.

'You get much of this type of business?' he asked. 'Large sums of money in cash.'

'You'd be surprised. It happens more often than you think.'

Jake sighed. 'I'm sure it does.'

'We pay all our taxes though,' CJ said as a final remark.

The fact that he needed to state that told Jake explicitly that they didn't. He made a mental note to get someone to investigate the business when he returned to the station.

'Cheers for your help, mate.'

'You don't need me to write anything down for ya?'

Jake tapped the side of his head. Then he pointed to the pyramid of metal. 'You mind if I have a quick look around?'

'Do what you gotta do. I'll be around if you need me.'

Right, Jake thought. CJ was growing more suspicious with every passing second, and the best part was that it was natural. None of it had been induced by Jake; it was just the young man's innocence coming through. There was more he wasn't telling Jake, but for now, at least, he had something to go on.

Danny Cipriano.

He ran the name through his head multiple times. It was impossible for Danny to have brought the car in for demolition. He'd been dead for just over a year.

Danny was just a scapegoat, an alias to cover the owner's real identity.

As soon as CJ disappeared from sight, Jake turned his attention to the piece of debris that had caught his attention earlier. He crouched and then reached for a small piece of white paper. It was a business card, bent and torn. On the front was a silhouette of a half-naked woman, with the name 'Diamond Geezers' printed on the side of it, and a contact number beneath. Jake recognised the card immediately. It was the same one that the Stratford Ripper, Lester Bain, had used to summon his next victims and brutally slaughter them. But Lester was dead. Had been for a few months; he'd died of a brain haemorrhage after being beaten inside his prison cell.

Dozens of thoughts raced through his mind. Were the pimps who solicited those women also behind this? Or was it just a coincidence? He hadn't picked up an accent from Baseball Bat in the nail salon, and he'd been sure that when he'd spoken to the pimps on the phone that one time, he'd heard an Eastern European accent.

And then another name popped into Jake's head. This time filling his mind.

The man who'd introduced him to Diamond Geezers. The man who'd told him where to find the prostitutes in the first place. The man who'd worked with Drew and Liam and Pete in the past.

The man who, it was becomingly increasingly evident, had connections to The Cabal in more ways than one.

Jake knew where to find him. The only problem was how to get there.

Chapter Sixty

TRIO

The sensations hadn't left her. Fear and worry, tightening deeper and harder into her stomach with every passing hour.

Before her was her father, resting, his eyes closed, the steady rise and fall of his chest signifying that he was still alive, several hours after the operation had been deemed a success. Opposite her was her mother and sister, both ignoring her. Martha was reading the newspaper and Tegan was on her phone, typing. Elizabeth recognised the deep blue Facebook logo at the top of her screen.

If they were going to be unsociable then so was she, and she pulled out her phone. For a long while, she stared vacantly at the image on her lock screen; at the photo of her, Jake and the girls on the beach in Cornwall. They'd visited some of Elizabeth's family down there for the weekend when Jake had been afforded some time off.

She continued to stare at the photo, her eyes homing in on Jake's face. He was smiling. *She* was smiling. As for the girls... well, they were always smiling; their innocence and age protected them from the reality of what was going on.

Two months ago they'd looked like a happy family. Now their relationship was on the brink of destruction.

She hadn't heard from her husband since their phone call last night. Plenty of time to think, to dwell on her reaction and behaviour. Had she been too strong? Had she been too quick to jump to conclusions? Jake and Stephanie were work colleagues. Yes, they spent long hours of the day together. But so did she, when she was working at the modelling agency. She got to know the photographers in a friendly way, so how was Jake and Stephanie's relationship any different? It was purely platonic. Nothing more, nothing less. He'd told her that explicitly. And she should trust him because he hadn't given her a reason not to.

Not to mention he trusted her to the moon and back. So it was an overreaction. That's all it was. Tempers frayed. Incredible amounts of stress. Easy to overcome.

The screen turned black. Elizabeth unlocked it and scrolled to her address book, found Jake's name and then pressed dial.

The phone went silent, and then she was greeted with his voicemail. She hung up without leaving a message and then tried again.

Nothing.

She hoped he was all right. It was unlike him to have his phone switched off or drained of its battery. He was incessantly trying to make sure that it had enough charge no matter where they were or what they were doing. Sometimes, she thought he was addicted to it. But it was only because the nature of his job demanded he be on call almost every hour of the day.

She tried a third time but got the same response.

Setting the phone down on the side of the bed by her father's frail, limp hand, she decided to leave it. Try again in ten minutes. Then she picked up her dad's hand and squeezed. His arm felt cold and his muscles weak, which she knew was because he was sleeping, but it didn't stop the temperature of his skin filling her with panic and convincing her that he was dead.

Elizabeth squeezed again. This time, she got a response: the beeping on the monitor beside her intensified and switched from slow, steady beats to rapid, torrential rainfall. Before she could react, her father's body started to convulse horrifically. His arms and hands were the first to move, followed by his legs and the rest of his body, while his head remained still but lolled to one side, lips parting as his tongue flopped out of his mouth.

'Dad!' Elizabeth screamed, jumping to her feet and placing her hand on his shoulder. She felt the vibrations of his body through her arm. 'Dad! Dad! What's going on?'

Her mum and sister jumped to their feet also, surrounding him in an instant. They frantically pressed and prodded the various buttons to summon the nurse as Elizabeth continued to scream, a paralysing fear inhibiting her from doing anything else.

Within seconds, a trio of nurses fell through the door and rushed over. Shoving Elizabeth and her family aside, they attended to her father, their movements swift and experienced.

'Is he going to be all right?' she asked. 'What's happening to him?'

The nurses wheeled the bed away from the wall, pushing her back.

'His body's having a severe reaction the kidney. We have to get him to surgery.'

Chapter Sixty-One

THINK

Jake begrudged using money that felt like charity. He didn't need people feeling sorry for him. If he got himself into a situation, he liked to get himself out of it again. Growing up, he'd never had someone fix his problems for him; as the man of the house by the age of fifteen, it had fallen on him to resolve them. People depended on him then, and people depended on him now. He couldn't rely on other people's generosity. It was a bad habit to get into, and an even harder one to get out of. Except, as much as he hated to admit it, in this particular instance, he had no choice. The money Stephanie had left him had paid for his train ticket from Birmingham to Stratford via London Euston, with little change to last him the rest of the day.

The two-hour journey had given him ample time to think. About his marriage. About his loyalties to the police force. About all the things he'd done wrong during this investigation, and how he was going to overcome the professional conduct review. About his father-in-law and the operation. About how Elizabeth had shut him out. About the kiss that he and Stephanie had shared.

A checklist of problems in his life.

But it was the last one that troubled him the most. A burning pit of guilt and regret roared in his stomach, reminding him of what he'd done, and what he'd sacrificed in doing so. No matter how much he tried to force the thought from his mind, it persisted, like a raging case of genital herpes. But the question that stuck to the fore was the one he was too afraid to confront. Who had initiated the kiss? Who had split the earth in two and created the gargantuan divide between him and the people he loved?

And then, as he wandered along the streets of London, heading back towards Stratford, the name appeared in bright lights on the billboard of his mind.

Jake Tanner.

At first, he'd tried to convince himself otherwise, that it was Stephanie who'd instigated it. But he couldn't lie to himself anymore. It was wrong.

He was upset.

He was lonely.

He was inebriated with low inhibitions.

He was in need of affection.

And Stephanie was the one to give it to him. *That's no excuse*, he thought as he arrived at a set of traffic lights, and determined to focus on the case, on the Diamond Geezers business card that had led him to this point. Without a map or a phone, and in possession of a terrible sense of direction, he checked the thirty quid he had left in his wallet and hailed a cab.

Within seconds, one pulled up and Jake hopped in.

'Where to?'

Jake searched his memory. 'I need to go to a phone box.'

'Plenty of those around the place, mate. There's one right over there.' The cabbie pointed to the opposite side of the road, but Jake ignored him.

'I don't know the name. It's near Carpenters Road, I think. There's an off-licence and a fish and chip shop nearby.'

Jake closed his eyes and thought harder. The name of the chip shop appeared in his mind.

'Sea-turday Night Takeaway!' He clapped his hands and slammed his palms on the seats beside him.

'I think I know it,' the cabbie said, and as they pulled away, Jake watched the man load Google Maps on his phone and type Sea-turday Night Takeaway into the search bar.

'Thought you guys were supposed to know where everything is,' Jake asked, leaning forward.

'When you get given vague directions like that, mate, it makes our lives a little more difficult.'

Jake said nothing and eased himself into the cushioned seat. He decided to sit the rest of the journey in silence. Unspoken unless spoken to.

Ten minutes later, they arrived. Jake thanked the man for his time, paid him fifteen pounds for his services and waved goodbye. On the other side of the street was his next destination: the phone box that he'd used when he'd tried to track down the Stratford Ripper, Lester Bain.

Jake looked both ways before crossing then skipped across the street and wandered up to the phone box. It was exactly the same as he'd left it. Derelict, disused and disgusting. Tiny shards of glass littered the entrance, smashed in by a violent offender or a drunk teenager with an anger problem. Amongst the shrapnel, empty nitrous oxide canisters rolled gently in the breeze.

Jake pulled the door open and stepped in. Above the phone was the same corkboard that had been there eighteen months ago. Attached to it was a selection of business cards. Jake reached into his pocket and held the one he'd found at Dale's Yard in the air, searching for the same card on the wall.

Then he found it, hanging from the top, hidden just out of sight behind another.

'Bingo,' he whispered, pulling a handful of coins from his back pocket and slotting them into the receiver. He removed the phone from its holder and held it against his ear as he dialled the number on the business card.

The phone rang and rang. Rang and rang.

Eventually, after the fifth ring, the person on the other end of the line answered, breathing heavily.

'Hi,' Jake said.

Then immediately seized up.

What was he doing? What was he going to say? As soon as he opened his mouth and asked to meet with anyone, he would give away his identity, he was sure of it.

No, it had been a mistake to call the number. There had to be another way.

Jake slammed the phone on the receiver, leapt out of the phone box and headed down the street.

Think. Think. Think. Think.

And then, as he reached the junction by the fish and chip shop, he realised what he needed to do. The answer had been staring him right in the face back in Birmingham.

Just as Jake came to the realisation, a taxi pulled down the road and started towards him. He flagged it down with a wave of his arm, climbed in and told the driver the address.

This one he knew.

Chapter Sixty-Two

JESSICA

Twenty-Nine understood everything clearly. And the thought of what was being asked of her made her feel sick.

The process was simple. Arrive, meet the client, do whatever the client demanded, with no questions asked, suffer, perhaps enjoy it (or at least pretend), then once everything was finished, accept the money and bring it back to the house.

Those were the rules. Non-negotiable. As clear as the number on her wrist.

'You do a good job, that'll be taken off you,' the man driving her to her first client said. 'Then we upgrade you to your real name, slowly work your way out of the debt. The fastest way to get there? Do what you're told. That's my advice.'

Twenty-Nine turned to face him. His head was bald, and looked as though it was shaved, rather than a result of genetics or baldness. His face was long and thin, and he had a lazy eye – the first she'd ever seen.

The car slowly came to a stop. The man beside her left

the engine running, reached into the door panel beside him and handed her a sheet ripped from a notebook.

'House number twenty-three. This guy likes role play, fantasy-type stuff. That tells you who he wants you to be. Names, backstory. That type of stuff. He's a bit retarded.' The man leant across her stomach and opened the door. 'I'll be waiting out here, listening, watching.'

To prove his point, and to show that he wasn't lying to her, he opened the glove compartment and pulled out a set of headphones connected to a small iPad. Beneath it was the unmistakable full grey of a firearm.

Calling out to her. Begging to be grabbed and fired, a bullet lodged in his brain, so she could—

'Come on,' he snapped. 'Out you get. Oh, and one more thing, he doesn't like it when you speak to him. It intimidates him. But if you do have to speak, you have to do it in a little girl's voice.' The man shrugged and pursed his lips. 'One of his requirements, not mine. I forgot to put it in there.'

Twenty-Nine said nothing as she stepped out of the car and closed the door. She stepped up the kerb and looked at the row of houses in front of her. She was in a quiet residential street, with small brick buildings lining either side of the road, a far cry from the towering blocks of steel and metal she'd grown accustomed to back home. A far cry from the dreary, drab, poverty-ridden streets, where everything was soulless and grey, a place where there were no trees and no signs of happiness.

She turned her head to the left, and at the end of the road saw an old shop that had been boarded up with a TO LET sign hanging from the fascia. Arnholt Galleries, the sign read. Then she looked in the opposite direction. Nobody in sight, and no sign of a car, bus or taxi approaching. No means of quick escape. For a short moment, she contemplated running, legging it down the street, but she knew she wouldn't make it very far. She was dressed in heels, a short skirt and a leather jacket. There was no doubt in her mind that her outfit would impede her.

The car window rolled down and the driver leant across. 'Don't think about it. It'll only be worse for you in the long run if you do.'

That was all the warning she needed, although a part of her still wondered what more they could do to hurt her, dehumanise her. They'd already managed to destroy her innocence, to reduce her to a number and a piece of meat. There couldn't be more, could there?

And then she set off for the house before she spent too long thinking about it.

At the front door, she rapped her knuckles on number twenty-three, the last house in the row. Beside the house was another street of similar-looking houses. A car was oncoming. A big one. She didn't know the make and model but it looked large and wide and heavy enough to kill her if she collided with it. The metal hitting her legs, then her stomach, then her chest as she rolled over the windscreen and—

The front door opened and she was greeted by a small man in a grey tracksuit. His hair was so greasy it reflected the light from outside. Red spots dotted his nose and jawline, and small patches of black and white stained his chest, crotch and legs. When he smiled, he displayed a set of black and yellow teeth, and he wiped his running nose with the back of his hand.

As she stood there, numb from fear and the elements, she felt his perverse eyes crawling over her body. She didn't want to imagine what he was thinking let alone what was going to happen between the two of them. But the longer she stood there the more she found out; his penis bulged into a large erection in his trousers, which he made no effort to hide.

'Pretty. You're pretty,' he said, slipping his hand into his underwear. 'What's your name?'

'Jessica,' she said, remembering the name at the top of the notebook page. 'What's your name?'

He grinned evilly. 'My name's Archie Arnold.'

Chapter Sixty-Three

MELANIA

'Here'll do, mate,' Jake instructed, pointing to a gap on the side of the road. 'Nice one.'

The cabbie pulled over and switched on a button overhead. In the middle of the glass partition, the meter read £9.30. Jake handed over a tenner and said, 'Keep the change, pal. You've done me a solid. Cheers, fella.' And then he stepped out.

As he set foot on the kerb, it suddenly dawned on him that he'd never said words like 'pal', 'solid' and 'fella' in his entire life. Perhaps it was because, for the ten-minute journey, he'd been talking cab speak – where the majority of the conversation was blue and filled with small talk – and so he'd assimilated his language to match.

The taxi pulled away and sped down the road. As soon as it was gone, Jake scanned the street up and down. The houses were silent, still, standing firm against the screaming wind that ripped through the narrow gaps between the buildings, carrying with it the distant sound of the inner city. The road possessed an eerie aura to it, as though it hadn't fully recovered from the monstrosity that had taken place at Steven and Jessica Arnholt's gallery at the other end of the road. He turned to look at the building, still boarded up and waiting for new owners, care and attention.

Images of the brutal murder scene flashed in his mind. The basement. The blood on the floor. On the walls. On the table. The corpse – dismembered, disfigured, decapitated. And then there was the other body hanging from the ceiling, Steven Arnholt's severed penis lying on the floor. The visceral, vicious images made him feel sick, history repeating itself. He'd thrown up then, and he was close to throwing up now.

He forced the sensation from his mind and brought himself back to the present.

As Jake stared up and down the row of houses on the same side of the street as the gallery, he recalled which house Archie Arnold lived in. As part of the initial stages of the Stratford Ripper investigation, Jake had been forced to conduct the house-to house-enquiries. Archie Arnold had been the last man he'd spoken to; Jake just hoped that he still lived there.

Jake sauntered along the pavement, his eyes flitting up and down, paranoia pitching a tent in his mind. Even though he had no reason to feel insecure, he couldn't help but feel like somebody was after him, chasing him – couldn't help but feel vulnerable and isolated with no way to contact the outside world. No money, no phone, no immediate way to let anyone know that he was still alive.

Jake found the house – number twenty-three. He wandered up to it and knocked on the door. Flashbacks of the same scenario two years before entered his mind.

Jake waited. A few seconds of nothing went by and then a white van pulled up behind him. Hearing the sound, he spun on his feet, holding his breath, clutching his hand into a fist.

DPD delivery. False alarm.

But as the driver slipped out of the vehicle, a man with a lazy eye climbed out of a Mercedes, irate, gesticulating, swearing loudly.

'The fuck you doing? Watch where you're driving, idiot!'

As he'd pulled up onto the road, the delivery driver had clipped the Mercedes, knocking the front headlight slightly. And the owner was letting him know exactly what he thought about it as the two became locked in a heated discussion.

Realising it wasn't his problem, Jake left them to it and returned his focus to the door. It opened. Standing before him was Archie Arnold, dressed in the same grey tracksuit he'd worn when Jake had first encountered him but with the addition of a few new stains on his trousers. His face was the colour of blood, his eyes wider than dinner plates. There was a slight bulge in his pants and—

'Do you remember me?' Jake asked, pulling his eyes away from Archie's groin. 'I came here a couple of years ago, asking you about the deaths of Steven and Jessica Arnholt.'

'Police,' he said, blabbering. His mouth was filled with saliva and he swallowed a ball of it.

'That's right,' Jake said. 'I was with the police.'

'Police,' Archie repeated.

As soon as the word left his mouth a second time, he swung the door shut, but Jake's reactions were too fast, despite the hangover. He threw his foot into the door frame and stopped the door against it.

'It's OK,' Jake said, leaning his body against Archie's weight. 'I'm not going to hurt you. You're not in any trouble. I just need your help with something. That's all. Friend, remember?'

After a few seconds of silence, Archie eventually relented, allowed the door to fall open and stepped back a little. Jake was unsure whether Archie was inviting him in or whether he was readying himself to launch an attack.

And then he saw something move behind the young man.

A figure – hidden, crouched, afraid.

Jake peered around Archie and noticed a girl dressed in a short skirt and an even shorter top.

Bingo.

'Can I come in, please? I won't take up too much of your time,' Jake said. 'I just need to ask you a few questions about something.'

'I have a—'

'I know,' Jake said. 'I can see her. She's one of the things I wanted to talk to you about, in fact. Can I come in please, Archie?'

Archie nodded carefully and then stepped aside. Jake climbed up the small step into Archie's house and placed his foot on the laminated flooring. A thick carpet of hair and dust covered the material. Usually Jake was courteous enough to offer to remove his shoes, but somehow he didn't think he'd be kind enough to extend the offer to Archie.

As he stepped deeper into the small house, the woman in the door frame scurried away. Jake followed her.

'Where are you going?' Archie called back to him. 'Can't go back there!'

Jake continued regardless. He followed the woman round the corner, through the dining room and into the living room, where he found her in the centre of the square space. The light pouring in from the bay windows hid her features, but he was able to discern that she was attractive. Long, flowing dark hair. Slim, supple and soft body. Gentle eyes, perfect teeth. And she possessed the innocence of a woman out of her depth.

She covered herself with her arms, wrapping them tighter around her body, crossed her legs over one another and swayed from side to side as she struggled for balance in her high heels.

Just as Jake was about to open his mouth, Archie appeared.

'Bad,' he said. 'Very bad.'

'What's going on here, Archie? Is this a friend of yours?' Jake stepped closer to the woman, holding his hands in the air in surrender. He meant her no harm, and he tried disarming her with a smile.

'Bad,' Archie said.

Jake mouthed the words, 'It's OK. Everything's OK,' as he removed his warrant card.

Eventually, the woman lowered her arms to a normal position by her side, and as she did so, she revealed the underside of her wrist. Jake glimpsed a red mark and noticed the tattoo stained on her skin. The same mark as the man he'd met in the nail salon. The same mark as the woman Jake had seen on his first visit to Archie's house.

Her number was twenty-nine. And there was a barcode beneath it.

'Do you have a name?' Jake asked, slowly stepping towards her, moving his eyes away from her wrist.

'Her name's Jessica,' Archie said behind him.

Jake closed his eyes and sighed. *Figures.*

'Do you have a name?' he asked again.

This time, the woman nodded. Slowly, as if she were a doll being wound up by a child.

'Can you tell me what it is?' Jake asked, his voice soft.

'Melania,' she replied. 'My name is Melania.'

Chapter Sixty-Four

DEAD IN A DITCH

The raging fire of guilt in her stomach showed no signs of relenting. And she expected it wouldn't. Not for a long time, not until her conscience was clean.

'I'm the worst human being in the world,' she said as she entered Darryl's office.

She needed someone to talk to, to vent to, to confide in, and right now he seemed like the best person for the job, not least because Ashley was still out at the warehouse and Brendan was still on leave.

Darryl was the best of a bad bunch.

'What're you talking about, Steph?'

'I'm the worst person in the world. When Jake finds out what I've done, he's—'

'You have no reason to feel guilty,' Darryl said, lifting himself out of his chair and placing his fingertips on the table to steady himself. 'You've done the right thing.'

'But—'

'Do you think Jake thought about hurting Liam Greene's feelings when he called you guys at the IPCC?'

She did. In fact, she *knew* he did. He'd confessed it to her the night before at the bar.

'Course he didn't,' Darryl continued. 'Because he was doing what's right. I mean, it's beyond ironic, but that's beside the point. He was doing what he thought was right, and that's exactly what you've done. It's professional, not personal. You need to remind yourself of that.'

Stephanie swallowed and stared at him. Her tears started to well and there was no amount of blinking that would get rid of them.

'What if it's already become personal, sir?'

Darryl returned her vacant stare. 'Oh, Christ. What have you done?'

Stephanie slumped into the chair nearest to her. She folded one leg over the other, placed one hand in her lap and rested her other on the arm of the chair, picking at her nails, resurfacing the habit that had lain dormant for fifteen years.

'Last night,' she began, swallowing before she continued, 'Jake and I followed a lead. In Birmingham. But it was closed. We were in no rush to get back, and Jake had a panic attack, so I had to look after him. I booked us into a hotel. Once he was all right, we… we had a drink. One led to two. Two to three. Three to four. Four—'

'I get it,' Darryl interrupted. 'You drank. Continue.'

'Jake was wasted, and I mean *wasted*. He's had so much going on recently, I thought it would be a good opportunity to help him forget some of it. But then, when we got to his room, he got your message.' She gazed up at Darryl. 'He broke down. It was the most fragile I've ever seen him. I didn't think it was possible for him to shed a tear, but he did. Lots. Droves of them. I told him everything was… was going to be OK. And then… well, we kissed. It wasn't a big kiss! Just a little one. It stopped almost as soon as it began.'

'Who stopped it?' Darryl asked, his face expressionless. It was as though she were looking at a painting of him.

'Is that important? I don't know. I can't be sure. It was all a bit of a blur.'

Darryl straightened his back and adjusted his collar. 'You do realise this puts you in a predicament, don't you? You understand the consequences of this, right?'

'I do, guv. But I… Is there not… I wondered if…' She hung her head in shame.

Darryl let out a long, heavy, lifeless sigh. 'Why would you do this to your career, Stephanie? I don't understand it. You had everything going for you. And right in the middle of the Matheson enquiry, as well. I never expected this sort of behaviour from you.'

The pain in her stomach worsened.

'Where do we go from here?' she asked, wiping a tear from her eye.

'I don't know. Honestly, I don't. You'll have to leave it with me. But in the meantime, I think you need to take time off. Go and spend some time alone, or go and see your dad. Something that's going to take your mind off everything. Where is the Matheson case up to? Are the team in a good enough position for you to leave?'

Stephanie dipped her head. Even that she wasn't sure of, but she agreed nonetheless.

'And where's Jake in all of this? He's got just as much explaining to do as you.'

'I don't know.' Stephanie shrugged. 'I left him in the hotel early this morning.'

'Alone?'

She nodded.

'With no money?'

She shook her head. 'I gave him all the cash I had left. But his phone was dead.'

'Christ, Steph. Take time off. Go away from here. Get your head straight. I'll try and find him. Let's hope he's not dead in a ditch somewhere.'

Chapter Sixty-Five

ARCHIE ARNOLD

'Take a seat please, Archie.'

Jake pointed to the sofa while he kept his eyes focused on Melania. 'I have some questions I need to ask you.'

'Trouble?' the young man whimpered.

'No,' Jake said. 'Not yet.'

Archie shuffled across the carpet and slumped into the sofa.

Staring at Melania, Jake pointed to the chair beside the sofa. 'Sit down please,' he said, and she did.

Once the room had settled, Jake turned slowly on the spot and faced them.

'Archie, I'm going to ask you one question,' Jake began, 'and no, you're not in trouble yet, but I need to know if Melania's life is in danger.'

Whether Archie was innocent depended on his answer. If Melania was in any way subject to force, through threat of violence or deception, which Jake already suspected was the case, thanks to the barcodes, then Archie paying for sex was a criminal offence, and Jake would have to treat him accordingly.

To Jake's surprise, Melania leapt out of the seat and clung to his arms, as if possessed.

'Quiet!' she hissed. 'Be quiet.'

Then she pointed at her ears with one hand and then the rest of the room with the other.

'Listen,' she finished. 'Listening. In the bedroom. Listening everywhere.'

Jake paused, closed his mouth and held his breath. How much had he given away? How much had he already said that had compromised him?

Before he could do anything, he had his answer. A figure, the same man from the argument with the delivery driver, stalking like he had a gun, emerged from the front garden and tiptoed towards the door. Without thinking twice, Jake grabbed Melania's hand and pulled her out of the living room, through the dining room and into the kitchen. By the time they entered the kitchen, the man had slipped through the front door, key in one hand, gun in the other. He was short, stocky and bald.

But the only thing Jake could pay attention to was the deadly weapon in his hands.

And then the man caught sight of them.

Weaving his way through the kitchen, Jake hopped over dried pieces of food and a tin of beans that had spilt over the side of the bin. In the far-left corner of the room was the exit into the back garden. Jake released his grip on Melania and readied both his hands for the door. It was made of thin metal, with a large glass panel running down the centre. In the split second that he stopped at the door, he felt a cold draft waft around his hands and face. Mercilessly, it was unlocked, and it opened with ease.

He yanked the handle and pulled the door open then shoved Melania through and closed the door behind them, just as their attacker closed in on them; the man on the other side banged into the glass pane with the butt of the gun, splintering it slightly.

'Run!' Jake screamed, holding on to the door handle. 'Get out of here!'

At first, Melania looked stumped, bewilderment slapped across her face. But after a few seconds of processing what Jake had told her, she spun on the spot, threw off the heels and sprinted towards the side fence. She clambered up a small plastic garden chair and hefted herself over the panel into the street.

Jake relaxed slightly knowing that she was safe, but then a banging sound brought him back to the present. It was the man, pulling and pulling on the door handle. By now the muscles in Jake's forearm and bicep burnt. He couldn't hold on to the door for much longer, and he knew that, if he let go, the man would be on top of him.

He needed to act, throw the man off guard.

The man gave another yank and, this time, Jake let him have it. But there was a surprise. Jake followed the momentum of the door and charged into the man's body, clattering into him with his shoulder and sending him flying back into the kitchen.

As the man fell to the ground, a bullet fired. The glass pane in the door beside Jake shattered and shards rained onto the floor. The sound battered his eardrum and split his head in two with a persistent ringing. Throwing his hands to his ears, he cowered and then sprinted out and back through the garden.

Adrenaline flowed. He was acting on instinct now,

giving no second thought to his decisions. The attacker had a gun, and he wasn't prepared to get shot.

Jake raced towards the plastic garden chair, steadied himself on it and then leapt over the fence. His midriff caught on the top and his body flipped over it like a rag doll. He clattered to the ground, his hip and backside absorbing the brunt of the fall. His shoulder followed next and his head snapped onto the concrete. A sheet of black flashed in front of his eyes and a searing pain swelled in the side of his skull. But he blinked away the darkness.

As he tried to lift himself to his feet, he felt a hand grapple him. Clenching his fist, he prepared to defend himself. Then he looked up and saw that the person trying to help was Melania, crouched down by his side, her feet already blackened with dirt and gravel.

She helped him to his feet.

Once he was standing, he nodded at her as a way of briefly saying thank you, then pulled her away again. Together they headed down the road, in the opposite direction to Archie's front door, as far away from a bullet being lodged in his skull as possible. A few seconds later, they were at the end of the street. Jake recalled from memory that there were a few shops nearby; he and the team had got themselves a couple of snacks from an off-licence while investigating the Jessica and Steven Arnholt murders.

'This way.'

As they crossed the road, Jake risked a glance backwards. There was no sign of the man with the gun. But he didn't allow himself to breathe a sigh of relief. Not yet. Not until they were in close proximity with another person or civilisation.

Eventually, after another hundred yards of sprinting, they arrived at a busy junction. Cars and buses and taxis and cyclists sped past them in a mirage of colour. Jake stood still, searching for the nearest place of refuge. To his left was a bus stop. One of the buses that had just driven past him was pulling in. Their ticket out of there.

Dragging Melania behind him, Jake sprinted to the doors, shoved past a young adolescent with his hood pulled up and a pair of over-ear headphones resting atop his head, and dived into the carriage.

'Oi!' the youth yelled, and before the kid had a chance to exacerbate the situation, Jake pulled out his warrant card and flashed it to the kid and the driver. 'You need to drive away. Now!'

The driver didn't need telling twice. He slammed his foot on the accelerator and pulled out into the street. The force of the two-ton bus moving faster than its usual glacial speed knocked Jake and Melania off their feet; together they stumbled back a few paces and Jake fell into the lap of a middle-aged man wearing a green Berghaus coat.

Apologising, Jake steadied himself and pulled Melania to the back of the bus where the seats were empty. As they approached, Jake peered through the window. Their pursuer was nowhere to be seen.

Jake slumped onto the nearest seat and looked ahead. All eyes, heads and attention were focused on him. He even felt as though the driver was watching him from the front. Paying them little heed, he turned to Melania. Her chest was heaving, and her hair was windswept, yet she wore an ebullient smile that illuminated her entire face, as though she knew that she was free, free from the persecution she had been and would have continued to be subjected to.

'Where we go?' she asked.

'We need to get you somewhere safe.'

Melania reached round by her hip and showed him her

clutch bag. She spread the lips open and allowed him to peer inside. Jake glanced down at a thick wad of cash inside.

'Where did you get that from?' he asked.

'We use it.'

Jake looked up at her, down at the money, then back up at her again. 'Yes,' he said, 'we use the money.'

Chapter Sixty-Six

WITHOUT WARNING

The taxi had cost them just over a hundred quid. And as Jake watched Melania hand over all the money in her purse, he wondered where it had come from. A down payment from Archie? Or from her previous appointments? One was as likely as the other.

Jake thanked the cabbie and stepped out of the car.

'Where are we?' Melania asked as she climbed out of the vehicle. With Jake's coat wrapped around her shoulders, some of the colour had returned to her skin.

They walked across the stony pavement.

'An old friend's,' he said and, glancing down at her feet, added, 'We need to get you cleaned up, and get you a new pair of shoes.'

Jake extended his hand and guided her the rest of the way. Together they walked arm in arm towards the driveway.

The house was positioned in a quaint street in the middle of nowhere, with the distances between each property so large you could fit another house in. But the one they were looking for was protected by a low brick wall and a row of trees, shielding it from view. Through the cracks in the branches, Jake saw a Jaguar, complete with personalised number plate, and the front door. Surrounding it, and buried in several corners of the house, were security cameras covering every square inch of the driveway. Small motion sensors were strategically positioned amidst the patches of unkempt grass, shrubs and trees.

The owner of the house was either severely paranoid or just a nut for security.

Both signalled to Jake he was in the right place because the man he was there to see had every reason to be paranoid.

They traversed the gravelled driveway, moving carefully over the stones. Melania was in agony – it was impossible not to be – but she didn't scream, cry or whimper. And for that Jake respected her. The only experience Jake had of walking barefoot along the pavement was at university when he and Elizabeth had been heading home from a night out. Elizabeth's feet were hurting from prancing around in high heels all night, so instead of offering her a piggyback the entire journey home, he'd given her his shoes. He very quickly, and painfully, learnt it would have been easier to carry her all the way home.

A small flight of stone steps led to the front door. On either side of the door were glass windows offering a view into two rooms. On the left, an office space – Jake glimpsed the Apple iMac sitting on a desk – and on the right, a living room, a fifty-inch flat-screen TV perched in the corner.

Jake rang the doorbell. The sound echoed around the house and then was lost before it reached the end of the driveway. The air in the street and around the house was still, serene. A complete contrast to the manic cars that were always speeding up his road. The neighbours' screaming kids. His own screaming kids. The police and ambulance sirens coming from the estate a few corners away.

A wonderful place to live.

I shouldn't be telling you this, Pemberton had said. *But his address is…*

In the taxi, Jake had asked the driver if he could borrow his phone. After explaining that his own was out of battery and that Melania didn't have a phone for reasons that were too private for him to understand, the man had relented and handed it over. Then Jake had called Bow Green and spoken with someone in the team who'd then patched him through to DCI Nicki Pemberton. It had taken five minutes to get through to her, and then a further agonising five minutes to convince her to give him the information he wanted.

Twenty seconds passed, then he heard footsteps followed by the sound of padlocks unlocking.

Eventually, the door swung open.

'It's good to see you, Bridger. Good to see retirement is treating you so well.'

Before allowing them to settle down in the dining room, Bridger had conducted a quick recce of the house, checking the CCTV cameras around the property and up the street, frisking them for wires and weapons, closing all the curtains, shielding them and their conversations from any unwanted visitors. His body was jumpy and his eyes wired, constantly ricocheting from left to right.

Bridger had changed drastically since the last time Jake

had seen him. His clothes hung loosely from his shoulders, his cheekbones appeared pronounced like cliff faces, and his hair was straggly and unkempt. Usually one for spraying aftershave every waking moment of the day, he now smelt of body odour. Bridger was the epitome of a man who didn't know how to look after himself.

'Bridge…' Jake started, as he watched the man peer through a small crack in the curtains that looked onto the back garden.

'How did you find me?'

'Pemberton.'

'That bitch. Stupid, stupid. Should never have… No, couldn't have… She didn't… Neither could…'

Jake listened intently to what Bridger was saying, trying to decipher his meaning. But he couldn't; his speech was shaky, disjointed.

Like the texts that had led him here.

Then Bridger yanked the curtain shut and stormed into the living room through another door. And then Jake understood the reason for all the paranoia, the disjointed and jagged speech and text messages. Sitting in the middle of a coffee table was a pile of cocaine and other drugs, sealed tightly in plastic bags. The leftovers of a hit remained in a line on the surface, interrupted by Jake and Melania's sudden appearance.

Bridger raced across the living room and peered through another set of curtains. 'How did you know it was me?'

'You didn't make it easy.'

'Point. That was the point.'

'The golf club. That was the biggest giveaway. But when you didn't show…'

'Couldn't. Couldn't show my face. Not the only one who

was there. As soon as I saw him, gone. Couldn't be there anymore.'

Bridger released his grip on the curtains and raced over to them. He studied Melania and then Jake. The man Jake had once known had vacated his soul a long time ago. As they looked at one another, Jake felt he was talking to a stranger.

'D,' he said.

'The one you want starts with D, yes. Have you done it? Have you found him?'

Jake pointed at Melania. 'Not yet. But I'm close, and I'm hoping Melania here can help us. But first, she needs food, a drink and some clothes.'

Without saying anything, Bridger tore past them and headed into the kitchen. Dubious, Jake stayed behind and waited until he heard the sound of a kettle boiling. Then they found themselves some seats in the dining room, away from the drugs.

A minute later, Bridger arrived with two cups of tea. As he placed one in her cupped hands, he warned her, 'Careful, love. Hot. It's really hot.'

She paid him no heed and downed the scalding liquid. Jake and Bridger looked at one another in disbelief. They both shared a looked that asked, *When was the last time she had a proper drink?*

Immediately, Bridger turned and headed into the kitchen. Not long after, he returned with a multipack of ready-salted Hula Hoops. He gave the bag to Melania, who tore open the first pack and poured the contents into her mouth as if her throat was a funnel.

Bridger reached out a hand and set it on her shoulder. 'Easy,' he said. 'You'll make yourself sick if you eat too much.'

Melania stared up at him vacantly, the bag hovering a few centimetres from her lips.

'She can understand me, right?' Bridger asked, looking at Jake.

'Yes,' Melania replied before Jake could.

'Lucky, lucky.' Bridger wiped his nose with the back of his hand and snorted heavily. 'Not safe you being here.'

'I need your help, Bridge,' Jake began. 'It's The Cabal—'

'Cabal?' Melania said slowly, her accent thick and her voice soft, delicate. By now she had finished the first packet of crisps and moved them to the side.

'You know him?' Jake asked.

She nodded furtively. 'He said to call him D, but I heard the others use that name.'

'Melania, I need you to tell us everything. What happened to you, how you know The Cabal. But there's no pressure. There's plenty of time.'

Melania quickly returned her attention to the crisps, scoffing another full packet and crunching on them loudly.

'This is a safe place. We're not going to hurt you here.' Jake paused a beat. He glanced down at her wrist. 'That tattoo. Where did you get it from?'

No response.

'Were you at the nail salon with lots of other people who had a similar sort of tattoo? Just like the one you have?'

Melania nodded.

'Were you brought into this country in a container, Melania?' Jake asked as softly as he could manage. This was a delicate situation that required an even more delicate approach.

She nodded.

'When did you come here?'

'I…' She hesitated, swallowed and looked down at her lap before continuing, 'I don't know. Two weeks, maybe, ago?'

Jake nodded understandingly. 'And all of the people inside the nail salon, did they come across with you?'

'Yes. Others, yes. Many.'

Jake swallowed. 'And what happened after then?'

'We were worked. Long hours. No pay. Sleeping on floor.'

'When did you meet The Cabal?'

She hid from the question.

'Did he do anything to you?'

She closed her eyes and nodded.

'Did he assault you?'

'Yes.'

'Did he abuse you sexually?'

'Yes.'

'Did he force you to become a prostitute?' Jake asked. 'Did he force you to go to that man's house and have sex with him?'

'Yes.'

Christ, Jake thought. Not only was she part of a human trafficking ring, she had also been sold into prostitution. He was looking at someone who'd been sold the dream of a secure and fruitful life in the United Kingdom, yet had been lied to and betrayed, the subject of someone else's abhorrent greed.

'Where did you get the money to pay for the taxi?'

'Dimitri. He give to me before I leave salon. He save me.'

The one you want is D…

D for Dimitri.

For a short moment, Jake thought about what Dimitri

had said during their meeting at the golf club, the way he'd acted. Sitting next to him then had been someone heartless, arrogant and evil. Yet, there, in the form of the money he'd given to Melania, was an example of his humanity, a desire to be better than he was.

Could Dimitri really be The Cabal?

Jake didn't think so.

Before he said anything, Melania opened her mouth and made a soft noise, a grimace, a sharp intake of breath. Then she pressed her hand against her stomach.

'Are you in pain?' Jake asked.

'My belly. It hurts.'

Melania sank lower into the chair, rolled the top of her skirt down her waist and gradually revealed a scar on the right-hand side of her body. At the sight of it, Jake stood and moved towards her, inspecting. The scar, red and inflamed, circled by a large black ring, looked fresh, as though it had been created recently. Jake was no expert, but it was by no means a professional surgery; the stitches were coming undone and the wound showed early signs of infection.

Melania groaned in pain again, which then turned into a howl. She clenched her teeth and her body stiffened. Without warning, her chest heaved and a thin layer of sweat coated her skin.

Her body began to shake and convulse.

'We need to get her to a hospital, Elliot. Immediately.'

'No. We can't.'

'*Elliot.*'

'It's not safe out there, Jake. The one you want is D, remember!'

'And I don't know who that is yet, do I? And if Melania dies, then I won't ever fucking know. So grab your keys and take us to a fucking hospital. Or I'll drive myself. And if she dies on the way, her blood will be on your hands.'

Bridger hesitated a moment. Looked at Jake, then Melania, then at Jake again. He exhaled slowly, seemingly undeterred by the severity of the situation.

'I'll get my keys.'

Chapter Sixty-Seven

SHIFT

It was time.

The room was filled with familiar faces, the same family members and friends who'd come to visit their loved ones in prison the last time she was here. A few of them recognised her and nodded at her as they shuffled through the tables and chairs.

Friends and strangers.

Yet she felt like the biggest stranger of all.

Jake was weighing heavy on her mind. But not nearly as much as her father's situation was. Ever since she'd visited Little Susie, she'd been putting it off. But now that Darryl had sent her home, ordered her to clear her head, she'd realised this was what needed to happen.

To clear her head.

To look out for herself, for number one.

And no one else.

In the corner of the room, a door opened and a dozen inmates bowled their way in. Some moved with swagger, while others – the more reserved, shy, fresh-faced inmates who were new and naïve to the brutal realities of prison life – walked with their shoulders hunched and their heads down, only looking up when they were standing next to their visitors.

At the back of the queue was Stephanie's dad, walking with his arms folded tightly against his body, making him look smaller than he was. His head snapped around the room, but something about his demeanour gave her the impression that it wasn't because he was trying to locate her amidst the sea of bodies.

A few seconds later, all of the other inmates found their respective seats and took them, leaving her dad the only one standing.

Stephanie rose to her feet and waved him down. Slowly, he shuffled over, moving around the fringes of conversations.

Stephanie remained standing, and as soon as her dad was a few feet away, she grabbed and hugged him. His body felt cold and frail beneath her arms, his ribs like she was rubbing her fingers up and down the teeth of a picket fence.

She pulled away from his hug and observed his face. The whites of his eyes were wild with fear. She smiled at him, but she knew immediately that he wasn't well. Nothing about him was well.

'You're late,' he snapped, his voice gruff. 'Where's your mother?'

'She's dead, Dad. She died twenty years ago.'

'Is that a joke?' he asked. 'Are you playing games with me?'

'No,' she replied. 'This isn't a joke.'

'Well, you need to tell her to get down here now.'

'Who, Dad?'

'Your mother. Sharon. The love of my life. Where is she? I've missed her.'

Stephanie swallowed. She decided not to answer the question. Instead, she placed a hand on the table and hoped that he'd reach out and grab it; he didn't.

Seeing him this way was like having a thousand knives plunged into her stomach, each one puncturing a perfect memory of him.

'I got in trouble yesterday,' he started.

'What? What for?'

'Marshmallows.'

'What?'

'You used to love marshmallows when you were younger.'

No, I didn't. Neither did Leah. That was...

She couldn't bring herself to think the name.

'And when I hear that word it always makes me think of you. How I'd do anything to protect you.'

The pain of knowing he was talking about someone else was becoming unbearable.

He used to sit me on his knee a lot, whisper things in my ear...

'What did you get in trouble for, Dad?'

'Drugs.'

A wave of shock rolled over her.

'They found them in my bed and mattress.'

'What were they doing in there?'

'Well I must have put them there, mustn't I? Why do you always ask me such stupid questions?'

Stephanie opened her mouth to respond but lost the words – and the courage.

Brian leant forward and then, just like that, all expression in his face dropped. The eyes, the cheeks, the mouth.

He stared at Stephanie almost as if he was looking through her, meeting her for the first time.

'They found spice and a phone in my bed,' he started again. 'Do you know who else likes spice? Susie. Little Susie from down the road.'

Uh-oh. Here we go…

Time to rip off the plaster. To look out for number one.

She steadied herself as she prepared to hear the truth that would confirm the suspicions and allegations she had locked away in her head.

'Little Susie always loved spicy food. I would always give it to her when she was a good girl. If I needed her to be quiet and stay quiet, I'd shut her up with spice. If I thought she was being bad, I'd give her some spicy food too. She loved spicy food. I miss Little Susie. She was so pretty; she had such a lovely bottom for someone her age.'

Stephanie didn't know what spice was a euphemism for, but as she listened, all she could hear were Little Susie's words playing in her mind again and again.

It always happened in my bedroom. Nowhere else. I suppose it was because he wanted me to be comfortable. But I could never sleep afterwards. Even then I realised what he was doing was wrong. And when he was finished he told me not to tell anyone. That it was our little secret.

A lump formed in Stephanie's throat. The knives were now joined by a dozen flames dangling beneath her feet, incinerating her toes and flesh, slowly devouring her entire body.

'Little Susie was my favourite,' her dad continued.

She wished he wouldn't, but she needed to hear this. For her own closure, for her own torture, for her own torment for what she'd done to Jake.

'I liked the times we spent together in the summer, with

the ice lollies and the swimsuits. And then when no one was watching, I would take her away and we would—'

Stephanie leapt out of her chair and raced towards the exit. In her career, she'd dealt with stories like that, of child rape and paedophilia, and over the years she'd grown numb to it. Part of the job. But hearing it from her father was something she couldn't fathom.

That it was our little secret.

There are things in life you don't want to believe. Can't believe. Because you'd rather live in blissful ignorance. Like the fact climate change wasn't your problem; that some smart arse somewhere in the middle of Los Angeles would find a solution for it and save the world. That you wouldn't get cancer if you didn't think about it. That you didn't need to help a homeless person on the street because someone else was kind enough to do it. But this... this was an inescapable and irrevocable fact she couldn't avoid.

Her father was a paedophile and a rapist, an abuser and a tormentor. The man who had protected her, cared for her, given her everything. The trust, the love they'd shared had all been a lie.

Her entire life had been a lie.

And she'd been naïve to believe him when he'd denied responsibility for the porn on his computer. She'd been naïve to think she could somehow prove otherwise and get him out of prison, that she could suddenly drop everything and look after him at home.

Leah had been right. The one to see through the veneer and lies, and call him out for what he was: a monster who deserved to rot in prison.

And then the thought struck her, had her father molested and raped her sister too? Had she been the lucky one to escape his grasp? Had she been the lucky one to avoid his clutches, his evil mind? Had she been the only one who wasn't robbed of her innocence and future?

She didn't know. But she knew that, by leaving him to rot in there, where he could get caught for as many drugs in his cell as he wanted, she was in some way denying his future and giving it back to the women he'd stolen it from in the first place.

Stephanie approached the guard standing in the way of her exit. As she drew nearer, she blinked the man into greater clarity.

'Everything all right, love?'

Standing in front of her was Williamson. The man she'd heard so much about and seen so much of – and in high definition, thanks to a young girl and a crystal-clear CCTV camera.

'S... sor... sorry,' she said, losing her train of thought. 'But I have to go. I can't be here with him anymore.'

'There's still twenty minutes left. You sure you don't want to hang around?'

She replied with a firm no.

Williamson reached for his keys. 'Let me escort you out,' he said. 'You'd be surprised the number of people that get lost in here.'

'Maybe they're doing it so they can see their loved ones for one last time.'

God knew that wasn't the case for her. She'd already forgotten her father's face and replaced it with that of the man in front of her.

Williamson led her out of the room, through a narrow corridor and into another. Then they reached the signing-out area. Stephanie scribbled her name, the date and her time of exit. She was patted down again by one of the female prison officers and then Williamson continued with her to the exit.

'Is this it?' she asked, feigning naïvety.

'Unless you *wanna* stay?' Williamson remarked. He moved his hands to his pockets and puffed his chest out in a display of ego and arrogance.

'I'd rather not. You hear horror stories, don't you?'

'Ah, they're not all that bad. Don't get me wrong, some of 'em are right wankers, but the majority of them just come in, keep their heads down and do their time in peace.'

'There's always a few that ruin it for the rest of us.'

'Couldn't have said it better myself.'

They came to a stop by the exit. It was a small door buried in the side of the wall. Next to it was a large HGV entrance, its shutters pulled down. She knew that this was where he left her, but she couldn't afford to lose him like that. She needed to ask him something.

'Through this door then across the promenade, through another one and you'll be out.'

'Thanks,' she said, choosing her time to strike. Now or never. 'You got long left of your shift?'

She said it as amicably as she could manage. Her pulse quickened as it felt like forever for him to respond.

'Nah,' he said. 'I finish in an hour.'

'Well-earned break, I'm sure,' she said with a smile. Then she nodded, ducked through the door even though there were acres of space above her head and strolled her way across the promenade.

In no rush.

She had an hour to kill.

Chapter Sixty-Eight

IMPOSSIBLE

Idiots. Everywhere. They were all idiots. The people working for him were idiots. Even the people working with him were idiots. None of them were competent enough to do anything.

'Fucking useless, the lot of you!' he shouted into the phone, slamming his fist on the desk. 'Do I really have to do everything myself?'

'What?'

'Are you deaf?'

'You didn't tell us—'

'I didn't realise I'd have to fucking spoon-feed everything to you too. Hold your knob while you take a piss? You're a fucking adult. You know how to defend yourself, and you know how to use a gun.'

'I do,' Anton said with a hint of misplaced defiance and smugness.

The Cabal sighed, placed his elbows on the table and leant forward. 'Do you know where they went?'

'On a bus somewhere.'

'Any idea which one?'

'No.'

'So you're blind as well as deaf. What are you gonna do to fix this?'

'Find him.'

'Too fucking right. Don't contact me again until you have something. Fucking imbecile.'

The Cabal slammed the phone down as a final parting gift to Anton. His hand stayed on it, gripping it tightly until he felt the plastic creaking under the pressure.

Anton had just lost his greatest asset, Twenty-Nine, to the one person in the world he shouldn't have. Gone. Just like that. Thanks to one man. The same thorn in his side. The cancer in his brain. Jake Tanner was now in possession of the greatest commodity The Cabal had.

The *only* commodity.

No more Crimsons, no more Danny and Michael Cipriano. No more Henry Matheson, no more E11.

No more empire.

Jake had destroyed it all. And it looked like he was closing in on The Company as well.

For too long Jake had impeded his every move. Now it was time to get payback.

The phone rang. He glanced down at the screen and answered the call.

'Yes?' he said plainly.

'Alan Clarke's just gone back into surgery.'

'Oh?'

'The operation didn't work. His body's riddled with infection, and it looks like he's rejecting the kidney in a really bad way.'

'Well done,' he replied, his voice filled with malice. 'You did a good job. Call me when he's dead.'

The Cabal rang off and dropped the phone onto the table. Then he dropped himself back in his chair and folded his arms across his stomach.

Alan's infection, and imminent death, wasn't enough for him. Alan Clarke wasn't a direct relation to Jake. It wasn't close enough, visceral enough to hurt Jake deeply.

In the past he'd tried removing Jake from the equation from various angles, none of which had worked. He'd tried to ruin him financially, destroy his career, tear his extended family apart. But none of it was having an effect. To get rid of Jake Tanner, it was going to take a 9mm and a small piece of lead.

He typed Jake's officer number into the PNC. Within a second, Jake's profile appeared, and he stared at the expressionless image looking back at him. Imagined lifting the gun in the air, aiming it directly at Jake – defenceless, weaponless – and pulling the trigger, the bullet penetrating right between the eyes and ending his life.

Before he was able to enjoy the fictitious moment any longer, his mobile started to ring again. Who was it now?

He glanced at the screen and smiled.

'I was just about to call you,' he said, placing the phone in front of him and setting it on loudspeaker. 'You've just saved me a few seconds of hassle.'

'And I'm about to give you a whole load more.'

'Sounds exciting.'

'I'm done. I'm out.'

Bless her, The Cabal thought, *thinking she has a say in the matter*.

'You're not out. People don't get *out*, not unless I say they do.'

'This time it's different.'

'Different how?'

'Because it's me.'

The Cabal sighed. 'What about your dad?'

'There's nothing you can do for him. There's nothing anybody can do for him.'

'So you're choosing Tanner over your dad? That's pretty fucking disgraceful if you ask me.'

'I didn't.'

'Imagine what that's going to do to him.'

'Not my problem.'

'But Jake is?'

Stephanie hesitated a moment, babbled through the speakerphone.

'Your intentions are true but misguided. Sometimes the ones we love hurt us the most. How long have you been in love with him, Stephanie? Weeks? Months? Ever since you laid eyes on him?'

'You won't lay a hand on him.'

So naïve. So, so naïve.

'You wanna bet?'

'Not when I know who you are.'

'Impossible.'

'Really? What about the little visit you paid to Amelia Wilmot the other day? She told me all about it. How you wanted to see her CCTV footage. She showed it to me, something about your presence giving her bad vibes. Sometimes there are things you men just can't do. But what were *you* going to do with it, sir? Destroy all evidence so nobody would find out who you really are?'

Chapter Sixty-Nine

OWL

The time on the dashboard signified she'd been waiting an hour. And then an hour had turned into a ten-minute delay. Ten minutes had turned into twenty. Twenty into thirty.

She was beginning to think she'd missed him somehow. But it was impossible. There was only one way in and one way out, and she'd been keeping a constant watch on it. Scrutinising every face that passed her in all directions.

It wasn't until an hour and forty minutes had passed that she finally saw him. Now dressed in casual clothes – a Superdry jumper with his hood pulled over his head and his sleeves rolled up to his arms, a baggy set of jeans and a belt that had the flap bouncing against his hip with every step – and carrying a backpack over his left shoulder.

Stephanie watched him slip into his Ford Fiesta and pull away. She then started the engine of her reasonably priced car and followed, keeping her distance.

Fortunately, the man didn't live too far away, a few miles down the road from the prison, in a town just on the outskirts of Dartford, near the crossing. Stephanie pulled over to the side of the road, maintaining her anonymity. As soon as the engine was switched off, she yanked the keys out and shut the door. The sound was drowned out by the *whooshing* noise coming from the M25 in the distance.

Williamson, still oblivious to her presence, strolled towards his house, a small semi-detached property with a children's bicycle chained to a drainpipe. She pounced on him and leapt at the door just as he was about to close it.

'What the—!' he said as Stephanie barged into him. As soon as he recognised her face, his expression dropped and changed from shock and surprise to fear.

'I need to ask you a few questions,' Stephanie said, placing her hand on the door.

'What? W… Why? Wh… Who… Who?'

'Are you an owl?' Stephanie snapped. 'My name is DI Stephanie Grayson. I'm from the Major Investigation Team of the Metropolitan Police and I need to ask you a few questions about Henry Matheson's upcoming trial. You wouldn't happen to know anything about it, would you?'

The man froze.

'Please…' he said, his voice neutral. 'Don't make a scene. My kids… they're in. My wife…'

Stephanie focused. She couldn't hear anything, save for the sound of a car passing by at that exact moment. It was after school time, so it wasn't inconceivable they were simply being quiet. In the end, she decided to give him the benefit of the doubt.

'You can come with me to the station voluntarily, or I can arrest you here. It's up to you. Which way do you want to do this?'

The man hesitated. Then stepped aside and let her in.

Stephanie crossed the threshold and surveyed the house. She wasn't one to judge, but it looked like he, and the rest of his family, could do with the extra hundred thousand pounds that had been deposited into his bank account. The carpet in the hallway was torn and stained, the skirting boards dusty and chipped. But what confused her most was the smell – as though the walls had been painted in bleach.

'Kitchen's down the end,' he said, brushing up against her in the narrow hallway. 'I'll put the kettle on.'

'No need. We won't be here long.'

He ignored her and continued into the kitchen.

As she followed behind, she glanced in and out of the rooms. A dining room to the left, facing the street. Next along the hallway was a small bathroom; the sink was positioned right against the toilet and there was little room for manoeuvring. Her reflection in the mirror above the basin caught her eye, and for a split second, she thought she saw a speck of blood.

Before she could give it any further thought, the sound of the kettle boiling distracted her.

'I thought I told you we weren't staying long?' she said, leaving the toilet and entering the kitchen.

'So what do you want to know?' he asked as he leant against the kitchen surface, nonchalant and brave, the countenance of a man who had nothing to worry about. On the other side of him was a draining board, a tower of drying pots and pans and plates and cutlery teetering on the edge of collapse.

'Who have you been paying off?' she asked and slowly approached the kettle, keeping her body and muscles tense, lest he decided to attack her.

'I don't know what you're talking about.'

As he finished speaking, she reached the kettle and depressed the switch, turning the device off.

'No tea,' she insisted and stepped away slightly, creating a gap between the two of them. 'No coffee.'

Like an insolent child who'd just been told off, Williamson inched his index finger closer and closer to the machine.

Closer and closer.

Until he turned on the kettle again.

Furious, Stephanie yanked the kettle from its podium and set it down on the surface. 'I thought I said no—'

Williamson brought a metal frying pan down on the corner of her head. The pain split her skull in two, she cried out in agony and surprise and dropped her into a black hole as she collapsed to the floor, her head knocking the underside of the cupboard door.

Before the light was completely consumed by the black matter, she heard him say, 'I'm sorry, but you forced me to do it.'

Chapter Seventy

D FOR...

Jake had made some fairly poor decisions in his life, but sitting at the top of the list was entrusting a junkie to drive himself and Melania to the nearest hospital while under the influence. Bridger had driven erratically and fast, pulling in front of people, skipping red lights, and creating havoc for pedestrians at zebra crossings, yet they had somehow arrived at the University of Surrey Hospital in the heart of Guildford in one piece. And thanks to Bridger's relationship with one of the staff members – as was frequently the case with police officers and medical professionals – they'd been able to rush Melania through A&E and have her seen by a doctor almost immediately.

For the past forty minutes, Jake and Bridger had waited impatiently, pacing from side to side, for the results of the surgery. There was no indication what was wrong with her, but the fact that she'd been admitted straight away set the alarm bells ringing.

Bridger, who was becoming increasingly paranoid, had been pacing from side to side, muttering to himself, checking his watch and his phone every two seconds, as the effects of the drugs wore off, then disappeared from the waiting room without a word.

He returned a few minutes later.

'Here you go,' he said, holding a cup of coffee he hadn't asked for.

Jake took it and thanked him, then tilted forward, resting his arms on his knees.

'Wash your hands. You should probably wash your hands,' Bridger said as he joined Jake's side.

Jake glanced down at the bloodstains on his fingers. Dirty. Indelible. A constant reminder of the drive to the hospital. Melania drifting in and out of consciousness, screaming, her wound opening, blood gushing out of her abdomen, soiling his hands and trousers and the back seats of Bridger's Jag.

If anything happens to her, the blood on my hands won't ever come off.

Bridger must have heard his internalised thoughts because he placed a wide, firm hand on Jake's back. 'You did everything you could.'

'What if it isn't enough? I could've stopped this from happening.'

'You can't save everyone, Jake.'

No, but I can try.

Jake lowered his head, closed his eyes and set the cup down on the floor between his feet, waiting until he felt the solid ground.

'The nail salon...' he said, speaking to himself. 'She must've been there. But I didn't see her. I didn't save her. I didn't save anyone. How many other women has it happened to before Melania?'

'That's not something you want to spend your time

thinking about, mate,' Bridger replied. 'The more you think about shit like that, the more it consumes you.' He removed his hand from Jake's back and prodded his temple. 'You need to dissociate yourself from everything. Take out all the emotion. Melania is a subject – a number. To The Cabal, she's a statistic, an asset that brings him money.'

'That's all this is about, isn't it?'

'It's all it's ever been about, mate.'

Jake stared into Bridger's eyes for a long time, searching for the answer. 'Why did you come back? Why did you help me?'

'Because it was time.'

'You'd decided you'd let too many people die?'

Bridger shook his head. 'There are things you don't understand.'

Given how deep he was into the investigation that was either going to make or break his career, he very much doubted that was true.

A door at the other end of the corridor opened.

'Detective?' came a shy, reticent voice.

Jake craned his neck up at the nurse approaching him. He was dressed in scrubs and wore Crocs on his feet.

'What is it?' Jake asked. 'What's wrong with her?'

'Your Jane Doe…' the nurse began.

'Yes? What?'

'She's got an infection. And her wound has split open. It appears that she had an operation not long ago, but whoever conducted that operation failed to sew her up properly and used unsanitary equipment. Her organs have ruptured and she has severe internal bleeding.'

'Is she stable?'

'For now. But we're monitoring her condition closely.'

'What was the operation?' Bridger asked, joining Jake's side. He felt the man's presence a few inches away from him, but his voice sounded as though it were right by his ear.

The nurse pursed his lips and his eyes danced between the two of them.

'Based on the position of the wound, and from the X-rays, it seems that whoever was responsible for the operation removed one of her kidneys.'

At that, Jake froze. His mind and memory blanked out and he drifted away, the sound of conversation around him becoming muffled and distorted as if he was underwater. Yet he was hyper-aware of everything else going on around him, drifting on the outskirts of the conversation.

'What?' he heard Bridger say, his voice muffled. 'I don't understand. Why would anyone want to remove her kidney?'

And then Jake snapped back to reality.

'For someone whose kidney no longer works. For someone who needed a new one.'

'Jake...' Bridger placed a hand on Jake's shoulder. 'Please tell me that doesn't mean what I think it means.'

Tentatively, Jake twisted and looked at his former colleague. 'My father-in-law. He needed a new one. I wanted to give him mine but I wasn't the right blood type. But then someone said that they knew a doctor, that they would be able to bump him up the list.'

The clearer it became to him, the more dazed he grew, the more he wanted to throw up and pass out.

'Who?' Bridger asked.

Jake swallowed before responding. He gazed up at Bridger's eyes.

'Assistant Commissioner Richard Candy.'
The one you want is D…
D for Dick Candy.

Chapter Seventy-One

HOLE PUNCH

The sudden realisation caused an avalanche of snow to fall over him, drag him six feet into the deep and trap him for minutes, hours, days, gradually suffocating him.

The next thing he felt, when he eventually regained consciousness, was the cold hard hospital floor against his back. Sticky, covered in dirt and bacteria. A breeding ground for disease and infection.

Like the blood on his hands.

The blood on The Cabal's hands.

An image of the assistant commissioner appeared in his head, sitting opposite him in Bow Green with Darryl, pretending to be sincere about Roland's death, offering support to his father-in-law.

Another image: Candy standing over him at the Met Excellence Awards, shaking Jake's hand. *We thank you for your service.*

Another image: the first letters of Candiru, Atomic Nails and Dale's Yard spelling it out for him.

C.

A.

N.

D.

Y.

He should have seen it sooner; the warning signs had been there all this time. And yet he'd been blinded by his distrust of Darryl.

For a long while, the image remained in his mind, but as it started to meld with reality, he realised he was staring at a completely different man. Bridger.

Different but not entirely.

He hadn't noticed until now, but there were similarities between the two of them. The wide nose, the receding hairline, the distance between their eyes, the width of their ears.

And then he dismissed the thought. Preposterous. Bigger things to worry about – like fending off this panic attack.

Out of nowhere, the nurse returned, holding a cup of water out for Jake. He took it while the nurse checked his pulse.

'I'm fine,' he said, swatting the nurse away like a fly. 'It was just a panic attack. I've had them before and I'll have them again. I'm fine.'

Jake stood, realised how fine he really was then sat back down again.

'Take a minute,' the nurse told him. 'You're no good to anyone if you're passed out.'

Jake smiled facetiously, and then they waited until he was feeling normal again. The nurse told them he was going to check on Melania, then headed out of the room.

The two of them sat at opposite ends of the room, separated by the elephant between them.

'You've known all this time, haven't you?' Jake started, unable to look Bridger in the eye.

'I... I-I-I don't know what you're talking—'

'The Crimsons. Liam. Drew. Garrison. You always said that *they* were after you. That they were coming for you. That's why you never said anything to me, isn't it? That's why you never told me what I wanted to hear. But it was never a *they*, was it? It was always one person. And you knew exactly who it was – and what he was capable of.'

Bridger played with his hands and started picking at his nails until he drew blood. Something Jake had never seen from the man before. For someone who reminded Jake of his dad, he was ashamed to look at him.

'There are things you don't understand.'

'Shut up with that bollocks. I've had enough of it. You've known all this time, and only now have you decided to help – when it's too late. When I've been left with nothing. My marriage is a mess, my career is in tatters, my family are being targeted. Have you been a part of this plan all along?'

Bridger sniffed hard and wiped his nose with the back of his sleeve. Jake didn't want to know what sort of germs were on it.

'It's not as easy as that. I wanted to tell you... I really did. But...' Bridger scratched his head furiously then leapt out of the chair and checked the various doors around the room, searching for signs of life. When none presented themselves, he returned to his seat, rolling back and forth. 'I told you about The Crimsons, didn't I? Remember? When you asked me if I was helping? I told you then, and I wanted to tell you more. But I couldn't.'

'Why not?'

'Because I needed to protect you.'

'Protect me from what?'

'From yourself. I knew that if you possessed the information I did, you'd go for everyone at once. But when you try to chop the head off, the snake is always going to fight back. I tried to warn you to stay away for as long as possible. Until the time was right.'

Bullshit excuse.

Bridger jumped up again, checked the doors and returned to his seat. Tapped his foot.

Taptaptaptaptap.

The cogs in Jake's delirious mind began to work faster and faster.

Taptaptaptaptap.

'Those parcels… they were *you*?'

'Some of them. I knew what Richard was doing, so I sent some more to persuade you. I was calling out to you all this time.'

Jake failed to understand how. 'By threatening my job and family and financial security?'

'I was doing what I thought was right.'

'Right? *Right?* You thought joining The Cabal and murdering countless innocent civilians, ruining hundreds of lives, betraying people's trust – you thought that was *right*? You're just as bad as him.'

Bridger reflected a moment, continued picking his nails. By now there was very little left, and he'd moved down his thumb to scratching the skin.

'It was never supposed to be this big,' he began. 'We never wanted it to become as widespread as it has. But he got greedy. Like he always did…'

Bridger checked the doors for the third time and returned to his seat. 'I wanted out a long time ago when I saw what type of things he was doing. But I only stayed… I only stayed with him because I loved him.'

Loved him?

'You were a couple?'

Bridger shot him an admonishing glance. 'No, you fucking idiot. Don't you get it? Richard Candy's my stepbrother.'

He hated hospitals. The germs, the diseases, the sight of the invalids lying on the beds, sucking in their last breaths, using up resources that could be better spared elsewhere. The way everything looked so clinical and out of a hallucination in a psychological thriller. The way the walls and furniture screamed death, death, death.

The constant reminder that his time on earth was finite.

What he hated even more than all that were the delirious and incontinent people coming up to him, asking for assistance. He was the furthest thing from a doctor, yet the dark blue shirt over his body suggested otherwise.

He was the destroyer of life, not the enhancer.

First Roland Lewandowski. Now this…

The corridors blended into one as he stormed down them, sweeping his head left and right into the various rooms and other connecting corridors. The place was well signposted, but when he didn't know where the target was, they were as much use as a lit match under water.

He made a left turn, no idea where. Following his instincts. Hoping they'd lead him to the one he was supposed to kill. The one connecting himself and The Cabal to the nail salon and Archie Arnold.

And with so much death around him, what difference would one more body make?

'Can I see her?' Jake asked the nurse.

'Not yet. She's resting. She's very weak. She's lost a lot of blood.'

And I've lost a lot of time.

'It's urgent. I need to see her.'

The nurse stood in front of him, impeding him from passing through the double doors.

'Is she awake?'

'Yes, but she—'

Jake pushed the nurse aside and charged through the doors. He rushed down the seemingly never-ending corridor, popping his head briefly into the rooms.

'Sir! Sir!' the nurse called after him.

Jake ignored it. Found what he was looking for at the end of the corridor. Melania was in her own room, resting on the bed, a white sheet draped over her. She lay with her back flat and her body rigid, her eyes closed as though she should be on the way down to a different part of the hospital in the bowels of the building.

Jake tiptoed in and, by the time he reached the foot of the bed, the nurse was standing in the doorway.

'Hey! You can't be in here!'

The sudden interruption stirred Melania. Her eyes fluttered open gently like a butterfly's wings, and her head tilted towards the source of the noise. As soon as she realised where she was and what was in front of her, she panicked. She crawled higher in the bed, throwing the white sheet from her body and scrunching her legs against her chest. The monitor beside her beeped rapidly to match the terrifying pace of her heartbeat.

'Easy!' Jake said, holding his hands in the air. Moving round to the other side of the bed away from the door – and the nurse – he continued, 'Remember me? Everything's fine. You're safe. Nobody's going to hurt you. Calm down. In through the nose, out through the mouth.'

To his surprise, she followed his instructions, and within a few seconds, her breathing stabilised and she stretched her legs along the bed.

'Could you get her a cup of water please?' Jake asked the nurse as he moved further along Melania's bed.

The nurse shot him a look of discontent, sighed and then headed out of the room. As Jake returned his attention to Melania, he found her rubbing her forearms and pulling the drips from her veins.

'Woah! Hey! Not so quick on those, all right. You need to keep them in,' he said, placating her with a hand on her shoulder.

'Doctor. The doctor. Last time I was in hospital, they cut me.'

'I know,' Jake said.

Beside him was a chair. He grabbed it, pulled it closer to her side and sat. 'I need to ask you a few questions about the doctor that did this to you in the first place.'

All thought of Candy and Bridger, and their brotherly relationship, had flown from his mind. In fact, Jake didn't even know where the man was – doing a line for all he cared.

'Do you remember what the doctor looked like?' Jake asked. 'Any distinctive facial features? Hair? Eyes? Scars? That sort of thing.'

He was greeted with a mute stare. Then Melania slowly turned her head towards the door. As if right on cue, it opened and a tall, thick-shouldered man entered the room. At first, Jake paid him little attention. But when he looked up at the new occupant of the room, he froze, stunned, caught in a snapshot.

Dimitri did the same.

D for Dimitri.

D for Dick Candy.

'What the—?'

Dimitri bolted before Jake could finish. He charged out of the room, slamming the door closed behind him with such force that it reverberated around the walls.

Jake, alert to the immediate threat and danger, gave chase, ignoring the shrill and coarse cries for help in Melania's native language. He made it as far as the end of the corridor before giving up.

Dimitri was nowhere to be seen, and with a fifty-fifty selection in front of him – left or right – Jake wasn't willing to take the risk that Dimitri might return to finish the job off.

The man was a master of the corridors and the disappearing act. Yet Jake sensed that somehow, as had happened twice already, their paths would cross again.

Besides, Dimitri wasn't the priority right now. Melania carried that baton; her safety, her recovery, her well-being was more important than chasing a human trafficker who had a habit of showing up wherever Jake went. If anything happened to their one key witness, the one who had first-hand experience of The Cabal's monstrous evil, their investigation was as good as done.

Jake turned his back on the chase and started towards the hospital room. As he arrived outside the door, Bridger appeared, jogging along half-heartedly.

'Where the fuck have you been?' Jake asked but already sensed he knew the answer. 'Let me guess, you told Dimitri where we were so he could kill her, didn't you?'

Wrong. The answer lay in Bridger's dinner-plate eyes and running nose.

'Un-fucking-believable.'

'I'm sorry, Jake.' Bridger wiped the underside of his nose. 'I'm working on it. I know it's a problem.'

That's not the only one.

Jake ignored the man and dived into the room.

There he found the nurse, frantically busying himself with the monitor beside Melania's head. Repeatedly prodding a button with his finger. Grabbing several tubes. Reinserting them into Melania's body.

And then there was Melania herself. Convulsing on the bed, like she was possessed by a terrifying demonic spirit. Head thrashing back and forth, arms rigid by her side. Stomach bending in and out like the lever of a hole punch.

Jake watched on, helpless.

Before he was able to comprehend what was happening, three more nurses and a doctor arrived and ushered him out of the room and into the corridor, where he and Bridger were instructed to wait in the waiting room.

Chapter Seventy-Two

DISEASE STICK

Elizabeth Tanner hoped that her husband was lying in a ditch somewhere. At least that way he would have an excuse for screening her calls and ignoring her messages. Her world was beginning to turn upside down, and he was nowhere to be fucking seen. Her body and mind were awash with anger and fear, two potent emotions meeting in the cauldron of her stomach to create a fiery combination.

She was inside a small waiting room on the east wing of the hospital. The room was no larger than a bus shelter, and in the centre was a coffee table that occupied most of the space. In the corner, mounted on the wall, was a TV. *The Chase* reeled off overhead, images flickering in the unending, infuriating silence. Beside her were her mother and sister, both of whom sat with their arms folded, staring into the vacant space in front of them.

Then Elizabeth threw her phone down onto the chair and jumped to her feet.

'Where are you going?' Tegan asked.

'For a walk.'

'You want me to—'

'No. I'll be fine.'

'What about Jake? Do you want me to try and call him?'

Elizabeth glanced at the mobile phone on the chair. She imagined the screen lighting up and Jake calling her. But she hadn't spoken to him in the past twenty-four hours, the point of no return. If he was in any real threat or danger, one of the team would have contacted her. Darryl. Ashley. Stephanie.

And then the images returned: the two of them checking into a hotel room, closing the door behind them, taking their clothes off, kiss—

She slammed the door shut behind her and stormed down the corridor, forcing her debilitating thoughts from her mind. They were poisonous, insidious. She should have been thinking about her dad, not her bastard husband's adulterous affairs.

Air. She needed air. And she needed it quick.

Elizabeth reached the end of the corridor, looked up at the signage and headed towards the exit. She strode through the network of corridors and waiting areas until, eventually, she arrived at A&E.

A large seating area sprawled in front of her, with dozens of people waiting to be picked off one by one.

Her eyes moved about the room; it was too busy for her liking. Not enough space to pause and reflect. But outside the door, on the other hand, was a small area with benches, a space similar in size to the room she'd left her mother and sister in. She ignored the Smoking Area sign and wandered through.

Gravel crunched underfoot and she trod on a weed growing through the stones. She moved to the bench farthest away from the door and sat staring at one of the plants that had been dotted around the enclosure. The air was filled with the lingering stench of tobacco.

As she withdrew her attention from the plant, the door opened and she was shortly joined by a man wearing a leather jacket. Black ink peeked out from its sleeves and collar. His jeans were ripped and he wore a chain around his neck. He stopped in front of her and hesitated.

'You lost?' he asked, his voice belying his appearance; her prejudices had assumed he would sound rugged and abrasive, but his voice was the opposite. It was soft, polite and possessed an endearing quality.

'Excuse me?' she asked, trying not to sound offended, even though she was.

'You look like you ain't ever smoked a cigarette in your life.'

'That's because I haven't.'

'Then what you doing out here?'

'Is that any of your concern?'

The man reached into his jeans pocket, produced a cigarette and ignited the end with his lighter. The tip glowed orange and a plume of smoke ejected from the man's mouth.

'If you came out here for some fresh air, this place probably ain't the best,' he said, taking another drag.

'Maybe I didn't come here for the fresh air.' She lowered her gaze to the ground at his feet.

The man dropped himself onto the bench opposite her. He sat with his legs spread apart and one of them outstretched. 'What you in here for?'

'Why are *you* here?'

'Visiting. Think the nurses might have something to say about me smoking if I was a patient.'

Elizabeth grunted.

'Bit weird, innit, this glass box? Everyone can see you while you slowly kill yourself with these little disease sticks.'

Elizabeth lifted her gaze. 'Maybe that's the point. Trial by judgement. Although you don't seem to mind. It hasn't stopped you.'

'And it ain't gonna.' He took another drag. This time longer. Harder. 'No point fussing what other people think of you. If I wanna do what I wanna do, then I'm gonna do it. But by the same token, if something ain't right, fix it. Simple.'

Elizabeth's brows furrowed in confusion. 'You mean like years' worth of smoking? You could always fix that by stopping.'

The man lowered the cigarette from his mouth and tilted it to Elizabeth. 'Do as I say…'

She rolled her eyes and lifted herself off the bench.

'So soon?' the man asked as she passed him.

Coming to a stop by his leg, a whiff of pungent tobacco climbed her nostrils. With a pretend cough, she made her discontent known, then wandered through the hospital, going back the same way she'd come. Two minutes later, she returned to her mother and sister.

'Any news?' she asked as she sat between them.

Tegan shook her head so she decided not to probe any further, picked up her phone and checked her notifications. A few Facebook friend invitations, and a *Clash of Clans* message notifying her that her fortification was under attack, but nothing else. Not a single message from her husband.

She opened her texts, found Jake's name and stared blankly at the screen. Her fingers hovered over the characters on the keyboard, clicking her nails together in anticipation of what to write.

The word 'divorce' entered her mind and lingered for longer than expected.

What the man in the smoking area told her played in her mind. Was Jake a disease stick in her life? Did she have to fix the situation that she was currently in so that she could be happier and live a better life in the long run? Or would she stick with the habit, even though she liked it, relied upon it, *depended* on it, even if it made her sick and could one day end up killing her?

Before she was able to answer that question, mercifully, the waiting room door opened. The surgeon stepped in, clasping his hands together by his belly button. A nurse followed behind and leant against the door handle, staying out of sight for the big news.

'I'm sorry,' the doctor began, matter-of-factly, cold. 'But there was nothing we could do for him.'

Chapter Seventy-Three

ARSEHOLE

The hour following lunch was Henry Matheson's favourite. It was the hour that he, along with the rest of the prisoners on the wing, was able to stretch his legs, get some well-needed exercise and blow off some extraneous, pent-up testosterone.

'I just get stiff sitting around all day,' Jason said beside him as they walked around in the playground. 'And you can only pull on your cock so many times in one day 'n' all.'

Jason nudged Henry in the arm and scratched the back of his neck before erupting into hysterics. Henry played along and pretended to laugh with him.

'You dirty fucking pig,' he said, bringing their laughter to a halt.

'Bet you can't wait to get out of here, bruv. See all them girls you been talking about.'

Henry smirked. 'There's a lot more to the outside world than girls, Jase.'

Like restoring his credibility and status as the biggest drug dealer in East London.

'Not when you been locked up as long as I 'ave, Hen. My balls ain't ever been so big in my life.'

Henry surveyed the little man. His short, greying hair that had been poorly shaved as though a child had done it, the rivers of red that drowned out the green of his eyes, the pores in his sagging skin. The unkempt facial hair that reminded him of hairs sprouting out of a potato. It wasn't Jason's fault that he couldn't grow any facial hair – he was at the bottom of the gene pool for that one. And then there was the burn mark on his cheek, the raised skin that was scabbing and flaking away, the freshly healed skin that was a different shade to the rest of his face.

Which reminded him.

'Any word on Dominic?'

Jason scratched his neck again. Even the mention of his name was enough to make the small man jittery.

'Last I heard he's due back today.'

'I'm looking forward to seeing him,' Henry said, but before he was able to continue, he was interrupted by Vinnie. The tall, imposing man waded over slowly as if his huge body was being met with a large amount of wind resistance.

'We've got a problem.'

'What?'

Vinnie reached into his boxers, stepped forward to within an inch of them and pulled out a phone.

'It's *him*. Saying that they know.'

'Who knows what exactly?' Henry asked, dumb-founded.

'The ones we don't want to know things now know the things we don't want them to know.'

Henry sighed and shook his head. Sometimes it was like talking to a brick wall. 'If I wanted a fucking riddle, Vin, I would've gone to the funfair. Talk in plain fucking English and then we might get somewhere.'

Vinnie nodded apologetically. 'The police found out about the jury. They're changing the line-up.'

'Fuck,' he whispered. 'He say anything else?'

Vinnie shook his head.

'It's all right, Hen,' Jason said, placing a hand on Henry's arm. 'He'll be able to sort it. He's bent – they've always got a way of doing things that the rest of us don't know nothing about. It's how they 'come coppers in the first place.'

Henry glared at Jason which instantly shut him up. Then he turned to Vinnie.

'How are your boys looking on the outside?' he asked.

'What do you mean?'

Henry massaged his jaw with his thumb and fingers. 'How quickly can they find out this new list? End of the day?'

'I mean… I'll have to see what they can do, but—'

'No "buts". I want it done. I'll pay them double. Just—'

'What you doing, Hen?' Jason interrupted annoyingly. 'What about the copper?'

Henry shook his head and pointed in Jason's face. 'Nah, I ain't trusting no bent copper no more. I trusted him to do it this time, but he fucked up. I've been in this shit for too long to know they ain't all as bent as they seem. Something's up, and he's just cost me nearly quarter of a million – the price for my freedom. Next time I'm sorting myself out. All right?'

He slowed down, calmed his breathing and placed his hand firmly on the back of Jason's head. 'I need you to do something for me, all right? During my trial, I ain't gonna be here, so I need you to keep an eye on the shit that we be bringing in, all right? Make sure you ain't snorting it up your fucking nose all the time, you understand me? And I want you to promise me you ain't gonna take no shit from no one, yeah? If anyone comes near you, you know what to do to 'em. You've got an example to set. After I'm outta here, this empire is yours to take over. And if you need help, you've got Vin – he's got your back.'

'Yeah,' said Vinnie, thumping his chest in further agreement.

'This part of my empire is yours now, Jase,' Henry continued. 'And there'll be an even bigger one waiting for you on the outside.'

The buzzer coming from the prison building sounded, piercing the air. It sent a shockwave through Henry and turned his body cold. He inhaled sharply and then released it gradually.

Back to the box.

'Come on,' Henry said, placing a hand on Jason's back. 'You better get back to thinking 'bout them girls. Hope you got enough tissues.'

The three of them ambled across the playground, in no hurry to leave. In fact, nobody on the spur was in a particular hurry, for the rest of the inmates were sauntering along, dawdling, pretending to finish conversations that had already ended a long while ago.

As they neared the entrance that would seal them inside for the next twenty-three hours, Henry gave one last look at the beaming sunlight overhead and grinned. If all went to plan, he would soon be out in it for as long as he liked.

The sea of inmates made their way through the building and onto the spur. Henry climbed the steps to the second floor, nodded goodbye to Jason and Vinnie, then entered his empty room. After the previous evening's search, old man Brian had been separated and sent to another cell, where he was being closely watched by some of the guards. Henry was sad to lose him. Over the past few days, he'd grown to like the man, and he thought they'd become friends. But he was in no way ready to lose sleep over him. Just the same as he didn't lose sleep over anyone else that had left him in his life. Des, Jamal, Elijah, Jermaine, Frank.

The only exception being Danielle.

Oh, Danielle, I wish I could see you now. Passing your exams, flying high at uni…

Henry caught himself before he brought a tear to his eye and headed straight for his bed, switched the TV on and reached underneath his pillow. There, he found Alex and all the other characters he'd grown to love.

Fifty pages to go, the home stretch.

He opened to the last page he'd reached and started reading. To his right, out the corner of his eye, bodies darted past his door, moving from right to left as the last of the inmates hurried back to their cells. It was nearly time for the doors to close.

Henry turned his attention back to the book.

Then something else caught his eye. Movement. Left to right. And he was certain it wasn't on the other side of the spur. No, it had been right outside his door. And he was even more certain that it wasn't one of the screws.

Henry tentatively lowered the book, climbed off the bed and wandered towards the door, his body rigid with anticipation. His fist was clenched and his hearing finely turned to his surroundings. Years of experience had taught him how to creep up to a door without making any noise at all, avoiding all the floorboards and creaky places, to see who was on the other side with a gun in their hand. This was beginning to feel like it was the same situation, different location.

As he approached the threshold, he saw two figures, one on either side of the door frame. He raised his arm to defend himself, but it was too late. The bodies rushed in, grabbing his arms and pinning them behind his back, while the figure on the left reached around him and held a shiv against Henry's lips. He tried to yell, but the metal blade dug into his lips and within seconds his mouth was filled with the taste of metal.

And then he stopped moving, stopped resisting, stopped breathing.

Dominic skulked into the cell. The light from the window illuminated the red and white scars that looked like small mountain ridges from where the water and sugar had corroded his skin. In his hands, he held a bottle of water by the lid. In the other, he held a toothbrush. Henry didn't need to see the bottom of the toothbrush to know what was attached.

Instead, he reacted instinctively. Wriggled and writhed and wormed his way out of it. But it was no use. The two men behind him were too strong and, as he shook his head from side to side, the blade in his mouth buried deeper and deeper. If he wasn't careful, he could swallow it.

'Bet you didn't think you'd see me so soon, did ya?' Dominic snarled, his yellow teeth bared. He was salivating, and strings of phlegm dangled from his incisors, bubbles foaming over his lips.

Even if Henry wanted to speak, he couldn't.

Dominic jabbed the end of the toothbrush in Henry's stomach. The small blade pierced his skin and stopped less than an inch in.

At first, Henry felt nothing, like it was a small prick,

somebody pinching him. But then, as Dominic moved the blade in and out of Henry's body like it was a punchbag, his stomach burnt with a furious stinging sensation. His blood pumped adrenaline, but it was useless against the pain. He took a deep breath, his chest and lungs rising, and screamed behind the blade, but then the man holding it wiggled it against his gums.

Henry let his body become a dead weight, hoping that it would disarm his opponents. He was wrong.

Instead, the men behind him kicked the back of his legs and he buckled to the ground. They then lifted him to his knees. Dominic moved down to his eye level, unscrewed the bottle lid and threw the cap onto the bed.

Without needing any instruction, Dominic's men tilted Henry's head back, ripping his hair from his scalp.

For a split second, Henry thought one of two things was going to happen. That they were either going to slit his throat and let him bleed out on the floor, or pour the water down his gullet. And then another thought flashed through his mind: they were going to do both.

'I hope you're looking forward to your court case, you little cunt,' Dominic snarled. 'You're going to look really pretty in front of the visitors.'

Henry's eyes flickered towards the bottle of water. The contents were milky and wisps of steam danced out of the top.

'If anyone's to blame for this,' Dominic said, lifting the bottle over Henry's head, 'it's you. You gave me the inspiration.'

Dominic poured. The liquid streamed from the neck and collided with Henry's face. He closed his eyes as soon as the water touched his nose and screamed in agony, but the scream only lasted a second, before he started to gag on his own blood and the water. His entire face – his cheeks, his chin, his lips, his nostrils, his eyes, the open wounds in his mouth, burnt and sizzled, sending a wave of nausea over him.

Before he was able to think straight, something landed over his face. It was soft, cold. Fabric. A piece of clothing or a tea towel.

History repeating itself.

And then it was ripped from his skin. The clothing tore away chunks of his flesh, and Henry dipped briefly into unconsciousness. He tried to scream but there was no air left in his lungs.

The men grappling him pushed him to the floor. Henry lay there, cowering on the ground, protecting his face and body, his hands covered in blood. He opened his eyes, but the world around him was painted a hazy red.

He heard movement around him. His attackers were still in the room.

'Pull them down,' Dominic said.

Without needing to be told twice, the two men yanked his trousers down, revealing his hairy arse. Henry continued to lie there, helpless, defenceless, coughing and choking on his own blood, his body consumed by pain.

Dominic knelt by Henry's side, grabbed his head and turned it so that Henry was facing him.

'Spread 'em,' Dominic hissed.

One of the men parted Henry's cheeks.

Keeping his gaze fixed on Henry, Dominic moved the toothbrush towards Henry's anus and shoved the blade in, rupturing his rectum.

'You're nothing but a piece of shit, arsehole.'

Chapter Seventy-Four

INSURANCE PACKAGE

As far as Jake could see, the only benefit of working for The Cabal was the financial side. In exchange for selling your soul and becoming a depraved, insidious, evil individual capable of murder and corruption, you were able to experience the finer things in life. Which, if you were Bridger, came in the form of an expensive house in a rich part of the country, two luxurious cars and access to copious amounts of high-quality class A drugs.

The middle-class dream. And Elliot Bridger was living right in the centre of it.

What wasn't a part of The Cabal's employment, however, was the innate paranoia, fuelled by the drugs, targeted at almost everything. Jake had driven them back to Bridger's house in Godalming, a small town a few miles south of Guildford, and on the journey, Bridger had chewed his nails so far back they looked like they'd been torn off in a bout of torture; he also shuffled and repositioned himself several times a minute, glancing out of the window every few seconds, and continued to wipe his nose, snort and clear his throat between every breath.

And then there was the talking. Non-stop, incessant, the drugs in his system beginning to take over his brain.

'I never wanted to be a part of this you have to understand. It's a part of my life that I regret, and if I could take it back then I would, but I don't think people should be judged based on their beliefs or actions even though that's what people do all the time, isn't it? They talk and they judge and they do and they say one thing and then do another and I'm guilty of that as well and I think we all are and—'

Mercifully, a snort, a wipe of the nose. Signalling they could both come up for air.

But the respite was only brief before Bridger submerged himself in his talk and disappeared again. It carried on like that until they pulled into Bridger's driveway. Before Jake could kill the engine, Elliot leapt out of the car and recced the house, checking the street, the bushes and the back of the house. Then he entered the front door, trying to hurry Jake along.

But Jake didn't play ball.

Not only was he devastated at having lost his only link between The Cabal and the nail salon, but he wasn't in the mood to entertain Bridger. He still hadn't forgiven him for lying all these years, for betraying him as he sat back and watched everyone die. The man was the epitome of a bad person. But Jake was also in no position to upset him; he needed a room, and with no phone or money to his name, the only option available to him was the most obvious one.

'You got two to choose from,' Bridger called as he sprinted round the house, checking all the rooms for signs of intruders. 'Take your pick. Don't care which one. Your choice. Both nice, really comfortable beds. You'll get a good night's sleep in there I reckon, probably the best you'll ever have and I'm not saying that lightly…'

Bridger continued around the house, talking to himself. Jake paid him little heed. The two of them needed to chat, to clear the air, but that would be almost impossible with Bridger as high as he was.

A little over two hours.

More than 120 minutes of talking before Bridger finally calmed down and returned to normal, whatever normal was for a man who'd snorted as much as he had.

They were both in the living room, sitting with the TV on, neither paying it any attention, yet both finding some comfort and solace in the background noise like it was a friend offering a weak hug. In the time that Bridger had been talking, all Jake had been able to think about was Melania, Dimitri, The Cabal. How close they'd come and now, with Melania gone, it was Bridger's word versus Candy's. And with Bridger's new-found proclivity for class A drugs, it was becoming increasingly impossible to think of a way out of the situation. Former corrupt cop turned drug user, versus upstanding hero within the police force with an immaculate history. No points scored on the reliability test there.

No points scored anywhere.

'Would you like a tea?' Bridger asked out of nowhere.

Jake glanced at his watch. Nearing midnight. He should have been sleeping, but with the thoughts rattling around his brain – Melania pulling the tubes from her wrists, her body convulsing on the bed – he knew sleep wouldn't come easily.

'Go on,' he replied. 'Remember how I like it?'

Bridger returned with two steaming cups a few minutes later. In his pocket, he carried a packet of milk chocolate digestives and set them down on the coffee table in front of Jake. The sight of them reminded him of his former colleague, DC Pete Garrison. The man was currently in a coma, serving his punishment for betraying Liam and Drew. But Jake's fondest memories of him were the packets of McVitie's biscuits he carried with him everywhere – on his desk, in his car, in his bag, in meetings. Wherever Pete went, a packet of biscuits followed.

Jake reached across and took one.

'I'm sorry about Melania,' Bridger started, even though the intonation in his voice suggested he wasn't sorry at all.

You're not sorry you did it; you're sorry you got caught.

'She… You tried your best. You did everything you could.'

'Which wasn't good enough,' Jake said, absently drinking his tea, his mind devoid of thought.

'I suppose you wanna hear what I've got to say, don't you? That's the real reason you stayed, isn't it?'

Jake would be lying if he said that it wasn't part of it.

Bridger took Jake's silence as his answer and said, 'Where would you like me to begin?'

'From the beginning is usually the best place to start.'

'Except for *The Odyssey*.'

With a hint of a smile, Jake let Bridger know what he thought about that comment. Bridger chuckled sheepishly then continued.

'It started back in the eighties and nineties, a few years before my time and before I realised what was going on.' Bridger took a sip and wiped his nose, the drugs' effects gradually wearing off. 'I was the only child of my birth parents. They loved me for a few years, but when I was about four, they got divorced. My mum told me it was because my dad didn't love me anymore, and from that point onwards, I never saw him again. He could be a billionaire businessman for all I care. Less than a year later, she found someone new, and less than a year after that, she married him. Nigel Candy. She took his name, but I stayed with my dad's. Couldn't tell you why, I just did.

'Nigel was a good man to my mum, as far as I could tell. He loved her, looked after her and provided for us. That's where Richard came in. He was Nigel's son from a previous marriage, older than me, and at first, we didn't get on. In fact, we hated each other, constantly fighting for our new parent's approval. Richard received it in droves from my mother, but Nigel... he was a hard, miserable bastard. And he had to be...'

'Why?' Jake asked, finding himself entranced by Bridger's story.

'Because he was a police officer. He treated everyone like criminals, except for my mum and Richard. So I struggled to fit in and find my place. The first couple of years were tough – Nigel was never home, Richard constantly received approval, and I stayed as I was, pushed further and further to the sidelines. What we didn't realise then was that Nigel was running a network of corrupt officers in the Met during the late eighties and early nineties. My stepfather was the original Cabal.

'Fast forward a few years, Richard and I joined the service. We'd spent our entire lives around it, so it was difficult to think of anything else we could do. And because Richard was a few years older than me, he was already excelling and progressing through the ranks by the time I joined so I saw it as a personal mission to do the same. I felt like I had something to prove.'

Bridger paused for a sip of tea. As Jake sat there, he couldn't help thinking one thing: that Bridger, his upbringing, and his relationship with his stepfather and stepbrother was a psychoanalyst's wet dream. It was all beginning to make sense now. The desire to win his stepfather's approval, to prove to himself that he was worthy of it, to do absolutely anything possible to earn it.

'The rest, as they say, is history,' Bridger finished.

'That's all well and good,' Jake replied, 'but it doesn't help me. I'm still no closer – *we're* still no closer – to finding out where your stepbrother is and how we can prove he's the one behind it all.'

Before Bridger responded, a loud snap erupted from outside the house. The sound sent a cold shiver up and down Jake's body. Silence quickly fell on the room, and he strained his ears to listen.

Nothing.

Nothing.

Had they found him? Were they coming for him? Or was he becoming just as paranoid as Bridger?

'Wait here. Don't move.'

Bridger slipped off the sofa and stalked out of the room, his movements slight and deft. And for the first time in a while, Jake did as he was told.

He waited…

Waited…

Straining his ears, holding his breath, trying to see through the curtains.

Until, a minute later, Bridger returned, flustered, short of breath. Beads of sweat popped from his forehead, despite the cold, and Jake was unsure whether it was from the adrenaline or the drugs.

'False alarm,' he said, sitting down on the sofa again. 'Was just a fox kicking a stone against the car.'

'Is the car all right?'

'Better than the fox will be if I find it.' Bridger let out a deep sigh. 'Now, what were we saying?'

'That we're still no closer to proving Candy's behind it all.'

'That's right, and that's where you're wrong.' Bridger perched himself on the end of the sofa. 'You're not gonna believe me when I say this, but I've got an insurance package: a storage unit of all the evidence you need. Everything from the history books. Everything I've managed to put together throughout the years. Somehow I knew it would come in handy.'

That wasn't the only thing Jake was wrong about; the other benefit of working for The Cabal was having the foresight to know you'd need an insurance package in the first place.

Chapter Seventy-Five

MANUALS

She awoke with a startle, the world around her snapping back into existence. The first thing she noticed was that her body was covered in a thin layer of sweat. There was heat. And a lot of it. And then she felt something digging into her back. Metal, sharp. The source of the blistering temperature radiating through her.

But another part of her was cold. Her lower half. From the waist down. Lying on the solid floor, her legs wet. Had she pissed herself? She squeezed her legs and couldn't feel any pressure on her bladder.

Shit.

She blinked again, trying to clear her head of distracting thoughts. She tried to remember where she was and what had happened before the darkness. Williamson. His house. The kitchen. And then…

Stephanie leant forward, peeling her body away from the metal spike digging against her. She rotated her body and realised she was pinned to a radiator. She saw the metal handcuffs cutting into her wrists before she felt them, but as she stared at them, her mind willed the sensation back. And the burning began. Unbearable, searing heat, melting away her nerve endings and receptors. She attempted to free herself from her constraints, but the more she moved, the deeper they sank.

She groaned in discomfort as she fought against the pain. Eventually, it became too much and she was unable to contain it any longer.

'Argh!' she yelled. 'Somebody help!'

The door to the room opened, flooding light in, illuminating her surroundings. Her eyes quickly scanned the room, absorbing all the objects and items that she could potentially use as a weapon.

There were none.

She was in a dilapidated bedroom with only a stained and soiled mattress to keep her company.

'Sorry about that,' a man said, entering the room. He carried a tea tray. On it was a mug. 'Peace offering?'

'What the fuck is going on?' Stephanie asked. She was no longer the police officer trying to defend others. She was the lonely woman out to defend herself no matter what it took.

Prey versus predator.

As the man drew closer to her, his features grew. And grew. And grew. Until she realised who she was staring at.

'Surprised?'

'I didn't think you were capable of this.'

'I'm capable of a lot of things, Stephanie,' Assistant Commissioner Richard Candy said with a wry smile. 'Some worse than this.'

'Where's Williamson?'

'Fixing you up a snack.'

'What are you going to do with me?'

'You're familiar with how ransoms work, aren't you?'

Stephanie said nothing but dipped her head slightly. She was afraid the terror in her eyes would give her away.

'We just need your disobedient pet to do as I tell him, otherwise you're the one who has to suffer.'

'Why?'

'Because life isn't fair. You either have power or you don't. And, generally speaking, those who think they have any sort of power, like you and Jake and the rest of the police service, are disillusioned.'

'I swear to God. You hurt him and—'

'And you'll what? Fight me? Kill me? Make me suffer?' Candy bent down by her side and placed the tray next to her knees. 'I've heard a lot worse from people a lot worse than you, Stephanie. Jake included.'

She spat in his face, a thick globule of phlegm landing on his cheek.

Candy smiled and wiped away the mess.

'Brazen, I'll give you that. But I always knew you were a coward from the moment I met you. Your poor dad…'

'Fuck off.'

'Is that all you've got? So you're a disappointment as well. They don't teach you this sort of thing in training, do they? Only when the shoe is on the other foot.'

'We both worked from the same course. We both know the same tactics,' she hissed.

'Oh, honey, they don't make manuals for what I'm capable of. They don't want you to know what's possible. They want to keep you locked up in your blanket of deniability and naïvety. That way *they* can plead deniability and naïvety.'

Stephanie shot him a menacing glare. In response, Candy leant closer to her face, his breath encroaching on hers. She retreated, but there was nowhere to go; her back eased into the spikes of fire, and the movement caused her bare wrist to touch the hot metal. She grimaced and gritted her teeth, trying to hide the pain.

Like she'd been doing the past few days.

'Easy,' he said, placing a hand on her thigh. 'We don't want any more accidents.'

Stephanie glanced down at her lap, at the dark patch on her crotch and the inside of her leg.

'Do you have a spare pair of clothes?'

A smirk grew on Candy's face. At once, it sent a shiver down her spine, and the hairs on the back of her neck stood on end, protesting for her to get up and kick the living shit out of the man in front of her.

'Stephanie,' he began, 'I hoped you'd ask that.'

As the man reached for her button and began to undo her trousers, Stephanie was beginning to wish she hadn't.

Chapter Seventy-Six

PLEASE FIND ENCLOSED

Even though he was physically with Bridger, their relationship operating and relying on a thin veil of trust, Jake had never felt more alone.

No phone, no communication with the outside, no money.

Nobody knew where he was, and the way his relationships were going, nobody would be bothered enough to find him.

Bridger and him. Alone in the middle of an industrial lock-up. Miles from home.

At this time of night, when the temperature was at its lowest, and the stars their brightest, Jake thought back to the only other time he'd felt this alone. Walking along the River Thames with Henry Matheson, wondering whether he would feel the piece of lead ripping through his body before he heard the gun or the other way round. A similar sensation seeped through him now as they traversed the car park and headed towards the lock-up, a small unit in a giant warehouse.

They strolled through the entrance, signed in their attendance and continued towards unit thirty-seven.

'I'm sure there was a list of dos and don'ts in the terms and conditions, but nobody reads those,' Bridger said as he unlocked the door. 'So long as you don't hide a body in it or anything.'

Jake was reminded of the scene from *Breaking Bad*, with Walter White and Skyler standing over their mountain of money from ill-gotten gains, not knowing what to do with it.

Sadly, the sight in front of Jake was nothing like that. No money to fix his problems; the queen had left him high and dry again. Instead, Jake was looking at something from the nineties. The unit was filled with old, dry cardboard boxes, a computer that needed an hour to start up, and a wooden chair that had faded and lost its paint since its creation in the sixties.

'It ain't about how big it is, it's what you do with it that makes the difference,' Bridger said, slotting the keys in his pocket.

Jake turned his attention to the pile of boxes and picture frames on the floor to his right. 'So what am I looking at exactly?' He bent down and grabbed an old picture of a toddler in swimwear beside a paddling pool.

Bridger snatched the photo and said, 'The past couple of years' worth of research. But *not* my family photos.'

'Why don't you keep them at home?'

'Because I like to keep them here, where I know they're safe.'

It was bizarre, but the way Bridger caressed and attended to the photo, as though it were a living, sentient being, made it seem like it was one of his friends. That all the evidence in there, all the pictures and furniture, were his only friends, and that he spent a lot of time in the unit talking to them, talking to himself.

If ever there was an advert for kids not to take drugs, Bridger was it.

'Is there anything specific you need?' Bridger asked.

An itemised list of everything you've got. Jake could only imagine the number of hours it would take to sift through and catalogue the evidence. Someone in the team would have to do it, and given his proximity to the case, Jake knew it should be him.

Time to get started.

Bridger spent the next hour showing him what was on the PC. A digital and physical copy of everything existed, the digital files backed up online, so if there was a fire, nothing was lost.

The evidence contained in the first file Bridger showed him was substantial enough: a copy of email correspondence sent between Richard Candy's personal email address and Rupert Haversham, detailing their movements and where they were hiding the Cipriano brothers in the witness protection programme. Also contained in the email were the names Liam Greene, Drew Richmond and Pete Garrison. Each with a different level of involvement.

Then they looked through several more emails and text messages between Candy and an overseas contact responsible for loading the containers full of humans; between Candy and Henry Matheson discussing the latest drug shipments; between Candy and Martin Radcliffe expediting the process of Jake's transfer from Hampshire Police to the Flying Squad.

The balance book of evidence against Richard Candy, incriminating him in every way imaginable.

Jake felt his body tingle with excitement.

'How did you get all of this stuff?' he asked.

Bridger glanced up at him, a smirk on his face – the first one Jake had seen all day. 'People think they're clever with their passwords, but they usually have something to do with the user's past. Given that I grew up with the cunt, I know him better than anyone else. After I guessed one, the rest were fairly easy to work out.' He typed furiously on the computer. 'And for someone capable of doing vastly difficult things with his phone and computer, his password security is frighteningly relaxed.'

Bridger prodded his finger on the Enter key. Somewhere in the room, a piece of paper churned and spat out the other end of a printer. Bridger leant back on his chair, located it with ease and handed the document to Jake.

In big bold letters were the words that had haunted him for so long.

WE THANK YOU FOR YOUR SILENCE

The email that The Cabal had sent him. The same one that had got Roland killed.

Jake was reminded of his former colleague. The tech wizard would have had a field day in Bridger's cosy storage unit. Although it appeared the hard work had already been done for him.

Another document. This time an image of Jake and Henry at the river.

Another document. Another image.

Slowly, as the pile of evidence grew, Jake was beginning to feel like Bridger. Each of these pieces of evidence was beginning to feel like friends to him too. Like each piece was there to support him and back him. In a world where he had little support, that was the motivation he needed to keep going, to keep pushing on until Richard Candy was behind bars.

Another printout. Another image. This time of Jake and Stephanie. The photo had been taken recently; at the bottom of the screen was a timestamp, dated the other night. But Jake didn't need to see that to know what the photo was.

'He must have…' Jake stared at it in disbelief. 'He must have followed us.'

'Or one of his contacts was there watching you.'

The next printout was the image of Jake clinging to Stephanie's shoulders, doused by the rain, being lugged into the back of her car.

The typing continued, growing faster and harder with each passing second.

'He's been busy,' Bridger noted. 'There's loads of new—'

The image on the screen changed. Jake's eyes snapped towards it, fuelled by a mixture of intrigue and curiosity. Something caught his eye. Just as he was about to lean closer, Bridger minimised the screen.

'Bring it back.'

'No, I don't think—'

'Elliot, do it.'

'But—'

'Do it.'

Reluctantly, Bridger brought the screen back. Then Jake leant in and read the document.

Darryl,

As discussed, please find enclosed a copy of my letter of complaint regarding Jake Tanner and the recommendation for regulation notice, along with all the supporting evidence.

Thanks,

Stephanie

Jake's stomach imploded. His throat dried and swelled. And his chest tightened.

The regulation notice. The complaint about his professional conduct. The reason for his internal review.

It had been *her*. Stephanie, the friend he'd relied upon for so much.

Jake looked at the date and time the email was sent – 2:12 p.m., 7th Jan. *First she destroys my career, then a few hours later she destroys my marriage.*

That bitch. That fucking, backstabbing—

'Jake,' Bridger said, bringing him back to the present. 'Calm down. It wasn't her fault.'

Jake glanced down at his hands. He hadn't realised it, but he'd crushed the printout he'd been holding, his nails ripping the paper in two.

'The Cabal put her up to it,' Bridger continued.

'How do you know?'

'Because there are emails between himself and Belmarsh Prison, talking about her father, Brian Grayson.'

Her dad's in prison? Why didn't she say anything?

Probably because if I told you where he was, you'd judge and have a lot of questions.

And then it all made sense to him.

The same way The Cabal had leant on Danika and Poojah, he'd forced Stephanie to do his bidding, either to ensure her father's release or his protection.

Jake could hardly fault her for that. There wasn't a situation in the world where he wouldn't have done the same for his family.

He placed a hand on Bridger's shoulder. 'I'm going to need several copies of these.'

'Coming right up.'

He watched Bridger move the mouse around several

times, click a couple of shortcuts on the keyboard, then said, 'Where are you getting all of these from?'

'Richard's hard drive. Problem with the cloud nowadays... makes it all so easy to access.'

'Speaking of which...' Jake began, the penny dropping in his mind. 'How is any of this going to stand up in court if you've hacked into your stepbrother's accounts?'

Bridger pondered a moment. Like Jake, the consequences of his actions were often an afterthought.

Better to ask for forgiveness than permission.

'Present this to your DCI and say you have reasonable grounds. Get the warrant and find everything before Dicky has a chance to remove it all.'

Because it was just that simple.

D for Darryl.

Please find enclosed a copy of my letter of complaint...

Part 8: 9th Jan

Chapter Seventy-Seven

NOOSE

The noose was loosening. Finally allowing Jake to breathe again.

Except one man's judgement decided whether it would tighten and kill him, or whether it would set him free.

All the hard work, all the evidence, all the friends he now had, hung in the hands of one man.

D for Darryl.

The same man he'd suspected of being in the wrong all this time.

Jake was so far in the doghouse with his manager he was beginning to hear high-pitched whistles, the car door closing half a mile away, the faint rustle of leaves in the trees outside. And he knew the only way back out would be to do a lot of arse-kissing.

A lot.

Hesitantly, he strolled through the office entrance at Bow Green, his eyes quickly scanning his colleagues. Searching for Stephanie but instead finding Ashley.

Keeping his head down, Jake slipped past the team and

knocked on Darryl's door. His manager's gruff voice echoed from the other side.

'Come in.'

D for Darryl.

D for Dick Candy.

Darryl had been exonerated of all the charges he didn't know had been levelled against him. Yet an element of doubt and suspicion continued to hang over him with Jake like a dense, ominous cloud, despite the fact neither he nor Bridger had managed to find any evidence incriminating him.

Jake's intuition had never let him down yet, and he didn't think it was the right time for it to start.

The door swung open, snapping him out of his reverie.

'You…' Darryl said, as though they were two lovers starring in a romantic comedy.

'May I come in, guv? I've got something I need to show you.' Jake lifted one of Bridger's backpacks in the air. The man had decided to stay behind in Surrey, thanks to his cocaine-induced paranoia.

It's not safe out there for me, Jake. They might come for me when I least expect it.

Because there was no possibility something could happen to Jake.

I wish I could help you more. I'm sorry.

Darryl stepped aside and Jake stepped in, found himself a seat at the desk and started fanning the documents from the backpack across the surface.

'How've you been?' Darryl asked as he sat opposite.

Great! Found out I might be losing my job. Destroyed my marriage with one drunken kiss. Almost got myself shot at point blank. Watched a woman die in front of my eyes. Need anything else?

'Good, sir,' he lied. It was becoming a habit now. 'I think the time away's done me some good.'

'I heard about what happened between you and Stephanie.'

Jake hesitated, his lips tightening. How could he know?

D for Darryl. Unless...

'Stephanie told you?'

Darryl nodded.

'She didn't have a right to do that. Elizabeth and I have been working on a few things. It hasn't been easy this past week.'

Darryl nodded again, this time offering a form of acknowledgement and sympathy. 'These things can be tough, but I'm sure you can work them out.'

He hoped so.

After a brief break, Darryl continued. 'I suppose you want to discuss my email...'

Had he not discovered the evidence suggesting Stephanie had been forced to report him, Jake would have stormed in there, guns blazing and ready to throw a few verbal assaults Darryl's way. But then Bridger had come to his aid and quashed his desire to make things worse for himself.

'I'm here about The Cabal, sir.'

'Jake...'

'I have evidence.'

'Jake, we discussed this...'

Ignoring his manager, Jake emptied the rest of the contents of the bag onto the table. 'It's all there. Everything you need to know. The Cabal has been working as a high-ranking police officer for several years now. He's been right under our nose. Or rather right above it. And we've let him get away with it for too long. Today that changes.'

Darryl studied the documents on his desk for a moment. 'What do you need?'

'A search warrant.'

'For who?'

Jake swallowed. 'I'm sorry to say it, guv, but Richard Candy.'

'The assistant commissioner?'

How many other Richard Candys do you know?

'The very same, sir, yes.'

'Bullshit!' Darryl exclaimed.

'Sir?'

He could feel the noose getting tighter again.

'You're out of your depth, Tanner. Clutching at straws. How dare you think you can throw an allegation like that at the assistant commissioner?'

Either Darryl was one of The Cabal's team or he'd been brainwashed into believing the assistant commissioner was a saint. Both were catastrophic.

'Sir, *please*. Just look at the evidence. It's all here, right in front of you.' Jake spread a couple of the documents apart, bringing them into closer view.

Darryl picked one up and examined it. His eyes glossed over the words on the page. 'This is an email. How did you access this?'

Jake swallowed again, his mouth growing increasingly dry as the noose drew tighter. 'A contact of mine, an old friend, found them for me…'

'*Illegally?*'

Jake had hoped he wouldn't say that word. But now it was too late.

Tighter… Tighter…

When Jake didn't respond, Darryl continued, 'You don't learn, do you? We have ways of doing things here. Not just

480

here, but in the police force. Ways that protect both us and the public. And this is exactly why I had to send that email, Jake. I didn't want to, but your behaviour forced me to do it.'

'Sir… I can explain…'

'Explanations are for those who deserve it. Now get out.'

As Jake left the evidence behind in Darryl's office, his throat closed up, his lungs suffocating as his brain switched off.

The noose had well and truly tightened.

Chapter Seventy-Eight

CRAWLING

But Jake had the courage to do something about it. Jab a finger in there, pry the noose loose and throw it around The Cabal's neck.

To do that, he needed to find the man himself. At his home. In his car. In his office.

The latter was the most likely.

New Scotland Yard was the second home to many of the most senior members of the Metropolitan Police; the commissioner, assistant commissioners, commanders and deputy assistant commissioner. It was the central hub for the forty thousand staff. Decisions, meetings and strategies were finalised within these walls. And on his first time visiting, Jake felt the overwhelming presence of the building. The modern fixtures, the cleanliness, the windows. Everything far surpassed Bow Green and its disfigured and broken chairs, faulty air-conditioning units, cloudy windows and filthy carpets. This was the place where the money was held, while the rest of it gradually trickled downstream like blood running through a fat man's veins.

As he waited his turn at the front desk, he couldn't help but think it would be a nice place to work. One day.

The person in front of him moved along, and Jake stepped up, clearing his throat before he began.

'I need to speak with Assistant Commissioner Candy,' he said to the staff member, whose false front-facing expression was beginning to wear down an hour after their shift had started.

'Do you have a meeting?'

Jake whipped out his warrant card. 'I should have one. He and I booked it together the other day.'

The woman briefly glanced at the warrant card then returned her attention to the screen. She didn't care who he was; he could have been the President of the United States and it wouldn't have made a difference to her. Jake was a nuisance, and an inconvenience.

Tell me something I don't know.

'There's nothing on the system,' the woman told him.

'Are you sure?'

She shot him an admonishing look that said, *I know how to do my job thanks.*

'Do you know where he is now?'

More typing. More scowling.

'His calendar says he's out of the office at the moment, but—'

'Do you know where?'

She didn't appreciate that. Not one bit. To show her discontent at his interruption, she knitted her fingers together and said, 'Let me just look into my crystal ball...' Then pretended to click the mouse. 'Nope, unfortunately, I don't know where he is. But if you spoke with him the other day, then give him a call, find out for yourself.'

Jake was glad the station didn't receive many civilian

enquiries, otherwise, he could only imagine the types of complaints they would receive.

As he moved away, wishing he'd said something clever to match her belligerence, Jake pulled out his phone and scrolled to the latest message he'd received from Richard Candy.

I've spoken with my contact and he's happy to do the operation at Croydon Hospital.

That reminded him.

Elizabeth. Alan.

He'd managed to charge his phone overnight at Bridger's, and when he'd checked it that morning, he'd briefly glanced over the deluge of text messages and missed-call notifications flooding in but had become distracted by the taxi picking him up outside Bridger's house.

Forty messages from Elizabeth. All saying his name, with varying amounts of question marks, begging for him to call her.

Then he found his voicemails – twenty of those – and started listening to them. Two days' worth of calls, each growing increasingly aggressive, malignant and short. By the last one, he was given a flavour of Elizabeth's current feelings towards him.

I hope you're fucking happy now, Jake. You better be lying in a fucking ditch somewhere.

He wasn't, but after hearing that, he felt like crawling into one.

What sort of husband and father was he? Two days without word – two days without at least letting her know that he was still alive.

Just as he was about to pocket the phone and head back to the car, the device vibrated.

A text message. From an unknown number.

Bridger?

Close, but not quite.

The text contained an image of Stephanie in a dark room, bound and gagged. Beneath it was a separate message:

She loves you dearly. But do you love her enough to save her?

Chapter Seventy-Nine

PUTTING ON A SHOW

There were no training manuals for this. No how-to guides that could get her out of her predicament. No amount of preparation that could have equipped her. The irony was that the only way to truly experience it and understand it was to live it.

Throughout her career, she'd heard from strong and powerful women brave enough to share their stories. She'd listened to them recount their ordeals, living the events with them as they retold them. Yet she'd always been one step removed, never fully able to grasp the horror and suffering of what they'd been through.

Last night and today, however, that had all changed.

Encompassing her was three hundred and sixty degrees of blackness and cold air. Great sweeping draughts brushed against her arms and legs. From the little light that filtered in around her, and as her eyes began to adjust to her surroundings, Stephanie realised she wasn't in the comfort of a small room anymore, like she had been twenty minutes ago. Instead, she was inside a large warehouse, with God knows what lurking in the empty void. In the distance, she heard water running from, she assumed, a gutter. She tried to move but soon became aware her arms and legs were strapped to a metal chair, so cold that it offered her some numbing relief to the burns on her lower back, wrists and between her legs.

'I hope you're not worried,' came a voice. It sounded as though it had come from behind her. In front of her. From her left. From her right. All around her, encircling her, closing in from every direction. The echo in this vast expanse of space wreaked havoc with her senses.

And then she heard footsteps. At first, she thought they were walking away, but then they grew louder, nearer. And the concrete they walked on sounded wet. Stephanie tilted forward and glanced around her. At the puddles on the ground, reflecting the white dots from the holes in the structure above.

And then she finally smelt it.

'There's no need to be worried,' the voice continued, this time louder, deeper, simultaneously right by her ear and on the other side of the warehouse.

She strained her hearing but the reverberations and echo disguised the voice. She failed to recognise who was talking, even though she was almost certain she knew who it was; her experiences in the last twelve hours told her it could only be one person.

Then, a few seconds later, she felt a pair of thick, firm hands touch her shoulders. The same hands that had covered her mouth when she'd tried to scream. The same hands that had pinned her arms and throat to the bed. The same hands that had torn her legs open and ruined everything inside her.

Stephanie snapped her head away in an attempt to

avoid the man's touch. As she did it, she caught sight of him behind her. He then grabbed the back of her head, squeezed and shoved it down into her chest.

'Someone's eager,' the voice said. 'Is there no romance in the unknown? Not knowing what's going to happen to you next? Not knowing where you are? Or is it just abject terror?'

Stephanie remained silent. The rule book on hostage negotiation, even though it was aimed at people who wore the shoe on the other foot, would have told her to converse with the abductor, to get him talking, to make him feel at ease because he was most likely just as afraid as her.

Sadly, she knew the reality was the complete opposite. The man behind her wasn't some sort of injured animal that had wandered into the house and couldn't get out. He was the animal who owned the house and everything and everyone in it. The past twelve hours had proven that.

Rule book, time to go.

And time for her to head into uncharted territory, in both mind and body.

'I wonder if our little friend has realised you're missing yet?' Candy asked.

'Which one?'

He edged round to her front and perched himself on her lap, his grotesque weight crushing her, transporting her back to that room. 'Your little lover boy. You know, I have a name for Jake that nobody else has ever heard before. I whisper it to myself in the bathroom when I get angry at him. Do you know what it is?'

Stephanie remained silent.

'Candiru. Have you ever heard of it?'

Stephanie kept her lips shut and maintained eye contact.

Eye contact was crucial. Eye contact allowed her to gauge his reaction. Eye contact allowed her to predict his actions.

Eye contact, unlike last night, was potentially going to save her.

She hoped. Prayed.

'A candiru is one of those little fish that swim up your jet stream when you're taking a piss in the Amazon. Nasty little fuckers, they are. They swim right up there and cause you a world of pain. That's exactly what Jake's done to me.'

'You named your business after Jake?'

Candy reached into his back pocket and produced a lighter. 'It was only fitting, given the amount of business that I've lost, the amount of money he's robbed from me. More money than you're ever going to see in your lifetime, especially with *your* salary.' He twiddled the lighter in his fingers. 'And here you are, one of the closest people to Jake. His damsel in distress—'

'I can look after myself.'

'If you say so… But just to be on the safe side, I think we should let him know you're alive and well.'

Candy dropped the lighter in Stephanie's lap, removed her phone from his blazer pocket and dialled Jake's number. She dimly remembered him demanding the code from her earlier, promising to stop the pain if she gave it to him.

'Let's put him on loudspeaker, shall we? See if he picks up.'

The call rang and rang, and every fibre in her being prepared herself to scream as soon as he answered. But then she decided against it; he was heading into a trap. There was no doubt in her mind that Candy was going to kill Jake. No doubt in her mind that—

'Stephanie, is that you?'

Candy held his finger to his lips, reminding Stephanie that she needed to remain quiet.

'Stephanie? Steph, are you there?'

An evil grin grew on Candy's face. 'Oh, she's here all right. She misses you.'

There was a long pause filled with silence, save for the sound of an engine starting in the background.

'Where are you?' Jake asked eventually.

'Might ask you the same thing.'

Jake's breathing grew until it was audible on loudspeaker. 'Trying to find you. At your office actually. You've got some pretty damning stuff on your cloud, Richard. And Twenty-Nine – I assume that's what you call her, judging by the number on her wrist – was very forthcoming with information.'

She admired him for the way he spoke to Candy. Years of pain and turmoil flowing through his words. Their long-standing battle finally coming to a head.

With her caught in the middle of it all.

'You found out then?' Candy responded. 'I underestimated you.'

'You always have. What do you want, Richard?'

'Time and a place.'

'Tell me.'

'Have you ever heard of benzene, Jake?'

Stephanie didn't need to hear his response to know that the answer was yes. In fact, all three of them knew what benzene was: the forensic analysts had found traces of it in the petrol Henry Matheson had used to burn Jermaine and Frank Graham.

Highly flammable.

Highly dangerous.

'Candy Cleaning Services warehouse, Coldharbour.

Thirty minutes. Otherwise, your little girlfriend goes up in flames.'

Candy rang off, threw the phone over Stephanie's shoulder and grabbed the lighter. As the device skidded to a stop, he struck the flint. A single flame danced in the air, putting on a show specifically for her.

Chapter Eighty

DEFY SCIENCE

Jake floored the accelerator. The one-litre engine of his Austin Mini Cooper screamed beneath his feet. He cradled the speedometer a few degrees south of 90mph as he ripped along the A13 towards Essex, ignoring the 70mph speed limit.

Thirty minutes. Otherwise, your little girlfriend goes up in flames.

Jake was dead to everything around him – the cars, the red brake lights of those in front of him, the road signs telling him where to go – while he thought of a contingency plan. He was heading into the same nest as he had at the Cosgrove Estate. The wasps' nest. Alone, without backup. Where, undoubtedly, he was going to get stung.

Very much aware of the risks involved, he thought of the worst and decided to call Elizabeth.

Make amends. Come clean. Be a better husband. Set the New Year's resolutions in motion a week late.

Keeping one eye on the road and the other on his phone, Jake unlocked the device and dialled Elizabeth's number. The ringing noise sounded through the car's speakers until eventually, it stopped. Voicemail.

Jake disconnected the call and tried again. Still nothing.

A third time. A fourth.

On the fifth, Elizabeth answered.

'Now's not the time, Jake,' she said. Her voice was still stern and firm, but it was laced with a hint of turmoil and despair. He sensed that she'd been crying and was struggling to stifle her sniffles.

'Liz, what's going on? I've got so much to—'

'I don't want to hear it. It's a little too late.'

Jake exhaled deeply and looked at the phone, wishing he could defy science and physics and reach through it to embrace her.

'I've been a shitty husband, I know I have, but you have to—'

'He's dead, Jake. Gone. Never coming back.'

'Liz...' Jake choked.

'I'm never going to see him again, and you're not even here!'

'I can explain—'

'Go fuck yourself, Jake.'

And, just like that, she hung up on him, filling the car with silence. Even the sound of the engine and tarmac rolling beneath him was muted.

Jake slammed his fist on the steering wheel. The force of the blunt attack knocked the wheel to the side, and he momentarily lost control of the car. As he righted the vehicle, he narrowly avoided the metal divider that ran along the length of the road.

But not before wondering whether he should let the car do its thing. See what happened as a result.

Once the vehicle was under control again, Jake tried

Elizabeth's mobile number. But there was no answer. He tried again and again. They all went to voicemail.

'Come on,' Jake said as he tried again.

Still nothing.

And then he had an idea. Elizabeth's mother, Martha. She would answer. Of course she would. He just needed to get through to her before Elizabeth did.

As Jake slowed the car to 70mph, he removed the phone from its cradle and scrolled through the address book until he found Martha's number. Just as he was about to press the call button, his phone rang.

It was Stephanie.

Without a moment's hesitation, he answered.

'Hello?' His voice was wracked with nerves.

'You sound a little bit scared, Tanner.'

'What do you want?'

'Just a friendly reminder you've only got twenty minutes. And I didn't mention this when I spoke to you earlier – I thought you'd be intelligent enough to not do it anyway – but I think it's probably best that you come here alone. For both your and Stephanie's sake. I know you're not good at following instructions, but it's in your best interest to do so now. It only takes one phone call and my people can be at your home in minutes.'

Elizabeth. Maisie. Ellie.

'Don't you dare…' he hissed.

'The power's in your hands, Jake,' Candy replied. 'Don't be stupid.'

The call disconnected. Jake increased his pressure on the accelerator, the speed of the car climbing to its maximum – 90mph. He passed beneath a structure notifying him that a 50mph speed limit was imposed further ahead. Mercifully, the roads were quiet, and so Jake was able to maintain his perilous speeds.

A few seconds later, once he was confident there were no cars in front of him for at least the next hundred yards, he called Bridger. He was the only person he could depend on now. The only person he could trust.

The liar. The corrupt police officer. The paranoid drug addict.

The only person he could trust.

The call connected.

'Bridger, it's me,' Jake said as soon as he answered. 'I need your help. He threatened my family. I need you to make sure they're all right. They don't know they're in danger. I'm relying on you. Please.'

'I…Jake… It's dangerous. Shouldn't you get—'

'Stop living your life in fear of *him*, Bridger. The more you let him into your head, the more control he has over you. Switch it off. Now people depend on you. *I* depend on you.'

Stephanie depends on you.

'Jake…'

'This is nearly it, Bridger. Once we're done, he's gone for good.'

Hesitation. Heavy breathing. A few hard sniffs.

'Your house. Croydon. Elizabeth and your family.'

'That's right, get them out of there and make sure they're protected.'

'And where are you going?'

Jake's grip tightened around the wheel. His eyes narrowed in on the phone.

'To finish this.'

Chapter Eighty-One

INTO THE WASPS' NEST

Jake relied on his smartphone to direct him to the location before his data allowance depleted entirely. After several miles on the A13, with Rainham Marshes running alongside him, he pulled off the slip road and continued on Coldharbour Lane. The road was a single carriageway littered with HGVs charging at him in the opposite direction. To his left was a landfill, with the stench of debris and rubbish rapidly replacing the oxygen in the car, and on his right was the River Thames. Small boats and cruisers slugged past. Jake paid them little heed and fixed an eye on the small blue dot on his phone.

Less than half a mile away, three minutes to spare.

In the distance, a few hundred yards ahead, was a towering beige warehouse with a slanted roof. In front of it were large squares of compacted garbage.

Jake followed the road round, and as he approached the building, the tarmac became uneven and ridden with potholes, wrecking the underside of his car and suspension, and in his forty-year-old motor, he felt every single last one of them jar his spine.

At the top of a small incline were mountains of wooden pallets stacked atop one another. They ran along the length of the road, varying in height and colour.

Without warning, the pallets signified the end of the road and the track switched from tarmac to gravel. With the warehouse on his right, Jake slowed down, keeping his eye on the dot. Just a few more metres to go.

Eventually, he slowed the car to a gentle halt behind the main warehouse, out of sight of the pallets, where he discovered a smaller annexe attached to the rear, so the entire structure was in the shape of an L.

Jake slipped the handbrake on and leant forward, peering up at the building in front of him. It was dominating yet at the same time unassuming, at least fifty feet high, almost as high as Bow Green. There were no other cars in the vicinity, save for a wall of tyres stacked atop one another and a broken and shattered door frame lying in the dirt. The factory, and the surrounding area, looked as though it had been disused for some time. The perfect place to slaughter people. Or perhaps the perfect place to run a drug and human trafficking cartel.

Jake stepped out of the car slowly, cautious and tentative. He kept one foot inside the vehicle and placed his hand on the door, swivelling on the ball of his foot as he surveyed the area, searching for any signs of movement or life.

Nothing.

He made a quick recce of his phone to see that it was working and that he had a signal and closed the door, making sure not to lock it. If he needed a quick getaway, he didn't want to suffer any delays, no matter how small or negligible.

Keeping his phone clenched tightly in his fist, he edged towards a small door at the bottom of the L, tucked into the corner of the joint. He trod lightly, keeping his feet flat so as not to displace any of the gravel underfoot. And to keep the noise to a minimum.

As he reached the door, he hesitated. Stared at it for a while. And then it dawned on him that he needed to be careful. Fingerprints. Footprints. Tyre tracks. Clothes fibres. Edmond Locard's spirit followed him. Anything he touched would leave a trace. And if – God forbid – anything happened to Stephanie, then he would become the prime suspect.

Even more so than he already was.

That was something he couldn't afford.

Jake lowered his blazer sleeve over his hand and pulled the door open. The rusty hinges squeaked, and any hope he had of being inconspicuous disappeared as fast as the scattering birds overhead.

The temperature inside the annexe was colder than outside, the metal structure radiating frigid air. Sadly, however, the temperature did nothing to alleviate the smell of garbage and manure that lingered in the air like shit on a shoe. Jake grimaced and rubbed his nose with his sleeve.

Immediately in front of him was an old machine. He didn't know what it was, nor what it had been used for, but he was unable to tear his eyes from it. The machine comprised of a metal circular tank with dozens of pipes sprouting from the top, equidistant apart. The octopus tentacles cleared his head by several feet and made their way through the corrugated metal wall to Jake's right, disappearing into the main section of the building.

Jake turned, saw another door in the far-right corner,

and advanced towards it, keeping his senses finely tuned to his surroundings.

As he placed his sleeve-covered hand on the door, he hesitated again. This time, he heard the sound of dripping. At first, he thought it was behind him, but after he glanced back at the octopus structure, he realised he was wrong. It was coming from the other side of the door. And then he heard the sound of muffled cries.

The sound of distress.

Stephanie.

Jake thrust the door open and stepped into the larger warehouse, his heart thudding in his chest and squeaking in his ear.

Dumf. Dumf. Dumf.

Dumfdumfdumf.

This warehouse was the polar opposite to the one he'd just come from.

For starters, it was ten times the size. Secondly, it was almost pitch-black, save for a trickle of light filtering in through a hole in the roof.

Thirdly, it was empty, but for one person in the middle – Stephanie, bound and strapped to a chair. Her mouth gagged. Her body hunched forward. Head dropped into her lap, her hair the only visible part of her.

As soon as the door opened, she lifted her head. Dazed and panting, a snapshot of delirium and fear caught in her eyes.

'Steph...' he whispered, letting the door close behind him.

He sprinted over to her, heedless of what was around him and what dangers lay ahead. The floor was slick with something that had been spilt upon it, but he continued regardless.

Rainwater, he convinced himself.

As he approached, Stephanie shook her head wildly and screamed, the sound muffled by the gag in her mouth. Her body shook violently.

He closed the gap.

Ten feet.

Five.

One.

Stephanie's features became more discernible. Her hair bedraggled. Black rivers streaking down her cheeks. Her eyes bloodshot, her wrists red.

'It's OK,' he told her, immediately crouching down behind her and setting to work on the rope that bound her hands together. 'I'm going to get you out of—'

A loud *crack* pierced the air and echoed around the warehouse. Jake froze. He sensed a figure standing near him, but he didn't know where. Left? Right? Ahead? Behind?

Lurking in the shadows.

Three hundred and sixty degrees of darkness.

Three hundred and sixty degrees of anonymity.

And then he heard the footsteps, slowly, carefully making their way towards him.

Jake swivelled on the balls of his feet. Twenty yards away, walking from the same door he'd just come through, was the man who Jake, at one point in his career, had admired. The man whose illustrious career he'd aspired to. The man who'd been kind enough to help his family.

The Cabal.

Richard Candy.

'Nice of you to finally join us, Jake. Things were just getting interesting.'

Chapter Eighty-Two

TICK TOCK

A draught of cold air nibbled at Jake's skin, reminding him it was there.

'I'm going to have to ask you to give Stephanie here some space. Ease up a little bit for me. There's a good lad.'

Jake glanced down at the rope tying Stephanie's hands together. For the first few years of his teenage life, before he'd been introduced to the world of video games and girl-friends, he'd spent his Wednesday evenings at the Scouts centre around the corner from his home. During that time, he'd mastered the art of knot tying, a completely useless and inapplicable skill for everyday life. Except for now. He knew how to unravel the bowline knot in front of him efficiently and effectively, and in the short amount of time he'd had beside Stephanie, he'd managed to loosen one of the loops.

One down, one to go.

That job was left to her.

Closing his eyes, he stood, exhaled and stepped away, then opened his eyes again.

'There's a good lad,' Candy repeated. He stepped forward until they were within five feet of one another, reached into his pocket and produced a lighter. With a growing grin, he sparked the end. An orange and yellow flame spat out of the top and flickered into existence. Their eyes remained locked on each other. 'You're a difficult man to track down, Tanner.'

'As are you.'

'I'm impressed you managed to figure it all out though. Very few have before you.'

'And were they all treated like this?' Jake gestured at Stephanie, whose eyes danced between the two of them.

Candy chuckled, his deep and throaty voice echoing around the space as he let the flame die. 'The opposite. They joined me. Many before you have been in a similar position to the one you find yourself in now.'

'Who's that?'

'Mark Murphy, Pete Garrison, Drew Richmond, Martin Radcliffe. They all started their careers by trying to get rid of me. And they were all willing to put their lives on the line to do it. But then I convinced them otherwise. I showed them what they were missing. Shortly afterwards, they were begging at my feet.'

'You're offering me a job?' Jake asked.

It was at that moment that he became aware of the distant dripping sound in one of the four corners of the warehouse again.

Drip. Drip. Drip. Drip.

'It's not a job, Jake. It's a career.'

Candy ignited the lighter again then hovered the palm of his other hand over the flame, warming his skin.

'The police force is a joke. From the low levels – the PCs who think they can abuse their powers to rape innocent women and assault criminals – to the high levels like me. It's all corrupt, like a disease. And now it's ingrained in the fabric of our identity. To be a police officer means to be bent. There is no honour amongst us anymore, Jake. And only when you open your eyes will you realise that.

'Nobody respects us. Nobody appreciates the work we do. Society has been conditioned to think we're the bad guys. That we're all racist, homophobic, sexist. Everyone thinks we're out to get them. But if they didn't commit crimes in the fucking first place, we wouldn't need to. Nobody knows the difference between right and wrong anymore. Everyone's out for themselves.

'You're dispensable. You can be replaced. Any one of us can. They won't have to look far to find someone just as eager as you, someone who was sold the same pipe dream as you were when you signed up. You're nothing more than a number.'

'But the same rules don't apply to you?' Jake asked.

'It takes a wise man to recognise a wise man, Jake. You know what I'm saying has some element of truth to it.' Candy lowered the hand holding the lighter. 'I've known about you for a long time. And I've watched you pick my empire apart, one officer at a time. I suppose you're wondering why I haven't killed you already?'

Because your stepbrother had something to do with it.

'First you offer me a job and now you're flirting with me?'

Candy chuckled but fought to suppress the smile that etched its way onto his face. 'You're a ballsy little gobshite, aren't you?'

He took a step closer, slowly reducing the gap between the two of them. 'And that was one of the things I admired about you. But do you want to know the biggest reason?

You highlighted flaws in the system, weaknesses in the infrastructure I'd worked so hard to build. The people working for me were beginning to get lazy, complacent. Prone to making mistakes. You exposed those and they suffered consequences as a result. You told me that I needed to dispose of them without even realising it, even when it came to some of the people I was particularly fond of—'

'But you couldn't do it for Elliot, could you? Not your own family.'

Drip. Drip. Drip. Drip.

Jake had been hoping to invoke a reaction. Perhaps a flicker of the eyebrow, dilation of the pupils, or even a little gasp. But there was nothing. Candy's face remained still, impassive, unfazed.

He stepped closer. Now he started to juggle the lighter in both his hands.

'Elliott's an exception to the rule. You'd do the same if it came to family and love.' He pointed at Stephanie. 'I mean, look why you're here.'

'Let her go,' Jake said.

Drip. Drip. Drip. Drip.

Like the ticking of a clock.

'You know I can't do that. Both of you are going to have to die. Unless, of course, you accept my proposition.'

Just as Jake was about to open his mouth, Candy clicked his fingers. Before the sound had finished reverberating around the walls, three figures appeared from the corners of the room. Out of the shadows. Out of the darkness. Like grim reapers in the night.

Each of them carried a handgun by their thigh. They slowly made their way into the centre of the space, and as they neared him, Jake discerned their features more easily. The three of them fanned themselves out behind Candy.

One of them stood on the left behind Stephanie, the second just behind Candy's left shoulder, and the third on the right, encircling Jake.

Three hundred and sixty degrees of darkness.

Three hundred and sixty degrees of danger.

As soon as they came to a stop, Jake observed their faces.

He recognised them all.

The man on the left was Dimitri. The bald head. The deep-set eyes.

The man by Candy's shoulder was the same man with the gun who'd pursued him at Archie Arnold's house. The Driver.

The final man was Baseball Bat from the nail salon. Jake would recognise the fury and anger in those eyes anywhere. The small shoulders and thin torso that belied the man's strength. The powerful legs that enabled him to sprint away quickly.

'I'm sure you recognise a few of my colleagues,' Candy said.

Jake shrugged, nonchalant. 'Our paths have crossed.'

'And I hope this isn't the last time they do either. But you need to understand, Jake, that this is a predicament for me. These people would like to hurt you; they'd like to hurt you a lot, maybe even kill you, but I want you to join me. Obviously, if you say no, then I won't have a choice but to shoot you and Stephanie here.'

'I thought you said you needed me?'

Candy shrugged. 'It would be nice. But you've already highlighted the expensive flaws in my business strategies, and these guys are going to fix them. I used to think that you needed brains to get the job done, but most of the time you just need brawn.'

'You do realise that… these… No… Forget about it.'

Candy took another step forward. 'If you've got something to say…'

Drip. Drip. Drip. Drip.

He was regretting having ever said anything now.

'Noth—'

In an instant, Baseball Bat pointed his gun at Jake, staring menacingly over the barrel.

Jake's heart started palpitating and his breathing intensified. He raised his hands in surrender.

'Speak,' Candy ordered.

'Listen, I don't want any—'

Baseball Bat cocked the trigger.

Jake swallowed.

'Twenty-Nine.'

At the mention of her name, Candy's wicked eyes widened. 'What about her?'

'I lied on the phone. She's alive. Dimitri will attest to that… You harvested her kidney, didn't you?'

Drip. Drip. Drip. Drip.

Candy shrugged again. 'It's a hundred and fifty-billion-pound industry. But what's that got to do with these guys?'

Tick. Tock. Tick. Tock.

With each passing second, they were closing in on him, suffocating their avenues of escape. Out the corner of his eye, he glimpsed Stephanie's shoulders and arms wriggling.

'Dimitri…' Jake swallowed daggers, the air drying out his throat. 'He gave her some money. A hundred quid. Something that might help her if she ever tried to escape.'

'I know he did,' Candy responded. 'I was the one who gave it back to her.'

'What?' This came from Dimitri, who was unable to hide the surprise in his voice.

'I'm not stupid,' Candy said. 'I know what you did. I know you tried to help her. And that was your third strike. I sent you into that hospital hoping you wouldn't come out again. But now, here you are. Ready to die like the rest of them.'

Before anyone had a chance to comprehend what was happening, Baseball Bat swept his extended arm ninety degrees and fired the trigger. A spark erupted from the end of the gun, illuminating the entire warehouse and the plume of blood and brain matter that blasted from the back of Dimitri's head. His body slumped to the floor and the gun in his hand clattered on the concrete. He was dead before he hit the ground.

The dripping stopped.

The ticking stopped.

But the ringing in his ears had only just begun.

Jake's body turned rigid. Beside him, Stephanie cowered, her screams stifled behind the gag in her mouth.

After a few seconds, his senses gradually returned. And then they were consumed again. By the pressure in his head. By the rapid rise and fall of his chest. By the hyper-ventilating, the air sucking out of his lungs. By the world becoming darker and darker.

Jake tried to block out everything around him and focus on his breathing. In. Out. In. Out. Until he fought the panic attack into submission.

Now he was fully aware of where he was, who was around him, and what had just happened. In the instant that he'd zoned out, however, the third man had charged towards Stephanie, his gun raised in the air. He brought the butt down on her face, lacerating her cheekbone, and she whimpered and buckled under the attack.

Jake lunged at him, but he was immediately stopped by

Baseball Bat, who pointed his recently discharged firearm at Jake's face again.

'Will everyone just calm the fuck down?' Candy bellowed, his voice commanding the attention of everyone in the warehouse.

Jake felt compelled to stop, and almost instantly afterwards, everything settled down. Stephanie's cries turned into soft whimpers. The Driver stopped shouting and retreated a few paces. And Jake's heart rate reduced.

Candy cleared his throat before continuing. 'You see, Jake, it goes back to my earlier point. Weak links in the machine. You point them out for me. You have the power to be a strong link sitting at the top of my many paper houses. And... well, I'm hiring.'

Jake glanced at the floor. Only Dimitri's feet were visible behind Stephanie – and the puddle of blood that was spreading around his body.

'You killed... He died because of me...' Jake started, shock beginning to sink in and bile rising from his stomach.

He tried to suppress it but it became too strong for him and he vomited onto the concrete, bile and clumps of food splashing onto his feet. Wiping his mouth with the back of his sleeve, he returned his attention to Candy.

'Better?' the man asked.

For the first time, Jake heard a hint of humanity in his voice. For a moment, it sounded as though he genuinely cared.

'I'm fine,' Jake replied. 'Please... just... just let us go. We don't want anything to do with this. You have our word. We won't—'

Jake was distracted by the sound of a door creaking open. Light flooded in from the far-right corner of the room and the atmosphere turned silent. The Driver and Baseball

Bat pivoted on the spot, flexing their weapons in the direction of the intruder.

But as they stepped closer towards the figure, Candy held out his hand and said, 'It's fine. Stand down.' Then he turned around and addressed the figure. 'I was wondering if you'd join us.'

Jake peered over Candy's shoulder, hazarding a glance at who it was.

'We never were good with family reunions,' the intruder replied.

Bridger.

'It's time to stop all of this, Dick.'

As Bridger's voice drew nearer, Stephanie squirmed and shook her head from side to side, almost as if she was trying to get his attention. Before Jake was able to move, Stephanie loosened the rope around her wrists, freed her hands and pulled the gag from her mouth. Then she undid the knots around her feet, leapt up and grabbed The Driver from behind. In one smooth swoop, she disarmed him, then locked her arm around his neck, incapacitating him. He attempted to fight her off, but he was no match for her, and as soon as she pressed the gun to his temple, he realised it.

The commotion alerted Candy and Baseball Bat, who turned to face Stephanie. Pieces of spittle and phlegm expelled from her mouth as she breathed heavily, almost demonically.

'Put the gun down!' she hissed at Baseball Bat. 'Put the gun down now!'

'You don't want to do this, Stephanie,' Candy said, taking a step nearer.

As he did so, Stephanie swung the gun at him, bouncing it between all three men.

'You don't look very confident with one of those in your

hand. Look at you, you're shaking. Think of your dad. What would he say about all of this? Why don't you just give it to me, and then we can deal with this in a more civilised manner?'

'No,' she spat. Turned to Jake. 'Call it in. Get the entire fucking army down here now.'

Backup.

The one word that tightened the noose around Candy's neck more than anything. And Jake wanted to be the one to cut off the air supply.

But as he reached into his blazer pocket, Candy called, 'I wouldn't do that if I were you. If your hand goes any further into your pocket, Fabian is going to shoot you just as easily as he did Dimitri.'

Fabian. A name to the face. Jake preferred Baseball Bat.

He hesitated, waited, watched.

Meanwhile, in the background of the conversation, Bridger inched forward, closing the gap between them, creeping along the floor silently. It wasn't until he was a few feet away that everything kicked off.

In a flash, Bridger leapt onto Fabian's back, knocking the gun to the floor. He wrapped his arms around the man's neck and his legs around his body, locking him in a choke-hold. Fabian collapsed to the ground, landing softly on Bridger.

To Jake's left, The Driver elbowed Stephanie in the stomach. She lost her grip on his neck, and he threw her to the ground. Then he lunged at her and they tussled for the weapon.

Jake prepared himself to charge at them, but by that point, it was too late. The gun had been fired. The bullet had gone off.

'Stephanie!' he screamed, hurrying over to her.

By the time he reached her, The Driver had rolled off her and onto the concrete, a flower of red rapidly spreading across his chest, blood and spittle foaming in his mouth. His fingers searched his body for the bullet hole. 'Please...' he whispered, his words muffled behind the contents of his mouth. 'Please...'

Jake paid the man little heed and lifted Stephanie to her feet. She dropped the gun to the floor. Her body was rigid, stiff.

To the right, Bridger and Fabian continued to wrestle, each fighting for their lives. Fabian had broken free of the chokehold and was repeatedly punching Bridger's face, colliding with his teeth, chin, cheeks and eyes.

As Jake helped Stephanie stand, Candy came into view once more. In his hand, he held the lighter. Saying nothing, he crouched down to the concrete and hovered it over a puddle. The liquid sparked and caught aflame, swallowing the chair in a ball of fire in a matter of seconds. Then Candy turned on the spot and bolted.

Jake's eyes were transfixed on the beauty of the dancing flames, battling one another for oxygen and fuel.

'Jake!' Stephanie screamed in his ear. 'Jake!'

His gaze darted to her.

'The fire! I'm covered in petrol!'

And so were his feet.

Together they started towards the exit. By now the blaze had engulfed the chair and spread across the floor to Dimitri and The Driver, consuming their lifeless bodies. The smell of burning fuel and charred flesh soon filled Jake's nostrils.

Have you ever heard of benzene, Jake?

Highly flammable.

Highly dangerous.

'Elliot!' he called, hurrying to the man's side before the flames reached them both.

'Get out of here!' Bridger yelled. He was straddling Fabian, beating him to a pulp, pounding his head against the concrete. 'Get Stephanie out of here!'

'You're going to—'

'Jake!' a voice bellowed above all other noise in the warehouse. It was Candy. He was standing in the doorway with a gun in his hand. In front of him was Stephanie, the weapon pressed against her head. Wrapped in his arms, she looked as though she'd ceased resisting, as if she'd lost all fight, as if she knew that Candy would blow her skull open if she decided to force her way out of his grip.

Jake quickly glanced at the space where Fabian had been standing. Candy was holding the man's gun, the one Bridger had knocked to the floor.

'It's over, my little candiru!' he called over the roar of the fire. And then, just like that, he slipped out of the warehouse and disappeared.

Jake didn't think twice. He bolted after him.

A line of fire split the building in two, and the rampaging flames spread rapidly, jumping from puddle to puddle. In the short time that the fire had been blazing, it had consumed nearly half the space. Already the entire warehouse was consumed with smoke, filling Jake's lungs and blocking his vision.

Hand over his mouth, Jake leapt over a burning puddle of fuel and sprinted towards the door. But as he approached, his feet caught on something and he tripped, clattering to the ground. The decrepit surface lacerated the skin on his palms, and his front quickly became sodden. Droplets of fuel matted his hair and ran down his face. He ignored the burning sensation in his hands and clambered to his feet.

Breaching into the open, he skidded on the gravel, panting, exasperated, gasping for breath. And shaking uncontrollably with adrenaline.

In the distance, to his left, he saw Candy and Stephanie climbing a flight of metal steps to the top of the structure. Stephanie's screams echoed in the distance.

Before Jake did anything else, he removed his phone and called 999.

Without giving the call handler any time to respond, he barked, 'This is DC Tanner. I'm at Candy Cleaning Services in Coldharbour. Shots fired, two fatalities and a hostage situation. Requesting immediate armed and uniformed support!'

'They're already on their way, sir,' the male handler replied calmly.

Jake rang off and started up the steps. His legs pumped higher and higher, breath coming harder and harder. His mind fought off any incipient fatigue and he continued regardless, vaulting the steps two at a time until he reached the top.

The roof of the structure was slanted and looked like a small rectangular pyramid. Patches of rust scorched the metal, and a walkway ran around the perimeter. Jake sprinted along the longest side of the building, then the shortest, and when he came to the longest on the opposite side, he slowed.

Stephanie and Candy were ahead of him, tussling with one another. He'd caught up with them. And now there was nowhere for them to go.

'Richard!' Jake yelled, tentatively stepping closer towards them, hands raised in the air. 'Richard, stop this.'

'It's too late for that,' he replied, coming to a halt. One arm was wrapped around Stephanie's neck, and the other was pressed into her lower back, forcing her to stand awkwardly. 'You know how this is going to end – how it has to end.'

'You deserve to go to prison for a long time. I'm not going to deny that.' Ten feet separated them now. Jake came to a slow stop. 'Nobody else needs to die.'

'Not unless you get me out of here.'

'I can't do that, Richard.'

In the distance, the high-pitched cry of police sirens wailed. Jake's mind turned to Bridger. He must have called them before he arrived, before he'd turned up out of nowhere and saved them both, before he'd—

Gunshots sounded around the warehouse, bullets ricocheting and pinging off the metal. Jake flinched. To his right, plumes of thick black smoke erupted through the holes in the roof and rippled in the air.

'You were saying, Jake? Nobody else has to die?'

'You can stop this, Richard.' Jake snapped his head back to the criminal overlord. 'Turn yourself in. We already have everything against you. The emails, the messages, the conversations you've had with your various colleagues. Liam, Martin, Helen, Rupert, Danny, Michael, Stephanie – the list goes on. We've got it all locked up in a storage unit. You can put an end to this if you just lower the gun.'

'You're more resourceful than I gave you credit for.' Candy's head moved from left to right as he canvassed the horizon.

Beyond the side of the building was a small alleyway. Piles of rubbish were stacked atop one another. The smell of decay wafted in the air and overpowered Jake's senses. Behind Candy, over his right shoulder, Jake noticed a set of fire-escape stairs. Vertical. Perilous. Ancient. They looked as though they hadn't been used in years. Covered in rust and graffiti.

'Come on, Richard,' Jake said, bringing the man's attention back to the present. 'Let Stephanie go and we can put a stop to this.'

Jake took another step forward. In retaliation, Candy strangled her with his arm. She yelped and clawed at him but it was no use.

'You need to learn boundaries, Jake. If you step any closer I'll throw her over the edge.'

'If you wanted to do that, you would have done it already.'

'Tempting fate is a dangerous thing.'

He knew he was playing with Stephanie's life, but he had every faith in his capabilities to save her. The only problem was working out how to do it. There were so many factors at play, so many variables. And there was no way he was able to anticipate what Candy might do next. The man had shown, throughout his career as one of the force's most corrupt and detestable officers, that he was a volatile and dangerous man, capable of anything.

The police sirens grew louder.

'They're on their way, Richard. They'll be here soon. You've been in this business long enough to know it's game over.'

'Unless I kill myself.'

'Nobody wants that,' Jake said, taking another step forward.

Because that was a coward's way out. Because that wouldn't count towards Jake's career of successful cases.

A few feet separated them.

'This won't go away, Jake. It will always be around.

There will always be someone to step into my position. You wait. And there will be nothing you can do until you find The Cabal.'

What?

Jake opened his mouth but nothing came out, save for a small cough that expelled from his lungs. Before he was able to react, Candy pushed Stephanie forward. Her body collapsed onto the metal walkway like a rag doll, her limbs flailing in the air. Then Candy vaulted the railing and disappeared down the vertical steps.

'Richard!' Jake called after him, rushing to Stephanie's side. He hooked his arm underneath her and hefted her to her feet.

By the time Jake reached the steps, Candy was nearly halfway down. But there was still a long way to go – a thirty-foot drop separated him from the bottom. Jake lifted himself over the ledge and planted his foot firmly on the first step.

One down.

Fifty more to go.

Then he started. Tentatively at first, cautiously, lest he—

A scream pierced the air. From Stephanie. Instinctively, Jake glanced down at Candy. The man had lost his footing and got his ankle trapped in the gap between the steps, his body upside down.

'Hold on! I'm coming,' Jake called.

He made it two steps closer, and then he saw it.

In slow motion.

Looking up at him with those wide eyes, Richard Candy wriggled his foot free from the step and plummeted to the ground, his dense body somersaulting through the air until he landed on his head.

The sound of his neck snapping cracked the air around him.

Tick… tock.

The ticking had stopped.

It was over.

Richard Candy wasn't moving.

Richard Candy was dead.

Chapter Eighty-Three

CROSSFIRE

But it wasn't over yet.

'Listen to me,' Jake said, grappling a despondent and disconsolate Stephanie by the shoulders with both hands. 'This is important. I need you to wait here while I find Elliot. Can you do that?'

Stephanie's hand moved to her mouth. She wiped her nose and rubbed away the tears streaming down her cheeks. 'Come back… please.'

Jake said nothing more and set off around the side of the building. Smoke continued to pour out of the small hole in the roof like a volcano, rapidly forming a thick black cloud around him, filling his lungs with toxic fumes. As he rounded the final corner of the building, he became worried. He'd heard nothing from inside the warehouse following the gunshots. It didn't even cross his mind that Fabian could be hunting them down, chasing them.

In his mind, Baseball Bat was dead.

When he reached the stairs, Jake lunged down the steps two at a time, using the railing for support. At the bottom, he sprinted towards the building's entrance and made it as far as the door frame before he slid to a stop. A dense wall of black smoke exploded through the annexe at the bottom of the L.

Throwing his arm over his mouth and holding his breath, Jake moved deeper into the outhouse. The smoke blinded him, clouding his vision. He bumped into the octopus machine, bruising his shoulder, but carried on regardless.

The atmosphere, temperature and air pressure intensified as he neared the door to the main warehouse. A furnace of orange and red and yellow and black blazed in the centre of the warehouse, flames climbing the wall in a furious attempt to escape. Jake opened his eyes and searched for Bridger. But it was no use. He saw nothing, not even the chair Stephanie had been tied to. The smoke and heat were so overwhelming they stung his eyes and the back of his throat.

Have you ever heard of benzene, Jake?

'Jake!' Stephanie screamed. He hadn't realised it, but she'd followed him down and into the building. She coughed violently and protected her mouth with her hand. Using the other, she grabbed his arm and pulled him out of there. To his surprise, he offered little resistance.

Whenever he'd seen a fictitious character bravely entering a burning building on a TV show or in a film, he'd always envisaged himself doing the same. Coming to the rescue, risking his life, saving others, emerging a hero. But life wasn't like the movies. The reality of the situation was that it was far too dangerous to comprehend. Which meant he wasn't as brave as he'd thought. Besides, he had a family to think about – what was left of it. And he needed to put them first.

If Bridger was still alive, he would have left the warehouse by now.

If not, he was as good as dead.

The two of them breached into the open, escaping the fire's clutches. Jake hurried away from the warehouse and bent double, placing his hands on his knees, coughing and spewing until his body and chest hurt. The rapid expulsion of air from his lungs made him light-headed, and he swayed from side to side. Spitting a ball of phlegm onto the ground, he stood straight and arched his back, opening his chest and filling his lungs with clean oxygen. Inhaling and exhaling deeply, slowly, smoothly.

'Are you OK?' Stephanie asked, placing a soft hand against his back.

He turned to face her. Her skin was blackened by the smoke, covering her tears and bruises. Over her shoulder, Jake glanced at his car. Beyond it was an entourage of police vehicles bombing towards them.

'You didn't kill anyone,' he said, staring into her eyes; her expression was lost, broken. 'You didn't shoot anyone. Any gunshot residue is from the other people in there. They shot each other, and you got caught in the crossfire. Do you understand?'

Stephanie's eyes glazed over.

'*Do you understand?*' Jake insisted, shaking her to attention. 'You didn't kill anyone. And you don't know who did. Stephanie, I need you to nod if you understand what I'm saying.'

The police cars skidded to a halt and a group of uniformed officers hurried over to them, barking orders into their radios, requesting more fire support and paramedics.

Jake glanced back at Stephanie. She never gave him a response.

Chapter Eighty-Four

BABY STEPS

Jake awoke in an empty bed, rolled over into the middle and traced his hands through the dip in the mattress where Elizabeth lay every night. When he'd got home, past midnight, he'd arrived to an empty house. No note, no food in the fridge. If it were under any other circumstance, he would have called and tried to reason with her, find out where she was and convince her to return. But this wasn't any usual circumstance. He was exhausted – physically, mentally and emotionally.

Following the incident, the paramedics had given him the once-over, made sure his lungs were healthy and in a good enough condition for him to carry on with his day, and then he'd been subjected to the mundanity of filling out witness reports, post-incident reports and just about every report there was.

And now he was paying the price for it.

His muscles were sorely fatigued, and each movement caused him considerable pain. Especially in his legs.

He rolled himself back to his side of the bed and

glanced at his phone through sleep-filled eyes. No notifications. No missed calls. No messages.

He checked the time – 8:42 a.m. The latest he'd slept in for years.

At first, sleep had eluded him, his mind plagued with thoughts of Candy, Stephanie, and Bridger. Running on repeat, and repeat, and repeat. But then as time wore on, his body gradually began to switch off and envelop him in the darkness.

The darkness of the warehouse.

Filled with fire and black and—

Jake grunted and groaned as he manoeuvred his legs off the side of the bed and shuffled to the bathroom.

After an intense and gruelling battle lasting several hours, the fire service had managed to extinguish the blaze. Shortly after that, they'd confirmed that four individuals had perished. Bridger, Fabian, Dimitri and The Driver. The news had made Jake sick, and thinking about it now was enough to spin his stomach upside down. Bridger had given his life for Jake and Stephanie. He'd sacrificed himself so that Jake could put a stop to The Cabal.

Which Jake had done. But it had come at a cost.

Stephanie.

Jake placed his palms on the basin and hung his head low.

Stephanie had shot someone. She'd killed in the line of duty, as an act of self-defence. But was it though? Jake wasn't sure. His mind was a blur. The actions surrounding that particular instant were a blur. And the more he thought about it, the more he wasn't sure whether he'd done the right thing in protecting her.

No, of course he had. It *had* been self-defence. She'd done it to protect both of them. Without her pulling that trigger, neither of them would have survived. That made it two for two, Stephanie and Bridger coming to the rescue, leaving Jake on the sidelines as an innocent bystander.

A coward, not willing to risk his life for others.

To stop his exhausting thoughts, he justified it to himself. Both Stephanie and Bridger owed him one. They'd threatened to destroy his career and had lied to him. It was only fair they make amends somehow.

By taking a life and sacrificing their own.

That was some debt.

Jake ran the tap and washed his face, the cold water shocking him awake. He dabbed his cheeks and eyes with a towel and returned to the bedroom.

The atmosphere was profoundly silent. It was unsettling, unnerving and set the hairs on his arms on end. Strange. He didn't like it. He'd grown so accustomed to the constant noise – shouting and laughter and crying and TV programmes and films and animated doll's voices – in the past few years that it made him feel as though he was a stranger in his own home.

Then his mobile rang, vibrating on the bedside table.

Jake snatched it and answered.

'Hello?' he asked, praying that the unknown number was somehow Elizabeth.

'It's me.'

Jake hesitated and tried to hide the discontent in his voice. 'How… how are you feeling?'

'Tired. In pain. Everywhere hurts. I haven't stopped coughing. And I hardly got any sleep.'

'Same,' Jake said and perched himself on the side of the bed. He ran his finger through his stubble and scratched the scar on the side of his jaw.

An awkward silence passed between the two of them.

Jake didn't know what to say, where to begin. And so he waited.

Until, eventually, she began to speak again.

'Listen... I've been thinking. I've been doing a lot of it lately, and... I've got some explaining to do. I just wanted to say I'm sorry for what happened in the hotel. I should never have done that to you. I should never have let it get that far. You have a wife and kids, a family, and I don't want to be the one to step in the way of that. I haven't been able to stop thinking about it since it happened. I'll understand if you can't ever forgive me. Christ only knows I wouldn't be able to if I were in your position, or even Elizabeth's.'

Stephanie hesitated. Jake took a moment to respond, to clear his thoughts.

'I'll pay back the money for the room and getting me back to London,' he said after a while. He hoped that his response would lighten the mood, but it was so dark and gloomy, he didn't see that happening.

'If you're going to give it to me in cash, then you'll have to do it quickly.'

'Why?'

'Because I'm leaving, Jake...' she said slowly. 'I've just handed in my notice. After everything that's happened – both at work and in my personal life – I think it's for the best if I fuck off and leave everyone alone.'

Jake was shocked but couldn't say he was surprised. He knew that as soon as Elizabeth found out about what had happened between the two of them, she would give him an ultimatum. Either Jake left the team or she did. And Stephanie had just made that decision a little easier for him.

'Steph... I don't know what to say.'

'Respect my wishes, that would be a start. I've been

thinking about this for a long time. Yesterday was just the catalyst.'

'What are you going to do?'

'I don't know. My dad doesn't need me anymore, and I don't need him. Leaving me free to do whatever I want. Maybe travel for a bit. Go and see some things. Learn new things. Experience a bit of culture. Or I'll find myself a new job. I don't know, but I think that makes it more exciting.'

'You're excited to be leaving?'

'Don't twist my words, Jake. I'm excited about the fact I don't have to live my life in fear of danger anymore. Working for the IPCC was much calmer than MIT, and you know it.'

'Well, we've lost an exceptional officer. You'll be sadly missed.' And he meant it.

He paused a beat to swallow. 'When's your last day?'

'I'm hanging around till the Matheson trial.'

Shit. The trial.

'That's today!' he said, thinking aloud.

'Relax,' Stephanie replied, her voice soothing him instantly. 'It got pushed back a week. Didn't you hear?'

'Hear what?'

'Matheson was attacked in his cell yesterday. Stabbed, beaten and had a bucket of napalm thrown in his face. He's currently in hospital. But I'm hanging around until the trial's over – that was my stipulation with Darryl. Seeing it through to the end. So it looks like you've got to put up with me for a couple more days, maybe even a week or so.'

A smile grew on Jake's face. 'I can deal with—'

The front door opened downstairs, disturbing the still air around him.

Panicked, Jake whispered into the phone, 'Sorry, Steph. I've got to go. But I'll speak to you soon, all right?'

He rang off before Stephanie responded, threw the phone onto the bed and bounded down the stairs in his boxer shorts, jumping them two at a time.

'Hey,' Jake said, smiling weakly.

'Hey.'

Elizabeth's hair was in a ponytail, and she was dressed in her favourite outfit: a double denim ensemble of jacket and jeans. Out of all the people he knew, she was the only one capable of pulling it off so elegantly. And that wasn't a biased opinion.

She gently shut the door behind her. 'I'm not here for long.'

'Where have you been? I've been worried.'

'Not worried enough to call?'

'I…' They both knew it was no excuse before he said it. 'A lot's been happening. Serious stuff – stuff I'll tell you all about – but I should have been there for you. And I neglected you.'

She dropped her head, sniffled. 'There's some food for you in the fridge. Unless it's gone off by now.'

Even when she hated him, she was still looking out for him.

Sensing the tears were marching forward, he moved closer. 'That's fine. I'll still eat it. Least I deserve.' Another step. 'Everything's going to be fine, all right? Everything's going to be OK. We're going to get through this.'

Jake reached out and touched her arm.

At first she flinched and retreated, but then, as he moved closer, she stopped. The dams in her eyes burst and sent torrents of tears streaming down her face. She blubbered and sobbed into his chest, submitting herself to his protection.

'I know you miss him,' Jake said. 'I know you're hurting.

But I'm here for you. And I'm not going anywhere any time soon.'

The Cabal was dead.

There was nothing left to worry about.

Jake massaged her shoulders, kissed her forehead and ran his fingers through her soft hair. Her sobs were muffled by their proximity. The closest they'd been in days, closest they'd felt in weeks.

The torment and misery of the past several months – years, even – disappeared in one hug.

Gone but not forgotten, however.

It would take some time to heal, Jake was aware. No overnight fixes. But right now he wasn't worried about that; he was focused on being in the present, on having his wife back, no matter how briefly.

'I love you,' he whispered.

'I love you,' came the muffled response. She pushed him away, sniffled some more and wiped her nose. 'But I need… I need a few days. I'm sorry. I need to process.'

'For how long?'

'As long as it takes. I need to be there for Mum right now.'

'I understand.'

'You can still see the girls. I won't stop you.'

Baby steps, he told himself. Baby steps.

Jake nodded and kissed her forehead. 'I'm not going anywhere,' he replied. 'Whenever you're ready to come back, I'll be waiting. You're the best thing that's happened to me, Liz. Take all the time you need.'

Chapter Eighty-Five

CROSSING PATHS

The rainfall reflected the mood and the solemnity of the day.

'I didn't think we'd be at this age until we were in our sixties,' Jake said.

'What age?'

'The age where the only time you see people and old friends is at funerals.'

Jake's second in less than a week. He'd received several notes reminding him of the details for Richard Candy's funeral but had ignored them all. For some reason, the organisers had coincided Candy's with Bridger's. To Jake, the choice was obvious: the better brother deserved his respect tenfold.

It wasn't even a competition.

'You should be grateful we're not burying you,' Elizabeth replied. She'd taken time out of planning her father's funeral to be with him, to support him. And he loved her for it.

In the intervening days, they'd spent their evenings,

once the kids were in bed, discussing their marriage, their mistakes, their faults. It was open and honest. And it was also the first time Jake had shared everything with her.

Everything.

Right from the very beginning. Liam, Drew, Pete and the drug money he'd unknowingly accepted. Henry Matheson and their conversation on the river. The parcels that had been addressed to their house. The parcels and photos that had threatened to ruin his career. The investigation into his professionalism. The kiss he'd shared with Stephanie in the hotel.

Out of them all, not unsurprisingly, the last one was the hardest for Elizabeth to take. The biggest betrayal.

It was, she'd told him, the wound that would take the longest time to heal.

Which was fine with him; the fact she wanted to stay and work things out was the biggest miracle. Her love for him ran deeper than the hurt he'd caused her.

They came to a gradual stop by the car. Jake placed his hand on the handle and gazed out at the car park; at the few people leaving the procession. Less than ten had been there, many of whom Jake recognised from Surrey Police's headquarters in Guildford, including Nicki Pemberton, who'd come over to Jake privately and thanked him for his help on the lorry container deaths. Thanks to the information he'd provided from Bridger's lock-up, each of the bodies had been identified and were in the process of being returned to their respective home countries, where they could be reunited with their families and given the funerals they deserved.

'It wasn't me,' Jake had told Pemberton. 'Bridger did most of the work. I'm just alive to share it.'

To continue his memory.

To make sure people remembered the hero that he was, in the end.

As Jake readied himself to enter his car, something caught his eye. A woman, tall, dressed in black – no, not quite black but a dark navy blue. A touch outside the dress code. Which meant she was either purposely doing it or she'd had no intention of attending the funeral in the first place.

Her hair was tied in a bun, and she wore a set of black sunglasses over her eyes, despite the rain and metal sky, making her look like a Disney villain.

But it was the bag resting on the top of her roof, getting sodden and wet, that Jake recognised.

'I'll be back in a second,' he told Elizabeth as he leant into the car.

'Everything all right?'

'I think so…'

Jake allayed her fear with a smile then hurried over to the other side of the car park.

'I didn't know you were a friend of Elliot's,' Jake began but then realised that, in the wider scheme of things, she probably was.

Veronica Bateman was one of Rupert Haversham's closest legal partners. The two had worked together with The Cabal to represent one Henry Matheson. Wherever The Cabal went, Rupert and Veronica followed, which meant her and Bridger's paths had crossed at least once.

'Funerals depress me,' she said. 'I prefer to honour people I knew in my own way.'

'I can only imagine how,' Jake replied.

Neither was willing to show their hand first.

'Was it a good send-off?'

'As good as any, I suppose. If you didn't come here for the funeral, are you lost? Do you need directions?'

Veronica stared at him unimpressed. Then she reached into her bag, and for a moment Jake thought she was going to pull out a gun. To finish the job off for Candy. Instead, she pulled out a small business card and handed it to him.

'I understand your wife's come into a bit of an issue with a photographer,' Veronica stared, her voice devoid of emotion. 'I've spoken with Rupert and explained the situation, so he's fully aware. He's just awaiting your call.'

How she could have known that Jake didn't know. He didn't want to think

Jake took the card and surveyed it. 'What am I supposed to do with this?'

As Veronica took her bag from the roof, she said, 'If you love your wife then you'll get her the best cover possible. And from what I hear, this one's on the house.'

'Why?'

'You'll have to ask him when you speak to him.'

'So I can incriminate myself down the line?'

'You were there when it happened, Jake, The Cabal's dead; he's not coming back.'

'So we just go back to our lives like nothing happened?'

Veronica opened the car door and climbed in. 'That's usually what happens at the end of these things, yeah.' And then she closed the door, started the engine and pulled away, leaving him behind in the rain.

Pocketing the card, he sauntered back to his Mini feeling a combination of shock and confusion.

As he climbed into the driver's seat, Elizabeth asked, 'Everything all right?'

He looked up at her. Smiled.

'Not right now, but I've got a feeling it will be.'

Chapter Eighty-Six

JUDGEMENT DAY

Judgement day.

The day that he, and the rest of the policing community – including those who had fought to prosecute him in the past – had been waiting for a long time

The day of Henry Matheson's trial.

Jake was standing in front of the bathroom mirrors at Stratford Crown Court, preparing himself. He washed his hands, splashed water on his face and dried it with a handful of napkins, tucked his shirt in so that it was flush against his body and adjusted his tie until the knot was pinned to the collar. Then he turned his back on the mirror and exited the bathroom.

The corridor he entered ran the length of the entire building, stretching as far as he could see in both directions. Immediately in front of him was the court's entrance. Darryl, dressed in his full police uniform, was addressing the media. Unsurprisingly, the case had drummed up a wealth of interest.

'You were in there a long time,' Stephanie said, joining his side from nowhere. 'Just in time. We're about to start.'

She was dressed smartly in a suit and her hair hung behind her ears, pinned to her skull by a clip. Her face beamed with a smile, the first he'd seen for a while.

'You're unusually excitable,' he replied as they entered the courtroom.

'Once this is done, I'm out.'

'You're still going through with it?'

'Too late now. Everything's booked. First stop Morocco. Then the rest of the world.'

Jake opened his mouth to speak, but something in the distance caught his eye. A woman Jake recognised instantly had just entered the room from another door. She wore a navy-blue blazer with matching trousers and a sky-blue blouse.

Veronica Bateman.

I've spoken with Rupert… He's just awaiting your call.

He and Stephanie found their seats and waited for the session to begin. As the bodies slowly started filtering into the room, Jake's nerves multiplied, the aches in his stomach intensified and the sweat on his back increased.

'Nervous?' Stephanie asked.

'That's one word for it.'

Jake had never been asked to appear in court for any of his cases before. But this enquiry was an exception to the rule. And it was safe to say he was shitting it. The mess he'd left in the toilet not too long ago was testament to that fact. He'd practised his answers to questions that would undoubtedly come his way in an attempt to discredit and confuse his statement countless times. He'd even gone to the extreme length of already imagining the courtroom naked to help settle his nerves.

Everyone except Stephanie.

A few minutes after everyone in the room was seated, the court began, and the defence and prosecution started the process of arguing, debating, convincing, discrediting.

When it was finally his turn to speak, he rose from his seat and made his way to the stand, keeping his head high and acknowledging every member of the jury. After everyone in the previous selection pool had been bribed, a new one had been put together, so none of the jurors drawn had had any contact with Henry, Williamson, or anyone else on Henry's books.

At the stand, Jake took his place and surveyed the courtroom. Beside him, to his immediate right, was the judge. To his left, the jury. Then he moved his gaze around the room. At the defence desks, at Veronica and her team, at the crowd at the back of the room, at the small booth of journalists and news reporters, at Stephanie, Darryl, Brendan and Ashley at the back of the room, at the prosecution desk, at the Crown Prosecution worker who Jake had spoken to in the build-up to the case to discuss the likelihood of their success.

And then his eyes fell on Henry, sitting in his booth, surrounded by police officers.

Up until this point, Henry had been a blur, but now they were close to one another, Jake realised how badly broken and beaten the man was. His features were unrecognisable. His left arm was in a sling and his face was heavily bandaged, the bits of Henry's skin that Jake was able to see disfigured and distorted from the napalm attack. His right eye was swollen and bruised, and there were small lacerations on his mouth, the side of his head and his forearms. The man before him was completely different to the man he'd arrested.

But there was still the same fire in his eyes. The same fire that burnt with malevolent intent. Jake knew there was no getting rid of the threat that Henry Matheson posed to society, not unless he was in an isolation cell or buried six feet under. But so long as he was locked behind bars, that was a start.

A court clerk to his left distracted him. In her hand, she held a copy of the Bible. Jake placed his hand on it without needing to be told what to do.

He swallowed and cleared his throat before beginning.

'I, Jake Tanner, hereby swear to tell the truth, the whole truth and nothing but the truth.'

Epilogue

Jake and Elizabeth, in the privacy and seclusion of their own bedroom, discussed their marriage. Tentatively, they sorted things out, and she and the kids have now moved back in. They attended Alan Clarke's funeral as a family.

The jury deliberated for two hours before finding Henry Matheson guilty of two counts of murder, five counts of GBH, possession and supply of drugs, money laundering and perverting the course of justice. In total, he received a life sentence, with a minimum of fifty-one years in prison.

Brian Grayson's body was found in his cell shortly after Henry Matheson was ambushed. His death was ruled a suicide. Nobody from his family attended his funeral.

After the Matheson trial, Stephanie began a tour of the world, starting in Morocco. Her exact location is currently unknown, but she's looking forward to finding peace, happiness and maybe even a bit of love. Since her father's passing, she hasn't spoken to her sister, but she continues to maintain contact with Little Susie.

The day after the Matheson trial, Darryl and Jake

arranged a meeting to discuss their differences and settle their disagreements. They both believe the outcomes were positive, and are starting a new working relationship with one another. Neither of them, however, confessed to believing that the other was The Cabal.

Williamson was later found guilty of perverting the course of justice and bribing jury members. He was removed from the prison staff and faces a lengthy trial.

Martha and the entire Clarke family continue to mourn the loss of Alan, while simultaneously trying to recover financially from the money stolen from her and Alan's accounts by The Cabal. To cope with her grief, and to continue paying the bills, Martha has busied herself with her work.

Brendan Lafferty returned to work shortly after Henry Matheson's trial. He continues to struggle with his mental health following the discovery of Roland Lewandowski's body.

Following Jake's guidance, an investigation into Dale's Yard was launched, and CJ and his father were found to have committed money laundering on behalf of The Cabal. They are currently awaiting trial.

All identities of the forty individuals found dead in the back of the lorry container were revealed to the public. Their bodies were released to their respective countries, and all those involved in trafficking them into the country were caught and prosecuted.

Twenty-Nine, who was later identified as Melania Pirlot, was celebrated for her heroics in the discovery of The Cabal's identity. Jake and several others from the team attended the small funeral held for her before her body was repatriated. Meanwhile, the rest of the inhabitants at Atomic Nails were found and settled into various parts of the country, where they are protected from any outside threat.

Thanks to a warrant and the evidence gathered in Elliot Bridger's storage unit, Richard Candy was proved to be The Cabal...

Next in the DC Jake Tanner Crime Thriller Series

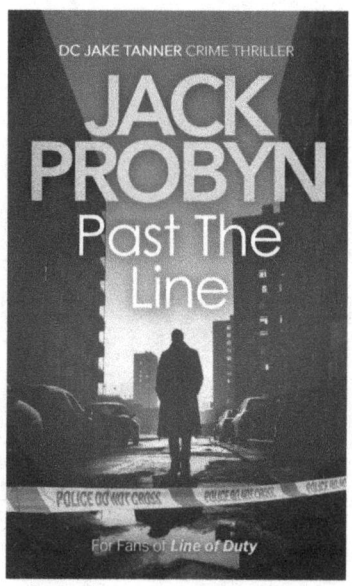

vinci-books.com/past-line

Sometimes the darkest evils hide in plain sight.

The Cabal is supposed to be dead—until a lawyer to London's underworld is brutally murdered. DC Jake Tanner realizes the empire still thrives, eliminating those who get too close. Jake must step outside the law and cross the line of duty to end this—once and for all.

Turn the page for a free preview…

Past the Line: Chapter One

ENVELOPING EMBRACE

For many, family was everything. But for Erica Haversham, that wasn't the case. She despised hers with vehemence and indignation. She hated the way they treated her. The way they acted around her. The way they made her feel. The way they belittled her. They were nothing but a bunch of insignificant, supercilious, no-good bastards who'd ostracised her for too long.

But now, in the same way the seasons rolled from one to the next, it was time for all that to change.

The air inside the car buffeted and pulsated in time with the heavy bass. The vibrations tingled her skin, arousing the hairs on her arms and legs. The seats and dashboard were pitch black, save for the blue and red strips of light lining the footwell and door frame. Like driving in a spaceship.

Beside her was Dylan; strong, powerful, beautiful Dylan. Pumping himself up to the music, beating his fingers on the steering wheel, swerving the car left and right as the female singer's voice rose and fell. Thrashing his head back and forth as the song approached the bridge. And then, when the bridge finally finished, he launched himself into the finale: the rap.

What they say they don't know they do

What they say they can't see ain't true

Whether I believe you, the result's always the same: I'm fucking come for you

Erica joined in, citing the lyrics verbatim. The result of days' worth of work in the music studio, fine-tuning the lyrics, the beat, the bassline, the melody and the role of the backing singer. The result of both hers and Dylan's efforts in making the song a worldwide success. One day.

As soon as it had finished, Dylan turned the volume down and swerved the car to the left, narrowly avoiding a bollard in the middle of the road. They were only two minutes away.

'What d'ya think?' he asked, turning to face her, one hand placed on the steering wheel while the other rested against the centre console. The epitome of cool. 'Good, eh?'

She smiled at him with glee. 'You know I love it, D.'

They continued down a secluded and remote street of East London until they arrived at a junction. Dylan switched the indicator on to signal a left turn, but Erica told him to head in the opposite direction.

'Trust me,' she said, pointing to the right. 'It'll be easier for us to get away.'

'But—'

'Trust me, Dylan. Please. I know what I'm doing.'

Dylan tapped the front pocket of his hoodie and said, with a wink, 'So do I.'

When Erica didn't respond, he placed his hand on her leg and squeezed. 'Everything'll be calm, aight? I got you.'

His touch roused the parts of her that were no longer

innocent. His hands were soft, yet strong, sensitive. They had the power to make her feel things she'd never known were possible. When she was around them, she felt secure, safe, a cub under the stoic protection of its mother. And in light of what they were about to do, they made her feel unstoppable – even if the gravity of their decisions hadn't quite hit her yet.

A few minutes later, they pulled up outside a row of terraced houses in a quaint residential street. Small blocks of yellow light punctured the building like holes in a grater.

Erica leant over Dylan's lap, ran her hand teasingly up his thigh to his crotch and glanced up at the house. The curtains were pulled across the living-room window, and the only other light in the front of the building was the bedroom on the third floor.

You little shit. Her body tensed, and she dug her nails into Dylan's thigh without meaning to.

The man grimaced and placed his hand on the small of her back, on the brief flash of skin on display where her top had ridden up. 'Relax,' he said. 'Don't stress. Please.' Then he reached into his hoodie pocket and produced a small plastic bag; inside was a handful of white pills. 'Think you need a little pick-me-up, don't you?'

Without hesitation, Erica snatched the bag from Dylan, rummaged through the contents, found the first ecstasy tablet her fingers could get hold of and placed it on the palm of her hand. Using her acrylic nails, she split the pill in half and attempted to crush it into a fine powder.

'What the fuck you doing?' Dylan asked.

'I…'

'Just swallow it. You'll be off your tits before you know it.'

Not wanting to upset him, Erica did as she was told and

placed the MDMA on her tongue. The reaction started at once, the tablet bubbling and fizzing on the surface, rapidly filling her mouth with the chemicals that would soon consume her entire body. She closed her mouth and dry swallowed, grimacing as she flushed the taste down her throat.

'Ready?' Dylan asked, pinching her cheeks with both hands.

'Time to face the music,' she said and stepped out of the car.

The humidity in the spring air had plummeted, replaced by an ominous chill that swept through the streets. The atmosphere was calm, untouched, unstirred like a sleeping baby. A dark and premonitory omen of what was to come.

As she rounded the front of Dylan's BMW, the moon bounced off the bonnet and blinded her. In her drug-induced state, she thought it looked like a giant football.

Ignoring it, she stumbled onto the pavement and climbed up a small flight of steps towards the front door. She retrieved her keys from the back pocket of her jeans and plunged the largest one into the door, her hands trembling with a combination of fear, ecstasy, and adrenaline. The sharp sound of the lock falling out of place amplified in her head, like the heavy bassline that continued to reverberate around her skull. Her senses ran wild and screamed at her from every angle.

The euphoria was kicking in. Faster than usual, she noted. Perhaps exacerbated by the splinter of fear creaking through the woodwork of her skin. Finally the door opened, and the crack sealed itself shut. The smell of recently cooked macaroni cheese – her favourite – wafted through the corridor and climbed her nostrils. She delighted in the scent and continued deeper into the house. At the end of the corridor lay the kitchen, and to her immediate left was the living room.

She advanced towards the kitchen. As she approached the threshold, the sound of a tap running and cutlery and plates ricocheting on the metal sink – a sound she'd been otherwise oblivious to – stopped suddenly.

'Erica!' Rupert Haversham screamed, throwing a sponge into the sink and spinning round to face her. The rest of his oversized body eventually caught up. 'Where've you been? We've been worried sick.'

'I'm fine.'

'Why didn't you tell anyone where you were?'

Before Erica responded, a figure appeared in the door frame to her left. Helena Haversham, Rupert's second wife.

Helena the Whore.

Helena the Homewrecker.

Helena, Erica's nemesis.

'Oh, Erica!' Helena screeched. The woman rushed towards her, flung herself over Erica's shoulders and squeezed with the false affection of a stepmother who cared more about her latest nail appointment than helping with her new daughter's science homework. 'I was *so* worried about you.'

Helena the Whore with the fake tits and teeth.

Helena the Whore with the skinny waist and perfect hair.

By now the drugs were fully making their way around Erica's system and she was entering what Dylan liked to call The Verisimilitude Phase. The fourteen-letter word was one that he'd learnt on a TV programme once and, after misinterpreting the meaning, had prescribed to be one of the side effects of ecstasy. The side effect that rendered the user with a slippery tongue capable of sharing their innermost and heavily guarded secrets as easily as a beaver building a dam.

But before she was able to unleash her tirade of vehemence, something distracted Helena, and she pushed Erica away and retreated.

'What is *he* doing here?' she asked, wrapping her cashmere cardigan tightly around her body, concealing the cleavage revealed by her low-cut top.

Erica spun on the spot, looked at Dylan, and then turned her attention back to Helena.

'*I* invited him,' Erica said with as much disdain as she could manage.

'I want him out of this house,' Rupert interjected, pointing at Dylan with a soap brush, flinging water and bubbles onto the floor.

'He has every right to be here!'

'Not without my say-so. He's no good for—'

'I can speak for myself, yo.' Dylan sauntered towards the granite island in the centre of the kitchen as though he owned the place and kept his hands submerged in his hoodie pocket.

As he passed, he gave her a quick blink.

The call to action.

'I can't be in here with him,' Helena said, then she waved her hand in the air dismissively and turned her back on the conversation. 'I won't speak to you until he's gone.'

Erica copied Dylan and placed her hand inside her hoodie pocket. Her fingers tightened around the item in there. She followed and slipped through the door before it closed, paying no heed to her father's cries.

Helena the Whore stormed through the dining room, through another door and into the living room, where she jumped onto the white seven-seater sofa, folded her legs onto the cushion and cast her attention to the TV that hung above the fireplace. Then she grabbed the remote and switched the channel to a home-shopping network. Oblivious to Erica behind her, edging closer, silent, graceful.

Like the leaves of autumn slowly dying.

Erica tightened her grip around the six-inch blade in her pocket until her knuckles whitened and her palm turned sweaty. For a very brief moment – and it was very brief, for it was only a flickering glance – Erica hesitated and contemplated her actions.

She asked herself: did she want to do this?

Yes.

Did she love the woman in front of her?

No.

Helena the fucking homewrecker whore with the big tits and the perfect teeth and the perfect smile and the perfect figure deserved everything she got.

Did she want Helena to be a part of her life anymore?

No.

The final one was toughest to answer: did she have it in her to do this?

There was only one way to find out.

Erica's body shook with adrenaline and excitement as she entered the Euphoria Phase. The rest of her body tingled as she pulled the blade from her pocket and stepped closer to Helena – closer to the chestnut-brown hair that Erica had always envied for looking so beautiful, even on her worst day. Closer to the stupid bitch who'd strolled into their lives and completely ruined everything. Closer to the woman who'd stolen her dad from her and manipulated him into making her life a complete misery.

From behind, Erica grabbed Helena's forehead, yanked it backward, opening up her airways, and slashed the blade across her throat, slicing cleanly into her carotid artery. A mist of blood projected into the air, showering Helena's legs and soiling the luxury sofa cushions and carpet in an explosion of red.

Erica glanced down at Helena's wild eyes. They were as white as the moon outside, and there was a pain behind them. Tears formed in the corners and eventually ran down her tilted forehead. Her arms flailed around, attempting to throw Erica off her, but her efforts were misguided, none of them making contact. By now, the letter-box hole in Helena's throat was overflowing with blood, running down her top and into her stomach.

As she watched over her stepmother, the guardian angel preparing to take her into the seven levels of hell, Erica wondered what the whore was thinking. Had she been shackled with guilt and loathing at having destroyed a happy family? Or had she been distracted by the disappointment of missing out on her husband's credit card forever more, of not being able to experience all the nice things he could afford for her?

Where she was going, she would never be able to experience nice things again.

Helena opened her mouth. Erica placed her hand over it and stifled the woman's final few gasps. Then she bent down beside Helena's head and whispered, 'You were never welcome in this house.'

And then, just like that, Helena lay perfectly still, calm, oddly serene.

Erica hovered over her stepmother, trying to comprehend how she felt. *What* she felt. The short answer was simple – nothing. Not even a morsel of guilt. The lines between reality and fiction, existence and death, had been blurred thanks to the waves of ecstasy rolling over her again and again, pulling her deeper, deeper.

And she didn't want them to stop.

She wanted to ride and ride and—

A sound came from the kitchen, shocking her back to the room. Erica swivelled on the spot and headed towards the noise, wiping the blade clean with the inside nook of her elbow.

As she entered, she froze in the door frame. Right in front of her was Rupert, Daddy, her hero, bent over the kitchen countertop. Slowly falling to the tiled floor, one hand clinging to the counter's edge, while the other clung to what remained of his existence. Dylan stood beside him, repeatedly punching the blade into Rupert's stomach and ribs and arms and legs and crotch and neck and head, making his way around the man's entire body until, like a wild gazelle that had been brought down by a lion, Rupert eventually breathed his last breath and collapsed to the floor.

What surprised Erica the most was that neither of them had put up a fight. They had been weak, defenceless, almost afraid to retaliate. For that very reason, they deserved to die – a minor consolation for the guilt she knew that she would no doubt feel later on. Weakness would hold no place in her life from now on. Not if she was going to survive the next few days.

'You good?' Dylan asked, panting. 'Helena?'

Erica nodded. 'She's—'

Something moved in the corner of Erica's field of vision. The movement came from the doorway to her right, leading into the corridor. She turned.

Froze.

Standing in the door frame, clutching a blanket against

her chest and a teddy bear under her arm, was Felicity, her four-year-old sister.

'Ecky,' she whispered, her nickname for Erica.

'What are you doing awake, Fleck? You're supposed to be asleep.'

'What's going on?'

'We're playing a grown-up game. Now go back to bed.'

Felicity's eyes dropped down on Erica's body. 'What's that?' She pointed at the blade in Erica's hand.

'It's a dangerous toy. It's for adults to play with. I... I want you to go back to bed now, please.'

She was rapidly sobering up. No longer were her fingertips vibrating with the ferocious beat of her heart. No longer were her ears echoing every sound around her. And the longer she stood there, she knew, the harder she would fall into the impending comedown.

'You take me?' Felicity asked, holding her hand out.

Erica opened her mouth, but a lump caught in her throat. She swallowed and sniffled, stifled the growing tears in her eyes. Shaking her head, she said, 'I'm sorry, Fleck, but I can't. I've got some... I've got some *adult* things to do. Dylan...' She sniffed – hard. 'Dylan can take you. He'll take really good care of you. Do you remember Dylan?'

'Yeah. Mummy said he's a bad man.'

Helena the Brainwasher.

'He's not a bad man. He's a part of the family. Do you want him to read you a bedtime story?'

'OK,' Felicity said, nodding. As soon as she finished, she rubbed the sleep from her eyes.

Before Dylan turned to face Felicity, he handed Erica the knife and looked her in the eyes. 'Leave it with me,' he said. 'Find your dad's car keys. And— Shit.'

'What?'

'The CCTV – is it turned off?'

Erica shook her head. After working with some of the biggest criminals in the country, her dad had thought it best to secure the premises and arm every corner of the house with twenty-four-hour surveillance. Not for the safety of his family, but for the safety of his documents and the work he was conducting. Rival gang members, psychotic killers and any other stranger could wander in off the street and abduct them, and he wouldn't have lost a minute of sleep over it. But when it came to his work and the security of his professional standing as the best defence barrister in London, that was where he drew the line.

For many, family was everything.

'Find the CCTV and destroy it,' Dylan ordered. Then he shuffled towards Felicity, placed his arm around her shoulders, and escorted her out of the kitchen.

'Night, Ecky. Love you,' Felicity called behind her.

Erica opened her mouth to speak, but the words were too heavy. She waited until they were upstairs before she moved again and raced to the other side of the kitchen, through a playroom and into another room to the right – Rupert's office. A bookshelf as tall as the wall ran across one length of the room. On the other side was an exercise bike. In all the years her father had owned it, she'd only ever known him to use it once. Twice maximum. At the end of the room was her father's desk. Resting atop it was a small computer monitor with rolling footage of the security cameras around the house.

Erica advanced towards the computer.

Experience from her teenage years had taught her how to erase certain pieces of footage from the cameras. Like the time she'd come home drunk from a party in the middle of a field when she was thirteen. Like the first time Dylan stayed over and left in the morning with no one knowing.

It was easy when you knew how.

Erica awoke the computer, logged into the CCTV software and scrolled back to the footage from six hours ago. She highlighted the gap between then and now, and pressed DELETE on the keyboard. Just like that, the footage was gone, lost into the ether.

Using her sleeve as a cloth, Erica wiped the keyboard and mouse clean of her fingerprints, grabbed Rupert's car keys from the pen pot on his desk, then hurried back into the kitchen.

By the time she returned to the hallway, Dylan was already on the bottom step of the staircase.

She paused at the sight of him, her body paralysed with shock.

'Did you…? Is she…?'

'I was kind,' Dylan said. There was nothing in his expression that suggested he'd just murdered two people in cold blood. 'Did you get the keys?'

Erica held them in the air.

'And the footage?'

'Deleted and removed from the hard drive.'

He leant forward and kissed her. 'I'm proud of you. Now come on – let's get the fuck outta here.'

They left the house and split up; Dylan taking his own car while Erica raced towards Rupert's Mercedes.

'Remember what I told you?' he asked.

'Put it in gear. Find the biting point. Easy on the accelerator.'

'That's my girl.'

'See you at the house?'

'See you at the house.'

She unlocked the car, started the engine, and sped away. As she roared down the road, she fought the urge to turn back and face the house where she'd grown up. Where she'd fostered many happy memories. Where she'd hoped that many more would come. But there was no way she could turn back now. She and Dylan shared a bond, a connection like no other. Her body – and soul – had crossed the point of no return directly into his enveloping embrace.

Dylan's blood raced around his body, fuelling the adrenaline in his cells. He increased the volume on the stereo and blasted his song. He screamed. Yelled. Pounded on the steering column. The song drowning out his noise.

He'd done it. And now he felt fucking euphoric. Like nothing in the world could stop him. Like he could take on anyone and anything.

And then he remembered he had a job to do. A call to make.

Dylan placed his phone on the dashboard, unlocked it, and dialled the number.

The song suddenly stopped and was replaced by the sound of ringing.

Brmph-brmph. Brmph-brmph. Brmph-brmph.

Eventually, on the fourth ring, the other line answered.

'Yes?' came the calm, soothing voice.

'It's me.'

'Is it done?'

'It's done. All of them.'

'And Erica?'

'Coming back to the flat with me.'

'Very well. You know what you have to do next.'

The line went dead.

Past the Line: Chapter Two

GOOD NEWS

Henry Matheson had been looking forward to tonight all week. Casino night. The only time he and some of the other acquaintances he'd made in Wandsworth, one of Her Majesty's finest, could put their money where their mouths were and relax. The night where turf wars and rivalries were left at the door.

And tonight, Henry had the luxury of hosting it in his cell.

With him was Andrew Bennett, one of the men Henry had heard about growing up. The man had owned almost all the gun trade in and out of South London, and it was rumoured he'd been the one selling weapons to the Irish and British during the Troubles. Both parties were willing to pay whatever it cost, and Andrew Bennett was more than happy to oblige them. Convicted of terrorism offences shortly after, the sixty-one-year-old was serving his fifteenth year of his twenty-nine-year sentence.

Beside him, with his jumper pulled up to his chin, was Reggie Mings, a complete nutjob who, despite never having been tested for it, possessed all the qualities of a sociopath. Severely unhinged and slightly deranged, he'd been arrested for the armed robbery of an entire high street. Jumping from shop to shop, his spree on the small road in Leicester had resulted in three fatalities and sixteen casualties. After a quick hostage negotiation, the police had eventually thrown him into the back of a police van and convicted him ten months later. He, too, was serving a life sentence. Year ten, with a lot more to go. But he'd resigned himself to his fate soon after his arrival and was notorious around the prison for re-enacting his initial crime: charging into inmate's cells and robbing them while beating the shit out of them. He didn't gain anything by doing it. No respect, no leniency on his sentence – he simply did it for the fun of hurting people.

The last member of the group was Roger Silverwood, a man in his seventies who'd originally been convicted of robbery but since his arrival in prison had developed a taste for blood and desensitised knuckles. Only supposed to serve a five stretch, he'd added an extra twenty-five years to his sentence for beating someone to death in their cell. When asked why he'd done it, he responded with: 'Because he looked at me funny.' But everyone on the spur knew it was because the two had known each other on the outside, and the victim had bragged about sleeping with Roger's wife behind his back. Whether or not true, Roger didn't care. It was a matter of principle. And soon thereafter, everyone quickly learnt the importance of keeping Roger's wife out of any and all discussion, no matter where they were in the prison.

Henry Matheson, on the other hand, was the newest addition to the small knot of acquaintances, and by extension the prison. Before his sentencing, he'd been involved in an altercation with a former inmate. And for the first time in his life, Henry had come off worse: a ruptured anus, which still caused him immeasurable amounts of pain; a dozen holes in his stomach that made him look like a punctured jacket potato ready for cooking in the microwave; and a torso of burnt and raised skin that looked like an ordnance survey of the Alps. But the worst injury of them all had been the Glasgow Grin. The scars on his face stretched from the sides of his mouth to the middle of his cheeks. Eating was a task, and talking not much better. If he wasn't careful, saliva would dribble from his lips like he was a baby. Following the incident, a decision had been made to separate him from the rest of the prison population, and so he'd been transferred to Wandsworth.

Sadly, however, upon his arrival, one thing had become abundantly clear to Henry: he was at the bottom of the pecking order. In Belmarsh, Henry had owned the prison, the prisoners, the guards and just about everyone else in it. He was the king, the king responsible for facilitating everyone's habits and trading favours for commodities. But here, he was on the lowest rung. A nobody. Those accolades were instead given to the country's finest: serial killers, and the likes of Andrew, Reggie and Roger. But none of them were on the same level as the Albanian and Romanian gangs that occupied more than half the prison. Because of the increasing epidemic of prison overpopulation, two of the biggest competitors in the drug trade had been thrown into the boiling pot.

And now Henry had been thrown into the mix, too.

'Your turn,' Archie told him calmly. His entire disposition belied the insanity and complexities of his working mind. 'You gotta lay eeva a six or a nine.'

'Thanks for the lesson.' Henry thumbed through his

cards and set down a six of hearts. 'When are we gonna talk about business?'

'What business?' Andrew Bennett asked. A cigarette dangled from his mouth, and wisps of smoke clawed into the air. The top of the cigarette jostled and shook as he spoke.

'Like getting me out of this fucking place,' Henry said defiantly, the arrogance and cockiness of his youth oozing through his ego. But deep down he was afraid, afraid for his life; the animals at the bottom of the food chain were always the first to go.

A chorus of laughter erupted from the men, the noise spilling out of the doorway and into the spur.

'Fuck off!'

'You're dreaming, kid!'

'You got more chance of Devlin giving you a successful sex change,' Roger said.

Devlin Cooper was a former award-winning tattoo artist responsible for stabbing a client repeatedly with a tattoo needle; he was the closest thing they had to a surgeon in the prison.

'You're stuck here for life.'

Henry joined in the laughter, keeping up appearances. 'In that case, I'm gonna have to see about getting me a couple of porno mags or something. I'm gonna need something else to look at for the next thirty years.'

Another chorus, another appearance maintained. Then it died down just as quickly. Almost as volatile as the four men's tempers.

It was Henry's turn again, and he laid down the four of diamonds. 'What's this I'm hearing about more Hellbanianz coming in?' he asked.

'Ain't much else to hear,' Reggie responded. 'Last I

heard, there was a big bust-up down in Winchester and a dozen of them are coming in. The feds are finally doing something right.'

Andrew, Reggie and Roger were from a different class of criminal. At some point in their lifetime, each had had an involvement in the drug trade, but back in their days, it had been more relaxed and there had been a certain element of cricket about it. Now, however, there was a new breed of dealer on the streets. One who settled feuds and rivalries at the end of a bullet rather than the end of a fist. Henry had been part of that new wave of criminal – and as a result, he was very lucky to be sitting at the table with these gentlemen, let alone be respected by them. He suspected there was a hint of xenophobia and racism behind their approval. But when it came to it, he was nowhere near as ruthless as the Hellbanianz, the Albanians' self-appointed moniker, or the Romanians. Not only had they been driving down the price of drugs for the past five years, they'd also wiped out several members of Henry's gang, the E11. They were like rats, rapidly infesting the towns and villages, spreading their diseases and running everyone out of town. And now they were occupying the prisons, a popular and fruitful revenue stream.

'I think I'm gonna need some protection,' Henry said, a lump caught in his throat. The words came as a surprise to himself.

His name was on the tip of his enemies' lips, and his days of casino nights and quiet breakfasts, lunches and dinners were quickly becoming numbered. Somehow he'd avoided a hiding, but he didn't know how much longer his luck would last; he was the zebra, a beacon of black and white amid the dreary grey of the prison uniform, and there were only so many times he could avoid a mauling from the lion.

Bottom of the food chain.

'If that's what you want, Hen…' Andrew removed the cigarette from his mouth, flicked the excess ash onto the concrete floor, and took a drag. He inhaled heavily, filling his lungs with the toxic chemicals, and eventually exhaled, billowing a cloud of smoke across the pile of cards in the centre of the bed. 'Then you know what you gotta do.'

Before Henry could think about it, his mobile phone rang. He removed it from his tracksuit pocket and glanced at the screen – Dylan calling ahead of schedule. *Vrrmph. Vrrmph.* The phone vibrated.

Henry held his finger aloft, silencing the men in the room.

'Yes?'

'It's me,' Dylan replied. He sounded exasperated, his breathing wheezy.

'Is it done?'

'It's done. All of them.'

'And Erica?'

'Coming back to the flat with me.'

Henry paused a moment. He nodded.

'Very well. You know what you have to do next.'

He rang off and placed the phone on his knee, then returned his attention to the card game. He was momentarily unaware of what was going on, and what had happened in the twenty seconds he'd been on the phone. And he was only slightly aware that he was smiling.

'Good news?' Roger asked.

A smile yawned across Henry's face. 'Guess you could say that.'

Past the Line: Chapter Three

BLACK 24

One of the things Jake Tanner missed about having his wife Elizabeth around the house, more than most, was her cooking. Despite never having studied professionally, she could create the most beautiful and delicious infusions from the meagre scraps and rations they had lying around the house. It wasn't until she was gone that he realised how much he depended on her to cook a decent meal, something worth spending time on and enjoying. Instead, for the past few months, he'd been reliant on his own abilities, which stretched as far as anyone in his position. A piece of toast with a smattering of egg lightly sprinkled with pepper was one of the most delectable feasts he'd had the pleasure of making himself.

That was as exciting as it got.

Except for this evening.

This evening was different. This evening he'd get to experience good food. Proper food.

Food worth eating.

Food worth enjoying.

The only downside was the company he'd be forced to share it with: Martha Clarke, his mother-in-law. The owner of the house that Elizabeth and his two girls, Maisie and Ellie, had called home for the past twelve weeks. Jake didn't mind spending time with *them* – in fact, it was the very thing he wanted more than anything else in the world – but the less he was near his children's grandmother, the better.

After arriving early from work – something Elizabeth had always insisted he was incapable of doing when their marriage wasn't a mess – he slipped out of the kitchen into the living room, where he found his daughters. Maisie was seated on the sofa, reading a book, while Ellie was colouring in with a varying assortment of crayons.

As he stepped into the room, the girls offered him no notice, no invitation to play or hug or even sit down beside them.

A stranger to his own family.

'Careful you don't get anything on the carpet,' he said, perching himself on the edge of the sofa next to Ellie.

'Daddy!' Ellie yelled. As soon as she laid eyes on him, she leapt up and gave him a brief hug before quickly returning her attention to her drawings.

For the first time in a while, all thought of work and the stresses of the past few weeks disappeared from his mind, and he focused on the present. He looked over at his eldest. 'How was nursery today, Mais?'

'It was OK. Miss Arrowsmith gave me a hug.'

'Why? Were you sad?'

'Yes.'

Jake lifted himself to his feet, picked up Maisie from the sofa and sat down, setting her on his lap. She continued to read her book.

'What was making you sad, sweetie?' Jake asked, his

mind whirring. He conjured images of another child bullying her, followed by more images of him storming down to the school, prepared to punish the child himself. Or the parents.

Fucking parents.

It was always the parents.

Maisie turned, her eyes a wide pool of innocence. 'When are we coming home, Daddy?'

It hadn't occurred to him that the distance between himself and Elizabeth had permeated through the malleable innocence of childhood. Perhaps he'd been naïve to think that they were oblivious to the realities of their parents' matrimonial turmoil.

Following the Matheson enquiry, the death of Assistant Commissioner Richard Candy and the personal attack on their finances, Jake's and Elizabeth's relationship had deteriorated. At first, things had seemed to be getting back on track, their marriage continuing with half-truths and a few white lies. But the straw that had broken the camel's back was when Elizabeth had discovered the news about his infidelity. The kiss that Jake and Stephanie, a former colleague, had shared one drunken night in a Premier Inn in the middle of Birmingham.

Now, she'd moved out, severed nearly all communication and taken the kids with her.

The childcare remained her job, while the mortgage, the bills and other expenses remained his.

So, in reality, it was as though nothing had changed at all.

Except *everything* had.

'Maisie,' Jake began, cautious on how to approach the topic. 'You know that Mummy and Daddy love you very much. And it's—'

'Jake! Maisie! Ellie! Dinner's ready,' Elizabeth called from the kitchen.

Saved by the bell.

Maybe there really was someone looking over him, even if it hadn't felt that way recently.

'Come on, girls – it's time to eat.'

Jake dropped Maisie to the floor, grabbed Ellie from the carpet and carried her to the kitchen, with Maisie trailing behind, holding his hand. In the open plan dining room, Elizabeth standing on her toes, reaching high into a cupboard, while Martha was on the other side of the kitchen, tipping ladles of spaghetti Bolognese into white china bowls. It was in that moment that Jake felt as though he were home, as though everything was back to normal again, as though the events of the past few months hadn't taken place at all and that it had just been a dream.

A dream that had turned into a nightmare.

'Jake,' Martha called, and immediately the feeling was crushed. 'Get the girls set up at the table. I don't want their food to get cold.'

And you think I do?

Begrudgingly, he did as he was told and found his seat at the table beside Maisie. A few seconds later, Martha handed the plates round, serving the girls first, then Elizabeth, then herself, and then Jake. He thanked her, sprinkled an extra serving of Parmesan on top, and grabbed his knife and fork just as Elizabeth finally sat down.

'Looks delicious, hun,' Jake said, glancing up at his wife and then down at his food again. 'Probably the best meal I've had in a long time.'

'Are you not eating properly?' Elizabeth asked before she shovelled a forkful of food into her mouth.

'Now and then. By the time I get home, it's too late to

cook anything substantial, so I just have a couple of packets of crisps – or a ready meal – and that sorts me just fine.'

'They're not good for you, Jake. You need a proper diet.'

'I'm trying.'

'Like you are with everything else?' Martha said derisively, making no effort to hide the contempt in her voice.

'Pardon?'

'Mum, *leave* it,' Elizabeth insisted.

Martha wiped the side of her mouth with a napkin and set it on her leg. 'It's been three months since Alan died, and you've seen us – what? – only once before tonight. Do you really care that little?'

Here we go. Jake readied himself for an assault. They were commonplace whenever his and Martha's paths crossed. But since Alan's passing, following a failed kidney transplant, Jake had struggled to remain civil and an upholder of the peace. It was about time they had an overdue argument. But then he realised where he was, and whose company he was in.

Tonight was a special night for several reasons. Best not ruin it.

'Things are complicated,' Jake said, tightening his grip around his dinner knife.

'You're entitled to your days off – there's nothing stopping you from making an appearance.'

Jake considered for a moment. And then it dawned on him.

'You don't know, do you?' he asked.

'Know what?'

As he was about to open his mouth and explain to Martha what had really caused their separation, Elizabeth's eyes flared, imploring him to remain quiet. He did – and scooped another load of mince onto his fork. 'I don't think this is a conversation we should be having in front of the children.'

'I have a right to know.'

'And I said *no*. It isn't appropriate for dinner. Afterwards, maybe, but not right now. I suggest we talk about something else,' Jake said, hoping the forkful of food he'd just shoved into his mouth signalled the end of the conversation.

To his surprise, Martha backed down. He didn't like shouting at people or speaking to them sternly – especially when it was family – but he was tired of allowing her to dictate conversations and people's emotions.

'Have you heard anything from Rupert?' Elizabeth asked. She was in the middle of helping Ellie focus and pay attention to her food.

'I saw him today,' Jake replied.

'And?'

Jake hesitated, looked into her eyes, and shook his head. 'I'm sorry, Liz.'

Elizabeth dropped the spoon on Ellie's plate and sank into her chair. Her brow furrowed, and she glanced at her food with a lost, vacant stare.

'I'm sorry, hun,' Jake repeated.

'Is there nothing we can do to convince him?'

'I tried.'

'Do you want me to speak to him?' Martha interrupted.

When both Jake and Elizabeth looked at her in mild disbelief, she continued, 'He and I worked together. He helped us with Detson.' She was referring to the tower-block fire that had taken place several years before due to unsafe cladding and a faulty hairdryer. The word was synonymous with the night hundreds of families had lost their lives as the fire spread rapidly throughout every facet of the building, and the subsequent government cover-up that had left them bereft and homeless.

Martha was the housing minister in charge of the decision and the one who'd received the biggest flak afterwards. Yet had still managed to keep her job.

'Why haven't you said anything before?' Jake asked.

Martha shrugged. Jake was soon beginning to realise that the more time he spent with her, the more he found out.

'So it seems we're just a family full of lies.'

'What's that supposed to mean?' Martha asked.

'Jake, *please*,' Elizabeth implored.

But he continued regardless.

'If you must know,' he began, 'Liz kicked herself out of the house a few months ago. Not because of whatever reason she gave you, but because she found out something that I had been trying my hardest to keep from her – not because I was trying to hide it from her maliciously, but because I was trying to protect her. Cliché, I know, but here we are.' He spoke to Martha, but his attention was solely focused on Elizabeth. 'A couple of months ago, while I was investigating Henry Matheson, I took a short trip to Birmingham with a colleague. Stephanie. We stayed in a hotel overnight, got drunk and then we kissed. It was a mistake, a stupid, terrible mistake, and there isn't a day goes by where I don't think about what I did to hurt you, Liz.'

Silence ensued, save for the sounds of delight and the clattering of cutlery on crockery coming from Maisie and Ellie. By now, Martha had set her knife and fork down and was gently dabbing at the sides of her mouth with her napkin. Jake prepared his defences for an attack.

'Was this before or after what happened to Elizabeth?'

she asked with an air of calm around her that unsettled him.

'After. And it kills me I can't be here with her while she's going through it all.'

'She has the girls. And she has me.'

'Is that necessary? Does she really need *you*? The Elizabeth I know is a strong and powerful woman who won't let anything like this faze her. She's perfectly capable of looking after Ellie and Maisie. She's been fine since they were born, so what's changed? Other than the fact that it might be soothing your ego slightly, or filling in the hole that Alan left after he passed...'

Another moment of silence descended upon the table. Jake reflected on what he'd said. Did he feel out of line? Maybe. Did he feel guilty? Not really. Did he regret what he said? Yes. But they were his feelings, and they had spent too long inside him to stay there any longer.

'I think it's about time we all started being honest with one another in this family,' he added, delivering the final blow to the jaw with a clean right hook. 'And I've said my piece.'

Martha's expression remained closed and impassive, a barricade in front of the castle. But Jake knew, deep down, deep beneath those walls, a fire raged throughout the castle. She began to sweat as she struggled to maintain her composure.

'And I think it's time for you to leave,' Martha said, her voice stern and authoritative.

'Mum, no, you can't. Let him stay.' Elizabeth placed her hand on Martha's arm.

'It's fine.' Jake lifted himself out of his chair and set his napkin down on the table. 'I can handle it.'

Jake kissed the girls on the head and said goodbye,

grabbed his things and then left. Maisie and Ellie called after him, but he continued regardless. He couldn't lose face in front of Martha, not if he wanted her to have any respect for him further down the line when all of this was over.

On the drive home, his mind wandered in and out of reality like a drunk walking in and out of an off-licence, thinking about what the future might hold for their relationship. He adored Elizabeth and the girls more than anything in the—

Was that true?

He considered for a moment. The whole reason they were separated was due to a combination of things. But at the front of it all was his obsession – and, dare he admit it, *addiction* – to work. What had happened with Stephanie was a direct result of that. Too many other officers in the force had suffered similar infidelity horror stories. Too many officers were addicted to the job. It was an obsession, and once it had a grip on you, it didn't let go.

Yes, there was nothing he wouldn't do for his kids and his family and his marriage. But, equally, there was nothing he wouldn't do for his career. Perhaps it was time to think about someone else for a change.

Before he knew it, he was home, parked on the side of the road, and walking towards the front door. He fumbled the key in his hands, then slotted it into the lock. When he made to swing the door open, he was met with resistance. The pile of shoes on the other side of the door. The mountain of bills and junk mail and newspapers that had formed over the past few weeks. The overflowing refuse bags that had missed the last collection and needed a new home in the local landfill.

Jake leant into the door, easing the mess out of the way, then waded through the corridor and into the kitchen. A skyscraper of dirty, unwashed plates rested next to the sink; beside it was a tower of plastic microwaveable meal and takeaway cartons waiting to be dropped into a refuse bag.

The recycle cycle.

Jake grabbed a dirty glass, ambled towards the fridge and poured himself a Foster's. As the cold fluid descended his throat, he stopped and gazed around the kitchen, searching for something in particular.

Eventually, he found it. Somehow in a different place to where he remembered leaving it. When he lifted the laptop lid, the screen illuminated on the last internet page he'd been on before he'd left the house that morning. And he was still logged in.

As he perused through the dashboard, he realised there were four Champions League matches on in less than ten minutes. He glanced at the top right of the screen, saw his balance was at £23.52, and placed a series of bets. Barcelona to win. Chelsea to draw. Both teams to score. Final score for each game. First goal scorer.

In a matter of seconds, he was down to his last £1.52, so he turned his attention to something more immediate. Something that would satisfy his urges. Something that he could enjoy watching. Roulette.

Jake hopped over to the live casino screen and gambled the rest of the money on black twenty-four. He clapped his hands in the air as soon as the bet had been confirmed and waited. His heart beat in time with the countdown clock, ticking down until the next spin.

Ticking…

Beating…

And then it began.

He watched the smartly – yet seductively – dressed

woman throw the ball into the wheel. It bounced and rolled until eventually...

'Yes!'

Black twenty-four.

He'd won, and when he refreshed the screen, an extra £53.20 had deposited into his account.

Elated, Jake downed his beer, grabbed the rest of the six-pack from the fridge and strapped himself in. It was going to be another exciting night. A profitable one too, he hoped.

In the weeks that he'd delved into the world of online gambling, he'd managed to burn through over a thousand pounds – more money than he owned in any of his bank accounts. His monthly outgoings chewed into what was left of his salary, and so he was relying on borrowed money – and borrowed time. He didn't know the exact figures because he didn't need to. There was a light at the end of the tunnel.

And that fifty pounds was just the beginning.

Grab your copy...
vinci-books.com/past-line